Echo of the
ABYSS

Siddharth Pandey is 26 years old. He is a writer and novelist who lives in Noida, Uttar Pradesh. *Echo of the Abyss* is his second book. His debut novel *Pilgrimage to Nowhere* was published in 2018. Siddharth is influenced by magic realism and existential literature, three cups of coffee and ice-cold water, melancholic jazz and classical music. He also enjoys mythology, manga, whiskey, and Muay Thai. He is currently working on his third novel *Delhi, Dolphins & Desolation* and expects it to be released late next year.

Echo of the
ABYSS

Siddharth Pandey

RUPA

Published by
Rupa Publications India Pvt. Ltd 2022
7/16, Ansari Road, Daryaganj
New Delhi 110002

Sales centres:
Allahabad Bengaluru Chennai
Hyderabad Jaipur Kathmandu
Kolkata Mumbai

This is a work of fiction. Names, characters, places and incidents are
either the product of the author's imagination or are used fictitiously
and any resemblance to any actual person, living or dead, events or
locales is entirely coincidental.

ISBN: 978-93-5520-537-7

First impression 2022

10 9 8 7 6 5 4 3 2 1

The moral right of the author has been asserted.

Printed in India

This book is dedicated to my brother.

∽

Chapter 1

L ife is a box of chocolates, and death, like circumcision. To experience death is a rite of passage. Like circumcision, the earlier the better. With time, the trauma of the event blurs and if it exists in the memory of an impressionable mind like that of a child, the event is easily pushed to the back, allowing it to fade while the child is distracted by the new-found world, and soon, only a faint indentation remains. Through this process, a person begins to acclimatize to the wretched reality of life. And in many ways, like circumcision, death too allows no choice in the matter. A dog, a cat or a relative, ideally age—much like a bottle of premium wine—only to become distant memory for those who outlive them.

Anant had his first encounter with death when he was seven years old. He too was fed lines that are shared after such an event takes place, including the classics such as how his uncle's time had come, that he was a favourite of god and was called back, that he had gone to a better place, but hiding beneath these hollow comforts, underneath the hysteria and the mourning, Anant with a child's intuitiveness wondered how so many different reasons could exist for a single death. That perhaps no one understood death any more than he did. Do adults lie from time to time, he asked himself.

Uncle and nephew were strangers long before death had a say in their relationship. His father's brother was no more than a face that would materialize during festivities before disappearing until another god was to be celebrated. There were a few random visits on other dates that weren't Diwali or Holi, and at times Ganesh

Chaturthi, but rarely outside of celebrations did his uncle even spare Anant a glance. His uncle would sit with his father, Sunil Vohra, drinking, watching old movies or the news, discussing politics where the brother did most of the talking until he was red in the face while Anant's father looked for witty remarks to make, and the more they drank, the more emotional they became, until politics took a back seat for more sentimental notions to surface. Like slurring about who had been the leader of their group, or remembering that girl in school who vanished one summer day after she got married, or whining about how strict their mother had been with them after their father passed away. Anant never found his uncle interesting, even with the sweets on Holi, the gifts on Diwali, and the snacks that were ordered on account of their visit. They both shared a common disinterest in one another. His wife and his children were rare guests, and the times that Anant might have spent with them was buried in the currents of time, never to be remembered again. It seemed to Anant that they all came into existence after his uncle had passed. An uncle who became interesting when Anant was woken up in the middle of night and bundled into the back of a taxi, weaving in and out of sleep throughout the journey, so much so that he woke up to the sight of his uncle lying on a white bedsheet spread on the floor, that matched the white clothes he had been made to wear. The first victim of what would tower over the rest of his life, was made more interesting for having been gathered by death than he had ever been when alive. This was the image of his uncle that remained with Anant throughout his life. Of cotton balls stuffed in his nose, as he lay on the white sheets, dressed in white clothes, his dark skin dry but smooth, strikingly in contrast to the white world imposed on him by the presence of death.

Death returned two years later to take away the neighbour's baby. Now a child of nine, Anant would see the baby in passing on his way back from school or the park. A blob of mixed emotions that remained in constant turmoil between laughter and crying. Anant couldn't understand what continued to aggravate a child so small. He had no school, no homework, and was free of all responsibilities—unlike the nine-year-old Anant. Naturally, his interest in the baby dwindled with every passing day since the only upside to all this was the baby's cuteness, which waned with every passing second, and crashed whenever he cried—which was all too often. And then one day Anant lost all interest in the baby, who as far as he was concerned was merely a radio playing in the background. The return of the mourning and the fountain of tears turned the radio into a baby again. In death, the baby was more than its laughter and cries. It was a reminder of his deceased uncle.

In death, the baby became a symbol for it, for the Titan. For the first time in his life, Anant was obsessed with something that brought him no joy. Death wasn't like cricket or Pokemon or sweets, and the weeks he spent ruminating on the subject suddenly seemed like an act of cruelty by his tyrannical mind. Yet, no matter how much he huffed and puffed, he could blow away neither his infatuation with death, nor the questions it brought forth. It didn't make sense to his young mind how a young baby that was, simply ceased to be. And the heaven where the baby was called back to came with its own share of questions. His uncle, perhaps, could still carry on with some heavenly activities, but what would a baby do in heaven? Cry and laugh for all eternity? To Anant, that seemed like a wretched existence. A torture that made him question whether reincarnation was preferable to heaven.

Was there a choice, he would ask himself. For the first time, Anant wondered what exactly happened after death. But his young mind faltered at the gargantuan task of deciphering death, and the larger question that clung to him, although it failed to make any sense, was how someone that was, just wouldn't be. What did dying mean?

Unbeknownst to Anant, his obsession with death was nursed in the unconscious mind. It kept coming back to him—on the bus, in the classroom, in the canteen, when he was writing an exam, or playing cricket, especially when he was fielding. His obsession stayed—it watched, and learned. It grew alongside Anant.

The next to fall was a friend his age when they were just teetering on the cusp of turmoil that was being a teenager. It was in his wake that Anant realized his relationship with death had fundamentally changed. If death could take away his friend— someone who used to play and go to school with him, and someone who used to cover for him every time he sneaked out of school in search of sweets that were given as prasad in a local temple—if his uncle could die, and if a baby could die, Anant felt that there was no way to know as to who was safe, or how the Titan, or Death, decided as to who would die, how they would die and when. From an abstract entity that Anant failed to understand, this Death that had been adopted by his unconscious mind surged to merge with his everyday life. It diminished boundaries between his more abstract unconscious and his self, mixing the conscious and the subconscious, and Anant began to see everyone imprinted with death—as if it was slowly stepping into role of a friend and becoming a constant companion. And soon, it would be his only companion. Everywhere he looked, from houses to families, death would stir in his mind and remind Anant of its omnipresence and ownership, until it became his second nature to live with the slithering and hissing of Death. Anant began to see Death that the inhabitants of this world carried on their shoulders like a weightless spirit which would tighten its grip as everyone aged, like a vengeful shoulder piece to be carried by the decree of god.

It was a terrible time in Anant's life as he suffered through his teenage years fearing the omnipresent snake that would bare its fangs and take whoever it wanted, whenever it wanted. This darkness flipped the axis of his world. It disconnected him from people while simultaneously evoking a strong sense of empathy in him. Sometimes in this tug of war of emotions, he would find himself struggling to breathe, as if the snake was coiling around his throat, preparing to take him. But the worst of his exertions resulted from his futile efforts when he tried to be brave against the all-powerful snake—to somehow face the Titan and wrench his loved ones away from it. With his spatter of a moustache and a voice that squeaked more often than he would care to admit, Anant would try to stand up to the overwhelming reality of life, and be constantly reminded of his impotence in the face of the Titan. Anant was never allowed to build an ego. But the currents of time softened the edges of such an existence. Anant learned to exist in such a world. He adapted to have Death as his companion, which took as sacrifice the prospect and possibility of a normal life for Anant. No longer could he maintain relationships. Death was an overbearing friend, family, lover, and enemy that demanded all his attention.

Anant became an infantile man who could not manage familial bonds except hanging on to the oldest relations he had, his parents, who were at the heart of the majority of his worries. People didn't understand him was a thought that he held close to him throughout his teenage years—proof that despite his ailments, he was still a teenager. But being suspended by the notion of Death, neither progressing nor being able to let go, impeded his chances of relating with other people. Years passed in a blur, a painfully slow blur, and Anant managed to wade through his teenage years right up to his graduation. The weeks leading up to his nineteenth birthday was when his parents began to worry that perhaps his troubles weren't a product of his age or a prolonged reaction to his friend's death. While they tried to convince him to go to a therapist, Anant realized that his parents constantly strove to understand him without knowing his plight, like shooting in the dark. The therapist ultimately did him no good. He was unwilling to divulge anything related to the Titan and the world he had created to escape it. There was a brief period between school and college when he felt he was in a limbo but it ended, and he shifted to the dormitory. The tension that singed his nerves whenever he thought of being bundled together with a bunch of people, constantly being in contact with one person or the other—the very thought that had on other occasions made him freeze in horror—gave way more easily than he had expected. While in college his desire to be a recluse grew, the existential turmoil was placated by living in a dorm surrounded by strangers. When unattached, Anant found it easier to accept the people around him. At whom the snake leered, it did not matter. The shadow of Death on their shoulders became a mere companion, like pirates with mute parrots. He learned to look at the wrinkles of his professors as if they were the soul's attempt to hollow the body to a point where it could burst open and be free.

This journey to his hermitage—this solitary cell—was built brick by brick in a place from where he could escape the world. It was only when he was faced with a therapist that he realized how impenetrable a structure he had created. Floating in his mind where once the sound of hissing and slithering could be heard was a shelter hidden from prying eyes. It was a simple room that had rough grey brick walls like Parisian catacombs, and plain mats covering the floor. A single window faced the unlocked door, both always open to serve as a reminder that this isolation was self-imposed, and to enjoy the dynamic view of his mind that brought him to new shores taken from his memories, dreams and reflections. In times of peril, his troubled mind would fall short of providing a view and he would have a starless night sky for company. After graduating from college, Anant worked under an interior designer for two years before starting his own business that somehow stayed afloat, with the help of clients who appreciated the lack of ownership Anant displayed over his ideas. It allowed him to afford a move to Mumbai, with his father's friend offering him his flat.

His retreat that existed in his mind, and the hyper-reality of his college and the dorm with students at every corner, prepared him for a life beyond college. But being an independent interior designer, with new clients and co-workers whom he had never met, suited him best. He found it far easier than the constant hustle and bustle of students, teachers, colleagues and bosses. He would meet his clients for interviews and briefs, and meet them again along with the labourers and contractors on site, and the darkness sitting on everyone's shoulders would fade behind them. He transferred a minimal rent to his father's friend whose search for a job had led him to Kuwait. On some days he went out for shopping—mostly whenever it dawned on him that he was about to run out of ration. This pretty much summed up his life in Mumbai. It was a life of limited interactions and Anant felt quite comfortable. The repetition of these events allowed him to rely on his instincts and experience to guide him through the conversations, almost like being in autopilot mode while remaining seated in his retreat. It was as if he had a sheet full of replies that he was choosing from, and later he would not have to put much effort into it. The only instances where life would pull him back to the front seat was when he was captivated by a scent or a sight, the culmination of his subdued interests coming together to serenade his senses, and other times when he would climb to the front seat himself when the autopilot couldn't be trusted to navigate through what he deemed to be 'treacherous roads', an inconsistency in the established pattern of conversation, an irritated client looking to lash out at the work, an envious contractor trying to upset the balance of power, or when he had, solely on account of being a face one kept seeing, moved up on the ladder of intimacy from a stranger to a familiar face, and thus had to take his time to adapt to the conversations again. There was also the routine visit to his parents, once every three months, for a weekend and a day or two. Anant explained it as a case of shaving a balding head, trying to get a semblance of control before the inevitable. He would rather be in control before the visit than have his mind spit him out and bar him from the retreat.

Chapter 2

The drive from Mumbai was routine for him. The same trees on the familiar wide six-lane expressway, the same trucks with familiar stickers working under the blanket of the moon, the same buses rushing ahead, the same cars racing past others, with the same expected movements to switch lanes just to avoid the trucks, and the same inevitable stop at checkposts for the trucks, buses and speeding cars. The drive from Mumbai to Pune was not too short to not be a journey, but not too long as to become tedious. Anant had woken up at a time when it was hard to tell if it was late night or early morning. He rushed to pack his bag and conduct a quick inspection of his car. Engine oil, air pressure, brake oil, and wiper fluid. He didn't drive his car in Mumbai, it was more convenient to take cabs and autos. And if the traffic got too bad, he could take the local. Which is why he had to inspect his car, and he had gotten better at it.

There was a rhythm to checking the car, as if you were dressing it. You began with the engine, and dressed it with the hood, and moved to the tyres, like stamping your shoes when you wore them, and finally an old tyre with rusty rims that was supposed to be a fall back option, but was in such a bad condition that Anant wasn't sure if he could use it during an emergency. A cursory pat around the corners of the car's trunk, to check for essentials, marked the end of his inspection. Despite this rhythm there remained in Anant niggling doubts about his car—he felt that one of these days, because of his haste, his car would give up on him. After he was done with the inspection, he jumped in and drove off. Out of habit, he turned off the radio and embraced the revving of the car engine—something he did quite often, but only when he wasn't sleepy. It wasn't much of an engine but because he rarely drove, the meagre speed that his car reached was exhilarating. For a few moments, he would hit the accelerator and burn through the road, or, well, singe through it while driving over the speed limit of 80 kmph. He would hit 100 kmph, even 102 kmph sometimes—that is if his engine could strain itself. He didn't pay attention to the speed. He would overtake buses and trucks while his beloved second-hand cherry-red Maruti Alto screamed and screeched, as if it were dying. Despite the risk, he would often survive because the buses and trucks, while mad in their own ride, were still in control and would avoid his tortured little cherry-red hatchback. When Anant had his share of exhilaration and thrill, although it only lasted for a few minutes, he fell in line and drove within the speed limit for the rest of his journey.

Anant reached his parents' home in Pune just as the birds had finished their morning chirpings and the neighbourhood was half alive with the humdrum of the last working day before the weekend. He parked his car on the road, in front of his parents' car, and remained in his seat—hands on the steering wheel, taking deep breaths, distancing himself from the cell in a bid to prepare himself for the days ahead, and the jarring darkness that would come to greet him alongside. An abrupt knock on his window snapped him out of his thoughts. Lips set in a perennial smile greeted him. The beaming face of his cousin Aarti, staring at him from the window on the passenger side of the car, caught him by surprise. For a moment, he was in two minds—whether to open the door, or reverse his car and take the drive back to Mumbai that would now take six hours. The roads would be busier and it was bound to be a longer trip. It would have been a fleeting choice, even if it were to be a viable option, but the moment had passed and Anant had taken too long to change his course of action.

Anant sat in his car contemplating the conversation that awaited him. He glanced at her again, and Aarti's rising eyebrows told him that every passing second was making this interaction more awkward, irrespective of her smile that was ever present. Aarti was the kind of person who perpetually wore a smile. She was the first person whom Anant had grown to dislike. This aversion that had been sown in his childhood had blossomed into something akin to a cursed tree that people would walk around despite having no ill-will towards it; but now that he was under her shade, he was cursed once again.

Following the days of her father's passing, a young Anant had tried to reach out to a young Aarti. The confusion he felt, the emotions he was trying to comprehend, it was given that she, only a year elder to him, would be plagued by the same confusion, if not worse. But what he saw behind her watery eyes was what his young mind comprehended as 'pretend sorrow'. That she was crying merely because there was sadness in her home, out of a reaction to the morose clouds floating over people's heads that filled her house, but ultimately, Anant believed that this tragedy was unable to pierce her heart like it had his. Unaware of the different ways in which people deal with shock, Anant observed her in the following days with a naïve cruelty that only children are capable of. He watched her turn to the TV, to music, eat whatever she wanted while maintaining that morose expression on her face, and decreed that she was unaffected. People would tug at her and pull her to their chests, and cry while rubbing her head; hidden from view, Anant imagined that she relaxed and wore her mask the moment she was given space to breathe, a mask that compensated for her lack of identity following her father's death.

Anant had stayed away from her ever since, putting distance between them whenever their families got together. When they would be seated around the dinner table, he would make it a point to not look at her, as if the mere sight of her made him uneasy. When she, her brother and their mother visited them during Diwali the year after, she had picked up a new expression, which he thought was an easy switch for her—almost like a change of clothes. A smile was etched on her face. It was the same expression she was wearing now, albeit with a few minor changes—the smile got wider, and the white teeth were more aligned. However, in essence it remained the same. To Anant, this smile was inauthentic, and plastered on. While the impassioned animosity that he had felt towards her in childhood had waned into a default preference to be away from her, the smile still had the same effect as someone chewing audibly, which, as it happened, had caused enough suffering throughout his college days. Anant opened his door and stepped out to greet her with a fleeting smile before he turned to pick up his suitcase and a shoulder bag. People who had once known him had learned to manoeuvre around his silence, as he had learned to manoeuvre through interactions. But not Aarti. It was another reason why he disliked her. He imagined that she believed that her pearly white smile could brighten anyone's day. 'How's the world of interior designing?' she asked while trying to take his backpack from him.

He tightened his grip on his bag and like an eagle circling her prey, she swooped down and snatched the suitcase out of his hand. 'It is fine. Same old. And the drugs?' He replied with a clenched jaw at having been defeated so easily.

'The drugs are always in demand,' she said. Taking advantage of the moment of silence, Anant turned towards the house to make his escape. Anant and Aarti walked the short distance from the gate to the front door in silence when Anant noticed a ring glinting on her finger. She was walking with her hand constantly moving in the front to make her new accessory obvious, as any newly engaged person would. A stylish gold ring with a single diamond that shone under the morning sun, filtering through the trees growing around the front gate.

'Congratulations!' he said with a pointed look at the ring and continued to walk. Aarti fell a few steps behind. In his march to the door, Anant missed the first time that her smile, since it had been plastered on, broke in his presence. And it was at that point in her life that she parted the blinds of her preconceived notions and saw the wretched being that resided within Anant. When Anant finally commented on the ring with a simple 'congratulations', without sparing a smile, or a courteous question, Aarti was caught unprepared and in her reaction, the mist of the tags of 'friends' and 'family' was lifted, and she saw their relationship for what it was. Far from a real sibling, not even a cousin or a colleague, he was worse than a stranger. A familiar face that was actively trying to put distance between himself and her. To her, this was a grave insult which was made graver because it managed to breach her otherwise impervious armour. More than Anant, whom she never really cared for and was a mere face that materialized from time to time when she visited her uncle and aunt, the ludicrousness of her reaction bothered her all the more.

Chapter 3

Aarti had arrived in Pune late in the evening when the city had already seen the worst of its congested traffic for the day, hours before Anant would start driving from Mumbai. She had taken it upon herself to deliver the invitations to those closest to her family, and to the extended family irrespective of their standing with her. Her late father's younger brother, her uncle and his family fell in the latter category, but they had remained close to them after her father passed away. Except Anant, but by the right of proximity, he was also included in this blanket term of extended family. The undeserving winner of the extended family tag wasn't particularly liked by Aarti. She found his unnerving silence weird, and unbeknownst to her, her subconscious had blown the magnitude of his silence out of proportion. The damning consequences of Anant's silence were a construct of Aarti's mind, but she refused to see it as such. She noticed that Anant had a pattern when it came to speaking with others—words and lines he used years ago would make their way into conversations. It was as if a tape recorder had been looped to the beginning once again. She would have rather not invited him, but her closeness to his parents won him an invitation as well.

As Anant stood by the door and rang the bell, Aarti glared at the back of his head and wondered why she had subjected herself to the torture of trying to have a conversation with him. She had wanted to be congratulated for her engagement, and after all, Anant was her cousin. That he wouldn't even have the decency to congratulate her was a scenario that Aarti hadn't even considered. Remembering his callous reaction, she tightened her hold on his suitcase to stop herself from flinging it on his barely-kept-together, red-blot-on-the-road car. The reality of her anger was staggering, and the acidic aftertaste of this negativity welcomed her in foreign yet familiar arms. Somehow, the bitterness she felt reminded her of her father, and his demise. She could feel the acid churning within her as she further tightened her grip on his bag, paving the way for her long-buried past to try and seize the stage.

It had been two decades since her father had passed away, two decades since she had chosen to leap away from despair. She remembered the days that followed vividly. Her home had become a house overnight. The delirium of her mother in her solitude once the guests began to clear, the hysteria under which she had burned all his clothes, it was obvious why as a child Aarti had chosen to bury herself in TV, toys, food and other wonders of a child's life. Her brother had recently begun college when he got the news of his father's death, and had rushed back home. He was a weeping mess as he stepped inside the house, but the question that made everyone squirm with discomfort was when he asked his mother whether he would still get the promised gift if he topped his class. He had asked the question the day after he arrived without understanding the seriousness of the tragedy, as if he were merely waiting for the people to clear out. The question held a chilling coldness that startled their mother. Perhaps the question had pushed her into further hysteria. Aarti wasn't sure if such had been the case, but she had blamed her brother for she could not tolerate losing two members of her family at once, and sunk in her bubble-wrapped world of manufactured joy where there was no time to introspect.

The next time Aarti's brother returned, he sold the car to sustain the family and continue his education. And the next, to the horror of their mother, he sold the gold that their parents had kept at home, even though at that point her mother could sustain the household working as a sports teacher in a local school. How she got that job, or what sports she excelled in, remained shrouded in mystery, but Aarti somehow seemed to remember those medals, trophies and plaques that belonged to her mother. She had a vague memory of having seen them as a child. Shortly afterwards, her brother left for America. In her present state of anger, still holding the suitcase, she could sense that an old fear had resurfaced—that after their mother passed away, her brother would return and sell the house. Alas, he was coming to her wedding. Suddenly, Aarti wasn't as excited for the wedding as she had been before meeting Anant.

Breakfast was had over typical questions directed towards Aarti, as is expected when a family member is getting married. Anant's family was quiet but unlike the son, the parents were familiar in the ways of the world and had accepted them as a part of life. Sunil Vohra, always delighted to host his brother's family, was exuberant over the fact that his brother's daughter had personally come to invite them to her wedding. In his eagerness, Sunil Vohra moved from one topic to the next, trying to discuss the venue, the clothes, the accommodation until Monica Vohra chimed in to direct him to stick to the questions that they thought would be apt, like how Aarti had met her soon-to-be husband, and how Gurugram was treating her. Throughout breakfast, constant exchange of questions and answers, and discussions, Aarti snuck glances at Anant and was reminded of her anger. It felt almost sadistic that she was compelled to look at him every now and again. Her smile dropped a little before she looked away. His presence continued to prick her resurfaced wound and kept it from healing. And if the wound hadn't healed in the first place, given how easily it had resurfaced after years of lying dormant, Aarti was confident that the therapeutic effect of simply ignoring it would have been enough to bring her back to the way she used to be. Her history was proof of the healing powers of ignorance. The bitterness that had left a strong imprint on her during her childhood, the feeling of abandonment that arose from the death of her father, the same absence also allowed these emotions to eventually, over time, wane along with his memory. They had no space in the world of joy that she had conjured. These memories were only alive in photos and these were pleasant memories—all of which had passed through the filter of nostalgia, and had been touched up and coloured over and over to such an extent that they were borderline make-believe.

Throughout breakfast, and lunch, Aarti continued to project every ill feeling that emerged from her resurfaced wounds on to Anant. The pent-up rage that she had exiled, already heightened with the upcoming wedding, had reacted with the enmity she felt towards Anant, and started to unearth dormant, long-forgotten emotions of her past. It had come to a point where she couldn't even look at him without feeling a scalding acid churning in her stomach, and it took all of her willpower to not flinch at the sight of Anant, who became more and more mangled with every glance. After dinner, as she prepared to retire for the night, while each member of the family was lost in their own worlds, she looked at him, if only to reassure herself that the brief tryst with her long-forgotten past had come to pass, and for a fleeting, startling moment, she was sure she saw her father's face instead of Anant.

That night, under the covers of an alien bed, Aarti wept the tears that had never been shed when she had lost her father. The cascade of tears bursting from a one-and-a-half-decade-long dam brought down the world that she had created. The next morning, she woke with the muddied feeling of a wet pillow and unruly hair that had managed to worm itself between the pillow and her face. She walked to the washroom with a clouded mind that was slowly piecing itself back together. She brushed her teeth, washed her face, and dreaded the breakfast—unsure if it would be Anant, or her father, whom she would be joining at the table.

'Why do they have to eat together?' she muttered, not without a little envy. She recalled how her brother would be more intent on stealing away her pieces of chicken before moving on to take all from her mom. In her cruel fantasy, she imagined her mother telling her that at least he had left the vegetables for them. And then she felt guilty for mocking her. It wasn't favouritism, she told herself. Her mom was a pushover when it came to either of her children. Her mom would have let her take her pieces of chicken as well. 'But she would have stopped me from taking his.' Aarti smiled and sighed at the same time.

She excused herself for the remaining half of the day after another unbearable breakfast at the dining table. Only midway through the meal when her uncle and aunt were talking to Anant did she feel compelled to look at him, that despite her anger, she didn't want to seem impolite. It was a noble excuse but in truth, she needed to find out who was sitting beside her, and upon seeing Anant's face, she let out a sigh. The relief that flooded her allowed her to momentarily step away from her own mind. She watched him as he talked about some new project that he might be getting. Some apartment in some area of Mumbai. Aarti hadn't lived in Mumbai long enough to know what was where. Being around his parents had done wonders for the solitary air that he carried; he seemed open, if not completely set in the world then not completely outside of it either. Aarti continued to watch Anant, enjoying the fact that her father's face was nowhere to be found, that it would not suddenly be superimposed on Anant's. This relief helped put the tears she had shed behind her, and return to the self that had arrived in

Pune, rather than what had become of her yesterday. Getting bored of listening to Anant, Aarti turned to her food. She could taste the flavour in the thick red-brown rajma sprinkled with coriander and pieces of ginger peeking through it, and steamed rice that had seemed bland moments ago, and slowed down to enjoy her food, rather than trying to chow down the rajma–rice combo and escape.

Chapter 4

When Sunil Vohra came to know about Aarti's plans of leaving after dinner, he was overcome with a paternal instinct that had laid dormant ever since Anant had succeeded in establishing his business and moved to Mumbai. He jumped in to remind Aarti that she should take care of herself. It wasn't an affront to her ability to handle herself, but Sunil, having received the invitation, had begun to think of his brother and how happy he would have been over the wedding. Sunil felt as if his own daughter was getting married. And in his eyes, Aarti and him shared similarities which could be taken for weakness. She had a penchant for being too nice.

Once upon a time, Sunil Vohra had been a shy man himself and understood how such niceties could be taken for granted. All that had changed when he received a call, late one evening, to tell him that his brother had died. Natural causes, he was told. What was natural about the passing of a healthy forty-two-year-old man? Sunil had had his share of ups and downs in his life. He understood the inevitability of death, and he simply tried to move on. His father had passed away when he was still in school, never to be mourned but for that brief moment when one of the Sisters from school had shared the news of their father's death with the boys. The moment his mother became the captain of the house, she ran the ship with an iron fist. She flew the flag of studying, of good hard work and dedication towards the rare opportunity that Sunil and his brother had of studying in a good missionary school while other villages like theirs would have to make do with more humble schools where teachers were stricter on conduct and values than teaching itself. His mother, the iron-willed lady who had decided that both her sons would become collectors, had died after both the brothers were married but before they had any children, a complaint she never got tired of raising. She died three years before Aarti was born, a decade before his brother passed away. The two brothers had mourned their deceased parents together.

Govinda and Sunil had relied on each other. In the quiet of the night they kept their dad's memory alive by telling each other the vague stories that they remembered. If one would concoct a fake memory to fill in a blank space where their father should have existed, the other would simply accept it, rather than papering over it with the truth. Their father's favourite memory was that of their grandfather, a freedom fighter with a great oiled moustache that Sunil's dad would stroke so that he would be noticed, and quickly lifted up and swung around. It felt like flying, their father had said while recalling the experience. But in the words of their mother, it was better than flying—at least that is what Sunil had learned over the phone from his mother after she had flown for the first time; it was one of the rare moments she mentioned his father. His mother never flew again, always choosing to travel by train thereafter. This grandfather's story being forgotten never bothered him, because he had never known him. His parents passing away was heartbreaking, but at least the brothers had each other to lean on and keep their memory alive.

As far as Sunil was concerned, the worst thing he had to experience was the profane lunacy of watching his brother's memory being forgotten. Govinda's death was horrible for Sunil, but to be privy to the wretched sin of time as it slowly blotted out his brother's presence seemed just as appalling, if not worse. His brother's aura, once full of confidence and brimming with energy so that it could be felt in multiple places at once, fading, being swallowed by the currents of time. Seeing his brother's story being forgotten along with his pictures, even by his own children which to him felt like a crime against humanity and all that was holy and natural, made him realize that he had become the last remaining monument of his childhood, with his parents and his brother dead and forgotten.

Sunil had deduced that the only course of action to take was to focus on the tangible, to push down his shy nature and build, with clothes as decorations, a persona that would be present in the memories of others, beyond his wife and child, whether out of jealousy or because of his charitable nature. Sunil too had a penchant for quiet, much like his wife and son. But unlike them and their perplexing quiet silence, his silence was loud, and became louder as time went by, demanding attention. One could hear his thoughts rattling in his mind even if he did not say a word. He used this silence to imagine the days ahead, and what he was on the track to do and what he should add to his life. To help others was just another task, along with work and mingling with the world around him. Aarti's marriage, where he believed he would give her hand, was another moment in life to be remembered. To intertwine himself in Aarti's memory of marriage and thus keeping not only himself, but his brother and their parents' memory alive.

After breakfast, Sunil walked Aarti to the front door and told her about a delectable café nearby before retiring to his office. It was once a parking spot with a green shed where the previous owner parked his cycles and scooter. It was made of concrete and turned into a storage room. When the Vohras moved in, the room remained abandoned until Sunil turned it into an office. For him, having a private space was a necessity. The presence of a guest in their house pushed both his wife and him out of tune with their respective worlds. Sunil needed an office to be lost in just as much as his wife, Monica, needed an undisturbed routine to lose herself in. Despite the limited budget and the small space, the office was well thought out and charming.

Anant had been sitting beside him when the idea of an office was conceived, and Sunil had pulled image after image on his laptop, muttering to himself the pros and cons of an office, before suddenly jumping to his feet and rushing out, leaving Anant to continue staring blankly at the television. Anant was used to his father behaving in such an eccentric manner. By the time Anant had visited the house again, the office was finished. He was told that it only took a month. The walls were painted a comforting off-white that breathed space into the room while the fake plants made the still cramped space seem homely. The canvas prints of obscure impressionist paintings were fitted in frames that were far more impressive than the paintings themselves, in terms of quality of print and not composition, leaving the colours stretched and distorted. The rich brown polish of the furniture, a bright blue lounge chair somehow fitted in the corner while the office desk on the other side had an executive office chair and two plastic chairs across the table.

Anant went to see the office that his father was excited to show him, and lost him to the praises he was gathering from people that weren't around. With a curt nod, Anant had left. Later when Sunil had offered Anant another tour of his office, he told him that he had done a good job. As Anant had left the office then, he quietly left the dining table after collecting the plates and putting them in the basin, and walked back to his room.

And while the two Vohra men were off to their own little slice of the world, where they could be alone, the matriarch of the family, Monica Vohra, the only one in the house to have found solitude in the real world rather than seeking peace by escaping the real world, observed them until she was alone at the dining table. She remained seated, tracing the floral pattern of the plate, and enjoying the quiet of the living room. She deliberated over a black tea. Perhaps with some lemon, she mused. But her internal clock struck and alerted her to the next task in her daily routine. She calmly got up, the tea forgotten, and cleared the table. It was this devotion to her routine and adherence to time that had allowed Monica to befriend rather than fight the flow of time, unlike the other two Vohras. The secret to her serene solitude was a simple one—she allowed herself to be carried by the currents of time, and thus attained the gift of never having to worry about making time to be alone. Every weekday was the same and so was every weekend, barring the ones when Anant would visit. Being one with her routine made her feel weightless as if she was floating down a stream—a continuous greeting and farewell to the seconds that continued to tick, with a stoic acceptance of the day that would be.

The three Vohras returned to the table for lunch when Sunil suggested that they give Aarti a token for the invitation. 'What a moment it will be!' Sunil was excited. 'It would be polite,' Monica responded after noticing that her husband would not deter from this decision. It was rare to have Sunil both excited and adamant. 'Yes, yes, polite. We must, mustn't we?' Sunil returned to his lunch, the same as always, living in the excitement of the moment, and the memory that it would become.

Sunil and Monica spent their time browsing through the gold almost every Indian family strives to collect over time. They picked out a beautiful pair of earrings that they would give Aarti at dinner. Once the decision had been made, Monica returned to what was next in her routine while Sunil held the earrings with a smile, his eyes twinkling as he relished in the memory that it would become. For everyone.

Upon being presented with the earrings, Aarti's face lit up—it was like the sun had suddenly emerged from behind the dark clouds. She even grinned at Anant, but her smile faltered within seconds of looking at him, as if it was no longer under her control but instead, it had become a rule for the muscles of her face to droop over in his presence. She did not let it bother her. She was moved by the thoughtfulness of her aunt and uncle, irrespective of the fact that the precious metal in her hands was maligned by the memories of her brother selling all the gold in their house. The rest of the dinner sailed past the four of them with the pleasant winds of the upcoming marriage that carried faint notes of the shehnai already, and Aarti could sense a feeling of belonging at the table with this extended part of her family. In the morning, before the birds began their chirping, even before the newspaper man made his rounds, Aarti slipped into Anant's bedroom and without a glance at the lump buried underneath the quilt, she left the earrings on the nearest table next to the door. She viewed it as reparation for the anger that she had pushed on to him. Though Aarti had not made her annoyance with Anant obvious, she did not want it to weigh on her conscience. She did not think Anant was important enough to be a bridge or a window to a world gone by. A world that she had carefully amputated when she had drawn the map of her new world. By paying him off, irrespective of whether it was needed or not, she decided that neither of them would be indebted to the other. As strangers ought to be.

Downstairs, Sunil and Monica Vohra had gotten up to bid her farewell. It was an early flight that Aarti had chosen. She planned to return to her office the very same day. Sunil was thinking of giving her another piece of gold, not as extravagant, but one that would really catch her off guard. He would whisper that this was from his brother. What a moment it would be, he had thought. But even thoughts weren't completely hidden from the observant eyes of Monica. She told him no without even being asked. Sunil nodded, the thought vanishing in the blink of an eye. It wasn't like him to be sullen over his unfinished whimsies. They did not have an abundance of gold, and giving her the earrings was already cutting into the amount that had been saved over the years. Sunil had thus managed to reason his way out of an impulsive decision.

Sunil wasn't sure why people saved gold, even his grandfather had a gold chain that had returned with his dead body when he was shot by the British Indian police. Sunil wasn't alive at the time, but the way his father had repeatedly told the story, it was as if he had seen the glint of the gold, and the oily moustache resembling the one sported by Chandrashekhar Azad. With no more gifts to give, Sunil and Monica hugged their niece and waved goodbye. Aarti left for the airport with a grin on her face that wavered and became a tight smile when she was finally alone, the work of her muscles more than her will.

Chapter 5

Anant was seated in the back of a cab looking out from an imaginary window of a paradoxical place that was both far away, and yet it merely took the awareness of it to gain entry. He sat in the cell throughout the ride, ruminating on nothing precise, nothing detailed. He was just mellow as he thought about the opportunity that was right before him. He already had a prior meeting with the then prospective client before he went to Pune, and was delighted to possibly have a new project so soon. Just a month ago, he had finished a simple design for the reception of a clinic. This project, however, excited Anant. It was rare for him to have an opportunity where he wasn't limited in terms of design, nor constricted in colours, or chained to a rudimentary layout of the space. The cab took its sharp turns and abrupt stops as they entered Juhu, the only constant was the traffic and the unchanging billboards of builders that cut down more trees to build apartments that would stall midway in construction in a city that already had a backlog of unsold flats, and hoardings of politicians who worked eighteen hours a day but should perhaps take some rest, and of heritage advertisements that might just outlast the whole city.

There were, of course, the usual as well. Heavy clouds barely hung in the air, awaiting a single pin or a gust of wind to burst. But somehow, they managed to hang in the sky with the warning of what could be, what soon would be, heavy showers in a minute or a day, one could never tell with Mumbai. The cab took him to a hotel called Sun-n-Sand, an aged white building that must have been modern once. Towards the back of the hotel was a courtyard that was elevated and overlooking the beach. There was a café to the side with large glass walls so you could enjoy looking at the ocean from the comfort of an air-conditioned room. There was a small pool to the other side of the courtyard, where people were splashing about and others had spread themselves over lounge chairs. Noises of splashing and chatter filled the air. His prospective client stood by the parapet on the far side of the courtyard with his back turned towards the door.

Anant walked over and paused beside him, observing the scene ahead in his own slow and deliberate way, as if to take in the details before he would look at the scene as a whole. A tractor moving across the beach with people running around it collecting the endless stream of trash that never abated, a person sitting right behind a lamp as if he had prepared to be in the shade if the sun ever peeked through the leaden clouds, the hustle and bustle to the left of the hotel was where the famous Juhu Chowpatty stood, attracting tourists and locals alike, the casual stroll of friends, couples, enjoying a pleasant Mumbai afternoon. 'Good afternoon,' Anant finally greeted him.

If the client hadn't noticed his presence till now, he didn't let it show on his face. Rajat was a comfortable man well in his thirties who seemed to be always comfortable, no matter the situation he found himself in. This was only their second meeting, but Anant got the impression that working with Rajat would be deceptively easy for it seemed like he knew exactly what he wanted. This made Anant wary of him. Clients who claimed that they knew exactly what they wanted rarely wanted what they said.

'Anant, my man, I spent the rest of the day after our meeting thinking about your ideas. You just toss them about. You know, a less honest man would have just stolen them and gone with them,' Rajat, the client, said in jest.

'Oh, thank you.'

'But I thought, if those were the ideas that you were carrying around like business cards, then what more would you have in mind for my flat.'

This almost made Anant furrow his brow, but he checked himself and focused on listening to his client—Rajat. He clenched and unclenched his jaw, and tried to focus on the prospective project. He didn't believe that he was carrying his ideas like business cards. It was true that he could be taken with a philosophy of design or an aesthetic, but that was a given for any person interested in design. Anant had only given the ideas that he was sure that Rajat could use. The thought of another man, more or less honest than Rajat, had never occurred to him. He was sure that even if someone did steal his ideas, it won't make much of a difference since they would not be executed properly. It would be like being measured by a tailor for a bespoke suit, and then using your memory of those measurements to find a ready-made one. Even with alterations, it would lack the personalization. 'So, I have the job?' Anant asked for confirmation, a flutter of nerves crawling up his spine.

'Of course, man. That's why I invited you over. My whole flat is at your disposal, but on one condition. Listen, I like your ideas and they're great. They really are. But I want the flat to be a space that I created. Now, of course, I may not know the fine print of it all, I leave that to you experts, but I want you to think of it as helping me create, you know...like you are the guide to steer me along.'

Rajat was only asking what every client asked any interior designer they hired. It was a given, the original unsaid clause of the contract between a designer and the client. Often clients would make small changes in an effort to put their stamp on the work, as if by doing so they were formally taking over the site, and turning it into their home. It was an added benefit that they could impress their guests by telling them how they had designed it themselves. 'Sure, there was an interior designer.' They would start their conversations like this, and then go on to say 'But I wanted something more me' or 'The designer just didn't understand me'. They thought their ideas were inherently unique. That the interior designer had but laid the groundwork, the playground for the owner to express himself. And they would have peace of mind knowing that the interior designer would never replicate what he had done to their home, not out of honour for the work or because a bespoke suit wouldn't fit the same on another, but because they were the ones who had brought it all together. Anant nodded and the client gave him a smile.

'You don't talk much, I like that. I don't talk much either.' Rajat turned and fixed his gaze at the ocean, as if to emphasize the silence. Anant took his cue and followed him. A group of people walked a long way across the beach, the tractor soon returned with workers moving around it as if they were in a procession, throwing the discarded litter into it. When Rajat was satisfied with the silence, he invited Anant for a cup of coffee so that they could admire the beauty of the ocean from the comfort of the café. There wasn't much of the beach to enjoy from the café, for a courtyard cut most of the view. But it was a necessary sacrifice for those who wanted to admire nature without exposing themselves to its suffocating humidity. The polished experience of nature without any hardships.

In the café, Anant ordered cold coffee while Rajat wanted to have coconut water. By the time the theatrics of cutting open a coconut ended, the cold coffee was already on the table. He focused on his drink while his client was taken with his fresh coconut water. Rajat would take a sip from the straw and look past Anant to admire the scene and sigh. Anant came to realize that Rajat had a taste for drama. They talked about nothing in particular, and Rajat did most of the talking with a few questions about Anant being sprinkled in between. He mainly focused on what he wanted his home to look like. However, one could guess what Rajat was about to say. Contrary to Anant's expectations that Rajat would know what he wanted, his new client was merely regurgitating objects from magazines and websites that any would-be homeowner who had dipped their toes into the world of catalogues would know. Anant could anticipate the course of the conversation quite effortlessly—art and music, the quest for a warm, inviting place, no risks, and assurances that he, Rajat, was the kind of guy to go with the flow, only to end the monologue by stressing on the fact that he wanted what was in his mind. But he couldn't explain exactly what it was. Of course, he couldn't. Rajat had merely plucked a feeling that was prompted by an array of images he browsed without ever trying to imagine the flat in his mind.

To begin was a daunting task, especially for a novice, and by making a decision on any aspect of it, from the layout to the furniture to even the stucco or plaster style of the ceiling, it would take him a step away from plausible deniability in case anything went wrong. If Rajat had taken the step, Anant thought, it would have eventually gotten progressively easier as he continued. A secret that Anant wasn't willing to reveal any time soon. And why would Rajat get caught up in the technicalities of the work when he had an interior designer to think for him. It was a good thing that he hadn't, for Anant had been bored on his previous job and was excited at the prospect of having a little more creative licence in the new project.

'Man, a friend of mine is hosting a party in his flat, and I like...certain things about it that we could make our own. Only inspirations, I mean. It's got a vibe to it, you know. Meet me the day after, I'll text you the details.' Rajat was done with the coconut water. He paid the bill and left swiftly without feeling any compulsion to ask Anant if he was available or interested in the said party. His parting words were reminders that Anant must observe nature, that he was missing the grandeur of the ocean by focusing too much on his coffee.

Anant merely sat at his table sipping his coffee, muttering a 'Bye' to no one for Rajat was halfway out of the café when he waved his hand. The cold coffee had turned watery by the time Anant finished a few fingers worth; he left the rest and went back to stand near the edge of the courtyard. A guard was standing there to stop people from sitting on the parapet. He hurried past Anant towards a couple taking pictures while standing on the edge. The parapet was made of stone and it was around two feet high, but one could never be sure who might fall and ruin the place, forcing the hotel to add fences or a net. Anant settled his eyes on the ocean, and soon his being followed suit. With deep breaths, the sound of chatter along the pool began to disappear and only the pleasant air, heavy with the scent of rain, and the pleasant sound of ocean waves along the beach remained.

The day after was a Friday with dark clouds hovering in the sky, and the promise of torrential rain. Anant was standing in the kitchen waiting for his sandwich to get warm when he received a call from Rajat to remind him of the party and share the details, which he later texted as well. It was a short call, and Anant could hear loud music in the background. The rain ended abruptly after the call. The clouds parted outside his flat. The sandwich had turned from toasted to extra crispy by the time he took it out.

In the evening, Rajat waited for him in the polished lobby of a high-rise tower in Parel. His friend stayed in a three-bedroom flat with his parents, and was hosting people in the living room and his bedroom, strictly away from the master bedroom and the kitchen adjacent to it. Such a set-up in a party often led to spills, broken bottles and damaged cutlery but his parents slept through it with little to no bother to them. Or so Rajat explained to Anant when they were in the elevator, also reminding him to not tell anyone of his occupation.

Sehaj Agarkar was a slim, smiling and solicitous man who greeted Rajat with a hug and Anant with a firm handshake, before giving them a brief tour of the flat. It was for Anant but Rajat tagged along. Sehaj stopped by a small corridor after showing the two bedrooms to them, a stern expression replaced the smile as he warned them like Mufasa from the movie *Lion King* to never venture to that side of the flat. Rajat was quick to point out with his eyes or gesture with his chin things that he fancied during the brief tour and when Sehaj left them, Rajat and Anant returned to all that had been marked—not to be copied but 'draw inspiration' from things, such as an inconspicuous accent light fixed on the off-white wall and falling on a sculpture of a tusk made with resin, or the ceiling with tube lights fitted in for indirect light, all of which seemed fairly standard to Anant. The only impressive piece of work were the masks decorating a wall, adjacent to which was a string curtain hung from a bar, with a strip of LED fairy lights tied to it; they sparkled, reflecting multiple hues, but the masterstroke was the play of light on the masks—it was as if the changing colours of the LED lights gave them an array of moods. Rajat was pulled away from the interiors and quickly seemed to forget why he had invited Anant, for he began to mingle with people. 'Anant, man, relax! You are in your own self too much. Look at the world around you. It will help you with your mind, you know. You must feed it constantly.'

It wasn't the first time Anant had received such an advice from others. In fact, he had gotten the same suggestion throughout his life, the reasons masked as 'not letting your life go by you' and 'being present in the world', as if the excuse itself was making an effort to not become monotonous. And as he took on the mantle of an interior designer, the advice became all about 'feeding his creativity'.

Anant found it peculiar how the same action was the one-stop solution for everything. He would have argued that looking at the world from the confines of a cell with only a window to look out from allowed him to cherish things that caught his eye and keep them alive in memory, that it was far more effective in stirring inspiration than living with an abundance of glitter and beauty, which no doubt would breed carelessness in one. But he consciously refrained from engaging with others on this subject—for he was sure that he would lose his sanity if he debated with everyone who had ever given him this advice. Anant fell into his routine of predetermined replies as he passed from one conversation to the next, until late into the night when he had to pause his cruise control. Late in the night, he noticed Rajat's face was flush and red after the countless drinks he had gulped down. He was surrounded by a group of people but his eyes were blank and unfocused. It felt like life was working to prove Anant's argument.

A cocktail of old Hindi and English songs played in the background while Rajat held a caricature of what could be deemed a conversation with two different people, moving his legs from time to time and looking around with drooping, red eyes in a hasty attempt to try and savour a world that, along with all its answers, had chosen this moment to reveal itself, and soon would be forgotten when he would wake up the next day on someone else's couch.

Chapter 6

Rajat woke up on a cramped couch in a barren room that he did not recognize. His weary eyes fluttered from side to side, hoping to remember the events that had led him to this room. He glanced at a huge leather wingback chair that stood near the foot of the small couch, and thought that the chair would have made for a far more comfortable bed than the one he was currently lying on. One where he could stir without the fear of falling out. The couch had barely enough cushioning to offer a pleasant seating, Rajat noted, let alone for a bed. Whoever had led him here had done him a grave injustice. And then Rajat looked around the strange, empty room with its dust-matted corners. The lack of a coffee table unnerved Rajat.

There was a small plastic stool in the far corner of the room upon which a record player was placed. Speakers stood on either side on the floor, with notebooks stacked on top of their flat heads. Beneath the plastic stool were a collection of vinyl records. The room did not look like it belonged to any friend of his, and the thought of being kidnapped triggered a panic and his mind started racing. Rajat sprang to his feet. The question why his captors would leave him untied became a statement that his captors had forgotten to tie his arms and legs. He questioned if he had been drugged. He didn't remember much of the night before.

He pondered over what to do next while having decided that he would bolt out the door. Close to working himself into a frenzy, his thoughts came to an abrupt halt when he saw Anant standing by the railing of a small balcony. Memories from the night before started flashing in front of him, in tatters, as if Anant's mere presence had raised the night from its grave. The hangover that had been alleviated because of the fear-and-anxiety-induced adrenaline rush had slowly made a comeback.

'Coffee? You want coffee?' Anant asked when he stepped inside.

'Man, what happened last night?' Rajat asked, rubbing the back of his head. 'And yes, black.'

'The world happened,' Anant muttered, his comment ignored or unheard.

He walked to his kitchen and poured water into a pot which he set to boil. He continued to observe the foreign presence of Rajat who was trying to make sense of the flat. There were a few comments on the night before from Rajat that Anant left unheard. When he returned with a cup of coffee, Rajat was staring at the record player.

'Man, for an interior designer, your own flat isn't your best work,' he said. 'Perhaps that is why you have your ideas as business cards.'

Anant took a moment to observe the darkness that sat on Rajat's shoulders as he registered what had just been said. The same darkness as everywhere else. One had to commend the Titan on its impartial ways. Death was a true liberal, despite being as old as time. Wordlessly, Anant gave him the cup of coffee. Rajat stared at him, waiting for a reply. The awkwardness of the interaction made the quiet feel heavy to Rajat.

If a home is the embodiment of its residents, Anant believed that the flat was apt for him. The grand wingback chair was a size too big for most furnished living rooms in Mumbai, and had been left behind in the flat by the owner. The sofa was a placeholder given to him by his parents until he found something better. For Anant, the grand chair and his corner of the living room were more than enough for him. But he understood that his philosophy was not for his clients. 'It is an empty space so I do not make copies of my own flat everywhere.' Anant was surprised at how easily the lie rolled off his tongue, as if he had practised it many times. He understood the necessity of giving people enough so they let him be, and practised it with unwavering dedication until it had become a reflex, but even he was surprised at how wonderfully it worked.

'You're very dedicated. So am I, you know,' Rajat said while taking a sip of his coffee. 'A record player, I would love to have one of those. You should make a space for this in my flat.'

Instinctively, as Anant did with any suggestion from his client, he ran it against the mental checklist that had been passed down to him from the designer he had worked under. It wasn't a need, hobby or passion that the client was fulfilling, and Anant was sure that the record player would collect dust in less than a quarter of a year. As could the client, Anant thought to himself as he spared another glance at the darkness. As could he. And he nodded in agreement, scrounging through the notebooks to find a fresh one where he put Rajat's name on the front page, and on the last page he wrote 'record player'.

Rajat left the apartment after downing the last sip of his coffee. He kept fiddling with his phone during his drive back to his residence. He browsed through turntables and vinyl records before he got distracted by brass sculptures available online and after much deliberation, he settled on one that he felt would perfectly describe him. The sculpture was of Atlas holding the world on his shoulders. He saved the brass statue to his wish list which had a sock and buskin sculpture. Despite nursing a headache, his mind was rattling suggestions and by the time he reached the hotel where he was staying, he deleted the sock and buskin from his wish list. 'It would be too common,' he thought.

Rajat had come to Mumbai on behalf of his dad to click pictures of a site and meet with the chief engineer. Rajat knew little to nothing about being a contractor, but he knew what was expected of him while he was representing the company. He had learned by accompanying his dad since he was young, and when he dropped out of college and found that the world wasn't bowing to his every whim and dream, he attended these meetings, always accompanied by other executives, to make his dad believe, and more so himself, that he was working. Yet, no matter who his teacher was, or which expert played the role of his babysitter, Rajat never learned the job.

He was content with being the face of the company and the management, a rank he was given at birth. It was a part-time job anyway, and Rajat refused to even court the possibility that he would sacrifice his own dreams for this job. His dreams that never ventured past a vague formless idea that would lead him to a scene and setting that had been shaped by television screens. These obscure dreams, the idea of dreaming rather than the dream itself, a dream of a dream and the illusion of a life post-dream, remained shrouded in mystery out of a fear that by declaring his grand idea, as if by writing it down and giving it shape, Rajat would begin to court the risk of failure. He explained his fear away by telling himself that to burn at the altar of any one goal would deprive him of everything else. The holidays he took for introspection and what he called personal work would change colour every now and again. Like a chameleon he would hide in the latest infatuations of his mind. The repeated building and rebuilding of his self, of keeping the distance between his goals and destroying them only for them to be made again, such a heroic task was built on the endless egotism of a youth beginning to fade.

The unwavering confidence in his ability to not merely make

a movie that would change the culture of the whole country and play in theatres longer than *Sholay* or *Dilwale Dulhaniya Le Jayenge*, but also write the next great novel and make an album worthy of being called a classic. But to keep these dreams vague, he spent more time fixated on stardom and acclaim, featuring on talk shows and spending the rest of his life living with this one project that would be a proof of the genius he had made himself believe. During these holidays, when the niggling reality would begin to force him to confront his own hollow identity, and the dreams that were slipping out of his fingers like grains of sand, he would promptly end the vacation in an effort to hide himself in the illusion that he was working with his dad until he would find the courage to venture out for a few days again.

Rajat had arrived in Mumbai to stay here for a week, but he was enraptured by the city and the week stretched into two, and soon he bought a flat. He had decided that Mumbai was where he could fulfil his potential. It was the city where dreams came true, or died. But Rajat had no doubt in his ability to succeed. He had called his parents to inform them about his decision. With a place of his own, not rented but of his own creation, he would find the peace of mind to finally fulfil what he had believed since childhood was his destiny. He convinced them that he would make it on his own, that he would live out of his own pocket and whatever pennies they would give him. Irrespective of whether his parents were convinced or not, Rajat had at least managed to persuade them to refrain from objecting to his decision.

It had been two months since Rajat had arrived in Mumbai, and he was yet to leave the five-star hotel where his dad's office had put him in for what was supposed to be a short work trip. He told himself that he would leave when his flat was ready. Of course, one night with a drink in hand, he had already considered buying a car and living out of it. But the romantic idea of a struggler's life, and what a promising story that would be to narrate to the audience at dinner parties and talk shows, cleared and he got a glimpse of the reality of his routine. He realized the amount of time he spent in his hotel room, availing the benefits of the hotel. Surely anyone could understand that they were a necessity until he had his own flat. The traffic of Mumbai became his excuse. Plus, all that petrol he would be burning, ruining the environment. Rajat would also use the credit card that his dad had given him, but only when the tab ran too high, at least that is what he told himself. Otherwise he would use his money— earned by being a director in his dad's company, plus the pennies.

After Rajat returned from Anant's flat, he told an attendant near the front desk to have a lemonade and a glass of any seasonal juice sent up to his room. Usually, he only sipped the juice once before keeping it away. He liked the image of it. It relaxed him. But the exhaustion from the night before and the unceremonious beginning of his day took an unexpected toll on Rajat and by the time he reached his room, he was completely drained. He could not even change his clothes and fell asleep on the bed before room service came with the juice and lemonade. Despite his exhaustion, Rajat had the clarity of mind to leave the door open so he would not have to get up from his bed and could simply shout for the person to come in, but Rajat fell asleep before this plan could be completed. With the door open, the attendant came in to find Rajat sleeping shirtless on the bed, the blanket draped over him and his neck disappearing into the pillow. The attendant quietly put the glasses by the nightstand and left.

On a Wednesday afternoon, Rajat remained in his bed watching videos on his tablet with the curtains drawn and the weather unknown. He had called Anant on Monday evening to ask him when he could see the rough sketches and drawing of his flat.

'Wednesday afternoon,' Anant had said.

When Rajat commented on the pace of things in an effort to warn Anant that he did not want half-baked ideas, Anant reverted with a simple and curt 'okay'. Rajat liked this decisive approach to conversations. Anant's quietness which when noticed made some uneasy, had the opposite effect on Rajat. He believed that he felt more comfortable with Anant because of his silence. To Rajat, Anant's quiet nature was not boastful or meek, but a steady state of constant acceptance like an automated hammering machine at the end of a conveyer belt that crushed any and all products into the factory standard size. Rajat liked to believe that he could do the same in his life. After a stream of infantile talk shows and videos of ostentatious speakers who preached the rudimentary self-help disguised as philosophy, he mused over this acceptance that Anant carried with him while he got dressed and made his way down.

Chapter 7

The lobby of the hotel was washed with multiple colours of marbles in mosaic. Celebrated paintings hung on the walls which only seemed at home because of the decadence of the hotel. A giant chandelier hung from the skylight ceiling and reached down to rest twenty feet from the tessellated floor, and finishing the lobby, in the corner was a collection of quiet round tables and a piano that seemed to have been cut out of a business hotel and pasted to this place. Rajat could see Anant standing by the entrance as he was coming out of the elevator. He paused to take a moment and observe him, wondering if he could learn his secret of acceptance via telepathic osmosis. Anant stood still with a small portfolio briefcase which had sketches and a tablet. He had a blank, almost dimwitted look as he stared ahead. Rajat found himself growing impatient with the lack of movement on Anant's part. It seemed like someone had turned his switch off, but as he walked closer, he realized that Anant's eyes were alive, taking in the hotel lobby in a way that Rajat believed was unique to Anant, or to interior designers as a whole. The mystery of the artist, Rajat told himself while ignoring Anant's tense posture. 'Good afternoon,' Rajat greeted him and Anant was quick to reciprocate the greeting.

The coffee shop at the hotel was an open affair with a pathway going across it from the lobby to the buffet where preparations for lunch were under way. The counter of the coffee shop was decorated with cakes, pastries, breads, cookies and cupcakes. As they walked to take their seats by the towering glass partitions overlooking a pool, Anant spotted a blueberry doughnut with sprinkles making a crescent on one side of the glaze. He could not take his eyes off it. Amongst the cakes, pastries, breads and cupcakes, this doughnut shone like the crowning jewel, as if a gingerbread emperor had been slayed to create the doughnut. The glaze seemed to twinkle as if it was refracting the light coming from the outside. The dough was thick, but airy, as if a cloud had been fried to perfection. While the two sat facing each other, Anant found it hard to tear himself away from the doughnut. He kept glancing past Rajat's shoulder, and at times, even through the darkness that rested on his shoulder to find the doughnut, illuminated by an ethereal light as if it existed to delight the gods. For a moment, the darkness that existed all around him, disappeared.

Anant's mouth had become dry and he rasped his order of a Vietnamese iced coffee while Rajat ordered an espresso. 'I didn't take you to have a sweet tooth,' Rajat commented, and it took Anant a second to realize that it was directed towards the coffee he had ordered.

Anant smiled, trying to blink himself out of this stupor and reached for his briefcase to pull out his notebook that had a few loose sketches of possible layouts for the rooms, and his tablet where he had saved a variety of images of heavy furniture that would allow him to further understand Rajat's taste. Rajat took two sips of coffee each time he reached for his cup while he flicked through the drawings and browsed through the pictures, and liberally complimented him constantly with 'nice' and 'love this'.

But by the third time Rajat declared his love for a sketch, Anant had come to realize that he already had something in his mind. This duplicity did not bother Anant. It was part of the job. Clients often began the interactions believing they were in front of a mind reader. Anant understood the way of the business, and turned to his coffee while he waited patiently, often stealing glances at the doughnut. At times Anant felt like he had been abducted by the doughnut to another world where the only separation between them was that of a wall created by Rajat's 'nice' and 'love this'.

The doughnut was like a lighthouse that guided Anant to safety, telling him that he was close to the shore and he needn't rush and risk this job, that he needed the money, and that the doughnut wasn't going anywhere, that it would wait for him. Anant was aware of the bliss that awaited him. His experiences with prior enchantments such as the doughnut helped him steer the waves of 'nice' and 'love this', amidst the noise of chatter from the buffet, and music from the lobby.

Rajat went through the notebook and looked up to find a distracted Anant, and used this opportunity to observe him up close. It was the same astute stillness he had seen in him while he was standing in the hotel lobby. He wondered if this was a practised look. Was Anant in the habit of standing in front of the mirror trying to perfect this look that he wore so often? Rajat wondered. Although Rajat wouldn't accept it in front of others, he had done the same in the past. The expressions he would wear when he was aware of himself were modified, if not created, to build an aura of the genius. What this genius meant, what all it entailed, changed from time to time, and so would his practised expressions. Rajat tossed the notebook on the table with a thud to get Anant's attention. With Anant's eyes focused on him once again, he squinted his eyes and fell silent, as if Anant had caught him in the midst of hatching a great thought.

'This is all great, Anant, I think we can take from here and there. But I...' Rajat paused, showing his penchant for drama once again. 'I don't know how to explain.' But explain he would, only later. Rajat turned around to see what was distracting Anant, and missed the doughnut entirely as if it was just a decoration to two attendants standing behind the counter—a man and a woman both of whom seemed to be nearing their thirties. They had neatly combed hair, as is the job requirement, and a smile that lied about how eager they were to be of assistance. It was a practiced smile—one that was a result of training and experience. 'Oh.' Rajat turned around to look at Anant as if he had dropped his train of thought. 'Someone you know?' he inquired.

'No.' Anant knew that Rajat couldn't possibly imply that he should talk to the doughnut. The two attendants were busy in their work, and when either would bend to take out a slice of cake that was placed on either side of the doughnut, the death hanging on their shoulders would act as a backdrop to accentuate the star-kissed colours of the doughnut.

'I know this is work but it isn't. I want you to be free in your actions and more so with me. That's how you will be creative,' Rajat said, having forgotten the numerous drawings Anant had made in two days.

'The lady reminded me of someone. Let's not distract ourselves.' Anant had gone through half of his iced coffee by now, and was hoping to end the meeting before his last sip.

'Oh, who?' Rajat inquired.

'Someone who died a long time ago.' The conversation came to a sudden halt.

Anant told himself that he hadn't lied to Rajat. That this wasn't a lapse in his system of automated responses. He wasn't sure if he believed in reincarnation but it was a convenient belief to pick up when he wanted to end conversations. The silence hung between them, stretched by Rajat who was no longer dramatizing himself, and dropping his planned act of pretending that he had just found one of the products in a flash of inspiration. He gave Anant his phone with the list and photos of design choices that he had saved over the weeks. The rest of the meeting picked up and for Anant, the meeting went swimmingly. It finished with only the last dregs of the iced coffee left. They shook hands and Rajat excused himself to retire to his room, carrying the silence that had dawned on him during the conversation. The mention of death had reminded Rajat of his old nemesis, his own mortality. As far as Rajat could remember, he never could grasp such a concept. He was, and then he wasn't, he deemed it impossible. Sometimes as a child, while playing video games, he would wonder if he would wake up from a previous checkpoint, a moment in life from where he would get to live it all again. And at other times he would believe in reincarnation or heaven.

There were times when he would use his own mortality as a shield, constantly reminding everyone of their impending death to inflict upon them the struggle that he was experiencing, and at other times it was an effort to evoke a reaction that he deemed fit, especially when a reaction from his end was missing. He wasn't sure if it was this struggle with mortality that bred the constant whisper in the back of his mind that he was destined to be great, to be remembered. To be immortalized by his work fit perfectly with his worldview. What work that would be, was another question entirely. This reminder of his mortality had knocked the wind out of his sails, and for him, the meeting had been painful. For Anant, Rajat's parting words were a placeholder until the doughnut he had ordered arrived on his table. The doughnut was sitting pretty atop a smooth white plate, as if it were floating on the remaining cloud that hadn't been used as dough.

'Can you believe that they might beat death in our lifetime?' Anant saw death sitting on Rajat's shoulders, vibrating as if snickering in glee at the self-importance of a man who believed that there would be no end. The doughnut despite being so close to divinity certainly did not believe that it would have no end.

Chapter 8

Sixteen days into the project, Rajat was mailed the sketch of his living room. Ignoring what he believed were minuscule things, i.e. the sparse false ceiling, the spotlights fitted in convenient locations to cast a soft light on the walls, the finely accentuated design of the doors with strips of wood running along its dimensions, except the door to the master bedroom which would stand out with a different polish and grains, Rajat focused on the general layout of the living room and the heavy furniture placed in it. The sketch and the supplementary pictures were such that they allowed him to visualize himself in such a room. Alone in the lobby of the hotel, he closed his eyes and managed with repeated effort to conjure something akin to the flat. The form, as it materialized before him, was almost like a ball of slime that refused to yield its shape to the whims of the one holding it. However, Rajat managed to conjure parts of the living room to life, each aspect causing the previous resurrection to disintegrate. He saw the living room piece by piece, slide by slide, as provided by the sketch and the images. A satin couch he had seen in a bar came to life where the couches were to be placed, the tube lights fitted above the false ceiling like in Sehaj Agarkar's flat bathed him in the colour of daylight, and standing on a console table in the hallway leading from the living room to the master bedroom was the statue of Atlas that he fancied, the wall behind it a textured grey. Sixteen days after the work in his flat began, when the plumbing and electrical work, both not Anant's forte, were being completed alongside the general work of breaking and restructuring the flat, Rajat chose the sketch that would be brought to life in his living room.

For Anant, these sixteen days were an unnecessary show of extravagance. He firmly believed that he could have done the same quality of work without any changes to the flat. He liked to design around the electrical map of a place. The general structure of a flat was a canvas to fill, an exercise to keep his mind sharp. But the contractor, Dandekar, insisted on rewiring, harping on the quality of wires and the need to explore options for electrical points, just in case they were needed. One must have the option, Dandekar would tell them. And once the flat was under his control it quickly fell under the blunt hammer until he cleared the flat of any and all excesses. Rajat was in constant touch with Anant throughout these sixteen days. If not for giving suggestions on design, Rajat also asked for his advice on the little things that Dandekar planned to do. With decades of experience, Dandekar could have easily made these calls but the fact that he was working for his contractor's son reined him in, and to keep the boss's son happy became his first and only priority.

Rajat had made it clear to Anant in the first few calls that he would always be quick to call him, that he needed Anant 24/7, and that he would pay him extra for his time. These demands were non-negotiable. Anant wouldn't be surprised if someone told him that Rajat had holstered his phone on his belt, like a cowboy carrying his gun, ready to whip it out any time to make the call. There were many calls in the odd hours of the night, often a slurred voice from the other side would fling ideas at him, and at other times merely circle around a vague idea of one thing or another. As the days had ticked on, Anant eventually realized where he was going wrong. It was the detail in the drawings that he had spent months of his life learning. These details were the bane of this project. Rajat was someone who by his own account looked at the big picture, which in this case meant he tried to look past the details. By adding them in, Anant was only putting roadblocks on Rajat's path and impeding his ability to visualize the flat, and accept the drawings. It was a drawing dressed in ambiguity that was accepted by Rajat. Anant had merely sent the e-mail with the scanned pages and wasn't present to see Rajat's eyes light up once he was done visualizing the room, and much like a child eagerly waiting to unwrap the present, Rajat couldn't wait to see how the drawing would materialize in front of his eyes.

After the drawing was chosen, Rajat concluded that it was vital that they meet right away. He called Anant, who fearing another long call felt conflicted about picking up the phone once he saw the name flash on the screen. But Rajat was the client, and given how often Rajat called him over the sixteen days, his body had unwillingly learned to adapt to his calls by pumping adrenaline and banishing sleep, which is how the invitation to meet at The Oberoi Hotel *'at once'* was thrust upon him irrespective of what he felt. The money also played a prominent role in his decision to allow himself to be put in this situation where he was always only a call away from Rajat. Despite his menial life, the city continued to extract an extravagant amount out of him. And thus, there they sat, on a cantilevered bar resting above the beach, right by the ocean alive under the moon which was only a crescent away from being whole again. It was under this moon that Anant learnt that his design had not only managed to finally catch Rajat's fancy, but it had also been selected. Before Rajat broke the good news, Anant stared at him with the budding feeling of powerlessness, like he had been watching a play that was directed and acted by Rajat, and midway through the enactment, despite his reluctance, he was pulled to the stage to be a part of it. The only other audience member was one that never left Anant alone. One that was seated in the back, and thus hidden. Only his hissing and slithering could be heard. Faced with his powerlessness, Anant believed, perhaps neurotically disposed to gather his thoughts around the Titan, that the only end to this play that he had gotten into, given the speed and the momentous build-up to it all and irrespective of how far his own role would last, would be death. Sitting in a bar, staring at Rajat who was building up to the moment where he would break the news that he had accepted the design, Anant was flooded with notions of death once again.

The volcanic man sitting in front seemed under intense pressure, of what Anant did not know. He was unaware of how deep Rajat's need for greatness ran, and his mind had long since forsaken the direction of the play and handed it over to his pride. Not that Rajat was malicious by any stretch of the imagination, at best he was deceitful. But a man who was deceiving himself by living this imagined truth that he believed was real. 'Would such deceit be insincere to anyone but himself?' Anant watched him in wonder, a sliver of curiosity in his heart over the man sitting in front of him, of the actor-director whose play would only end in death. The death of his ego, and the death of his being. As Rajat continued to talk, Anant wondered about the number of deaths that a man is fated to live, and which one would finally bring the curtains down. He wondered about himself, briefly, but never one to contemplate his own passing, his thoughts returned to Rajat, and his plays within plays.

As the night grew darker and the glass emptied quicker, Rajat had his fill of suspense and drama. An earnest smile appeared on his face and he broke the news that the recent e-mail was what he wanted. Before relief could settle in Anant's heart, it took a moment to sympathize with Rajat. As if sympathizing for him was an attempt to check his thoughts and where they were inevitably leading to. That by thinking of his death, he was subjecting Rajat to it. Everyone goes through many deaths in life, Anant told himself. 'Aren't we all meant to be destroyed,' he thought. 'Perhaps he won't be. Maybe it will be as simple as pushing away a speck of dust. And if he survives, he could create himself again. What a gift that would be.' With that thought, Anant finally allowed relief to settle in him and smiled back at Rajat.

'This one right here, man. This one right here. Wait, let me draw for a bit.' Rajat scribbled on the pages he had printed out. 'And you see this TV area, I was thinking that maybe we can have a floor to ceiling structure of sorts. You know, keep some of the artsy pieces I have. And wait, I gotta draw this too,' Rajat continued. Slowly, Anant began to drift away from where he sat in the bar. It was a magnificent night, the great expanse of water shone silver in places, and in others the light of the moon illuminated the darkness of the ocean, making the dark darker by having a light for it to consume. In the mystic ways of the doughnut but more successful, Anant was captivated by the ocean that seemed to have come alive. Anant rarely drank, his way of life did not account for lapses in awareness where death could sneak up on him. Perhaps a social drink here and there, yet such was the synergy of the divine moon and the eternal ocean that even he had gotten a repeat and was waiting for another. He drifted away not to his retreat, but to be one with the ocean. The vividness of this image made him pat his arms and legs from time to time to remind himself that he wasn't wet from being in the water, that the ocean was a few feet away, and had been throughout the night.

He was pulled away from the ocean by Rajat who showed him the modifications he had made sketches of. 'This is it. I want you to call me, any time, to ask me about anything related to the project. Any ideas simmering in your head at night, man, you gotta tell me. I want to know. I will season it. And I will do the same, so you can cook it as you like.' Once again, Anant had been given the task rather than an offer. 'We will make something great, I know it.' Rajat turned to the page where he had scribbled a bunch of inspired yet, as of now, incoherent ideas. 'This. It could be full of patterns and be really vibrant and colourful, maybe. I'm not sure about it being too colourful.' Anant thought a vibrant set-up in the living room would suit the design and layout Rajat had selected. Rajat pushed the paper with his drawings and waved it in front of Anant. 'This is it. This is what I want, man. Think of this. You and me, our minds together. I have to go home, you know, need some alone time to think. I know I don't talk much, right now I am f***ing excited, but apart from this moment, I can be quiet. But I want you to know that this is exactly it. Perfect.' And a handshake later, Rajat was gone carrying the darkness on his shoulder with him, leaving Anant behind with the ocean weaving coy couplets for the yearning moon that continued in its ceaseless ministrations.

After another drink, Anant forgot the papers on the table. By the time it dawned on him that the papers were missing, he was sitting in a quiet corner of his living room, listening to 'Forsvinder' by Bremer/McCoy on his phone connected to his speakers. When the moment of revelation came, he flipped through the notebook he had dedicated to Rajat's flat, sighed, took a moment to mourn another untimely death in the world and a moment after, he hunched over the notebook to try and re-create the drawing out of memory while changing it at the same time. Rajat's wayward ideas filled the gaps left by his creative lapses and when he was done, he came up with a new design altogether. Inspired by the old, accentuated by Rajat's energy for the colourful and the vibrant, but changed fundamentally.

Chapter 9

Ever since the night Aarti broke the news of her marriage, Sunil Vohra's mind steadily picked up steam and compelled him to be faster every day. It had reached a point where he was now running around as if his own child was getting married in a month's time and the burden of the preparations fell solely on his shoulders. But while the ceremony was to take place in Varanasi, his fervour was confined to his house in Pune where he would skilfully thread every possible story leading to the marriage, and the day of the marriage around him. His primary wish was for Aarti to have the perfect wedding, but close behind, as if stuck to it as a combo deal, was his wish to play a distinct role in the perfect wedding. He would spend hours in the office with chai to give him company in the morning, and jasmine tea in the evening. He had shed a few centimetres off his waist by living on tea. On his desk rested a rough notepad full of ideas, many scratched out and others circled before meeting the same fate. Most of the time, he would sit tinkering on a puzzle or a Rubik's Cube, at times playing carom with himself, something to keep his hands occupied while he lost himself in his imagination.

Having seen how demanding and unpredictable Rajat was, and uneasy over the fact that it might just get worse, Anant decided to visit his parents a month and a half sooner than his usual three months, just in case his presence might suddenly be demanded by Rajat when the expected trip came around. This break from his routine of visiting his parents every three months was not given much thought at home, the palpable energy brimming in the house seemed to take up all the attention. The vibrancy of the house was noticeable the moment one crossed the gate and stepped into the world of the Vohras. The source of this life, Anant noticed, was his father's office. While Sunil sat in his office drinking tea, making models, toying with puzzles and playing carom, lost in a dream of things to come, his mind knitting moments on their way to becoming memories, and hoping to crack the case that was the search for the perfect gift for Aarti, the rest of the house, separate from the office, was ticking on under the watchful eye of Monica Vohra.

Anant had brought 3D renderings of Rajat's flat that the owner himself hadn't seen. When the three Vohras sat down around the table for a late breakfast, Anant shared these renderings for breakfast entertainment so that he wouldn't be required to engage in conversation. He knew from experience that nobody would be more excited than his father before the unveiling of what Anant had brought as an offering, and like a child or a genius, when the mystery was unveiled, Sunil would get bored and move on to the next thing. But the extent of his indifference surprised Anant. Sunil barely gave the renderings a glance. He was staring at the pages from the future, from his memories-to-be, while taking a peek at the drawings without comprehending any of it, more interested in eating his diet cereal and reminding himself to sip water after every spoon or two. 'You know what you should do.' Sunil broke the silence, taking the attention away from the images Anant had prepared as an ideal starting point for a conversation. 'You should get a suit made. A sherwani. One of those long ones, like a kurta,' Sunil told Anant. 'I should get one too. I...' Sunil paused, briefly calculating his finances on his phone before a smile appeared on his lips. 'Yes, I will get one.'

'What do you think, black or a colour?' he asked to no one in particular.

'You should go and see for yourself. You might find black

too dull. Maybe a colour,' Monica said without looking up from the renderings, knowing her husband just needed a noise in the background to continue holding his one-sided conversation.

'Yes, but black does look good. Now that I've shed so much weight, I'll look like a sleek car. Like one of those nice ones. Do you think they have those in Varanasi? We could arrive there in that car.' Having spent his life in Lucknow and Pune wasn't an excuse for Sunil's ignorance of other cities, but ignorant he was.

'We are with the bride, not the groom. We will be there beforehand,' Monica reminded him.

'Shame, is it not? It would have looked good. And I think we are modern enough to move past these traditions.' Sunil was further gone in his endeavours than he had ever been, Anant noted. It did not bother him that the small talk he had prepared while packing was for nothing. Any small talk was good enough. Anything to keep him from floundering in his attempts to make conversation. Sunil finished his meal and walked over to the kitchen to boil water for some tea. Monica had finished her food, but she continued to linger at the table long after Anant had retired to his room. She had the renderings in one hand and an empty plate in the other.

Sprawled on his childhood bed, staring at the pristine white coat of the ceiling, Anant found himself asking an age-old question. What does a room say about a person? Anant believed that a room said nothing about the occupant, given his dealing with far too many people who no longer viewed a room as a place of living but rather an extension of someone they could be, or more importantly, who they liked to be. Like an uncomfortable but flattering piece of footwear, perhaps a heel that was an inch too high, but more often than not, a shoe that was a size too small. What Anant failed to see was what a lived-in room showcased about a person. Like a river shaping the neighbouring rocks, the routine of the occupant shaped the identity of the room in its image. More than how it was decorated, more than the designs that he based his livelihood on, more than the flooring that could 'make or break a place', more than the precious artworks and strategic lighting, it was the creases in the chairs and sofas, the impression on the mattress, the spills and stains, the walls drilled with nails or stuck with posters once upon a time that left a residue on the wall. It was the furniture and how it had aged. Books scattered on the sofa or the table. The claw marks of a pet. Dust distinguishing what was used and what wasn't. Things left in a jumble or neatly organized. The room always had stories to tell, in parts that when collected made a memoir of the person living in the room, and his own room in Pune told a story that was in stark contrast to his flat in Mumbai. It told a story of hoarding.

To an outsider, it would seem like two different people lived in the respective spaces. Such a notion wouldn't be completely false. The Anant who had resided in the house in Pune was someone who had in his misery desperately coveted a retreat, had built a cell, and exiled himself to it. He had struggled against the prying hands that would try to pull him out. It was before he had learned to traverse the waters of the world and become comfortable in the cell, unlike a much later phase in his life when he moved to his flat in Mumbai. His college days were the shallow waters that prepared him for the deep waters of the world. And the dorm room too was muddled with stories—a myriad tales criss-crossing one another, lives compressed together to form a vague idea of those inhabiting the rooms—that were there for anyone to pick and choose what they wanted from it. And Anant had chosen a life beyond.

But the room in Pune was made for one, made by one, made of one, and every nook and cranny only had Anant's invisible hand on it. Here, Anant had lain when he was unable to shed any tears for his friend, with the pillow clamped to his face while he tried to release the sobs stuck in his throat, and never did the tears reach his eyes, like the unrelenting pain of a bruise under the nail. Here, Anant had broken up with his girlfriend for the darkness on her shoulder terrified him. Like an invisible weight pressing him down, slowly crushing him. Here, he had spent countless sleepless nights, plagued by the Titan. And here, washed by a multitude of stories of his dorm room, he had slowly begun to realize that he was coming to a life that had gone by. His descent into himself led to a detachment from his past, and the strings that remained became sanctified. Here, he had begun to see his parents as separate planets altogether, but ones whose orbits criss-crossed with each other and his own. In his dorm, he had learned that these were the only planets in the whole solar system.

In Mumbai, Anant understood that planets need not cross paths with each other all the time to communicate, that it was possible to converse from across the orbits, if only the other planet would pay attention. In this room was his life that came to accept the darkness on everybody's shoulders, and in Mumbai, he arrived having already learned to coexist.

The room was a relic of the past, and his only reminder that the past had been his. That the stories in the room, of the room, and from the room, of a life gone by, aged to seem like another lifetime, even though they had been his stories. And till this date, this reminder would tug at his heart, bring the truth that he was not detached, that he wasn't an island.

Anant met the thoughts with a sigh, as if he were an old man who had weathered countless storms created by the Titan. There was a hint of a pompous disdain in him, a pretence of knowledge that had made greater men hollow, but Anant believed, foolishly or otherwise, that somehow the consistency of these thoughts proved their validity. This was the story he believed, and thus, this was the story. Whether with ignorance or arrogance, Anant managed to keep the feeling of being shaken at bay. A ray of light slipped through a gap in the curtains, providing a stage for the dust to dance. He could hear the cars whizzing by, but his own house was quiet. Anant briefly contemplated if the speck of dust was his friend, dancing in his new form. He had never been one to dance, but who was to say that death hadn't made him think differently about dancing.

The truth was that Anant no longer had any recollection of how his friend had passed away. The memories of his friend had faded from his memory, like clouds that had disappeared after pouring down rain for hours, leaving behind puddles of water on the road, as if to convince others that it had rained after all. For Anant, the stories he was left with were like those puddles. He knew that the boy was his friend with as much certainty as that the earth was round, or that there was a sun up there, or that there was a doughnut with the blueberry glazing and sprinkles in the shape of a crescent, or that the ocean that bathed in the silver of the moon that night in the bar with Rajat had been other-worldly. He knew the act of turning to dust brought a decisive end to the events. It was only his cell that laughed in the face of such a fact. As if in contempt of all that was natural, the cell would turn to dust whenever Anant would come across a scenery or an object or a person that seemed like an artefact from another world, the bolt of thunder, the enchantment would spread like wildfire, and this magic infused in the cell would allow it to disappear, and then it would return to its former glory.

Sunil Vohra returned from the market around eight o'clock and Anant came back from his stroll fifteen minutes after him. To the naked eye, the house was ticking on—Sunil was in the kitchen making tea, Anant was lounging on the couch—but the routine of the house was in an inconspicuous upheaval for Monica Vohra was nowhere to be found. Nobody was searching for her yet, it would take the absence of the routine goodnight wish for the father–son duo to take note of the house that seemed to be weeping for being ignored. Such was the enigmatic meticulousness of Monica that even her absence could be believed to fall under her routine. But it was still a point to be made between them that she wasn't around. Sunil had been too engrossed in his world to be certain if this was part of her routine or not. He made his tea and went to his office, believing it was. Anant took a shower and sat on his chair in his bedroom, dripping down on the floor that he would later wipe, fingering the gold earrings that he was sure had been given to Aarti. Why he found them on his nightstand, he did not know. Nor did he try to explain it. If he could see no obvious reason, or a possible trail, he believed that there was no point in rummaging through his mind in an attempt to squeeze any explanation out of it. In another part of the house, Monica Vohra had arrived from the terrace to the first floor without anyone noticing the two hours she had missed of her routine. It was as if her presence had seeped past the walls to wash away any sign of the momentary worry that father and son had shared. It was only her in the house who would have mourned for the lost hours, but surprising herself, she merely jumped forward and continued her routine from 9 p.m. rather than hurry through her routine to reach a steady 10 p.m. as she would have done in the days gone by. When the family came together for dinner, Sunil talked about the loot that was bespoke suits. Anant would have given out small talking points for his parents to gather around like it was the hearth, playing the part of the entertainer to somehow make up for the lost time he spent being away from them and from his phone, had his father not already had something to talk about, and Monica, unbeknownst to either, had moved away from observing the world and was lost in her own world. A world that had been left behind far too early in her childhood. When they were finishing dinner, the quiet descended over all three like a heavy fog that hid everyone including each other. Sunil was lost in calculations to see what he could afford, how much he could stretch, and if it would 'make the moment' that was still a month away. His thoughts were so meticulous that they might as well have already happened, the memory itself couldn't be any more detailed than his imagination. Anant retired to the cell with the darkness on the shoulders of his parents to give him company. Monica pulled herself away from her own world to the world around her for a brief moment in time, and after noticing both, she let the fog cloud her eyes once again and let the other two disappear as she leaned into the flow of her world that ran parallel to the currents of time, and let her be carried through the night.

Chapter 10

In a month, Aarti was getting married in Varanasi. It was a simple, concise statement that did not allow any subjective observation. She was getting married and the location was Varanasi. If one were to ask what was happening in Aarti's life, this would be the answer. No layer of fat on it, nothing that the Occam's razor could cut from it. Yet Aarti had trouble coming to terms with such unambiguous facts, just like she had trouble accepting that the woman sitting in the dim marbled bar, post her evening workout, was in fact her. With a sigh bubbling in her chest, she leaned into the bright red satin chair, staring at herself through the reflection of the lacquered glass of the bar. The glass of wine in her hand wasn't helping. It had stopped helping a week ago. Her workouts that she had doubled to be in shape for the red lehenga the way she dreamed of, or perhaps, she briefly courted the prospect that these dreams had been made for her by advertisements that imbued the idea of the perfect day to sell products to not only the bride and groom, but their families and their close friends. These workouts too had stopped helping. Her work as a high-level manager in a pharmaceutical company had stopped helping too. There was a time when it was clear as day to her that her troubles blossomed in that trip to Pune, when she had seen her father's face in Anant, but with time acting as a buffer between her and the emotions that rose in her during that trip, she began to nurture suspicions on whether her troubles were really rooted in that moment. She had begun to contemplate whether she was blaming a symptom, that her anger had existed in the depths of her being, and that it had merely chosen to reveal itself when she met Anant that morning. She pulled out her phone from the gym bag she had hauled in the bar to get a better look at herself from the front camera of her phone. She smiled instinctively, out of habit, paused, stared at herself, and then, in an action that would be sacrilegious had any of her acquaintances or friends seen her, she dropped the smile. She wasn't herself, and it seemed to her that nobody had noticed. Not her colleagues, not her acquaintances, not her mother, and not her soon-to-be husband.

The previous evening in the same bar, she had debated if these changes were the result of the notorious pre-marriage jitters that plagued so many. But thoughts of the marriage itself were so scarce that she found it hard to believe. When her musings did wander over to marriage, all she had was apathy. Like the feeling of an impending unneeded exam, one that didn't scare her or help her build confidence, one that didn't get a reaction out of her at all. An exam that despite all the noise, meant nothing to her, and yet, since it was an exam, she felt obligated to sit through. She had brought up the idea of eloping with her fiancé. She knew that she was being cruel knowing how grounded Ravi was in his family customs and traditions. They were getting married in Varanasi because they met each other on a company getaway in that city. It would have been romantic had Aarti not felt impervious to any and all reactions that her marriage tried to evoke in her. 'It might still be romantic,' she told herself. Ravi was a manager just like herself, in the head office in Mumbai, while she worked in Gurugram. The idea of running away was so absurd in Ravi's eyes that he failed to consider it as a serious suggestion, and chuckled at what he deemed was a bad joke. Maybe that was what she was trying to do. To crack a joke, to churn some humour into her life, to conjure the now elusive smile.

Yet here she was, no closer to any semblance of joy, no flash of a smile, the bubble she had wrapped herself in ever since her father passed away slowly coming undone. She sat in the bar going through her reps of wine as she would go through reps of burpees in the gym. An exercise for her soul that seemed to be slowly forsaking her, or she forsaking it. Aarti refused to believe that she had abandoned her soul already. When she called for a cab on her phone, a peculiar thought struck Aarti. That the world was missing common sense. And it wasn't anybody's fault. People looked around, trying to pin the blame on someone, and after they failed to find a culprit, they simply assumed that they weren't missing it. Aarti thought that just like her, the rest of the people just didn't get it either. She cancelled the cab and returned to the bar to order another glass of wine, wondering why in the hell did everyone behave like they 'got it'. 'Life could be so much easier if everyone revealed that they were full of shit,' she told herself as she placed another order at the bar.

Aarti woke up in her own bed early in the morning before the sun reared its ugliness. For that was how the sun now seemed to her. A new day meant facing the same all over again. She was greeted with a feeling of emptiness, like a dream half forgotten whose effects lingered. She slowly began to stir on the bed. She turned to check the time, and realized that she didn't have to go to the gym on a Saturday. She yawned and rubbed her eyes, making a face when she remembered the ludicrous tip she had given the waiter for just getting her glasses of wine and how she had stumbled while trying to get into a cab. The image of that single stumble made her cringe. The bottle of wine she had opened in her flat last night sat on her bedside table with three fingers of wine left. The bottle seemed morose to her, as if disappointed for being treated with such callousness. When she put weight on her legs, a shooting pain made her wince and she sat down. There was a light bruise on her knee. She managed to pluck the memory from the flickering jumble of last night, and remembered that she had hit her knee against the kitchen drawer when she bent down to pick up the dropped wine opener. Quick to see the bright side to this predicament, she relished the good excuse she now had to cancel the lunch with her two colleagues without the weight of guilt on her shoulders. While texting them, the bruise became an injury, and the dull ache from the hangover became a searing headache. And thus, Aarti escaped the lunch that she herself had suggested to them. Strangely, she felt better that she had cancelled the plan, rather than soldiering on and going to the café. She began to wonder if it actually felt better than that moment when she had found the prospect of going to a new café exciting. Sitting on her bed, she browsed the web on her phone, searching whether the café that she wanted to visit delivered to her address. The pizza wasn't the reason why she had cancelled. There was no reason to direct her anger towards the pizza. Drifting away with her thoughts while she searched for the café, she diagnosed herself with solitude as if it were a communicable disease she had contracted by being around Anant. And melancholy was merely a symptom of the disease. Keeping the phone away, she got up and carried the bottle of wine to the freezer. She popped a Crocin to ease the dull headache that was making her eyes water, rummaged through the drawers of her kitchen while keeping her knees at a safe distance. She found a packet of Maggi amidst the array of masalas and packaged dry fruits, the one pack that had managed to survive the gathering she hosted in an effort to get every food or drink that might entice her to cheat on her workout into the stomachs of her friends. She set the water to boil. She chopped chillies, and added the masala to the water. She got rid of the broken pieces of the noodle cake and the rest she slid into the pot.

'Something old and something new,' she muttered to herself when she placed the bowl full of Maggi and a glass of wine on the coffee table. The noodles were a comfort, the hangover was from last night, and the day drinking was new. She spent her morning watching early seasons of *Friends* when the group hadn't been weighed down with their love lives and occupations. A carefree world, every episode brought trivial problems that were solved by the end. She remembered that she forgot to brush her teeth and took another sip of her wine, swirling it around her mouth as if she were in a wine-tasting. She did it once more, the alcohol cleansing her teeth, or so she told herself. There was a swell of pride in her when she looked down at the empty bowl after she was done with her meal. She had perfected the recipe of Maggi long ago. The secret was adding a hint of chilli oil and chaat masala at the end. She poured herself another glass of wine, berating herself for not keeping a beer in her fridge. 'A cold brew as a *digestif* would have been perfect,' she muttered. When the air conditioner got too cold, she dragged herself to her bedroom to grab a blanket, filled her glass with more wine from a previously opened bottle that was in the fridge, and buried herself on the couch with the blanket over her, perfectly cool and warm. 'Something borrowed and something blue.' She liked to believe that this solitude was borrowed from Anant. As for something blue, she was feeling pretty blue herself.

Chapter 11

Anant returned from Pune to a site that had come alive with workers. Another platoon of men had arrived with a new contractor at the helm to assist the experienced Dandekar. This dramatic increase was the result of Rajat's incessant demands to his father that the work on his flat ought to be completed sooner, that the seams of his mind were coming apart from the abundance of ideas that could only be brought to life once he had his own place. His dad decided in favour of these demands, either to indulge his son or by making the simple calculation about the costs involved in expediting the work and letting Rajat stay in a five-star hotel on company money. Rajat had also instructed Dandekar, a company man through and through, whose first name was a mystery as old as him because everybody had collectively agreed to only refer to him as 'Dandekar sahib', to inform him whenever Anant returned to work. His holiday had been abrupt, and Rajat wasn't the kind to be lax with those working for him. He had high expectations from everyone who worked around him. If you work hard and aim for perfection, you rise to the top, he was quite fond of saying. Work hard right now, party hard later, he had told the workers on the site during the first meeting. As Anant introduced himself to Iqbal, the new contractor, and exchanged cordial greetings with some of the workers, Dandekar sahib stepped out to the small balcony to notify Rajat.

Of the workers Anant recognized, there were two who had made a distinct impression on him during his early visits when the interiors of the flat were being broken and reduced to rubble.

Anant had noticed that the elder of the two was interested in what he was saying while he explained the design, while the contractors seemed to only care about keeping the margin of error in inches. In the early days of the project, Anant learnt that the two, the stonemason who was popularly known as the mistri, and his helper, were Dandekar sahib's men. Kartik, the mistri, was a bespectacled man with salt-and-pepper hair that carried an aura of a therapist. He had a penchant for listening, and was averse to the trivial rivalries of the subcontractors who fought in an effort to seem like the head chef of the site, rather than what they were, the station chefs of a dish that was only a part of the menu. Given his comprehension of the drawings, patience in dealing with other workers, prior relation with Dandekar sahib and Anant's fondness for his ways, Kartik was the unofficial sous-chef of the project. This development suited Anant. Kartik's paternal guidance made him the ideal choice to be a natural extension of his presence on the site.

Every mistri came with a helper, and Kartik's helper was a Maratha man born in the wrong century and under the wrong circumstance, yet his earnestness earned him the nickname 'Marathi'. His beginnings mirrored the early inhabitants of Mumbai. He came from a fishermen community not unlike the Kolis. But while the city had grown to become a great metropolis, somewhere in the city's apathetic pursuit of refinement, his family had been left behind. He had the choice to work the same job his father had, and his father before him, and on and on, or to venture into the city that buried people in its sheer density. Such were his options that led him to being the man who would often be called 'the right-hand of Kartik' rather than the warrior he was meant to be in another life. Marathi was a vocal man who would rush to fix things while Anant would still be in the middle of his explanation. He had a pep in his step that papered over the pepper of his tongue. With the two, Anant had a duo balancing each other and crucial in the implementation and management of the site, a work that Anant didn't know he had signed up for while taking up this project. Never before had the implementation of his designs fallen on his lap, but at the behest of Rajat, or rather his habit of not asking but informing others as to what had to be done, he who Anant had promised all his time, compelled Anant to make sure his designs were done justice, and this baffling duty was made easier with Kartik and Marathi by his side.

The day Anant returned from Pune, Kartik was quick to direct him towards a third man who he believed ought to be included apart from the duo. Aamir was a carpenter by training and had a glint in his eyes that reflected his ambition and a strong smell of marijuana. Kartik warned Anant about his contractor Faiz, who had a tendency to interject out of an insecurity that any attention paid to any of his workers was an affront to his own skills. And Aamir, unconfrontational to a fault, was quick to distance himself whenever the subcontractor jumped in on the conversation. 'Just include him in our conversations,' Kartik had advised Anant. And so, when Anant wanted a brief on what had happened while he was away, Kartik had roped in Aamir as well. 'Let me call Faiz bhai.' Aamir excused himself when he realized that it was just the four of them. Aamir returned with Faiz, and the other contractors began to gather around when Danderkar-sahib entered the fold. The brief conversation centred on the queries that the subcontractors had, and Dandekar sahib—who had noticed Anant's tendency to gravitate towards Kartik and Marathi, who were considered to be 'his men'—in a bid to extend his influence over the peculiar designer helped Anant in answering the questions. The molding was uneven in the guest bedroom, two electrical points needed to be lowered, and the excessive use of MDF had to be curtailed. 'Maybe we can use brass strips here,' Anant offered.

The conversation was brought to a close when Dandekar sahib was alerted that the marble had arrived and awaiting inspection. 'Sir, I will call the elevator for you, Iqbal sahib and Faiz,' Kartik said, leaving Anant with a chance to talk to Aamir.

When the crowd cleared, Anant and Aamir stood discussing the use of brass. Despite his lack of grey hair, decades of experience and his proclivity to being a yes-man, Anant trusted Kartik's judgement and thus indulged Aamir. Perhaps it was only the product of Kartik's influence, but Anant began to see that Aamir was honest at his work, and had a resolute style that Anant could not sway easily, and therefore bounce ideas off him.

'You mean like those old Bollywood films? Record player, big CD, thick oak furniture, dark polish, maybe a lion statue and all.' Aamir's inquiry was confirmed with a curt nod.

Rajat had chosen to stray away from the Swedish minimalism in favour of a modern take on Indian-Victorian abundance. 'Modern or traditional?' Aamir inquired.

'I will consult with Rajat. For now, think *Kalichaaran* or Vijay Verma.' Rather than explaining how he envisioned the entertainment centre to be, he gave Aamir a starting point for him to flex his creative muscles. Such a heavy piece of furniture would play a major role in the ambience of the living room, and while the basic design had been cleared by Rajat, and Anant believed that he knew how to get Rajat to agree to it by following a step-by-step routine, he wanted to do justice to his work and not merely collect his paycheck by exploiting Rajat's desire for the obscure. 'Tomorrow,' Anant said and left Aamir to continue his work. And thus, the duo become the trio.

Anant took his time around the site and paused in every room. The master bedroom, the guest bedroom, the third bedroom where Rajat wanted a home theatre, the two bathrooms, the living room and the kitchen. The headphones he wore played no music. The noise cancellation helped him concentrate. When the absence of sound had settled, everyone and the darkness on their shoulders faded away. He could still feel certain machinery and tools that made the floor tremor and the walls vibrate, but now moving to exist on the cusp of his retreat, the sensations began to feel like the echo of the past. Like the death of a star that sent fading shockwaves to his world long after the star had disappeared. Never away from a morose thought, the death of the star reiterated Anant's belief that they were all ghosts at the end of it. When the work was done and dusted, he reminded himself, these people would become faceless, and he too would be a phantom to them. Some might manage to prolong their existence by hiding in the trenches of memory, but for how long? Sooner or later the memory itself was washed over by time, and left behind a memory of the memory that once was. A blur of colours and outlines indicating what the painting must have once looked like, without any possibility of having it return to the original. Anant made the round around the flat again and again. With the general layout and the colour pallette, marble, false ceiling and plasterwork on the walls of the living room decided, and some of the other work nearing completion, he imagined pieces of furniture in the living room; side tables, console tables, coffee tables, dining tables, accent lights, pendant lights, lamps, sofas, chaise, poufs, and on and on, going over the styles, from deco to nouveau, Parisian to Persian, Victorian to mid-century modern. Rajat wanted choices, he wanted changes, and so Anant coated the walls with paints and wallpapers until he was made aware of himself by the buzzing of his phone. A sharp stiff inhale, a slow relaxed exhale, and repeated until he left the limbo that existed outside the cell and returned to himself.

He turned off the noise cancellation feature on his headphones, and took a moment to adjust to the world that flooded in. The sound of machines now piercing, the thud hammer, the whine of the wood being scraped, the sound of chatter, tables being dragged, the creak of the scaffolding. He pocketed the wired headphones. The whole process took him fifteen seconds, and the phone continued to ring. It was Rajat.

'Anant, we gotta meet,' Rajat told him. 'Tonight, or maybe tomorrow. I'll fill you in with the details in an hour. Don't make any plans man, all right?'

Anant could have already had plans. It was five minutes to four, which was when he would generally leave the site. But Anant did not tell him that. At least now Rajat had the courtesy to not be transparent in his demands. Anant noted that he had arrived at the flat quarter past one and after greetings, he had pulled the duo to the side. At ten minutes past two, he began talking to Dandekar sahib, Iqbal and the subcontractors. Thirty-five minutes later, he was talking to Aamir. He had been walking when he next checked the time, five minutes past three. 'Call, don't text,' Anant informed him, a by-product of the infuriating habit Rajat had of texting him, after having called him, incomplete sentences and questions.

'Absolutely. The last time, it just slipped out of my mind, you know. It was just once or twice before, or whatever.' Or whatever it was.

'Okay,' Anant said and waited for a reply. When nothing came from the other end, Anant cut the call.

Rajat was still on the line when Anant ended the call. He was expecting a retort or some comment, even if it was about the weather. Instead, he was greeted with the unceremonious sound of the call being cut.

'That guy needs to relax.' Rajat firmly believed that there

were only finite chances that a person had to be infinite, and it was important to be perceptive of when and where such a moment may arise. Unlike Sunil Vohra, Rajat firmly believed in the infinity of greatness. That to be remembered, as Sunil wanted, by those close to him and cherished for the memories he would leave behind after his demise, wasn't enough. That a generation of love wasn't acceptable. To not fade away within moments of passing away, or succumb to a few meagre years like the memory of Sunil's brother, was aiming too low. Rajat's desire was centred on immortality through genius. He wanted to be remembered as far in time as he could imagine. The people were a mere audience to his greatness. He worked on the sole belief that once his work was idolized, and such a feat would be accomplished before his death, not posthumously, more often than not in the prime of his years that had been knocking on his doors already, that this idolization would absolve him of being him, of his shortcomings and failures. That all his actions and struggles would be justified on the highest realm once he could traverse to immortality. In pursuit of this higher plane of existence, without any work that could bear the burden of being remembered from time immemorial, Rajat began to dress his meetings with strangers and friends alike as a place to perform, to be in the memories of the people he had come to know. For the more the audience believed it was magic and not a trick, that it was the greatness of a genius and not some imposter, the more concrete his own idea of the self would become.

Chapter 12

Rajat and Anant met the following evening at a modest pastel café with abstract murals painted on the walls. Acoustic versions of classic rock songs played in the background to complement the hushed nature of the café. Rajat was drinking a soda with lemon and ginger, hunched over his chair staring at the rendering of the living room. A few hours before they met, Anant had sent designs along with a rough sketch with measurements erased in case Rajat found the details to be jarring. He had added the styles of the bed for the two bedrooms that he envisioned, which Rajat announced along with his greeting that he had accepted. The rendering of the living room had furniture that could be locally sourced, imported or made. An emerald lounge chair adjacent to the windows, a small round side table encased in a muted grey stone. On the wall facing the lounge chair was a sprawling media centre that he had added alterations to after a conversation with Aamir, alongside a place for a record player, a small television, books, plants and sculptures, perhaps records if Rajat did indeed take a liking to the record player. He added some closed shelves with opaque lacquered glass to go along with the open ones. And finishing the sketch was his brainchild, from the bottom of the centre were two lines of empty spaces turning and tapering symmetrically, as if in a dance that brings a couple together only to separate, never meeting until the end of the song, at the very top of the structure. It was a space for ambient lighting, and small strips of wood to hide the source of the light. Each time these empty spaces turned away from the middle and then back towards it, it provided a space to keep diffusers, bottles, small statues and whatever else Rajat had on his wish list. Anant explained the sketch to try and gauge Rajat's feelings towards the design, and continued with the explanation despite Rajat's shrugs and nods and his repeated 'I got it'. Anant did not want obscurity to entice Rajat into accepting designs that were not to his liking.

'I know that you dabble in many things,' Anant said, 'and you are quick to understand, but I am just explaining for my own peace.' He was oblivious to the fact that he had already uttered the unforgivable to Rajat.

'I don't dabble,' Rajat boomed, lowering his voice to a vehement whisper and not giving Anant the opportunity to say anything further. Rajat's menacing whisper would have been a screech had it not been for the almost oppressive silence of the hushed café. His eyes flared with irritation and only further widened after he took a large strenuous sip of his drink. 'This isn't good work. It's lazy.' He said, pushing the papers away from him. His attacking words failed to register like Rajat had hoped. Seeing Anant remain still, untroubled and silent in face of his outburst further enraged Rajat. The hammer of his anger struck again, his eyes widened further and his voice strained to remain a whisper. 'Even the asymmetry is jarring. The ambient lights adjacent to the window, I mean come on, even a child would realize that it's counterintuitive.' Rajat met each person with an earnest enthusiasm to have them believe in his greatness, and thus become a shareholder in his dreams. Nothing enraged Rajat more than a heckler, a person dismissive of these aspirations. 'Man, I am sorry but this is kind of unoriginal too. I really thought you were special.' Rajat spat with a smile in an effort to mask his anger, but the smile did not hold for long. 'You have to do better. Work like this is done by men who will be forgotten when they die. The moment they drop dead, poof. They disappear. Come on, you gotta, I mean, really, I hope you will do better next time.'

Anant squinted as he tried to keep up with the barrage of words that Rajat continued to fling at him. With a clenched jaw, he was somehow able to control his urge to scream. Somewhere along the outburst, Anant had stopped being a part of this theatre and turned to autopilot. 'Yes, I will. As will everyone,' Anant muttered under his breath, not realizing that he had spoken until he had, and regretted it immediately. There was no need, he told himself. The transition from the cell to the real world had caught him unawares, and the world quickly ensnared him.

'I will not be forgotten,' Rajat replied with a quiet confidence brimming from him. 'I will be remembered... You will see.' Rajat asked for the bill, but before the bill arrived, as if coming to a realization that he couldn't stand Anant for a second more, he took his exit the only way he knew how, with a dramatic push of his chair and disappearing before the door to the establishment could close behind him.

Dumbfounded, and annoyed with himself, Anant sat in his seat waiting for the bill. He was unsure of what to think. It wasn't the outburst that annoyed him, but that he had been tripped by the world, that he replied despite knowing better. His autopilot had failed him. Anant leaned into his seat and shook his head. The outburst itself reminded him of his younger days, and the image of himself wallowing in pretend rage against death. It was the odour of a busy humid evening in Janta Market that he had stumbled into when he had first shifted to Kasaravadi. Now that the image had spread, it had clung to him. The thought of Nandini made his stomach flip and turn acidic. He felt vile remembering his ex-girlfriend. Your problems are our problems, she had told him after he had locked her in the room in an attempt to save her from the darkness on her shoulder. But they can't be my problems. Anant shuddered at the image of her frantic fearful eyes and held his head with both his hands. Recalling Rajat's parting words, the ones that weren't directed at Anant but were the only part of his outburst that evoked a response in him, Anant hoped that he would not be remembered. That he had already been forgotten by all who knew him. That the spread of his word was contained within him.

A stocky man in a loose orange and yellow sunset shirt brought him his bill. Removing his hands from his head, Anant automatically went through the movements and paid in cash. Yet, he remained seated. Quickly glancing over the menu, he asked for another cold coffee. 'Please make it sweet,' he said with a courteous smile. In an attempt to block his marauding past, Anant found himself more and more fixated on Rajat's parting comment. He closed his eyes and turned his attention to his breath. Breathe in, and breathe out, he repeated to himself. Slowly, he began to stretch his breath like a rubber band, inhaling deep and pausing as if to wring the air of every thought. And exhaling, filling the air with his thoughts and thus, emptying himself. With these repeated movements, Anant retreated to a world paradoxical in its distance. Mere breaths away, yet another world entirely. Anant's joints creaked without making a sound, the result of this sudden appearance in the cell. His disarrayed mind took its time to adjust to the new world that surrounded him, as if he hadn't existed on its borders just a few moments ago. Eventually, Anant got to his feet. The mats covering the floor were without texture or any feel to them. He could have been floating if it wasn't for his own weight. Anant tackled the meaning behind Rajat's parting words with fervour, crowning it as the quintessential question of existence, all in an effort to distract himself from his own past.

'To be remembered, what did it mean?' His mind rung with the question, but before any sound could reach the cell, it was swallowed by the world that existed around it. The question existed, and remained in the distance. Anant stepped out of the doorless cell to venture into the world beyond, from where the sounds originated. He briefly considered whether he ever felt the need to be remembered. 'No,' he replied. He had never had any aspirations of immortality via memory or in the more fantastical sense.

Treading dangerously close to his own past sins, Anant quickly directed his curiosity to whether he had ever conceived such a thought, and what sort of immortality could one chase. The conundrum of being remembered had aroused his mind so much that the cell had washed up to a new shore altogether. Like the doughnut. Like the moon. It hadn't been too long ago when the cell rested on the beach overlooking the ocean with his memories pinned to the sky like stars. Now the cell was on top of nothing, as if floating in the air, hanging in a limbo, and beneath his feet, at the bottom of the world that was separated from the immediate darkness around him, his mind had unravelled to present him all his memories. Some existed above others, superimposing themselves, while others, further down were blurred and washed out of focus. When Anant stepped out, he did not fall down. He felt weightless as he was met with the invisible steps, just like the time when he walked on the mats in his cell. As he descended down the invisible steps, these memories, thoughts and dreams bloomed in the distance.

As Anant continued to descend, taking one step at a time in an almost meditative state of mind, the multitude of screens playing different silent movies beneath him began to overwhelm him. He began to exert an effort to focus, to keep to the memories that may contain the notion of being remembered, but soon, the impervious tides of his mind forced Anant to kneel, and be swept into a wandering rumination. It began at the start which seemed like a fair place to begin.

What is life, Anant asked himself as he stared at the myriad mute memories playing beneath his feet, and thus, staying alive in his mind. Stripped down to its core, Anant viewed life as a simple journey from point A, birth, to point B, death. This was his absolute truth. From pets to trees, the sun and the moon, even plastic, eventually, ceases to exist. From point A to point B, people trudge on, carrying memories and tagging moments, and events, as if the the meaning of life was solely based on the act of collecting baggage. Some bags were chained to the neck, some to the wrist, bags were glued and bags were pinned. Some memories mutated to become a part of the being, thus shaping the person as he/she continued his/her journey to point B. The rest was discarded, either by callousness or inattentiveness, sometimes with a prick, and at times without any pain at all. In this pilgrimage to death, there existed archetypical monuments that made one believe in the presence of higher beings. A person could be intertwined with a higher common consciousness by being in the presence of these monuments which, by the decree of its everlasting nature, became the product of a higher power. A being that awaited the person at point B. A power whose continued existence negated a shared point B. With this being, this power, a person could go even further.

Anant had never paid much attention to the afterlife. He had struggled with the Titan itself for so long that when the thought of an afterlife first occurred to him, he did not have the fortitude to delve into the concept of life after death. Anant had always been too preoccupied with the end to even try and make sense of god. It made him averse to praying, and thus, by discarding the ready-made answers to death, the weight of his own existence rested on his shoulders. Whenever religion was brought up around him, the sole thought Anant had was of the uselessness in wanting to disturb such a being. Its apathy was clear to Anant, otherwise god would have listened to him. If god existed, he had to be apathetic, either to all humanity, or simply to him. Anant understood why gods would not take an interest in him. In his eyes, he was at any moment less than a billionth of a species, living what would be a span of a second, and making very ordinary use of this fleeting second. Anant had no grand notions about himself. Whenever he looked at himself objectively, he would come to the conclusion that he was rather average. Even at his peak, Anant knew that he would remain average. And there was not an iota of him that desired for anything more. It wasn't the degree of his ability, but the effort that resulted in satisfaction. If he happened to cook a meal, there was a high probability that he would enjoy the meal. The quality of food ceased to be the most important part of the meal, when he cooked it himself. And Anant knew that there existed many that had a better palate, and that needed more flavour, a variety of textures and a synergy with the ingredients, and he was content to leave the weight of excelling to them.

Beneath him, a memory began to grow. He noticed that it was a childhood memory that had been squished by the plethora of other memories. As it expanded, the memory gave birth to the route from his house to the local café known for its delectable smoothies and the long stretch of a two-lane road that steeply inclined at one point, where he would step out of the rickshaw and walk up before getting back in. There was a pre-nursery school midway, close to a small local temple surrounded by greenery. Closer to the market stood a mosque, with an imam who seemed to disappear until Eid came around. The world of seviyan was revealed to him when he was in middle school. But before seviyan, before the café with its scrumptious smoothies, it was the local temple that incited an undying flame for sweets. It was common knowledge to all kids that prasad was available daily, but what many of them did not know was that the temple was relatively closer to Anant's home, allowing him to step out and get back, with his friend covering for him in case the mission turned sideways. These visits continued for about a year or so until the priest was changed and the new priest denied him the little sugary bubbles of diabetic heaven. The respect Anant had for faith, his inclination to form a viable explanation for god's existence, and even to forgive god for his teenage years when he prayed in vain, emerged from this priest who had an amicable disposition and indulged him, thus making him fonder of the possibility of a higher power. Anant felt indebted to the priest for affirming his belief that the gods he adored existed. It was merely a vague year of Anant's life, an elusive moment in time that was largely forgotten in memory, that only his parents' house in Pune could validate the fact that it had indeed been his own life where he had met the priest. He recalled the little game they played, where he would try and act like an antagonist to the priest whenever their paths crossed. A typical Bollywood villain sporting a popped collar. More Sanjay Dutt than Ajit Khan, more Al Pacino in *Scarface* than Al Pacino in *The Godfather*. When the priest disappeared, he was told that he had been transferred, as if there was a farm for the priests after their retirement. It seemed so convenient how time swept away this memory of the first circumcision. A time before the hissing and slithering. The only memory of the local priest that remained was of him playing a man in distress to his antagonist until he would begin reciting the Hamuman Chalisa and despite Anant wanting to continue their game, they had agreed that once he began the recitation, Anant would scurry away. The Hamuman Chalisa protected him. It was his safe verse. The memory of a time that had vanished altogether, much like piecing together moments from a blackout, seemed akin to a child's imaginary friend. Seeing it in front of his eyes was nothing more than a brief tryst between what had gone by and what now was. He wondered who remembered the nameless, faceless local priest. And the thought of being forgotten led him back to his ruminations about Rajat and this need of being remembered.

Anant could not understand why someone would try to immortalize a life that was inherently fragile and fated to be devoured by time. People carved their names on trees and monuments because they stood the test of time, but life in itself was a drooping branch that bent a little more with every passing day. Strangely, the monument that came to his mind was one that he had seen on a school trip to Delhi. The monument he remembered was the Qutub Minar. He recalled other tombs and forts that seemed to be littered in the capital city, the result of a plethora of empires vying for control. He distinctly recalled standing over a Mahatma and an emperor. In Pune itself, he had seen flags bearing the face of another emperor. Were they remembered? The kings were fated to be mere names, either a part of an empire that had become the sum of its rulers, or part of a struggle that outlasted them. It was the accolades people remembered, but their individualities were forgotten. And the former had been dead less than a century and Anant had seen the stories around him begin to change already. There was a stark distinction in being remembered, and being remembered as you were. To be immortalized, one must accept to be mythicized. And in myths, the individuals were subject to change in accordance with the feelings and beliefs of the people. An eternity of being subjected to the will of the people. Such a distasteful immortality seemed counterintuitive to Anant. He argued that perhaps in art, which stands the test of time, every artist could preserve an essence of themselves. A purer, more noble form of immortality. Rabindranath Tagore had embedded his own values in Nikhil as he wrote *The Home and the World*. But was the immortality of Tagore pursued by Tagore himself? And weren't the arts firmly subjective, and thus even more subservient to the feelings and thoughts of the audience. Rabindranath Tagore had written in his memoir about how his memories could not be weighed on its validity, but only on its impressions, and Anant agreed that memory could not be merely history, but history churned in the many emotions and thoughts of the individual. There were others that reached immortality outside art. In science, Einstein became an adjective. But his work by nature impersonal, objective, did not allow any room for something as trivial as individuality. Was Einstein only his work? Was that the sum of his self? Did Rajat mean to be remembered in his field? Like a device named after its inventor? But was that immortality, or merely stamping a name in history? A name that would cease to belong to the person, and become a formula or a device or a medicine. No stretch of his imagination allowed Anant to see how the individual could be remembered as more than their work, and the work itself was either vulnerable to this audience, or did not allow any room for individuality. Thus, negating the self. The more Anant followed the train of thought, the more he began to question the train itself. What did it mean to be remembered at all? The answer eluded him. The different kinds of immortality confused him. And the worst of all immortalities was the fantastical one that would take away death. By removing point B, life was made hollow. A never-ending escalator where you were privy to the deaths of everyone you ever knew, and would come to know. Such a life was worse than his worst nightmare. Some are born at dawn, some at noon, and other unfortunate ones at the dusk of their lives, destined to die the next hour. This was acceptable. To not live in a world where death was a mere theory viewed from a distance, but have the primeval being so close that you could hear its sinister hissings, that was why he had built a retreat. It was immortality that mandated his presence for the death of everyone around him, for all eternity, was hell. Anant shuddered at the thought and decided that he would simply ask Rajat the next time they met. Once the blindfold of thoughts was removed, Anant came to the realization that despite all the walking he was no closer to reaching the world beneath him. The memories seemed to match his every step and coyly drift away from him. He continued his descent down the steps, the tranquil repetition helping him put the thought of immortality to the side. One step after the next, like he was descending from a Buddhist retreat hidden in the mountains down to the world that could no longer disturb the serenity that he had found. When he was content with the distance he had put between himself and the thought of being remembered, he turned around to the cell that was only a few steps away. But before he entered the cell, he took a moment to stare into the void that had covered the sky after his memories abandoned it to appear beneath him, and he prayed for a priest that acted as if he was perpetually distressed by a child.

When Anant returned to the café, 'Wild Horses' by the Rolling Stones had begun playing. The cold coffee in front of him had made a puddle on the table. But the coffee was still cold. Anant closed his eyes before every sip, in an attempt to enjoy the somewhat watered-down coffee.

Chapter 13

Anant and Rajat crossed paths a week after the fated evening in the quiet pastel café. During the week, Rajat kept receiving daily updates of Anant's comings and goings from Dandekar sahib, and much to his bewilderment, he found that Anant remained a stalwart to his routine. Rajat could not ascertain whether it was dedication to his work, or an effort to show his indifference to the quarrel, which had simmered in Rajat ever since. The thought drove Rajat to plan his visit accordingly so he would cross paths with him, to see with his very eyes whether he had made a mistake in hiring Anant.

Rajat arrived at his flat at a quarter past three, when he was certain that Anant would be present. At the door, he was greeted by Dandekar sahib and Iqbal, who were ready to show him the shape that the flat was slowly taking. Anant was at the tail-end of his stroll around the flat, his headphones securely in his ears, oblivious to the world by cloaking it with music. He continued to colour the walls in a variety of paints, sticking wallpapers, scrolling through the saved images to stop on a shade or design before closing his eyes. He diligently made small notes of the shades of paint and styles of wallpapers that he liked, to make a list that would later be sent to Rajat. Upon finishing his walk, he noticed Rajat standing by the kitchen door, in discussion with Faiz, Dandekar sahib and Iqbal. He stood by, waiting. Rajat noticed, and made him wait longer than required, stretching out the conversation, out of spite. 'You're finishing up?' Anant asked when the four disbanded.

'Yes, just about. Giving my two cents.'

'Well, do you want to go grab a drink afterwards?' Rajat was hard-pressed not to smile, believing that Anant's invitation was a peace offering. Rajat agreed before excusing himself, much more apologetically now that his anger had been placated by what he believed was Anant's repentance, and going back to Dandekar sahib who had brought the man who had taken the electrical contract for a quick discussion. Anant waited by the main door of the flat while Rajat breezed through the conversation, endearing himself with the subtle pauses and expressions of deep focus. After the electrical contractor, there was the one who had taken the plumbing contract, but Rajat had had enough already. He pulled Dandekar sahib and Iqbal to the side to give them some money, something Rajat had learned from his dad. They were reluctant to accept the money from him, but it was all an act, and Rajat excelled at drama. He complimented them on their work and thanked them for their attention and time. When his words had cast the desired effect, he gave a small but respectful bow and said that he needed to leave, following which Dandekar and Iqbal took their cue and promptly accepted the cash. In the cab on their way to a bar, Rajat half apologized for his behaviour at the café. Anant waved it off. 'I've forgotten all about it,' he said. As if the mere sentence had pulled Rajat back to the searing realm of anger, his mood had soured again, the thought of his outburst being forgettable seemed criminal to him. His half-apology was a half too many. The cab itself was an affront to him. Having already decided on distance rather than extravagance, they approached a nearby bar, an old joint with square, four-panel wooden windows and an air of abandonment that seemed to seep out of the entrance.

A waiter promptly arrived with the menus as they took their seats. 'What do you mean by being remembered?' Anant said after they were served their drinks. Seething at having had his outburst consigned to oblivion, Anant's question was a cold splash of water that made the burning hellfire of his anger a mere illusion.

'What?' Rajat managed to muster, unsure of whether he was leading a drama, his drama, or acting his part in the play of another, or that maybe, just maybe, there was no theatre at all at this very moment.

'When you told me that you will be remembered, what does being remembered mean to you?' Anant inquired, leaning on the granite table top, a glass of tequila in hand, with lime and a splash of ginger ale, all his attention focused on Rajat. The bright lights were soothing to him, they banished the shadows that weighed heavily on one side, the spotlight brought him back to himself, it corrected his axis.

'My man, you ought to drink more if you want to understand,' Rajat replied with an ease that came from the belief that there was no need of a response that he did not have, irrespective of the alcohol poured between them. This notion of being remembered was second nature to Rajat, but to articulate his feelings in a way that did them justice, or express them at all, seemed beyond him. He would have more luck explaining his childhood events that paved the way for him to be the man he was. Yet in his bravado he also believed that if he had to, he could articulate this need just the same, only he needed a little time to find the right words, and the right motivation would be alcohol.

'I'm keeping up with you, then.' Rajat smiled, admiration and interest from Anant or anybody sitting across him was what his heart craved. And the added relief that Anant had not forgotten about his outburst, that it must have been a figure of speech elevated his mood.

'My man, you are finally listening. When we give ourselves to the world, the answers come to us.' Rajat lifted his drink and

Anant reached to clink his glass of beer with his tequila. 'Is that good?' Rajat reached forward and waited for permission. A nod later, he took a sip from Anant's glass and rubbed his tongue on the roof of his mouth. 'Needs olives. But we'll both have this the next round.'

Anant and Rajat sat in the bar till sunset. They listened to the songs being played at the bar, and also each other—although it was mostly Anant who was listening. They went from discussing their taste in music and flats to sharing the titbits of the past that became more and more introspective and personal with each round. From Rajat's treasure chest of stories, there was one of a fight in his first year of high school where according to him, he took on three seniors, and the time he had jumped off a bridge in Florence. There was also the time when he had seen a herd of elephants while he was walking through an open hotel lobby in Zambia. As per Rajat, the mighty creatures were on their way to their favourite spot. There were half sentences about his struggles where he would liberally take dramatic pauses, and as the night ascended, a slurred sentence spaced out and peppered with sighs in between, he muttered to no one before falling mute.

'I don't know. My dad, my mom, my friends, I know that I need to show that I can do what I have always said I could.' It was his lowered inhibitions that allowed the thought that would have drifted away to reach his mouth. Anant let him move on to silence in peace, knowing better than to try and unearth thoughts that were not his to inspect.

Anant shared a few stories of his own. He told himself that it was needed to continue the conversation, and the conversation had to roll if he wanted to learn about what it meant to be remembered. But the truth was that the rush of tequila was formidable and his mouth had become loose. While he could not control his mouth, a fact that bothered him every couple of minutes after he had shared a story, he held on to the reins of his mind and kept to work and college, of incidents where he was an outsider, borrowing from a stream of observations rather than dipping in the river of his own memories. He described them as if these were stories he had been told. There weren't many, and Anant plucked people that were once a part of his life and turned them into characters that he thought bloomed and weaved, but rather stumbled through vague half realities. He told Rajat about an uncle who had fought against nature itself, when he found himself lost on a trail in the hills. A friend who had disappeared that one day. There were rumours that he had left for a protest against corrupt mining companies, and then he went missing. His stories quickly lost the touch with fiction, and became dull, like the college boy that cuffed himself to the gate, for what reason, Anant did not know, nor did he attempt to fill in the blanks with his imagination. In the latter rounds, Anant briefly touched upon the Titan, but perhaps he was too abstract for Rajat took it as some story from Greek mythology. When Anant believed they were ready to discuss what it meant to be remembered, Anant went on to express ideas of sacrifice and immortality, leaning on a translation of the Rig Veda that he had read. After the story about Purusha, a cosmic entity that had been slayed to give birth to the universe, Anant returned to the question at hand. 'It seems to me that not even all the gods have stood the test of time. Even Brahma dies when the universe comes to an end.'

'Yes, my man, we are a part of god, are we not? Then why can't we follow in their steps?' Rajat replied, his words rolling one after the other. Soon, his speech would begin to slur.

Anant was drunk enough for his explanation to make sense, for a brief moment in time, gone in a flash as his mind came up with a reasoning. 'Would the whole not be remembered instead?'

'Yes, but a part can be too,' Rajat replied.

'But what does it mean to be remembered? You mean, for years, a century, a millennium? Till humans exist? Remembered by all? Some? I don't get it.' Anant put forward his queries as if he were talking to the customer support of Immortality Ltd.

'No, you do. You get me, man. You do, we don't need to put it to words. It is just to be remembered, to be immortalized. Socrates, Alfred Hitchcock, Mir Taqi Mir, you know, The Beatles.' An odder quartet had never been put together. Anant attempted to make sense of what was being said, and perhaps deceiving himself, in the guise of understanding, he wove his own interpretations to his answers. To be remembered in any way possible, to however limited or expansive an audience, to be adored. But before Anant could inquire about what Rajat planned to pursue to fulfil these hopes of being immortalized, it dawned on him that by evening, Rajat had begun to drift away from him and into his own world, the question at hand fading into the background. Looking across the table, Anant noted, seemed akin to staring across a roaring sea. Where Rajat now existed, or perhaps what the alcohol revealed was his place of existence, answers took different forms. Their table that once seemed intimate had become a border separating the two, and the surrounding tables of the bar that had become increasingly busy as the day went on, with all its noise, existed in a different realm altogether. Anant stared at him in this moment of clarity. There were more questions to be asked, much of what Anant had built was merely his own comprehension of Rajat's half answers. But he could see that they would lead him nowhere because Rajat wasn't at a loss for words that he masked by undermining words themselves, but by trying to diminish words he was making an effort to mask his inability to answer, or at least answer in a way that Anant understood, for answers themselves seemed different on his side of the world. Anant took a moment and hoped that

Rajat would indeed achieve these goals, whatever they were. Perhaps one day, Anant thought, he would look back and see that it was his own failure to understand greatness that had been the roadblock to comprehending these dreams that Rajat had. But for now, everything said and done, Anant's rendezvous with the evening had come to an end. Rajat would have liked to order another drink and continue the conversation, but for Anant the failure to find an answer that offered him some insight into his own memories was too great a hurdle to overcome. For him, this called for an unceremonious end to the evening. Anant no longer had any interest in whatever world Rajat claimed to be a part of. He made his way through the drink, painfully aware that the purpose of this conversation had been defeated. It became a struggle to remain seated, the place began to claw at his sides and chest. He didn't want to be in the bar, the thought thudded with every beat of his heart. A world of his own called out to him. The noise that had mixed with music, that once remained in the background had seeped in and was ringing in his ears. The presence of Rajat seemed too heavy a weight to hold, the darkness on his shoulder hurt Anant's eyes like he was being pricked by pins and when Anant closed his eyes to relieve himself of this pain, a paradoxical world serenaded him. But Rajat was quick to tap him on the top of his head, twice. 'Don't pass out.'

Declining the offer to stay at Rajat's, even with the added incentive of passing out in his room, Anant and Rajat got up after paying the bill and shook hands before Anant was pulled into an awkward hug. The hug in itself wasn't awkward until he began to pat Rajat on his back. Perhaps in his world across the ocean, these were what hugs were. 'Take care, okay,' Rajat told him.

Anant woke up pleasantly surprised to find that he was without the ailments that followed an indulgent night. There was no headache that pricked his eyes, no sign of a foul morning breath, he couldn't make out any scent from his breath at all. The anxiety over the night before was absent and the concert of his stomach had also been cancelled. The usual suspects that had made him wary of drinking were not tormenting him this morning. His mind pleasantly devoid of thoughts and of any attempts at reconstructing the memory of last evening, as if by waking up in the cell, he had left his body and its baggage behind. Anant assumed that these luxuries were the benevolence of this structure. He didn't remember how he passed out, but clearly, he had done something right as he had managed to cut many tedious corners. Getting to his feet, he noticed that the mats of the cell were oddly softer under the soles of his feet, and he glanced down to make sure he wasn't standing on a mattress instead. To his surprise, the floor of the cell had changed. He was now standing on a rich mahogany floor. He began to stretch out of habit despite none of his muscles aching, and his mind trying to come to terms with the change in the flooring. His habits still followed his morning pattern as if he had woken up in the real world. He strolled over to the window of the cell and was greeted by nothing. There was an absence outside the window so dark, he had to put his hand out to make sure the cell hadn't been transported to a box. When no boundary met his hand, he looked up and down, side to side, and stretching as far as he could see was a starless space, pitch black as if god had turned the lights off. Anant turned away from the window to face the exit and his pleasantly empty mind let out a soundless yelp when it registered that the always open door of his cell, if there was a door at all, that led to the world outside was closed. Never before had Anant seen the door shut. A flutter of unease made his stomach squirm. Anant tried to open the door, it budged only a few inches before it got stuck. Anant tried to apply force but the door refused to cooperate. He inspected the door and found that the hinges were darkened as if something had been poured over them. Returning to his spot in the cell, he sat down and closed his eyes. By waking up in the cell, he told himself, he had obviously stumbled into this world before his cognition was prepared. The strange events unfolding could only mean that he had dozed off, and somehow made his way to the retreat. Anant decided that he'd rather be with the ailments of drinking than in this world that was not yet ready for him. He closed his eyes and began to control his breath. There was no prerequisite to move from one world to another, but if there had to be one, Anant would say that it would be being mindful. When Anant opened his eyes again, he found that he was still in the cell. He got back to his feet and walked to the window and looked out to find the unwavering void was absolute in its presence, stripping Anant of any and all sense of direction and location. He closed his eyes to try and listen to time, in ticks, in the flow, in the winds, anything that could represent time. There was nothing. He tried to bring about a change of scenery but the sense of impotency remained in him, enveloping him in its cold, inhumane arms. He turned to see the door shut and the hinges still soaked. He tried to open the door again. With the jerk of his back, he pulled at the door, but to no avail. He pulled a few more times out of frustration, before he crouched low to inspect the hinges once more. The hinges were still wet and the scent of tequila that in the real world would have acted as chants for his stomach to begin the concert, still lingered on it.

Anant lost track of time sooner than he expected. But how much time had really passed? He never paid much attention to time, the blanket categorizations of morning, evening and night were more often than not enough for him. Yet in the cell, suddenly cold, which made him feel that he was an unwanted lingering presence, he began to try and keep up with time that no longer seemed to be uniform. In this world, there was no way of tracking time apart from counting it. And when he started to count the seconds, he would only go as far as counting till forty or fifty before he would be distracted, as if his mind was unwilling to let him complete the minute. As if his mind had ordained that no minute would pass inside these desolate walls. He wondered if time was flowing at all, or whether all this was happening in the time it took for a grain of sand to filter down to the bottom of the hourglass. He got up again, counting the seconds that never reached a minute while he looked out of the window, and again he tried to open the door, with force, and other times, without it, as if imploring it with caresses to open. He crouched down to the hinges to smell them. Still tequila. When he sat down once more, it dawned on him that he had never closed the door after it budged a few inches in his first attempt, nor in the efforts that followed, and when he glanced back at the door, it was shut once again. He continued his staring contest with the door as his mind began to formulate a daunting thought. His mind took its time deliberating, weighing the thought, feeling its texture, listening to it in incomprehensible whispers, measured in seconds that never amounted to a minute, before finally, the thought was unveiled to him. A thought that had been stirring in the back of his mind while he repeated this cycle over and over. Finally accepted and pushed to the forefront, dressed as a question. Anant asked himself if this was the afterlife.

Chapter 14

It was a cloudy morning in Mumbai. The scent of rain clung to the air from the night before, and people on their way to work, on foot, on bikes, in autos, in cars, and in trains, would look up every now and then expecting the clouds to burst. A single crow sat on the railing of the balcony, black feathers swept back as if they had been combed after he was drenched in rain, gawking with matching beady eyes at the clothes that lay on the sofa inside the living room. Past the door where the crow could not see, Anant lay lifeless on his bed. The faint buzzing of the AC was the only sound inside the flat. The sound of screaming from a plethora of news channels playing in surrounding flats, the horns of scooters and cars at regular intervals, the conversations on staircases and the cawing of the crow, were unable to penetrate the flat and remained on the periphery of it.

In another world, Anant opened his eyes to a rich mahogany floor instead of the floor mats. The grey brick walls of the cell were soft against his back, just like the mahogany floor was soft on his ass. In a world where seconds never amounted to a minute, Anant was oblivious to the time he had spent in the cell. He was neither hungry nor thirsty. He would stand by the window hoping for a sign, even for a whisper in the wind but the all-encompassing abyss remained impassive. There was nothing but this everlasting void that the cell was floating on. He scratched another line on the bricks, the lines he had made prior had disappeared. 'Five. It is five.' He said out loud to himself, not to make it easier to remember, but to merely hear the sound of his voice. The only sound in this world was the one he made.

It had been five times that he had attempted to return to his world, five times he had closed his eyes, with a diminishing belief that he would wake up from this nightmare, five times after he wondered if he was dead. Five times of how many seconds? How many minutes? What were minutes in a world where seconds never ticked on and culminated in a minute? In the time, however much it was, he had scratched five lines on the wall representing the hope that he still clung to. Was it hope? Or had the reality become so surreal that he was merely trying to hold on to what he knew? Five times, and in these five times, Anant learned that he could make changes to the interiors of the cell, to an extent. A lot of modifications would simply disappear within seconds of appearing, and that he couldn't make any changes to the door or the walls for even a second, no matter how much he tried. Not even the hinges that he had cleverly tried to open were bending to his will. He couldn't outsmart his mind. When he had jumped out of the window, he just drifted away from the cell, as if his would-be fall was cushioned by melancholy, until he blinked and he was back in the cell.

He had prayed once, and another time he had sat on the wood and listened to the sound of his breath till he felt, imagined, energies within him soothing his body, one last parting gift before they left to reunite with a higher power, join a cycle or return to the universe. What now?

'What now indeed,' Anant said out loud. 'What do you think?' he asked himself. 'It seems like I have been in this retreat forever,' Anant replied.

'Forever is a long time,' he reminded himself.

'Yes. But what is time any more?' He glanced at the void outside the window. He paused, and then added, 'What can you do here?' he asked himself. 'Time is change. From time to time, the world outside the cell changes, like seasons. You're new, aren't you?' he responded to his prior question.

'Yes and no,' Anant replied, the act of talking to himself slowly losing its preposterousness.

'Ah, I see. You're the one who used to step in and out at your convenience.'

'Yes.' Anant nodded, further and further believing or deluding himself that he was in a real conversation.

'How is the world out there?'

'It's different.' Anant was unsure of how to proceed with his answer.

'Don't be cryptic. It's just us here. Different how?'

Anant went blank, and started looking for an answer to alleviate the crippling silence of the cell. 'It's hectic. Like you are caught up in a storm.'

'Then why do you step out of the cell?'

There was silence, but his silence did not put an end to his own questions.

'Is it something you do?'

'No.'

'Loved ones?'

'No.'

'This other world has something this world doesn't?'

'No.'

'Not much for words, are you?'

'Enough to have a conversation with myself.'

'Touché.'

Anant made a sound and nodded in agreement, sighing. The only change since he had been trapped in the cell was this conversation. Was he losing his mind? 'Why did I step out?' The question had circled back to him once again. He was no longer sure if he was asking the question, or replying to it.

'Forsaking your laconic tendencies, good. Why did you step out? Was it your work?'

'No.'

'Was it your family?'

'We've been through this.'

'Was it the world?'

Anant was quiet.

'Was it the world? Does it hold something for you?'

'It wasn't.'

'Were you even alive or are you simply trying to hoodwink me? Maybe you aren't the one that steps out. You have no reason to.'

'Hoodwink… Yes, I was…I am alive.'

'Were you living?'

'Yes.'

'What made you leave this place?'

'I don't know.'

'Was it your work?'

'No.'

'Was it your family?'

'Are we going to keep moving in a circle?'

'Who knows, perhaps time is a circle. Like you said, what is time but change. Who is to say it doesn't circle back. Was it the world?'

'Maybe,' Anant replied. He refrained from correcting the voice about who had said that time was change. Perhaps, he thought to himself, it might have been him.

There was silence on the other side, and so Anant continued, 'So what if I was alive and living my life. What's wrong with that?' Anant couldn't believe that he was earnestly defending himself against himself. He could not understand what he was guilty of.

'Nothing. I was just making conversation, but you don't seem too keen.'

'You sounded accusatory. Who exactly are you?' Anant was getting more and more curious about this mystery voice.

'You.'

'Touché.'

'What's it like? This world of yours that you keep draped in obscurity.'

Anant took a pause and then turned his head to see more grey bricks. For a moment he had expected to find someone talking to him. Anant decided that he was done with the conversation. But the waves of silence were formidable, and quickly began to overwhelm him once again. It felt as if the waves were seeping into his sanity, into his heart, attempting to silence it.

He promptly returned to the conversation with himself. 'Is that why you were asking? To know about the world?'

'I have only seen it through the window. Let's not pretend that you haven't when you scurry over here. Is it really preposterous that I would like to know what this other world is like?'

Anant refrained from jumping into his defence and 'scurrying' against a voice in his head. 'What do you want to know?'

'What makes you step outside this cell? I myself am quite chuffed about my surroundings.'

Anant ignored his chuffings and took his time to articulate his thoughts. 'The world, I mean, sure it's hectic, but it can be a good hectic too. I enjoy working, I like to make that trip every three months, and…you remember the ocean?'

'Yes.'

Anant continued his probe. 'The doughnut?'

'Yes, and all the others. The record player, candle, the breath, the roller shoes.'

Anant chuckled at the mention of 'the roller shoes'.

'She was transcendental.'

'I suppose. What do you remember about the breath?'

'Well, I was certain that I wasn't drowning, even though the cell was flooded. But once the water disappeared the breath felt like a gush of divine wind that soothed me. Like a crisp, cool wind coming through the window after having sat in a smoke-filled room.'

'Every time I finished swimming that month, I would take a few moments to appreciate my breaths.'

'They were good times for me.'

'Yeah, moments like these. That is why I step out. I savour them. They're like pieces of my soul scattered around the world.'

'I relish them too.'

'Hmm. I suppose someone has to go find them.'

'Indeed.'

'What now?'

'I don't know.'

'Oh.'

Silence descended on Anant once more, but during the conversation, whether it lasted a blink of an eye or many blinks, or in obsolete measurements, seconds or years, he had grown accustomed to the world and the silence itself no longer tried to perforate his consciousness. He did not peek out of the window, nor did he steal glances at the gate. There was no memory of markings lingering on the wall. He just sat there, and existed. It was time to deal with the question. 'Am I dead?' he asked out loud.

'I don't know. Would I be dead if you were?'

'Yes. Are we both dead?'

'I'm not dead.'

'How would you know?'

'How would you?'

What if he had passed out on the bed never to wake up again? Anant had always considered death as an end, a full stop rather than a comma. To find himself in afterlife, in a space to contemplate his own passing away, never once in all his years of courting the Titan had such a possibility occurred to him. It had never been about his own death. Looking back at his struggles with death, it dawned on him that the darkness rested on the shoulders of everyone but himself. Had he taken his mortality for granted?

'I always thought you'd have the answer.'

For a moment, Anant wasn't sure who was speaking to whom and it was only the curt reply that followed that he figured that the one speaking now must be him.

'What kind of an answer?'

'You know, death, meaning of life and the afterlife.'

'Like a god?'

'Are you inclined to save the Queen?'

Anant couldn't ignore it any more. 'Are you trying to be British?'

'No, well, I suppose so. I amuse myself by using slangs of different regions and countries from the books and movies you consume.'

'Oh!' For a moment, Anant forgot about his struggles.

Left speechless, the voice continued, 'You do appear out of nowhere and take control of this body. And you change the cell with a thought.'

'The flooring? Yes, I did do that.' Anant said, wondering if it had been him. 'But most of the changes disappear. So, as amusing as that would be, I am not god. This...this place...it is just my imagination.' Anant didn't believe the words he said, but hoped that by continuing to make light of the situation he could somehow delude himself into believing it. That this wasn't the afterlife, but merely his cell, same as always. No reply came from the other side, as if he couldn't be bothered to comment on a lie. 'Okay, maybe this isn't my imagination.' Anant seceded from the lie.

'It's my world. I would hope that you see why I find it a little condescending for it to be called a figment of your imagination.'

'I suppose so.'

'And?'

'And what?'

'Apologize.'

'I am sorry.'

'You are apologizing to yourself, you know.'

'I...yes. I am.'

'So, do you have any other sins you want to repent for?'

'Repent to myself?'

'Well, if you consider them sins, you let yourself down too.'

'You like to try and sound profound.'

'Yes, but that isn't part of my theatrics. Just making conversation and keeping you on your toes.'

'What do you do when I am not here?'

'Sit. Without the noise of your presence, it's pretty good. Look out of the window sometimes...you know, when there is something to look out to. I suppose I also wait for you to find these pieces of your soul.'

'Because it becomes pleasant?'

'Or interesting. But yes. Like little nuggets of bliss in an otherwise mundane existence.'

'I'll keep that in mind.'

'If you aren't dead.'

'Hmm.'

'Oye chokre, you over that already?'

'No, I feel that you are tying me in knots. And please, not from my college.'

'You remembered his nautanki.'

Anant wasn't going to forget the class that began with a greeting and ended with scarring, and having sworn to desist from these memories, he returned to the topic at hand.

'You are trying to distract me.'

'Why would I do that?'

'To entertain yourself? Keep me on my toes?'

'Guess I am not incapable of such an action. But I am just trying to pass the time. Your presence, while not undesirable, and I don't want you to think you are unwelcome here, but it has become icky. A bother, in the best of ways. I would much rather you leave.'

'I have tried.'

'Would it be distressing if you were to never return?'

'It would but the thought hasn't completely registered with me yet.'

'What about the body?'

'What about it?'

'Well, when you are not here, I continue going about my existence. There isn't an abundance of ways to tell time, but I have grown accustomed to it. And I have grown alongside you. I have had the horrible shaggy hair, and what I personally suspect is the smelly beard. My body mirrors the growth of yours, but I continue on my own. Do you believe that body you left behind would do the same?'

It was a ludicrous idea, the thought that his body would simply discard him and continue to live, it could not be justified by words, and yet, when Anant tried, he found that no set of words put in any order could explain why this wasn't possible either. And yet he said, 'No.'

'No? Why not?'

'I never had someone with me in that body.'

'Unlike this.'

'Yes.'

Another round of silence to let the implication of this situation settle on him. That unlike before, he had never been trapped outside his body either, and the resident seemed to be aware of this.

'Where do you think the body is?'

'On the bed.'

'A bed, must be nice.'

'It's not very different, these bricks are very soft. But a bed is nice.'

Silence ticked on, and the conversation came to a mutually agreed end. Anant could not entertain any more conversation with himself. He could not risk being convinced of what he labelled an absurd theory. But more so, Anant could not begin to contemplate his own death. The bricks were indeed soft, he thought to himself. They were reminiscent of his mattress with the springs that were jutting out here and there. He thought of the AC that he had a habit of switching on minutes prior to entering the bedroom. He tried to remember how he had passed out last night. He had discarded his clothes in the living room and stumbled his way to his bed. Anant remembered the fine cotton bedsheet over him and, dare he say it, he believed that the resident could feel it too. When he opened his eyes, he found himself in his bed once again, as he had imagined.

He looked around his room confused and when he could finally register his surroundings, he jumped off his bed as if it were about to open up a wormhole that would suck him back into the cell. Had it been a dream, Anant wondered. It seemed the farthest thing from it. Anant pondered over what he had gone through while he clenched and unclenched his hands.

It seemed as real as this world. It was the retreat, the cell, he was sure of it. And while the time had passed normally, seconds had become minutes, and he hadn't woken up particularly late that day, he was certain that he had spent a long time in the cell. Longer than he had been asleep. Unfortunately, in a place where the usual units of time were obsolete, he could not ascertain how long he had been in the cell. And unbeknownst to him at the time, Anant brought back a new thought growing from the tomb that, at one point, his cell seemed to have become. A parting gift from this surreal tryst with his retreat. A notion that had been precariously overlooked ever since his first dealings with the Titan—that of his mortality. What would be the ramifications of his death? He could no longer ignore the thought. The gift was a jack-in-the-box that kept popping up every now and again, like the venomous plant that Mario tries to avoid, growing larger with every peek-a-boo, bearing the flag of death.

Chapter 15

Subtle changes took place in Anant after his last experience in the retreat. The first was a disregard for sleep. Given how treacherous dreams had become, and that his mind had started to function like a jack-in-the-box or a cuckoo clock that is just moments away from popping out a surprise, which in his case was the thought of a tree that grew from a shallow grave that was meant for him, Anant actively tried to avoid sleep. But since no one had accomplished such a feat, and the inevitability of sleep was an immediate truth that Anant could not argue away or retreat from, he accepted that he would succumb to the will of his body every now and again. All Anant could do, and all he did, was try to prolong his days as much as he could. On the first night, he sat on the mat in the corner of his living room, listening to an old John Coltrane record, where he passed out after his body disregarded his wish to abandon sleep and imposed its rest on him. His eyes snapped open and he jerked awake an hour later. He walked around the flat, making sure he was in the real world. The jack-in-the-box gift that his cell had given him, like a cuckoo clock striking the hour mark, popped open and images of a tree bearing his own death flashed before him.

The following day, Anant felt the next change in his body. Though he was sleep deprived, an abundance of energy compelled him to venture out of his flat even without any work. It was as if he were in a constant state of vying for his survival, and his body that had rejected his will the night before, chose to indulge his wishes, and burned itself trying to keep him going. Stepping out of his apartment, Anant knew he could not go to the site like this. He hardly felt he could talk on the phone and not seem insane. Gopal, the apartment guard, had informed him of the unavailability of water, when Anant nodded with such vigour that caused Gopal to repeat himself, in case Anant had misheard him.

This inexplicable rush of energy made it unbearable to remain still, but the same energy confined him to himself. He did not leave Kasaravadi simply because he could not call for an auto, or a cab. He could not accept rejection, or cross-questioning. He expended his energy walking around the Janta Market, and the Shivaji Mandir where a small huddle of people was standing outside smoking. He reached as far as Matunga before turning around in the direction of his apartment. He wandered in different directions the next day, and the day after. The small pockets of sleep that he got were not enough and it left him drained, so he got burnt out faster, and the distance he walked shortened. He would return to his apartment having walked a kilometre, and pass out for half an hour before he snapped awake, the cuckoo clock striking every now and again, worsening his state of mind.

One sunny day later in the week, with his body suffering under the brunt of this change in lifestyle, Anant left his apartment with the intention of burning himself completely. He looked to reset himself by swinging to the other end of living. It wasn't in his nature to act in this way, but he had a site to go to, a site he hadn't visited the past few days.

Stepping out of his apartment, he steadied himself. He called for an auto, with a stoic affirmation of accepting the present situation. He told the auto driver to take him to wherever he was going. 'I just want to...I mean, let's just go. Wherever.'

'I'll drop you at Borivali,' the auto driver said after eyeing him suspiciously. 'No funny business. Don't think I'll let you get off without paying.'

I will pay. Of course.' Anant tumbled in. From Borivali, he plunged into the deep waters of travel. He joined the swarm of people waiting at the station and got on the local, unsure of where it went. The journey was the medicine, he told himself. He could always take a cab back. Not many cab drivers had a problem going to Dadar, especially in the late afternoon. There would be minimal cross-questioning. He even contemplated getting into a cab and pretending he was mute. He was carried in along with the swarm of people waiting at the station, and carried out when the majority of them began to leave. He patted his pockets, he was becoming forgetful but was glad he had a token. He walked on the streets of Malad where there were more cars and bikes on the road than people. Anant walked. Half-abandoned shopping malls littered around the area. The denser alleys were full of people. He spotted a mean-eyed skull on the hoarding of a shop in a deserted plaza. Just past the hoarding, three men with progressively denser beards removed their shoes outside before entering a tattoo shop. For a moment, Anant contemplated getting a tattoo. He thought that constant pricking of the needle would be a shock enough to the system to reset him. That perhaps the tree could be poked out of his head. But Anant was unsure of what he wanted. The moment he began to contemplate on what tattoo he would get, the cuckoo clock struck. The tree flashed in his mind, and he jumped back at the sight of it. He could feel the thoughts building in his mind, growing in weight, making his head heavy. Anant promptly called for an auto and jumped in. The urgency on Anant's face or just the long-distance trip had the auto driver race off with a roar that was more sound than speed. Anant took deep breaths to collect himself. He was confused over what was happening to him. He could not comprehend how a thought could so thoroughly affect him in this manner. But he did not ruminate over his condition, for he feared that every thought invariably led to the tree. Instead, his eyes settled on a small idol of Ganesh resting near the dashboard of the auto. The idol stared at him, and Anant stared back. He wondered if the festival was around the corner. It would prove to be a helpful distraction. The festivities could be a reset for him. The unwavering eyes of the elephant-headed god soon made him uncomfortable. He began to feel as if he was being judged. A fleeting mirage of the tree consistently prodded his mind, as if demanding that it be examined, that it be given the attention it needed to become concrete. But in reality, it was but a false alarm. When the cuckoo clock struck, the thought imposed itself upon Anant, seizing attention and forcing him to ponder over it.

Anant shifted in his seat till he was pressed against the metal grille in the corner, away from his eyes. Questions of his mortality, and its ramifications began to stir in him. The cuckoo clock struck again. The tree rising from his grave. He shook his head and asked to be dropped before the gate of his society, by a cigarette stall that was built on the remains of a rickshaw. Anant bought some cutting chai and moved to sit on the concrete bench when he caught himself about to comment on the weather to the people around him who were on their breaks, chatting and going through their phones with a cigarette burning between their fingers. Words were slipping off his tongue easier than ever. He feared what he would say. Till now, he had only been nodding and shaking his head. He had managed to rein his tongue in. But the change was only worsening. Anant could barely sip on his chai without getting restless. Until this moment, Anant had struggled against these changes while believing they were momentary hiccups that would soon disappear, that the tree was just an infatuation, or a way for his mind to punish him. But as he sat unable to revert to his old habits, having made the trip and returned without any improvement, he considered the possibility that perhaps he wouldn't return to normal. That there was no normal to return to at all. It felt like someone had tampered with his wiring and then welded the wires together, thereby making the alterations permanent. Throwing half his chai in a dustbin, he made his way up to his flat. He wanted to use the stairs, but he held himself firm to his routine in hopes of taming this excess energy rather than submitting to it. He dared himself to use the elevator. He needed to fix himself and the only way was to rewire himself. He shut the door of his flat, and rushed to his bedroom, locking himself in it. There were plenty of excuses that these new connections prompted in his mind, but he dismissed them before he could be swayed. He sat on his bed with a resolute declaration that he would not move until this energy ceased to affect him. But the energy only rebelled. It grew until he was forced to see that like a raging bull, this energy would not be tamed. This strife only lasted for fifteen minutes.

Doubt began to creep in. Anant wondered if he had no chance. Seeking an asylum in his washroom, he took a longer shower than usual, and spent time combing his short hair this way and that until it pained him to remain still. He refused to sleep, and he refused to seek comfort. He decided that if he was looking for normal, he would find it in the normal. He settled on returning to the site. He would not be transparent in his troubles, but rather keep a check on himself. He would not nod, at least not emphatically, and his tongue would be still. He could do that. He had learned to be still while building his retreat.

Anant called for a cab. He waited by the society gate trying not to glance at Gopal. Stay still, he told himself. He sat in the cab and greeted the driver with a smile. Stay still, he reminded himself. He arrived at the site without his headphones. He smiled all around, overcompensating for his current state of disarray. Stay still, he whispered to himself and his smile became more courteous than happy. He could not work, but the fact that he had arrived on the site and could move freely was success in itself. Still, he declared. Once he had completed his rounds, he packed up for the day. Feeling better than he had when he arrived at the site, he chose to wait for the elevator without a second thought. Stay still, Anant celebrated. When he reached the ground floor, he called Rajat and realized after he picked up the call that he had nothing to say. Even Rajat was surprised by the call. 'Cool. This is rare,' Rajat said. 'You haven't been around lately.'

'Yes, I was sick. I was wondering if you wanted to grab a drink,' Anant said before he realized what he was saying. Stay still, Anant questioned himself.

'Some tequila, eh amigo?'

Anant understood that he was a quiet man, and one who disliked using words needlessly to compensate for the silence. That was his normal. Stay still, he drummed into himself. He bit his tongue to stop the words that were trying to worm their way out of him because to change now would be to give in to his tampered wiring. Rajat inquired after the quiet had stretched on for quite a bit if he wanted to repeat that day again, and considering what had followed, Anant was quick to suggest whisky instead.

'That's fine with me. I know a good cocktail bar. I'll send you the details in a bit,' Rajat said.

Anant cut the call with an 'okay', if only to stop himself from blabbering more. Stay still, he snapped at himself. He walked out of the lobby and relegated himself to watching the dull greenery of the society. The day was alive with sounds, of television, of children running around in the park, of the hustle and bustle of the basti adjacent to the society, of a collective chatter that grew the longer Anant tried to remain suspended in the sounds. The cuckoo clock struck. The tree flashed in his mind. Anant did not flinch at the thought, he merely moved on from sounds to colours. His eyes were out of focus, and he stared at nothing but a vague silhouette of colours, greys of the buildings, whites of the cars through the black wrought-iron gate, the olives of the fluttering poncho raincoats worn by people on bikes who expected the clouds to burst open at any time, and sunshine yellows of the auto that mirrored the sunny evening. Foolishly he ventured into his mind to remember the moon-kissed ocean. The clock struck. His thoughts quickly drifted towards death. All roads led to the same cursed tree, to thoughts of his mortality. No matter how ludicrous the jumps his mind had to make, it would turn into an Olympian and make those jumps. This time he had moved from the ocean to the full moon and to the sacrifices during the full moon. From sacrifices, the natural progression was towards death, his death and landing on the familiar thought of its ramifications.

Anant returned to the site. Kartik met him at the door with a register of deadlines that he kept by his side at the behest of Anant. 'How are you?' Anant asked, no longer trying to monitor his smile.

'Good, sir. The work is going on.'

'The rains gone for today, huh?' They both paused for an uncertain moment where neither of them knew where this was going, before Kartik smiled, nodded and commented that while it wasn't ideal weather, the sun today was a respite from the overbearing humidity.

Anant met Rajat on the site and in an effort to expel more energy and even tire his tongue, he took his time to explain Rajat what was being done by the workers—the carpenters were busy making the furniture, the wiring for the lights had been done, and what kind of lights would be fixed and where had also been decided. An hour later, they were seated on chairs draped with a velvet-like cloth that bore an abstract print. The trick had worked. Rajat had called for the cab, he had picked the bar, and he made conversation during the ride there without being bothered by Anant's silence. He had filled his quota of conversation. The time was passing as it would have had Anant not stumbled upon the wretched tree. Anant recalled how weightless he felt while sitting on the chair as he continued to drink. He had liked the seat. The cushion was adequate and the glossy brass-finished back support curved along his spine. The abstract print looked like some transcendental being had swept down in a fit of inspiration and in frenzied brushstrokes created what he had created. Anant's focus oscillated between the seat, the bar and Rajat, who was enveloped in a fit of emotion and was telling Anant how he appreciated his belief in him. 'I am telling you, man. You seem to have a pep in your step. Finally, you are living.' Rajat's parting words had left an impression on him.

Was Anant living? Anant sat in his living room corner with a pencil in hand and his notebook open. The nib of his pencil was sharp, the pencil rested just over the arch between his thumb and index finger. A crisp blank page stared back at him. Such Sweet Thunder by Duke Ellington played in the background. Yet, he was unable to draw. In the comfort of his apartment, he dared to ruminate over the statement, tiptoeing around his treacherous and increasingly despondent mind. These past few days he had hardly felt like himself. He didn't remember much of what had happened. Was he, the person sitting on the mat beside the record player, twiddling with the pencil, the real Anant, or was he an imposter while the real Anant was still in the cell along with the other that resided there? Was he the product of his mind birthing a new consciousness that the resident had warned him about? Was he the tree that grew from that Anant's grave? Anant lay there on the mat, the soft drums, the sensuous saxophone, the languid piano, nothing moved him. It felt mindless. Lifeless vibrations of the air. Dare he say, he always found the music needless. It was his muscle memory to pick up the notebook and place the pen beside the record player, to sharpen the pencil and place it on the notebook. The body worked as it should have, it was he who resided in the body that seemed to have changed. He considered the possibility that perhaps the wiring felt tampered with because it was connected to a new being. Meanwhile, the dreaded tree that grew from the thought of his grave had become a behemoth. The reason he didn't flinch at the thought of the tree was that its existence was no longer vague. Its branches were sturdy, and it was bestowed with a thick crown that light couldn't penetrate. The shade it cast over the quarantined part of his mind was edging closer and getting darker, almost mirroring the void that surrounded the cell in his previous visit. Anant closed his eyes and heaved a deep sigh. Now that the tree was a staple of his mind, the desperation to draw, to use his mind, to be comfortable within himself once again, grew with each passing breath. The fear of the cuckoo clock ensnared him. The thought of venturing into his retreat did not seem plausible. Not until the tree remained. He was ceding a part of his mind to the tree. But now that he had grown to accept its existence, Anant realized that he still needed to move on. He needed to draw, to use his mind, to have the retreat.

Rather than waiting for the thought of the tree to strike, he ventured towards the tree. Now that he had come to accept its existence, now that it had embedded itself in his mind, Anant allowed himself to ruminate over the tree. The first thing that occurred to him were the possible ramifications of the tree.

Would there be shrubs and bushes and vines that missed the tree? Would the ecosystem that thrived because of it perish? Or would the tree merely be forgotten. Like his uncle was. Like his friend. The little he remembered about his uncle or his friend, focused on him, how he felt, his emotions, his reactions, the overwhelming stranglehold of the Titan on the world, in relation to him. But now, thinking about undergrowth and wild bushes, he stumbled into their families. What had they gone through? There was nothing to do but feel the grief, to mourn the loss, and to accept the end, but ultimately understand that what they had gone through was just part and parcel of living. Anant scoffed at the deceptive nature of these words. How easy did his mind make it seem. It almost sounded like the side effects mentioned at the footnote of any description of medicine found on the internet. Like this pill may cause stomach ache, headache, dizziness, depression, and worse, the side effects of life were pain, suffering and mourning.

And what of the one meeting his end? Anant's brief flutter of empathy disappeared and he returned to focus on himself. What of him, he asked himself. What would happen to him? Anant gazed at the wretched tree from the other side of the border he had set up when he had divided a piece of his mind for the tree to be contained. He stood at a point where light still touched the ground. A wide expanse of greenery existed behind him, and past the vast plain lands that would slope down into the depths of his mind, existed his retreat. In front of him, the tree stood covering the land past the border in darkness. Indifferent, towering, impervious, Anant suspected that the tree hosted venom under its shade. He imagined ugly ghoulish creatures with bent spines and hair growing out of their sinister eyes, shrieking in a manic fervour of desire that wanted to bury him in the grave as an offering for the tree. But these ghoulish creatures did not scare Anant. He stood in the domain of his mind, and therefore, either side of the border fell under his jurisdiction. It was his land where the tree had roots and was growing. The fear that had tormented him all his life existed outside of him, its authority was absolute in the real world. Its flag erected on the shoulder of every person he came across. Yet, he had barricaded death to remain outside his retreat. This was Anant's realm. The thought that he would be held hostage by a mere tree was shameful to him. He had exiled his biggest fears. He could not accept defeat against a smaller enemy. The terror he had unearthed when he was trapped in the cell was that of the Titan setting its gaze on the living. His death, Anant thought to himself. It wasn't the notion of death, but a specific notion of his own death that scared him. 'Yes, my death, and what?' he told himself. He ran through the banal script of sayings, 'the game must come to an end', 'what had a beginning must have a finish', 'why worry about the rules that had been ordained since birth' and strangely enough, these sayings that he had mocked when his uncle was on deathbed, what he termed banal and pedantic, seemed to work. The classics made sense. His shoulders began to feel looser. The grass underneath his feet seemed to extend past the border, into the unknown that existed beneath the tree. Perhaps it was the time he spent staring at the tree, but the monstrosity itself seemed lithe, and the ghouls seemed to be an illusion of the dark. Perhaps it was just the confidence that the whisky had given him, but he asserted himself in his world, the empty fields of his mind where he hadn't built a retreat was still his mind. He couldn't recall the tree ever swaying before, but it moved now. It drifted away from him, as if the whole world was being tilted. The shade the tree had cast within the quarantined land receded, as if the rising sun had cast away the shadows to the other side of the tree. Wide-eyed, Anant watched as the light revealed the tree's gangly, thin, and shallow roots. That despite its thick trunk and wide branches spreading out over his mind, the roots of the tree did not run deep. It felt as if he were being led by a primordial understanding that had bloomed after a lifetime of sowing and caring.

Slowly, with only the remains of the fear he once felt lingering in him, Anant made his way to the tree. Thoughts of his mortality struck him like a whip. But what was worse, his death, or the death of his loved ones? To the infantile Anant who had ceased to make connections in the world, his world existed on two columns and the mere thought of them breaking was utterly devastating. His death was half of the contract of life that had been signed for him. He realized that he had been too focused on the shade, the trunk and the crown of the tree to check the roots. That the right to mourn his death, not what happened to him afterwards, but the moments following his death, did not rest with him. That the humdrum after him wasn't in his fate to partake. What he feared of death was not directed towards him, but centred around his world. Him dying was just a fact. The game mustn't go on, Sherlock. It must end.

But before he reached the trunk, the world began to tilt back and realigned itself to its axis. The dark murky shade of the tree enveloped him in absolute darkness. He was reminded of his fear. The disarray, the desolation, the cuckoo clock, the jack-in-the-box that only had a plant that grew into a formidable tree. But he had seen what lay in the dark was nothing but a shallow tree. He reached out to place his hand on its trunk to bend down and inspect its roots. But a fleeting push was all it needed, applying less force than when he had tried to open the door, the tree was uprooted and began to fall. Anant watched with mute fascination as the tree, before it met the ground, no doubt in a thunderous fall, began to drift away. Like he was viewing the

Flying Dutchman in its last moments before it disappeared, he saw the enormous tree carry its venomous fruits along with it, into the sky and fade away. Light embraced his mind in grey once again. Just like that, he could think again without fear weighing him down. It was as if he couldn't put two and two together until now, and all he needed was a reminder of how numbers worked. The ramifications of his death which seemed large and daunting were after all the aftermath of mortality, the never-to-be experienced side effects of life. The words that made it all sound deceptively easy proved to be true nonetheless. Given his long-standing struggle with the Titan, it did not take much for him to accept its effects. That was easy. Cowardly perhaps, for he could not revel in the bravery he bestowed on those around him, yet, perhaps because he was cowardly, it was easy. Anant didn't have the strength in him to be brave. But he had enough to go on. And that, for Anant, was good enough.

Anant opened his eyes to find himself in his living room, his breathing shallow and laboured, sweat trickling down his forehead and his shirt sticking to him. The world oscillated as it had when he left the bar. He hadn't gone to sleep, he hadn't retreated to the world of the cell; it was merely a dream, a lucid one, but a dream nonetheless. The world still moved, it seemed to be dancing to the music that had come alive. A weight had been lifted off him, a weight that he wasn't sure where he had picked up, or how it had floated away.

Anant woke up at noon, twisting and turning in bed, trying to go back to sleep again. The parting gift of the cursed tree, as it drained every bit of energy out of him, leaving him exhausted. Cramps in calves, spasms in his thighs, stiffness in his spine and arms, blisters on the soles of his feet and a constant ache in his body were all the presents that had been left by the cursed tree. It was an intolerable hangover from the abundance of energy that had been injected into him. But Anant knew that the pain would subside, and that it was a badge of honour after having defeated the cursed tree and returning his wires to their original connections.

The warm shower was pleasant. If his muscles could make noises and his blisters choose a colour to express themselves, the warm water cascading down him would have made them purr and turn a joyous violet. He stood beneath the shower with the pleasant realization that the restlessness no longer plagued him. He took his time to change into fresh clothes. The AC caused a wave of goosebumps to erupt on his wet skin. He booked a cab while he had a cup of coffee, and arrived at the site with a refreshing lull in his world. With his headphones firmly placed on his ears, he seamlessly fell back into his routine. The nightmare that seemed to have lasted for weeks, but in reality was but a few forgotten days, was already leaking out of him.

He greeted Dandekar sahib and Iqbal, Aamir and his subcontractor Faiz, and the dynamic duo before he began to walk around the site. The marble had been set on the floor, and covered with plastic. The ceiling was complete. Furniture was in the works with the cupboards, nightstands, side tables and beds already built. Rajat had been sent the shortlist of paints, wallpapers and polishes. The work in the flat should have taken another few months, but with the volume of work that was being completed each day, Anant deduced that the flat would be done in two weeks, maybe three depending on how long it would take for the polish to dry, and how many coats of paint would be needed. Of course, there was the likelihood that Rajat would want certain changes in the flat. Unless it was polish or paint, the work would run simultaneously. He walked around the flat for an hour with no music but only the noise cancellation turned on. His phone buzzed to notify him of a message. He ignored it. He was slowly bleeding into his wirings and he was pleased to find that it all seemed to be connected as it had been before the tampering. He called Kartik when he was about to leave, and gave him some money to buy everyone Coke and samosas. It was promptly snatched by Marathi with a declaration that he would get the food after the work was over.

'Is there some good news?' Kartik ignored him and asked.

'What news, sir?' Marathi boomed with a grin.

'No news,' Anant replied after a brief moment of contemplation.

'You were in a good mood yesterday, that is why I asked,' Kartik explained, seeing that Anant was more like himself today.

'Was he? I didn't notice.' Marathi glared at Kartik as if he had been betrayed by not being privy to this observation.

'I am in a better mood today.'

'It's hard to tell sometimes.' Kartik smiled.

'If sir was a teacher, I tell you, no one, not a single student, not even the parents, would know what was happening.' Marathi chuckled and only after Anant joined in did Kartik allow himself to allow his bubbling laughter to surface. 'But he would get results,' he added as an afterthought, in a rare moment of awareness of his proclivity to be offensive. To Anant, it was all blissful. It was the normal that he thought he had lost. The normal was blissful.

'Now get to work before he fails you,' Kartik told his right-hand man.

Marathi pursed his lips as he contemplated the meaning of Kartik's words. 'Might as well graduate somewhere.' He smiled his toothy smile and returned to measuring the level of the slab of marble fixed on the windowsill in the living room.

'Sorry about that, sir. I will order the food in an hour. There's still some work to be finished,' Kartik said.

'You know best.' Anant nodded, shook his hand before making his way out of the site. He decided to take a walk around the area. It seemed like a good day for a walk, despite the pain he was experiencing.

Chapter 16

Even if nobody but Monica Vohra and the walls of their home noticed the time Sunil invested in planning the ways to make Aarti's wedding better, he would have no remorse over the past few weeks given it resulted in Aarti's day being better because of him. To create memories wasn't limited to work, the work merely paved the way to creating memories. And he had worked till he had an arsenal with him to use at the wedding. With foresight, with flourish, with muted gestures, Sunil Vohra was confident he would make her wedding memorable. And in the process if his efforts and his new slimmer body went unnoticed, well that was something different altogether.

Sunil was seated in his office scrounging through a tattered brown box full of old photo albums, certificates and other memorabilia, small trophies and medals, an odd broken sunglass and a discarded discoloured watch, looking for the perfect gift. He had pulled the box out with an aim to find a token that would touch Aarti's heart. Perhaps even bring tears to her eyes, Sunil had thought with glee. In the box lay the artefacts of his life, and some items of Monica's had ended up there as well. It was a sobering reflection of a life that seemed to have gone by too quickly, a melancholic malady that he exchanged his tea for whisky and soda to combat. Aware of the time of day, Sunil poured soda and whisky in a steel glass in case someone, namely Monica, entered the office, which he knew she wouldn't, for she almost never did unless she specifically had some work there. Sunil put the box to the side and began to drift away, began to reminisce. All those memories which the memorabilia were merely tokens of, the stories behind the photos, Sunil couldn't shake the feeling that all of it existed solely within him. That he was the sole survivor of a terrible plague that would be forgotten once he passed away. What other fate could these memories of old have? What would happen to the memories he was trying to create, if they were only remembered by the old relatives at Aarti's wedding? Wouldn't they too meet their end? 'And judging by the state of them, a lot sooner than I.' Sunil was lost in thought, taking a large gulp of his drink before sighing.

Sunil Vohra's parents lived a quiet life on the outskirts of Lucknow. His father enjoyed learning English and even though he had learnt it in bits and pieces, the fact that he could understand the language endeared him to the nawabs and begums who were always looking for opportunities to parade their generosity in the parties that they hosted. Of course, this was before the parties really begun. Nobody wanted the real life to cling to them when they had decreed that it would only remain outside their beautiful mansions, only to be brought in and led out at their command. His father, Lakshya Vohra, an honest postman, never became a showpiece for them, and was content to be met with a smile. The gifts on Eid and Diwali, in embroidered mauve envelopes with their titles and names foil-pressed on the front in gold or silver was all he was willing to accept, because it would be indecent of him to refuse. Perhaps there was a semblance of honour that remained ingrained in him. He was satisfied with delivering letters and his broken English that he learned from his nearness to letters. It was honest work. It was good work. The twinkle in his eye when he met people he recognized, and a sharp memory when it came to remembering faces made him a popular and welcome figure at the houses on his route. He was more than who he was. He was a postman. A deliverer of messages, like Hermes but on a flimsy bike that needed work, but could do without it. He was a mourner and a celebrator; and at times, judging by the manner in which the letter was received, a silent yet comforting presence. But Lakshya's humble life was not what had been envisioned for him. In the eyes of Lakshya's father, the freedom fighter, Lakshya was destined to lead India to independence. But he was a man born too late to fulfil the destiny that his father had charted for him, and the mantle had to go to the Indian National Congress and the supergroups of placated figures that branched out from there, and others lost in time. He was a child when India got independence, and his father gunned down before he could see the day. Before Lakshya became a postman, in his teenage years, if such a term even existed in the wretched years following independence, he was a daily wage worker on a wide stretch of farm. Unlike his father, and later his sons, Lakshya seemed to be one without dreams. Born with the dreams of his father that had been slipping away from him since the day he was born, he viewed dreams and destiny to be wicked and deceptive, and chose to bask in the simpler pleasures of a gruelling life. Of pleasant winds at night and meals two times a day. Of seeing his children grow up, knowing, unlike his father, that it wasn't a given that a parent would have time to spend with his child. And at times, of betel leaf and chai. Lakshya worked throughout his life while making time for his family at every step of the way. His wife Beena was a pleasant woman whom Lakshya never quite understood in life. Perhaps it was the demure mask that life had taught her to hide behind, or the goals that she let slip, goals bigger than Lakshya could imagine in his dreams. It was Beena who after the premature death of her husband ran the house with an iron hand. Behind the mask stood an imperial autocrat, under whose guidance the Vohra brothers, despite Lakshya's teachings, were enticed with dreams. Of being a big man, a collector, Beena would say. Neither she nor the Vohra brothers knew who a collector was, or what he did. But only that this collector was a big man, with a sarkari job, which was enough for all three. Studying under candles and lanterns, the Vohra brothers grew distant while sitting beside one another, while sleeping on the same cot, and walking to and from school together. Sunil remembered very little about his childhood, the price of ageing. All he had were recollections of moments, the stories he and his brother filled in together, but his memory of his past blurred long before time got involved. He was never one to pay attention, more often than not his eyes would be downcast, and he had learned to act the part when more and more people called him shy. He had bought into his mother's aspirations and was vicariously living through them even with the books open in front of him. 'I have done well,' Sunil Vohra commented in the present time to no one. Alas, he wasn't a collector, but at least he knew what a collector was. Feeling the same as he did when he was a teenager, alone and with one foot in reality and the other in dreams, Sunil ventured out of his room to look for Monica. All these thoughts reminded him that he didn't have many tomorrows left to give his attention to his beloved wife, and he hadn't been fully present in the past few weeks. That he wasn't alone. The house was in order as it always was, the trail that Monica left in her path. A matte black writing pad sat on the arm of the sofa in the living room, and another on the dining table. Sunil wondered if Anant had left these behind. He could feel the silence oozing from beneath the bedroom door, and found the source of the silence in the house hunched over with a notebook resting on her lap, and a pencil in hand. Sunil watched her for a few moments till she lifted her face to meet his. 'Do you want something?' she inquired.

'No, no, just wanted to know how you are.' Sunil tried awkwardly, unsure of why he had come, and if there was whisky on his breath.

Monica stuck the pencil in the holder on top of the pad and set it beside her, turning to give him her full attention. 'I am good, Sunil. How are you?' The fact that the otherwise astute Monica had noticed a change in him only after he had put it into words was the result of her own new-found hobby that she had picked up.

'Just going through the box,' Sunil replied.

'Still looking for the perfect gift,' she stated and waited. She knew that he wouldn't have come asking for advice on a sentimental gift.

'Yes, I am trying and...' Sunil checked himself from saying anything further. He wanted to resist the temptation to start blabbering about his needs. He went to sit on the chair adjacent to the door. 'When did we get old, Monica?'

'You got old when Anant left the house,' Monica replied as if she were telling the time.

'And you?'

'When my mom passed away,' Monica said in the same tone.

'You were eight.'

'Yes. Being the leader of a circus ages you.' Monica's uncanny ability to be concise, for her observations to be voiced without any noise, yet not sacrifice the authenticity of her observations could be jarring to some, but Sunil had learned to appreciate it.

'What was it like?'

'Sunil, you already know.'

'I just...I don't know.'

'Here it is, the reason why he had come here.' Monica could see him floating away once again. He had only returned in fear that he may fly too far, or too high, that it was too soon to be met with Icarus's fate. That Icarus had already met the fate, and thus, it wasn't a novelty.

'Who will remember your memories when you pass away? I know there is Anant, but he will remember his version of you and me. What about our memories?' Sunil whispered, wondering to himself.

'Nobody, Sunil. Memories are already recollections of the past. They are gone. If life itself ceases to exist, what good will be the memories.'

'I suppose. Well, I don't want to disturb you.' Sunil was only being courteous, Monica knew that he had already begun to drift off again.

Back in his office with a drink in hand, Sunil brought the box to the centre of the table once again and took to reliving his memories with a clenched jaw, knowing his wife had been right, yet determined to not let them simply drift away like the remains of a life gone by.

Chapter 17

Monica Vohra, once Monica Trivedi, was the fifth child in a small house where renovation work had started with the birth of the fourth child but was never completed. Two sons and two daughters before her, a daughter and a son after her, Monica came to a home that had already been burdened by out-of-grasp dreams. Apart from their parents' work, her father a teacher and her mother a housewife, and making babies, her parents lived a fairy-tale life that did not reflect the reality that surrounded them. If the renovation of the house was a manifestation of this fairy tale, the non-completion of the imprint of reality. Every Saturday, the Trivedi parents would step out of the house, leaving the kids at home. And as their numbers kept increasing, the one in-charge only became crueller, their numbers continuing to increase, while the one in-charge only became crueller. It was the second eldest child, the first daughter who was left in-charge. Because unlike the eldest, the parents believed she was responsible. Till date, Monica could not ascertain how Indrani had managed to fool their parents. It wouldn't have made much difference to the rest of the Trivedi children whether it was the eldest or the second eldest who was made in-charge, for both were needlessly cruel to the rest, believing they had taken food from their plate by being born. As if they had any say in the matter of their birth. Perhaps they were struggling just the same as the rest of them, and given that they couldn't take their anger out on the parents, they chose to be cruel to whoever came after them.

To weave this fairy tale, the parents would scavenge whatever savings they had managed, and go to the temple on Saturdays. But more than the inside of the temple, the parents were interested in the outside where neighbours and colleagues would gather after the evening prayers to spend time drinking tea and treating themselves for a hard week. The savings that they chased so desperately would be spent with an open hand, a gnawing need to appear more than they were. This fairy tale was built on a few notes and change, of which most of the denominations had disappeared already, and on delusions that their children were always happy despite their troubles growing up in a household where the parents seemed to live two lives at once, where the food that was barely enough for the hungry mouths was a lavish banquet. The early memory Monica had of her life was of queuing up for money for the village carnival along with her brothers and sisters. The five of them back then, the sixth in the stomach and the seventh yet to be gifted by some angel or deity, benevolent or malicious Monica did not know, were given ten rupees each, a hefty sum of money at the time, especially for them. But appearances at carnivals, which the whole town would be privy to, outweighed appearances at the temple. On the hierarchy of fairy-tale locations, the temple was sacrosanct, but the carnival was divine. After all the carnival came around Dussehra, when Rama killed half-man half-rakshasa Ravana, and before Diwali, when the Vishnu incarnate returned home. So it could be estimated that as Rama was making his way back to Ayodhya, the Trivedi children set out from their homes to take a glimpse of, and perhaps even play a part in, this fairy tale that their parents had created. The impact on their finances was terrible, and for the coming weeks they would live on a meal a day and the Saturday temple visits would be put on hold till the next salary, but the night when the curtains parted was a hallowed magical night, for most. Monica never understood why they repeated this cycle every year, knowing the fate that awaited them. Because while Lord Rama's return from his exile was celebrated, the Trivedi children's return to their lives was despaired. The self-indulgence of their parents stripped away any celebration of Diwali outside of the prayer and a handful of diyas, which taught Monica the value of finding joy in the little things in life. It was in the wake of the third night of sleeping on a growling stomach that Monica questioned not only the sanity of her parents, but the intelligence of her siblings. To be accompanied by an empty stomach for a week after the carnival ended ripped away the magic of a fairy tale from her. Ripped away the magic of the carnival itself, and to a greater extent, the carefree of childhood. The annual carnivals that followed were no more a wonderland, knowing the price to be paid for the luxury of a fairy tale was too steep.

She remembered looking in the eyes of her own siblings, and she resented them for believing in this fairy tale. Hated their innocence which she branded as stupidity. She detested the rest of the kids too, for being swept away by the magic, for being wide-eyed in wonder, hated their privilege at being allowed to possess such marvels. All she could do was stand at the periphery of the magic that had been wickedly revealed as a trick by life itself, the ten rupees held in a tight fist, her face getting progressively older with every passing hour. The ten rupees she saved, crumpled by being clenched in a fist, would be spent throughout the following week buying and inspecting diyas from a vendor who would push his cart across the street on his way to the marketplace. And at night to distract herself from her crying stomach, when she wasn't cursing her own morality that stopped her from buying snacks seeing as the rest of her impractical family members, whom she had cursed throughout the day, were starving themselves, paying the price that the fairy tale demanded, she dreamt of diyas. Plain old earthen diyas, and where they would be kept on Diwali. This cycle continued two years after the sixth was born; shortly after the seventh child, five away from a football team, her mother passed away.

More than mourning, the house descended into chaos following her passing. With the active partner in the fairy tale snatched away, the fairy tale itself that her father had built his life and routine around disintegrated, leaving him with the biting realities of his life that he found unbearable. Following his wife's passing, he couldn't stand to be in the house that no longer seemed like home. He would remain in school long after the rest of the teachers went home, and often took detours on his way from work, detours that wouldn't have been kindly received if others got to know about them. Until one Sunday morning, weeks after his wife had passed, as he walked around the house while Indrani tried to salvage something from the ingredients in the kitchen, he noticed that the house was in order once again. Not only in order, but in a serene ethereal harmony. The source of this order, and the one who had instructed the second eldest to cook, the one now in-charge, the one who perhaps should have always been in-charge, one who wouldn't have been cruel to the rest, was the fifth child of seven, Monica. Overcome with shame at his own immaturity and irresponsibility, that Sunday morning Daksh went to shop for rations and returned with a pledge along with food that he would pay attention to the other children and be a father to them once again. That he would no longer take detours after work, no matter the dread in the pit of his stomach. By the time the next carnival was set up in town, Monica Trivedi had become the unsaid matriarch of the family, even the rowdy eldest and the cunning second fell in line, and flinched at the first hint of anger in her voice. That year, for the first time in the Trivedi household, no one was given ten rupees when the carnival was set up in town. Thoughts of dissent that bubbled among her subjects would fizzle out of fear of the child-turned-chief, whose sanity prevailed in the following days when there was no starvation in the camp. And any remaining dissent was swept away when she invited everyone, her father included, to five diyas of their choosing, decorated around the house as they saw fit.

All said and done, married life suited Monica far more. She stepped into married life at nineteen, when Daksh finally gave in to societal pressure and began to look for a groom for her. In a way, Monica always believed that her marriage allowed her to return to her life. Until then, despite the power she had and the different traditions she established, she had put Monica away to toil as the chief to keep the work of her mother alive.

Given her history, Monica always pushed Anant to be more like Sunil. If she could unfold all the experiences of her life as a chief, or perhaps more apt would be to name this partnership a diarchy, she might find the exact moment when Anant began to show traits like hers, but alas, neither could she remember all her past, nor was there a way to be certain that she could have made a difference had she known sooner. When she had noticed this development in him, she reacted by not only allowing him, but actively encouraging him to live in his life, whether he was struck by sadness or happiness, so he would not do what she did and lose years of his life living as someone else. She was happy that Sunil and she could provide the privilege of choice to Anant. Did she agree with how Anant turned out? She was content that he was his own man. She was happy with both, her husband and her child. She continued to work, content in her own job. She enjoyed watching people, she had a routine and hobbies. Even if certain duties did not change from her past to present, she was satisfied with the present because unlike the past, the present was hers. And it was all she ever had for herself. But there remained in her the little girl who yearned for magic, the magic that had been lost too soon in her childhood. That she never had a chance to be wide-eyed in wonder and be lost in awe. Until that day around the dining table when Anant had shown them his sketches and renderings of a flat he was designing in Mumbai. One look at the sketches that were in one hand, which materialized into the renderings that were in her other hand, Monica found the magic she was looking for. She had kept the drawings to herself, and when she retired to her bedroom, she broke into tears staring at how the sketches became these 3D renderings. It was cathartic for her to realize that she had been part of the magic after all, the ineffable ways of life had brought her son to work in a field that in another life she was certain she would have pursued as well. To understand the house, to care for the house, to have an eye for the needs of the house, to spot in the midst of the gratuitous, as she had done decades ago with ten rupees in her hand, what would enrapture her and increase the energy of the house, she had spent her life understanding the house and how it could be turned into a home. The sketches and renderings spurred her, the feel of the lost magic compelled her and she began to doodle in an empty notebook she found in Anant's room, resting alongside a pair of gold earrings that she shrugged off as luggage lost in transit, thinking that Anant must have accidentally brought with him from Mumbai. For once in her life, rather than observing the world while floating on the languid currents of time, Monica was lost in her own world. In her notebook where she drew small furniture with grains in a certain pattern, columns with simple and intricate designs that would not be comprehensible to anyone but her, but they were real to her, so were entire rooms that would never become reality, and diyas. Diyas with different patterns and flames that perpetually ended up looking like cotton candy. The shortcomings of her drawings never once deterred them from coming alive in her imagination.

Chapter 18

To celebrate the return of the old world before the tree, Anant decided to take a walk to commemorate his free will. Anant wandered along Rajat's small society with its piercingly high towers looking for a cigarette shop. The modern-day towers of Babel seemed to grow higher and higher before his very eyes, more interested in putting distance between the adjacent bastis that came into existence because of the very towers that relied on them, for their construction and their working, than in any attempt to try and close their distance to god. God was for the spiritual, or the advertisers. Near a new construction site along the main road, Anant found a shop. Amidst a collection of hawkers stood a cigarette stall fitted to the trunk of a tree, a tree not as large, nor as vicious as the one that had vanished. He bought a cutting chai and deliberated over some egg fry that was being sold by another hawker. There was also vada and bhatura, and in the background, a kid with darkened eyes and a man's hands, rugged because of the dishes he had to clean. Dogs scurried between the vendors hoping to come away with some crumbs or entirely relying on the benevolence of the people. It was always a source of wonder for Anant that he had ended up in Mumbai. It was clear that the city wasn't for him. That its sheer density was counterintuitive to his need for solace. Yet, here he was. Like any person who had grown up in the more comfortable parts of cities, Anant too had his musings about 'living in the hills' or a self-sustained existence in some village in Goa. It was the second year in college when he briefly harboured the romantic notion of escaping from the world. If he couldn't cheat death, the least he could do was escape the normalcy. Alas, Anant moved from one dense city to an even denser one. The city gave him a chance to work, and he enjoyed his work. He even considered the possibility that he was meant to be in this city—that the duality of Mumbai reflected in him. Just like there existed two sides of Mumbai, so were there two sides of Anant. Him in this world, and him in his imaginary world. Simple, Anant told himself. And in a sense, it was very Mumbaikar of him to come to such a basic equation. Mumbai, the city of dreams, dreamt while its houses got flooded and streets clogged, and loud barrel-chested men with guts hanging from their belly, wearing gold watches with the gold fading, tried to cordon their idea of Mumbai from those most easily preyed on, the meagre-earning immigrants, while louder-in-action politicos profited from the 'filth of the west' while deriding it. The city of dreams was a city that was built on dreams, and sustained itself on the insistence of its citizens to keep dreaming. And like the city, Anant too had a dream. The delusion that had withstood the disruption caused by the tree. That his two worlds existed separate from one another. Where the unreality of his retreat allowed him to hide from the wretched truth of reality, of death. Anant reflected the city in his refusal to grow, to hide himself from reality with illusions of a great king or a leader, like a parent, to comfort. The duality of man and city was a great mirage of separation, that the dual sides did not form a single nature.

Anant shrugged in an attempt to put the carcass of the tree behind him. That it had existed, no matter how shallow its roots, made him uneasy. He turned his eyes to the people around him. There was a hectic nature to the Mumbai walk where people seemed to become a collective, and Anant tried to peer past the whole and look at the individual. He eyes fell on a girl with a high ponytail who was rushing back from the market, and a group of friends that had bought bright orange and cola ice-cream sticks. The striking white uniform of a group of schoolkids caught his eye as they headed home from the bus stop with a coach or a tutor waiting on the horizon. And in contrast, his eyes followed a trio of kids—two of them had neat uniforms while the third one's looked shabby and dirty, but none of them carried the shine of starch. He wondered if they were now going to work. Groups of twos, of threes, of fours, collected around the tea stall. Property dealers, local shop workers, plumbers, teachers, and the array of professionals who existed in every city. Watching them, Anant began to feel like a voyeur. He sighed and concentrated on the sounds. Of bikes, buses, and cars, the sipping, slurping, and chewing, the walking, the running, the laughing, and the arguing. The strike of matches and lighters, and the sizzle of eggs on a searing pan.

Anant sipped his chai quietly, not the celebration of his freedom from the tree nor the city itself could distract him from the new event that had sprouted up in his life. When he was on the site, he had received a text from Aarti asking him to meet her tomorrow. She was in Mumbai for a conference. His first thought when he saw the message was to find an excuse to avoid meeting her. In hindsight, Anant knew that he could have found one eventually. But the autopilot wasn't working to its full capacity, and words that not too long ago tried their best to worm out of him, abandoned him in his time of need. Much to his own irritation, he had replied with an 'okay'. Her wedding was two weeks away, and Anant was unsure if this meeting had anything to do with it. It seemed natural to assume that she could be in need of another pair of working hands or legs to help with her wedding. He knew the dances that took place in the events preceding the wedding, people needed to be set up like inflatable balloons at petrol pumps to greet the guests, and also become porters carrying the palanquin if that was the desire of the bride, the groom or their families. An Indian event was incomplete without the comments, constructive or snide, by the families and quasi-families that were the neighbours and friends who have grown up with just as much interest in what others around them were doing as they were in themselves.

Finishing his chai, he turned to the site that had been reinvigorated by the energy of a single man. Rajat walked around the flat, flanked on either side by Dandekar sahib and Iqbal, delighted at how the flat was coming together. Anant learned that Rajat was treating the workers today, and had instructed the two contractors to make sure everyone was invited. The flat had begun to take shape. The tasks Anant was most afraid of, the management of it all, had all but come to pass. All that remained were the finer details that he was most comfortable with. There was delivery for furniture that was made to measure, which was pending for when the work would be finished. Rajat wanted the flat, in his words, 'to show his eccentricities'. For a home to reflect the owner was always the desire of the client. Hitherto Anant had managed to walk the fine line between comic, outlandish, and eccentric. But with Rajat, a part of Anant was worried at what awaited him. He had managed to convince him to keep some of the more creative choices away from the living room. And so, there were ludicrously high thread count wallpapers with wild geometrical prints being stuck in every room but the living room and the master bedroom. The lack of beige in the living room was a matter of pride for Anant. It was very rare for a homeowner to stumble away from the dull comfort of the brown palette, and Rajat, in his pursuit to be different, had taken a braver step than he realized. The grey floor and the navy and pale blue walls of the living room were soothing to his eyes, the entertainment centre with all the razzle and dazzle that Rajat might want, and still empty spaces for him to hang or keep whatever else he wanted, was a meeting point of utility and aesthetic. But of course, Anant had no doubts that if anything went wrong, or what was right now suddenly became wrong, he would still be blamed for it. Such a relationship was part of the job. People paid as much for the design as they did to outsource the blame while keeping all the praise. The big problem of the flat that jumped at Anant was that there wasn't an office to work from, but instead a home theatre in one of the rooms. Anant was sure that after living in the flat for a few weeks, Rajat would rue the fact that there wasn't an office to work from. Anant could already hear Rajat conveniently thinking out loud in passing that there was no need for such a big TV, that TVs were a waste of time, even though Rajat was an enthusiast of the many streaming sites, of shows, movies, cricket and F1 races.

There were also the nails that Rajat had gotten drilled in the living room. Despite Anant's repeated insistence that he could hang any painting whenever he wanted, that all that he needed was to check the electrical drawing when drilling a nail, or even getting someone to drill a nail, Rajat was adamant that he already knew he'd buy plenty of artworks, and didn't want to go around looking for a carpenter every time he came home with one. The thought of hanging it himself never crossed his mind. Rajat wanted to find the paintings organically, and only original artwork that would inspire him. A noble thought considering Rajat had never been interested in paintings before. Weeks later, when the housewarming party would be right around the corner, Rajat would forsake these noble beliefs and order prints of the classics.

Out of the three bedrooms, the one that had been turned into a home theatre had a thick faux-fur rug over a bamboo wooden floor and the wall behind the sleek leather sofas was a trompe l'oeil wallpaper of what could only be described as mandalas on acid being shot from a roman bathhouse. Anant wasn't even sure where Rajat had found such a wallpaper, but the more he looked at it, the fonder he became of the absurdity of it. He hoped that Rajat would not be pressured by the nails, and take his time to find the original artwork he was looking for, for it would be a sight to behold. Rajat had a fascinating but endearing taste that Anant hoped would be plastered all over the flat.

The master bedroom and the guest bedroom were alike, with marqueterie side tables and thick, low beds. The only difference was the wall behind the bed. Merlot paint in the master bedroom complementing the oak hardwood floor. Tissues and papers had been used when the wall was wet to give it texture, and the result was a wall that looked like it was weeping, or a bundle of clouds overlapping one another had appeared on it. A geometric pattern in gold with mauve highlights had been pasted on the guest bedroom.

At 4.30 p.m., the work was paused and the feast began. Anant had always found Rajat to be good-natured, and it showed in the treat he was giving everybody on the site. There was biryani with mint, tamarind, and coconut chutney, along with samosas, pithas, vadas and batata bhaji set on the grey counter of the kitchen in large burnt containers courtesy of the local restaurant that Rajat had ordered from. Bottles of Coke, Limca and Fanta rounded up the feast. Rajat sat on a plastic chair, which was the only piece of furniture that had been there since the beginning of the project; and everybody around him had aluminium foil plates full of food. The contractors had reined the workers in so everybody watched the food on their plate with doting eyes, but nobody began to eat. Everyone waited for Rajat to leave or for his permission for them to leave and begin their feast. Despite the celebratory mood in the apartment, Rajat's presence, at the behest of the contractors, stifled the cathartic relief from the weeks of hard work. It was a day before everyone in the apartment would be shifted to different sites and projects, with new people that could be crueller, and workers who were unaccepting of them. Alas, hunger eventually defeated decorum, and after a certain amount of time had passed, one by one, everyone went ahead and ploughed through their food. The contractors steadied themselves between their lip smacking to give mindless compliments to Rajat, and pat each other on the back. Anant had worked on enough sites to grasp the importance of these compliments paid to the workers who had toiled away night and day without letting their focus waver and with a deadline hanging over their heads, but the time Dandekar sahib and Iqbal spent kissing each other's asses, perhaps out of an insecurity at the lack of work they had to do considering Anant had been burdened by most of it, one would have thought that the two had built the flat with their bare hands. Alas, the show of communal harmony in a capitalists' utopia with the sign of the rupee replacing their pupils came to an end when Anant invited Rajat for a drink. It was the least he could do for all of them who had worked under the good cop–bad cop management of Kartik and Marathi. When Anant and Rajat stepped out of the flat, Kartik trailed behind them.

'What is it?' Rajat asked him.

'Nothing sir. I wanted to talk to Anant sir for a second,' Kartik replied.

'Well…' Rajat motioned for him to talk, glancing at the elevator that finally ascended to their floor.

'I'll meet you downstairs,' Anant told Rajat and allowed himself to be pulled by Kartik.

'Must be some questions about the remaining work,' he added on behalf of Kartik, and followed him inside. Some of them had taken a second helping and were busy finishing what was left on their plates, but they all eventually stopped eating, most after Marathi bellowed at them. Nobody took his screaming to heart. Anant had noticed how frequently they would try to make him laugh while he screamed.

'Good job everyone. Some of you really upset me, but all's well that ends well,' Dandekar sahib began. Marathi hurried to and fro, with his glass of Coke in hand, and managed to get Kartik and Anant a glass of Limca each. 'I know we had to work through a lot, but we did it. Rajat sir is happy, and so is sir ji,' he said, and when Marathi came close to the contractor, Dandekar sahib nudged him away with a smile and a shake of his head. 'One day, age will slow you down. Maybe when you are eighty,' he said to some chuckles. Anant took a gulp of Limca and cherished the relief he felt at having successfully finished this daunting and unholy alliance of design and management that had been forced upon him. Caught up in his own world, it soon dawned on him that the room was quieter, and that he had become the subject of interest. They were waiting for him to say a few words. Not because they were particularly interested in what he had to say, but simply because he had often been equal in rank to Dandekar sahib. And for the second time in two hours, the words revelled in their treacherous nature.

'Sir, we have all worked for a long time, on many sites and with many, many designers. You know how they are,' Kartik began, pausing for the chuckles as if he were a maestro conducting the audience. 'Really sir, everybody pays attention to the site, well, most do, but they don't show interest in how we work. They want to snap and have the work done, without even a margin of error in millimetres. You could have done that too, but you didn't, and we appreciated that.' Kartik once again showed his management skills by setting up, in a few lines, all that Anant needed to say. Marathi stood by Kartik's side, agreeing most enthusiastically with every word. Anant was unsure of what he had done that deserved such a compliment. Was it really that he hadn't snapped, and screamed, but quietly, with Kartik carrying the weight of the work, enforced the designs, that they appreciated? Anant hadn't even realized that he could have screamed, it wasn't in his nature to raise his voice. And Marathi had screamed at them every step of the way, but they seemed to forget, or forgive him. Anant glanced at Aamir who still stood close to Faiz who had managed to rope him in once again. He forced himself to begin speaking. He understood that there was no need for a big speech, that all he was required to do was thank them. Good job, well done, Anant thought that something along these lines would suffice for the moment at hand. They all wanted to return to their food, sooner than later. The quicker he would get through the sentences, the better it would be—for him as well as for others. Most didn't care. They were there out of professional courtesy, rather than personal affection.

It was just then that Dandekar sahib had decided that he would speak. He was feeling a touch sentimental, but was unsure if it was because of the people, the amount of time he had spent on the site, the strange work that he had to do, or the upheaval in his own world during work hours. It felt like the closing of a chapter. He hadn't felt like this even during his first on-site assignment, or the first time he had his own project. All paled in comparison to this moment. Eventually, as seconds, that had become obsolete in another world, ticked on, time thawed him out of his stupor. 'You all worked very hard on this project, and I know at times what I said might not have made sense, but you made it work. If you work like you do, you'll all go far. Good job. Thank you.' No sooner had they finished their drink than they forgot all about Anant and the contractors. The biryani was getting cold. The pithas had been made with fresh curd. 'You eat too,' he told Kartik who was still standing by his side. 'And Kartik, give me a call once your work is finished here.'

'Yes, sir, yes, I will.' Neither Kartik nor Anant knew what this was about, but both were swept by the emotion that hung between them. Both of them nodded to each other enthusiastically, thinking that the chances of crossing paths with each other, at some point in the future, were rather high. However, that never happened and they continued on their separate ways.

Chapter 19

Rajat conversed with the security guard in the lobby while he waited for Anant. Inquisitive about the rules of the society, mostly because he had heard from Sehaj about the stringent rules concerning noise and music past a certain hour, eleven in certain apartments and twelve in others. Rajat turned to the recently arrived Anant. 'My man, is it too late to soundproof walls?' Rajat asked an oblivious Anant, who for a moment struggled with the possibility of another three months spent in this flat with the dreadful dual job of designer and manager. 'Or maybe I can park my car in the lobby to listen to music. No flat, no problem, right?' Anant managed to breathe again when he realized that it was in jest, and the security guard began to chuckle as well. 'Sir, if you want, park it in the lobby.' He said with an affable smile before greeting Anant and returning to Rajat. 'I have never seen this many people work in a single house, in a flat. It feels like a whole project, you know, big project. Whole building project.' Rajat struggled to put forward a dispassionate front, his smile threatening to break into a grin, but he managed to keep himself in control, and after a half wave of a goodbye, walked out with Anant close behind him.

'Where to?' Rajat asked once they were out of the society, waiting for the cab.

'I thought you'd have some place in mind,' Anant replied.

'You invited me,' Rajat exclaimed incredulously. 'Come on, I won't judge. You know I won't judge. What's your usual pad you know? Where do you put up after a hard day at work?'

Home, but Anant was averse to having him in his flat once

again. The only place that came to his mind was the bar where he was to meet Aarti tomorrow. She had sent him the time and place, and he suggested the same to Rajat, The Harbour Bar in Colaba. The Taj Mahal Palace suited Rajat's extravagant taste, and even more was his curiosity about Anant and his ways. He was unsure if Anant regularly visited the bar, or if he had suggested such a venue because of him. The latter seemed more likely, or Rajat was more inclined to believe the same, always one to enjoy if he had an effect on people.

Upon entering the lobby of the said hotel, Anant paused to take in the banquet spread of aged luxury, his eyes lingering on the lamps and pendant lights and chandeliers, languidly sweeping the carpet to admire the ensemble of flowers that seemed to him would always remain in the prime of their youth, no matter the day or time. Rajat noticed the pause, he waited momentarily, and continued to walk. What disappointed Anant were the corridors of nearby shops, in a cut-and-paste marble selection, the cream, the beige and the coffee, that may have had a novelty once, but now were lost in the crowd, even if they were the original. The brown walls with the utilitarian division that complemented the ostentation made up for the choice of flooring and its highlights. Anant noticed that Rajat had moved on. He followed; though his pace was slow, he remained on his trail. They sat on high wooden chairs by the bathroom white counter of the bar, and in their new-found tradition birthed after one day of drinking together, they ordered the same drink. The burden of choice fell on Anant, who wasn't much of a drinker. And with the limited knowledge that he had picked up along the way, he chose an old-fashioned, and ordered two. Now came the hard part. Without the site to discuss and nothing prepared for the conversation ahead, Anant was devoid of any material, and the awareness that his conversational skills did not thrive in spontaneity further crippled the words that could have been. Anant had built himself to bring conversations to an end, not stretch them. He just sat sipping his drink while Rajat struck a conversation with the bartender about a beer he had seen being served at a table—it was served in a glass that had the name of the hotel imprinted on it. Anant on the other hand found his thoughts seeping past the tourist's choice of a bar in Mumbai, past the glitz and the ornaments of the building, and into the structure itself. He courted a peculiar thought, one that brought this grand structure of Bombay, standing grander in Mumbai despite any evil that may have once tried to crumble it, and his burnt and scattered great-grandfather together.

He knew very little about this great-grandfather except that he had been a freedom fighter, and had died for this country. He wondered if he died knowing the kind of riches people on the other side of life, including certain Indians, enjoyed. He wondered if this fact should have left a bitter taste in his mouth, but the lifetimes between them made them unfamiliar to one another. His own flesh and blood, washed away by the currents of time. To be bitter on his behalf, Anant felt like it was more of a choice. The thought of his great-grandfather returned Anant to the thoughts of the Titan, and instinctively his eyes began to wander, gazing around the room, inspecting the darkness that sat on the shoulders of everyone present. He felt the weight of the world on his shoulders as history and the present mingled together in the hallowed hotel, as if corpses were being served liquor by ghosts. The only question that remained was which world was it that burdened him, whether it was this world or the one where the cell existed. Rather than risking being lost in the other world in front of others, he turned to Rajat hoping to strike a conversation to distract himself, however long the conversation may last.

'Can you imagine the luxury of those times?' Rajat took the baton with which Anant couldn't move, and dashed it as if it weighed nothing. 'My grandfather began his company with contracts from the British. For bricks, and later labour as well. I can't imagine the lives, the music, the women, the different powers at play.'

'Most of the country was starving.' Anant thought while Rajat spoke. 'A lot of the country is still starving.' He finished the thought. It did not make him reluctant to enjoy his drink, why should he expect otherwise from the men of the past? It was what made the ones that did fight all the more special. Rajat was only talking from his perspective of the world, and to ridicule his unfiltered honesty for just being untouched by the moods of the general public seemed hypocritical. He wondered whether Rajat was lost in a world of his own, like he was. A very different world it would have been. 'He must have been a very smart man,' Anant said, referring to Rajat's grandfather.

'He was, very astute. And I am from the same genes. I am just as smart, in a different way. In my way,' Rajat said. 'One day, with all I have, I will build something astonishing,' he murmured under his breath. Anant realized that Rajat was indeed lost in another world, and while it was different in how it had unfolded, it had been built with the same desperation that had moved Anant to put the first bricks of his cell.

Fear is a strange emotion, it has a lingering presence that sweeps even the calm and the stoic away. With every sip of his drink, distracted as he was with the conversation, fear continued to spread in Anant. This residue of fear gave rise to other worries, and the worry that surpassed them all. Worry of what may happen if he had too much once again, of where he would wake up. He believed the alcohol was the catalyst that had led to him being locked in the cell. It couldn't have been coincidence that the hinges that refused to move more than mere inches were covered in tequila. He managed to excuse himself after two drinks despite Rajat's insistence to drink into the night. At first, Rajat had been unwilling to let Anant leave, he made it seem like he was abandoning him but his ego that had progressively grown over the evening, with thoughts of his grandfather and what he believed was the reason Anant had brought him to the bar, did not allow him to resort to his usual antics and instead, he shrugged and waved a hand when Anant declared that he was leaving.

The taxi drive to his flat was over an hour, and with nothing better to do until the traffic cleared up, Anant walked around Colaba, taking the longer route around the hotel to the ocean. He could see Rajat's titbits about his grandfather and British India come alive in parts of the area. Many buildings of a time forgotten had managed to remain standing, even if the foundations were rotting and the buildings themselves were hunched over like old men. Under the lens of the past, they all seemed to hold a hundred secrets each as they gazed into a blank space, unwilling to answer, or perhaps incapable of replying. Anant wasn't sure whether the buildings had been built under the British, or the contempt and disregard they were treated with aged them. But for the evening, anything old simply became part of the time of British India, a time before Maharashtra was torn on the lines of language, a time when the seeds were being sown for the whole country to be torn on the lines of religion—handing over the playbook for electoral success to the political parties. The air carried the smell of smoke, wet dirt and grass, but the nearer he got to the ocean, the more the air carried the whiff of salt and water.

The Gateway of India was littered with people taking photographs on their phones, ignoring the photographers standing with their antiquated cameras hanging from their necks. These cameras were not old enough to be a part of the years following independence, but Anant imagined the camera lens pointing at a world entirely different from the one in front of him. What pictures would come out if the camera captured snapshots of the past, if it plucked a moment in history out of the cascades of time rather than create a memento of what would become the past? Would the people jogging past the monument be replaced by a paper boy shouting about news trying to sell newspapers? Would there be smug governors and heartless policemen that had sided against their own countrymen? No doubt the forgotten founders of Mumbai, the Koli men and women would have still been forgotten. The only thing that wouldn't have changed would have been the carnival of people attracted to the monument like moths to a flame. Going against his first instinct of moving closer to the monument to inspect it, he chose to walk around it until he could see both, close enough to pretend he could see the view from the harbour that is a staple in most postcards of Mumbai, the hotel in the forefront and the monument jutting out by its side as if the land itself had spread to accommodate it. A modern tower in the distance stood over the palace, both sharing the same name. Anant was sure that there was something about time to be learned here, about history and the many facets of culture as it changes, but Anant had already turned towards the ocean and was preoccupied by the shore of Mumbai.

As far as the eye could see, the towers in the distance lit like lanterns hung atop each other. He imagined himself standing on a boat, or further away amidst the strong tides of the ocean, looking at nothing but the monument, the hotel and the tower from a distance. The world he imagined was an apocalyptic world where only the three buildings had managed to last. He planted wild trees, creepers and vines running up and down the buildings till one couldn't make out the first ten to fifteen feet of any of the three. He alternated his vantage points until he was further away so he could add the ocean to his view, with its vigorous tides, untethered and undisturbed by the changes in the city. The traffic began to clear, but Anant knew that even the Google map could be deceptive and the traffic could come to a halt at any moment; he decided to call for a taxi, thinking that it was as good a time as any to take the chance. On his way to his flat, he basked in the afterglow of it all. His mind had come alive, and he took the last ten minutes of his ride to look up the Gateway of India. How the British had built it to commemorate their arrival. The name was a giveaway, and yet it never occurred to Anant that the Gateway of India was indeed as the name suggested, a gateway meant to represent the arrival of the British.

Back in his flat, Anant put a Brahms symphony on the turntable and took to the mat with a hot cup of instant choco-mocha. He was sketching a gate inspired by the Gateway of India, with a triumphal arch, an automatic shutter and engraved at the top would be the name of the house or the house number. Anant spent an hour or more toying around with arches, and his favourite was a bookcase with a hollow arch where one could keep bottles, each bottle separated with wooden partitions. It was like an altar with books and whisky looking over it like angels. He went to sleep after midnight, and woke up to find a moonless sky visible through the only window in the room, with a mahogany floor underneath him and grey brick walls around him.

Chapter 20

As the reality of his surroundings dawned on Anant, he tried to argue that he shouldn't have been here, declaring over and over that he hadn't had too much to drink. He stressed that he remembered the manner in which he had gone to bed, he had washed his face with warm water and brushed his teeth to rid them of the stains of the choco-mocha. He even remembered how the mint of the toothpaste complemented the aftertaste of the coffee. He had placed his clothes on a chair in his bedroom before going under the covers. The cool breeze from the AC, the warmth of the covers lulled him to sleep. He argued with the grey brick walls, with the mahogany floor, with the void petulantly gazing at him through the window, as if he could or would talk it all away. He turned to the door to continue the argument that had quickly descended to imploration, and was startled to find that the door, along with its tequila-stained hinges, had vanished. Anant marched towards the vanished door for a closer inspection. If it was a crime, no clues had been left behind. There was a clean break, and even the nails had been removed and the holes filled in, or perhaps the bricks themselves had healed. Anant didn't know any more. If the cell had swallowed the door, he did not find a change in the walls. If the cell had spat the door out, he could not see it floating in the void beyond the cell. He peeked out to his right and to his left, the all-encompassing darkness was absolute, and having choked out time, a door must have been child's play. Perhaps it was the fact that Anant knew the way back to the real world that made him daring, or maybe it was the mystery of these abrupt visits that coincided with changes happening in a place that had hitherto been a constant throughout his life. Comfortable in his knowledge of escape, Anant put aside any notion of self-preservation, took a deep breath and stepped outside the cell to find solid ground under his feet, as if the void that he was walking through was the same void that he was walking on. He took dreaded steps into the abyss, conscious of his actions, aware of his steps that he placed one after the other with trepidation, the fear that the next step may not meet any solid ground clung to him. These fears were in vain. For he walked and walked till he could hardly make out his own body. The darkness enveloped him, it coiled and swallowed him, it seeped in through his ears and nose, through his mouth and eyes, through his skin, till he felt the emptiness plucking away at his veins, matching the beat of his heart. Yet his invisible legs did not falter in their stride. It was the radiant cell that he frequently glanced back at that, unlike him who had merged into the void, remained visible as if it had the ability to simply repel the darkness. The cell shining down like a lighthouse gave him strength to not fall in despair or ennui or desolation or a hundred other emotions that the void carried in its bosom. Anant walked on through the deafening silence of the abyss, wading through a myriad emotions, protected and in danger at the same time. Danger of what, the abyss, Anant thought, or the cell?

He began to look back less often. The crushing darkness, Anant realized through experience, did not really crush him, but instead felt liberating. As if he was slowly melting away into the infinite void, and slowly spreading himself around the whole world, his whole world. Somewhere along his march, Anant had relaxed enough to close his eyes, it was hard to tell since it was just as dark either way, but one moment he was in the dark, and another, when he opened his eyes, which meant he must have closed them, he was met with familiar grey brick walls, and seated on the mahogany floor as if he had never left the cell. He looked around the cell, he looked at his hands and legs, at his body and touched his face, wondering but strangely not fearing if any darkness had managed to cling to him. He tried his march once more, this time trying to make out something, anything, from a door to a nail that may have been drifting amidst its depth, yet he met the same result. At some point, the darkness overwhelmed him, it swept away any reluctance of being bound together as one person, he melted away, scattering here and there, everywhere, and he would close his eyes, and open them to find himself sitting in the cell. Anant wasn't sure if he was blinking or the darkness that surrounded him made him close his eyes, but without realizing that he had shut them, he would open his eyes to find himself back in the cell. The fourth or fifth time he found himself back on the cool wooden floor, he finally saw through his stubbornness and decided to remain seated with his eyes closed. Taking deep breaths, he consoled himself with the fact that he could return to his world at any time. All he had to do was imagine his bed, his room, how he was sleeping, and he would return. The power to step out of this world with a few thoughts placated him, and rather than running around in circles trying to stumble on to the answers of this mystery, he paused and reflected on why he was worried about the changes in the cell when he was the creator of it. The world that the cell resided in was his own mind. He had lived his life retreating to this cell without any troubles. His previous visit when he had been stuck was more likely to have been an anomaly than some sinister alterations taking place in the cell. As if to convince himself of the same, and to unearth even a vague notion that he could use to explain what was happening, he shut his eyes and began with the deep breaths. His attention wavered from time to time but ultimately hung on the rise and fall of his chest. What now? Anant ignored the thought and continued to breathe in, his lungs expanding, his chest rising, and out, his lungs contracting, his chest falling. He opened his eyes expecting clarity to bow before him, and something akin to it may have washed over him for a few moments, gone before there were any answers, leaving behind only the ever-increasingly sinister 'what now?'.

Anant tried to think of a topic to preoccupy himself while he waited for something to happen, anything that could help him understand, but like the treachery of the words before, the thoughts turned their back to him and he was unable to scavenge any. He tried to remember the arches that he was fascinated by the night before, or perhaps the same night, but other than his memory of them, he found himself incapable of generating a single thought that could pass of as original. He could only dig out mundane facts, like the Gateway of India was old and that it was a monument. That it commemorated the arrival of the British. He tried commenting on the engravings and the style of construction, but he was merely dressing the old as the new in an effort to believe that he was thinking. It was as if his voice had been taken from him, and like a broken tape recorder he could only repeat his old thoughts. Anant questioned if thoughts of danger, desolation and death were the only ones he was capable of while he was in the cell? He found the question ridiculous and tried to remember a time when he had done his work in the cell, but none were present in recent memory. How long had it been since he fully immersed himself in this world to work? At last he managed to latch on to a thought, but which concerned the cell itself. He did not let go of the thought, fearing that he would be left with dreadful facts once again. He wondered how the cell had been built by a man...by a child taking his first steps into his teenage years. The foundations of this very place had been placed when his friend had passed away. One could say the first brick had made the imprint of death in it. Anant shook his head. Was this constant awareness of the Titan present in the cell finally leaking into him? Anant looked past where the door once stood open, and into the abyss. Perhaps losing himself in the void wasn't a bad idea. But what if he wouldn't return? What if he would? Anant wasn't sure what was worse. He returned to confront the insidious nature of death, something he hadn't thought of in a long time. He had always considered the cell to be a clean break, he had built the cell to be insurmountable, for the real world to never find its way here. Perhaps what he had built was Troy, and he was the Trojan horse. And Helen too. And Paris with no Aphrodite to save him. No god was present inside these grey brick walls. His eyes lingered on the walls, and then swept down to the mahogany floor; it was only then that he was able to perceive what he saw—that in his absence the place had gone through renovations. Thereafter, everything seemed obvious to him. These changes weren't to the interiors or the structure, but to the nature of the cell itself. The cell felt different. Or perhaps, Anant ventured further, he had been distracted in all his previous visits and he was only coming face to face with what the cell had long since become. 'How long ago could it have been?' Anant thought, feeling a sense of fear scraping his back. He considered the possibility that perhaps the cell had always been this way, that with the first brick carrying the mark of the Titan, he had damned this place from the beginning. Anant shook his head, he scratched off the thought at once. The cell must have changed, he told himself. And yet, looking around, past the window where lay the abyss, inside where he lay drifting away, he found a place devoid of life, living on the passive experiences brought on from another world.

Anant did not dig further into the past. He knew where the path led. He feared what he would find, feared what the signs pointed at, feared what he would find in the foundation of this structure. He knew of the comfort in introspection—when it was done masterfully with blunted tools or with a stoic mind— but he was nervy and the tools in his hand dangerously sharp. Anant chose to flee because he felt he might just bring the roof down on himself. Only just having returned to normal from his previous interaction with the obscure parts of his mind, with the tree that grew from his grave, Anant felt the weariness of a journalist who had been exposed to more than what he or she could stomach, or a seasoned traveller who had travelled and seen too much at the expense of his knees. The price to pay for further admission could be too much for him to bear. This was a journey that might have excited him once upon a time, and could excite him at a later date, or so he told himself, but in the moment, all he had was apathy. Anant thought the ideal choice to make was to flee from the cell. But much like a seasoned traveller who caught the whiff of a new destination, for such a traveller couldn't have been completely sane to pay for his destinations with his ligaments and cartilages, Anant with his finger on the eject button, felt the disinclination of one that must accept defeat. He couldn't stop now. Perhaps his reasons were different from those of a traveller, that rather than the noble pursuit of his heart, he was merely avoiding leaving the cell in cowardice. Or maybe it was a mixture of both. Maybe after a certain point, the traveller, the journalist, they continue on because they don't find the right reason to quit. A reason that surmounts their ego. Alas, for an addict to continue his addictions, the reasons are always aplenty. Anant told himself that he believed that there was nothing to life but to experience more of what his existence had to offer. The irony of which, standing in a cell built by his past, did not occur to him. For better or for worse, Anant got to his feet once again. Like any addict, the traveller paid the price in the health of his ligaments and cartilages, the journalist with morality and sanity, the alcoholic with his liver, Anant wondered what price would be asked of him.

Before Anant could embark on this adventure, prepare to embark on this adventure, prepare himself to prepare to embark on this adventure, he paused and began to look around. Where was the resident of the cell, the other him? Was he merely refusing to indulge him? Or, and he found this unlikely, had he been a figment of his imagination? 'You can't leave.' Anant tried with no reply. He made his way to the window as if to look for him who had never taken a form outside of Anant. He stared into the void, wondering if he could hear him, dramatizing, imitating, perhaps with a stranger accent, and before it even registered in his mind, his eyes settled on a light that revealed itself from within the depths of the void. A barely twinkling light struggling to assert itself amidst the vast expanse of darkness. In between squinting and rapidly blinking to focus his eyes, Anant tried to ascertain what lay in the light. In the ocean of the abyss, the light like eyes seemed the window to its soul. He thought he could find a possible answer or explanation within it. A little light, struggling to peer through the robes of the abyss, but a light nonetheless, on the edges of the void, causing the unabashed darkness in its immediate surroundings to appear midnight blue. The further he stared into the light, the more the midnight blue revealed what lay in it. A glimpse of a silhouette of what appeared to be a formation of rocks of sorts, so far away from his cell that it felt like it existed in another world altogether. Upon further investigation, his eyes bouncing and straining, his pupils dilating to hold on more and more of the precious light, on top of the formation of rocks, at the edge of the precipice, stood an archway that no matter how many times Anant told himself that he was being deceived, resembled the Gateway of India.

Anant took deep breaths to steady his racing heart that had gone into a flurry at the sight of the precipice and the archway that stood on its very edges. He pushed himself against the window and squeezed himself out of it, expecting to land on familiar grounds like the time he had discovered when he had stepped out of the door. But the ground seemed to have disappeared for he never stopped falling. Without any wind on his face, without any ground beneath him, without any feeling of gravity dragging him down, devoid of all senses that would alert him to a fall but the fact that cell was moving upwards, he floated and fell, fell and floated, the cell disappeared into the sky, and finally, the darkness overwhelmed him, he melted, he scattered away, he blinked, and just as before, Anant found himself back in the cell. He was quick to his feet and quicker out of the door, unwilling to waste time processing information. He walked around the cell with a finger tracing the grey brick walls, and found ground where previously, when he jumped out of the window, there had been none. He did not waste time dissecting this change. Turning around expecting to face the distant midnight blue, the little light, he found the daunting abyss staring back at him. He blinked and returned to his place in the cell. Once again by the window, pupils dilated straining to focus on the light, and he found the precipice, and the silhouette on the precipice. Out and around the cell, he was once more met with the abyss. Desperation had begun to jumble his thoughts, he fought his body's inclination to hurry. Feeling clever and having confirmed that ground existed, he entered the cell through the window and turned around, expecting to see the silhouette and was disappointed when he found the same void staring back at him. No doubt if the abyss had had a face, it would be smirking at him. He blinked and found himself seated, the spot where he returned to every time he blinked outside the cell. It seemed that stepping out of the cell meant that he would be returned, even if only in ceremony, to the spot where he had appeared from the real world. He returned to the window with failure looming over him. The light, the midnight blue, the silhouette, the precipice, and then the archway. Even the hues of dark blue around the silhouette seemed to be waving sardonically, as if relishing his failure. What was he to do now? Anant had no answers, and his desperation had given way to frustration. He did not know how long he stood by the open window straining his eyes without any pain or discomfort to see as far as he could to make out the silhouette of the precipice. If the seconds could turn to a minute, and minutes to hours, Anant was sure that hours would have passed with him standing by the window. But alas, seconds that ticked on never turned to minutes and all Anant had was his unwillingness to leave until the dilemma was solved. He waited with bated breath for a new clue, for the David light to defeat the Goliath abyss, or to merely make it bleed some more.

Anant wondered if the light had been present when he woke up in the cell that perhaps he had missed it, however unlikely that seemed. Maybe the light could, and would, do more if given more time. Perhaps some notion of time did exist in this world. Yet, nothing moved outside the window no matter how long he stood. Even the hues of blue as the light continued to strain itself against the abyss seemed stationary. The light was so minute that it could have been the result of his eyes watering from focusing into the distance for so long. But unlike the chicken and the egg, Anant knew that he strained his eyes staring into the distance after the light appeared. Given the lack of clues, the fact that he had indeed plateaued, Anant thought it was better to leave with the progress that he had made. A tactical retreat from his retreat. Perhaps the light needed more time, time of a world where seconds ticked on and became minutes. He didn't consider the light losing this battle by the time he arrived next, leaving behind no trace of ever having existed, meeting the same fate as the door and its hinges, the precipice once again swallowed by the unwavering abyss. He returned to sit in his place in the cell, where he had appeared these past two visits and where he would be placed every time he blinked after venturing out of the cell. It seemed as if his own mind was enforcing its own rules as a reminder to him that he wasn't in complete control of his existence in this world.

Sitting down on the soft mahogany floor, Anant considered the two roads ahead of him, even though he had just decided to return to the world. If he wanted to put an end to his dilemma, he would require conviction—which he knew he was lacking. The two roads ahead, one of which he had considered as cowardice and the other that he knew was of distress. To escape, or to stay. Was it ego that compelled him to remain in the cell? That his ownership of this world was being questioned by forces that wanted to subjugate him. A king's last stand. Anant liked to believe it was curiosity. He conveniently left out the third, most likely, road, one of fear. Fear of this loss of control over the cell spiralling into ruin. To wake up from sleep with these grey brick walls for company, unsure of what to do, where to go, and how to return. And hiding from this fear would have given it validity, made it concrete. With this fear in his heart, dressed in the garb of curiosity, he argued with himself that if he could return at any point, then why not wait in the cell for the light to emerge victorious? Perhaps he could tackle both his problems now, Anant thought, by simply waiting and introspecting. With nothing to distract him, no clues being revealed and the light continuing its static fight with the abyss, he returned to the only thought that he managed to conceive, the one that he had looked to avoid. He thought of the nature of the cell and the possibility that desolation was inherent to it. That the cell was meant to be devoid of life because it was created as such. To tackle the why, Anant took a moment to contemplate the structure of the retreat. How had he ended up building a cell? Had he been influenced by prison while he made this structure? But without a door, what purpose did the cell have? What significance did it hold? Or was it merely the limited imagination of a twelve-year-old who had not yet understood the concept of the retreat? Anant found it hard to stomach the thought. To blame it on ignorance was too convenient. Could it not have been a grander place, or if he was going for the bare minimum, without any distractions, why was this not a room with a simple bed or a bench? Surely an empty room inspired by his own bedroom would have been much easier for a child looking to escape. Anant was left with a barrage of questions, but he had no answer. Anant took on a different approach, and considered the futility of such questions. They were targeted at a child whom he had long since forgotten. Even if their thoughts ran on the same tracks, they clashed in experience. Anant in his mid-twenties wasn't the Anant that was stepping into adolescence. Even if he could peer into the past, he would have his experiences clouding his judgement and making it impossible to be his past self once again.

While Anant was looking in the right place, he continued to ask the wrong questions. By diving into his past and chasing ghosts of answers rather than questioning the existence of the cell in his present, he continued to look past the answers that he was seeking. The answer that the cell was devoid of life because it had been untouched by his present, which at times managed to overpower or squirm its way into the world outside the cell, but in essence remain a mere spectator, a screen showing another world. That the cell wasn't a monument to the past but a place, like an embassy car with diplomatic immunity of an empire that was no longer alive, existing in the present while still in the jurisdiction of the past, something that by natural order should not exist.

Anant wondered why the only change he had made in recent times to the cell was the floor, and it occurred to him that he had only done so in his previous visit, when he had been trapped. 'How far can one take ownership of a thought?' Anant asked himself. He argued that the cell had never been just a thought. Even before it held such prominence in his mind, when he could come and go as he pleased, Anant had allowed it to exist in its own corner, and the cell had established itself as a part of this world. It dawned on Anant that perhaps the cell had never been completely in his control. That a thought put out into the world takes its own course, finds its own constitution, becomes its own entity. And now that it had come alive, having battled and won the test of time and become a staple of his mind, Anant swallowing his pride, questioned if he had had any ownership at all.

Two trains of thought arrived at the station where he stood waiting, and he could only board one, to either believe that the cell was its own entity or accept it as a retreat and make changes. It was the last remnants of pride which convinced him to take the latter train. He surveyed his surroundings with a rekindled interest. The grey brick walls were comfortable, and he had grown to like them, much like the new floor. Furniture would take up too much space, the cell was only about 5 square feet in size. He had no intentions to try to make changes to the structure that was a part of history, not that he could, having already tried in his previous visit when he was looking at ways to escape the locked door. He could fit a corner bed but what was the use when the floor itself felt like a mattress. Anant did not have to flick through images to know what he wanted. A mat and a turntable sitting atop a small stool. He added the details, the square mat would be two feet, scarlet in colour, the front legs of the walnut stool would curve outwards at the bottom. They appeared in the cell, in the perfect location, the mat underneath him and the table beside him. Anant closed his eyes and opened them, and again and again, relieved to find that they didn't disappear.

What kind of music did the resident enjoy? 'Johnny Cash,' came the reply, surprising him. The resident finally made himself known. Anant was unsure of how he felt towards the existence of the resident now that he was no longer searching for reasons to remain in the cell.

'You're here,' Anant replied.

'Well, I couldn't ignore the gifts you have brought me, even though I was led to believe that the nature of the gifts would be different.'

'The world, I have been looking for it.'

'I sincerely hope you have.'

'Do you listen to music when I do?'

'I don't know. How frequently do you listen to music?'

'It must be similar to the doughnut.'

'The doughnut theory.'

'Johnny Cash, when did you first hear it?'

'Don't ignore the doughnut theory. I quite like the name, how about you?' The resident was met with a resolute silence.

'I can be silent too, you know.' The resident was not silent for more than a few moments.

'Fine, fine. I heard it when my body was younger. I had a scraggy patchy beard which was very unbecoming. Might I say, it was downright ugly.'

'Thanks. So, college.' The same principle about what he saw was applicable to what he heard. All it needed was magic. For him to be entranced. And he distinctively remembered the moment when he first heard Johnny Cash. It had been divine. 'Can you taste what I eat?'

'I'd like to keep the sovereignty of my mouth. Thank you very much.'

'Did you taste the doughnut?'

'I know the taste of the doughnut,' the resident replied. 'What do you think of the doughnut theory?'

'The texture?'

Silence. The resident, while invisible, had figuratively crossed his arms and pressed his lips into a tight line.

'I think it is dismissive. But if you like it, you like it. The texture?' Anant asked again.

'No, not the texture. Do you think it should be doughnut or donut, you know, with a "ugh" or the short version?'

'How about the smell?'

'Of the doughnut, with a "ugh"...or without it?'

'Are you doing a bit again, like the last time? Is this imitation of someone I have heard or met?'

'No, I have moved on from merely replicating the linguistics and donned myself a character. No longer will my personality waver, my semantics be fickle, subjugated to my immediate whims, but rather be concrete in my convictions.'

'If that's what you want. Now, the smell of anything. The ocean or fresh grass after rain.'

'Yes, there is no reason to doubt my olfactory system. All three.'

'But not anything to touch?'

'I know the feel of this wall, and the floor.'

Anant didn't have the heart to tell him that real walls and

floors did not feel like a mattress, especially considering the pride and joy that Anant heard in his voice while playing his current character. Glancing at the turntable, Anant tried to remember the songs he knew of Johnny Cash. The sound of the needle meeting the record cut through the momentary silence that had settled between the two. 'The Man Comes Around' began to play. It was the first Johnny Cash song Anant had heard. Hearing the song again, he was taken back in time to the pungent smell of weed that turned his stomach, with thumping music blaring from the speakers barely able to withstand the bass in the other room of the small two-bedroom flat, and to the relative quiet of the balcony attached to the master bedroom. Someone had played the song on their phone. The song was promptly changed due to complaints, not allowing Johnny Cash to complete his first verse. But Anant was mesmerized with the melody, the composition and the American twang—the heart and soul of all Johnny Cash songs. He left the flat for his dorm at dawn, in an auto driven by a driver named Harish, the popular choice amongst the college students for his willingness to wait outside flats and houses, and even more popular with Anant for he too liked to remain quiet. Anant repeated the tune and mumbled the words that he wasn't sure were the lyrics along the way till he reached his dorm. The guard was asleep, and when he wasn't, he was paid to pretend to be asleep. Anant had the choice of sleep himself, not the peaceful deep sleep that the guard slept, but one that would be disturbed within an hour when the rush for classes began. With the tune playing in the back of his mind, Anant decided to soldier on. He longed for sleep but with the melody accompanying him, he went to the communal shower area where he used most of the hot water, which was hardly much. He went to the morning classes with hooded bloodshot eyes that yearned to rest, and feet alive to the sound of the tune playing in his mind before he skipped the remaining classes to sleep. He was floating before he hit the bed.

When Anant opened his eyes, he found himself lying on a mattress. He was struck with a peculiar crisis of identity that made him ignore his surroundings and rush to the washroom. Recognition of his aged self looking back at him from the mirror eased his worries. 'I am me,' he thought. He was Anant Vohra, aged twenty-seven. He was in Mumbai. He had to meet Aarti today.

Chapter 21

Once upon a time before her life had become weary, Aarti felt at home in the events and conferences hosted by her company during the annual company offsite. She understood social dynamics better than seasoned professionals. She exuded positivity, had a rather refreshing smile—one that seemed effortless and genuine—and reprimanded with tact. The HR personnel would have grown envious of Aarti because of her unique abilities, had they already not been in awe of her. She was liberal with compliments, but understood the fine margin of complimenting someone and kissing someone's ass. She paved the way to put her well-framed thoughts forward, while being mindful of both the timing and context of her actions. Like a farmer who understood which seed to sow when, she used all the tools at her disposal to produce the best results. It seemed the work of a person with an entirely different skill set that she no longer understood. As if the English language had donned a new set of alphabet overnight. That was a time when Aarti understood that presentation was as important as substance. Nay, presentation was paramount, it was blinding, like magic, while substance was delayed, it was labour, and most were interested in the immediate splendour of the trick, and those who perhaps cherished or understood the importance of labour, at least some of them, could be deluded into believing there was substance that didn't need inspection. That the dazzling trick meant that there must be work put behind it. Ideally, for there remained in her company and in life those that dealt only with substance, or those that dealt with both, compartmentalizing the two separately, Aarti brought forth both substance and presentation, both of which were lost to her now.

The conference in Mumbai began to drag on the moment she entered the hotel, as if the hotel itself had come alive to warn her of what the meetings to come would bring. Aarti persevered. Although she knew what needed to be done, there seemed to be a lag in her that constrained her, that weighed her down. Her fiancé Ravi, with the wedding coming up, had taken leave so he could use this time of the conference to distribute invitations. Unlike Aarti, he had a large family and an even larger group of people that considered him family, so he was running around personally giving invites not only to close family and friends, but to all family and their friends. He would regularly tag along with his parents, his uncles and his aunties to visit people he did not know. He had tried to get Aarti to come with him. Her work wouldn't suffer during the time of the conference, the company would understand and his parents would have appreciated it, but the increasing agitation he could sense whenever Aarti would interact with him, and what he put down as pre-wedding jitters, made him wary of even discussing the possibility of her travelling to Delhi to stay under the same roof as his family, instead of being in Mumbai for the conference. He had to lie to Aarti about why he wasn't attending the conference despite it being hosted by his branch. So instead of sharing the real purpose of his visit, which was to hand out invitations of their wedding, he told her that he had to travel to the venue and finalize certain changes. To lie to her left a bad taste in his mouth, and made him feel a certain shame even though he knew he was doing things the right way. And the disinterest that Aarti exhibited to these changes he was travelling to Varanasi to make, worsened his mood. Thus began a cold war between the two, both expecting apologies,

Ravi because he felt he was treated unfairly, and Aarti because she had begun to feel that the world owed her an apology.

On the final day of the conference, when the last of the meetings and events were coming to an end, the employees were making plans for the party that the company hosted. They would book a section or a floor of a prominent bar in the city, but never the hotel they were staying in. It was an HR policy to limit the liabilities of the company in the event of foolishness, no doubt born out of the alcohol and the drugs that managed to find their way past security, as they it was best to look the other way. The last thing a pharmaceutical company wanted was to ruin its ties with a hotel given how many doctors and chemists were hosted in any worldwide chain. Employees were also advised not to drive post-conference, but occasionally there would be a few who would go rogue and court trouble for ignoring the precautions set by the company. A select few speeches and one or two cordial drinks would begin the party, before the dance floor was left for the employees to get shit-faced. Despite the HR actively tackling the issues, the drugs and the awkward office hookups remained a prominent footnote of the party, only because there were always worse incidents that would take centre stage. People passed out on the floor, being led to their cabs in a haze, and once or twice, heated debates had turned physical.

In the hours preceding the party, Aarti's colleagues wanted to get drunk on company money before going to a club but the number of group-bonding activities, branch-bonding games and employee meetings going on all at once had diminished their numbers and the ones remaining included Aarti's friends who started talking of a bachelorette party. Aarti was quick to nip the talk in the bud, much to everyone's dismay. She had become increasingly defensive about each and every conversation involving her—a personality change that had not gone down that well with her friends since they had considered it to be a reflection of who they were. That her disinterest had more to do with them than her marriage that was knocking on the door. One of them commented that she was already becoming an aunty. And of course, she meant well, that it was said out of concern and no ill intent hung in her words, that it was only said in the presence of everyone because everyone was just as concerned. Aarti was just tense, one of her close friends said in her defence. 'She isn't even smiling as much' and 'Come on, this could be the last time we hang out while you are single' and 'If you girls have a bachelorette party, do us guys have to leave', rang around the group. Aarti would have liked to put forth an oblivious front, that she merely didn't understand why her impending marital cuffs were of any consequence to her colleagues, most of them were married or in long-term relationships themselves. But she knew. She understood that there was a prevalent culture of gossip in office, no matter what age, relationship status or gender. It wasn't merely sacrosanct, but also indoctrinating, and the longer one worked in office, the more they conformed to this culture. Everyone, even the ones with little or no connection with the subject, or subjects, in question, lived vicariously through the gossip. There was a time when Aarti enjoyed this office culture, she felt a camaraderie seeing everyone around her wearing masks that bore smiles much like herself. But while what lay behind her mask was make-believe happiness, theirs hid sinister judgements. Everybody was chomping at the bits to criticize others, colleagues, friends, interns, maintenance and management, nobody was safe. Nobody knew when the seeds of this culture were sown, everybody must have been trying to pass time, once upon a time. But the once upon a time watercooler conversation became something worse; as the world became smaller, the gossip became a staple, and these scandalous-but-almost-never-really-scandalous topics became mundane, people got desensitized and the bars were raised higher and higher, and more forbidden topics were shovelled into the firebox to keep the train running. People spent more and more time indulging in these scathing remarks, and it slowly changed the foundations of the people themselves. They became a caricature of these activities. Aarti believed that she had known more interesting people in college, but there was so much to do in college that perhaps nobody spent enough time with one another to lose their individuality. It wasn't everyone in office either, the upper echelons of upper management were too removed from the office culture, and there were the fresh faces. But everyone who had been present in the office long enough knew that they were merely lambs on their way to slaughter, because over time they too would either relinquish themselves to the culture or leave. As if within the office was a pencil scribbling over them, making them into a doodle, a satire of themselves. Everybody lacked an exciting life, no matter their adventures. The friends she had weren't any different, neither was she. But she had lived in her own little bubble for so long that she had, to an extent, managed to hold on to a piece of her individuality in face of this insidious culture. Her friends and her, the very same that were being ignored when they brought up a bachelorette party, remained an interesting bunch despite it all. She enjoyed the time they spent talking over tequila and they shared her passion for good food. She liked listening to their adventures, and they listened to her stories all the same. While it wasn't a given that they wouldn't leak this information, caution hung over them, but they managed to share a bond despite the roadblocks. They were there for her birthdays. She was there for theirs and their wedding anniversaries. She appreciated the excitement that came over them when she broke the news that she was getting married. Over the years she had done the same for them. But alas, on that

Friday, she had to step away from them. She had plans, and plans that she could not share with them.

It would have been relatively easy to explain that she was meeting her cousin, but there was a chance that they would have invited themselves, or worse, invited him. And while she was certain that Anant would have declined, she couldn't risk his presence muddying their friendship, or worse, her friends contracting solitude from him and spreading it through the vines of communication to the rest of her office. Aarti herself hadn't known why she invited him, or why Anant had agreed to meet her. Didn't he have anything better to do on a Friday evening, she thought. She had prepared herself for a last-minute cancellation, looking on the bright side that she could use it as a ruse to sit in her room drinking wine and reading a book that she had bought at the airport while waiting for the gates to open for boarding. She had purchased *Metamorphosis* by Franz Kafka, a short book that she thought she could finish on the flight. Or, at most, that she would finish three-quarters of the book on the flight, and the rest in the room. And she'd purchase a new book on the flight back. She had not read ten pages when the book became overbearing, the loneliness of Gregor Samsa, as he struggled with what he should do, and what he could do, pushed Aarti to the brink of tears, and she turned to talk about nothing with two of her friends sitting beside her. Their conversations began on the topic of her wedding, but she was adept at gently manoeuvring the conversation along to what they all wanted to talk about, and on that day, it began with politics and ended with what once used to be a hearty discussion and now a one-sided conversation about the documentaries they had seen. Despite everything, when their conversations weren't muddied with office culture, Aarti enjoyed herself with them. 'Perhaps going out with them wouldn't have been the worst idea,' she thought. It would have been better than sitting in the Harbour Bar all alone, like the other time in Gurugram. She had arrived ten minutes early. It was five minutes to six in the evening, and drinking alone in a bar unreasonably bright made her feel like an alcoholic.

Anant arrived two minutes past the agreed time, almost as if he were waiting in the lobby and it took him two minutes to walk to the bar. Anant and Aarti greeted each other with an affable smile. Or rather, Aarti's lips curled up in their best imitation of a smile that once adorned her face. Despite being in the best shape she had ever been, Aarti was finding it rather difficult to control muscles that she never knew existed—like the muscles around her lips that had wormed out of her control. Nor did the fruits of working out to look her best at the wedding include her feeling the best, which seemed absurd to Aarti. It felt like she had been lied to once again, and by whom she still did not know. She had even begun to feel sceptical about this idea of trying to look her best at what was said to be the best day of a person's life. If the wedding day was the peak of her life, she had thought one late evening with a whisky sour in hand, it was given that the sense of personal achievement associated with marriage, which could last for days, weeks, or months, would begin to fade, and the marathon she had run would have turned pointless because there would be no cathartic finish. It was as if the awards had been given halfway through, and the runners were expected to merely keep on running. Surely, then, these intensive efforts to look her best was the worst thing she could have done, for not only would the life that followed never be comparable to the best day of her life, the sun a little bleaker, the winds a little coarser, the laughter a little heavier, the relationships a little duller, but she would perpetually look worse.

Aarti had begun to think that the only sane choice for the bride and the groom, for a healthy, successful, happy life after this dreaded best day, was to let themselves go in the weeks leading to the wedding. So, when they looked back at the photos of this ordained day, better health would at least be a comfort to them. Aarti kept to shaking her wine glass as they shared a greeting that was barely there, the phantom smiles vanished. She felt a hint of trepidation in meeting his eyes at first, a lingering fear that she would see her dad once again. A fear that she immediately squashed by staring him square in the face. 'How are you?' she asked. Anant shrugged and repeated the question. 'Good', 'Fine', 'Well'. Aarti thought of all the one-word replies ingrained in anyone who had worked with a team, but chose a response that sounded like a jumble of words. She ended up mumbling it before they walked from the bar to a table.

Silence. What else did Aarti expect? He ordered a drink, there was a polish and an assurance in his actions that Aarti hadn't seen before. She was amused by his behaviour, like he had been a patron of the bar for decades, instinctively knowing when a waiter would look and raising his fingers to call him, declining the menu with a curt shake of his head and ordering a cocktail. Certain habits that had been formed after visiting an array of bars with Rajat. The Vohra cousins waited in silence. The old-fashioned arrived. They raised their glasses, and Aarti thought to say 'cheers' but it never left her mouth. Silence stretched on. Anant was quiet, his eyes lacked focus and would hover around without ever fixing on anything for long before settling back to a dazed look. Aarti realized that it was the first time that she wasn't uncomfortable with his brand of silence, that for once it was a shared silence rather than one he was imposing and she trying to break.

'How are you?' When Anant broke the silence, Aarti was thankful for the lack of control over her mouth because surely, she would have smirked, relishing the fact that she hadn't tried to make conversation.

The question posed a new dilemma to Aarti. They had gone through the greeting already. It was as if by asking the question again, he wanted to know the details. And Aarti wouldn't have shared the details with Anant if she had any. How was she? 'Agitated, confused, uncertain.' Aarti flicked through a Rolodex of words hoping one would fit, but she was unsuccessful in finding the right words. She decided that she did not know how she was. It was the reason she had picked up the Kafka book with the particularly nauseating cover. She had been looking to find the right words or to find a character that she could empathize with and try to wear the emotions the character would feel. Alas, she had nothing. She was not an insect, and she didn't feel like one either. Instead, what she had was anger and dejection, and a peculiar sense of helplessness that was choking her. 'Well, how are you?' She didn't mean for her question to sound like a retort.

Anant had plenty on his plate now that his retreat was unavailable to him. After his return from the cell, return perhaps would be too kind, after he was spat out by the cell, a giant sign hung in his mind at the thought of the cell, telling him to come back later, that it was going through renovations. Little-light-at-work, the sign read, or so he hoped. There was the added weight of his belief that he could no longer go empty-handed with the resident in the cell living through him. The cell had become less of a retreat and more of a house visit. And any time he tried to venture into the cell, as he tried once she asked the question, he found himself light-headed and momentarily weightless. 'In two worlds, recently,' Anant replied.

'Really?' Aarti said inquisitively, surprised that he had answered honestly. She wondered if the change in the dynamics between them could have something to do with her seeing her father in him.

'Work has been stressful,' Anant managed. 'So, you're getting married.' It was a statement placed like a diving board for her to jump off and speak. To lead him to whatever was on her mind, and no doubt, to why she had invited him.

'Yeah, it is something,' Aarti muttered while she edited her thoughts. 'How is work stressful?'

'This and that.' Anant shrugged, and they returned to silence, one very different from the silence they had shared previously. Unsaid words and thoughts hung between them, making it difficult for Aarti to concentrate, making Anant uncomfortable, as if he needed to speak but had nothing to say. With the possibility of him being affected by the moment when she saw her father in him, she had questions that made the silence heavier, and she neared her limit to tolerate the quiet. She wanted to break the silence, much like she did in the days gone by, or her co-workers tried in recent weeks. She hadn't expected Anant to continue, and when he did she started watching him intently. 'I have an interesting client.' Anant was used to preparing for when he could be required to fill in the overbearing silence that he carried with him, but unlike before, he was met with thoughts drifting in his mind, thoughts of suspicious origins. Wrapped in gift paper to pick and choose to serve for a source that may or may not be him, the only way to know what these thoughts were once they were unwrapped. And to unwrap these thoughts was to put them into words, and he was unwilling to share the recent upheaval and turmoil with anyone. 'And the work in itself has more responsibilities than what I am used to.' He ignored the thoughts that weren't his, or at least believed that they weren't his.

'How so?' Aarti inquired, letting him decide which scenario he wanted to detail.

'What are we doing here?' Anant asked instead. It wasn't like him to be blunt, but the prospect of fishing in his mind and catching an alien thought in front of Aarti aggravated him. 'I didn't take you as someone that would be flustered with silence.'

The biting comment took Aarti by surprise. While she still held some disdain for the morning outside his parents' house, which once upon a time she had believed was the start of her troubles, she had come to terms with the fact that her troubles ran deeper than Anant and his self-serving introversion, and even him donning the face of her dad. It was more than the reminders of her dad and his absence from her wedding. It was about the wedding itself, for she hated every time anybody told her that it would be the best day of her life, like all she could aspire to after that day was a gaudy imitation of this best day that had been served and that was that. But even the wedding, and she kept this thought tucked away in the recesses of her mind, she knew was only a catalyst to her troubles rather than their source, that again boundaries were being drawn around her, as she had done once by living in a bubble-wrapped world. But not again. And especially not by anyone but herself. The wedding was the platform and Anant merely a tipping point from where the bitterness was quick to spread, but the bitterness had been nurtured since long before. He was insignificant in the grander scheme of her life, Aarti mused to herself. And the wedding itself was the product of a past that she had floated by. As the silence between them served as a reminder of the disdain of that morning, she allowed herself to revel in her anger, anger that had been subdued but not extinguished. Once she opened the Pandora's box, thoughts she wasn't sure she ever had began to cascade her consciousness. As if another self, a shadow or her unconscious mind was drowning her now that the floodgates were open. From insulting to violent, all unfolded with a frightening calm. From cutting him with words, throwing her glass on the floor to punching him. It wasn't just Anant, she wanted to punch the waiter too and break the bottles lined up at the bar. In the empty bar that seemed far too small to contain her, Aarti allowed the disgust in her stomach to swell and rise, like the kundalini rises to the sahasra chakra, her disgust completed its insidious climb till her eyes darkened with rage that barely hid in her dark eyes. She had been learning boxing in the gym, and thought it would be a good time to practise her hook. She wasn't great at twisting her body and punching through. As she had been told repeatedly, the power is generated from the hips. She imagined the hotel security coming to the scene of the crime with two bodies on the ground and her with her glass of wine, she had decided against breaking the glass, leaning back, relaxed, the monster in her stomach taking the form of bruised and bloodied hands, maybe a cracked knuckle. How long would it take for them to realize what had happened, that she had knocked two people out and then returned to her drink. She wasn't an imposing presence; would they question who had done this, ignoring all the obvious signs before their eyes until a waiter or someone on the edge of their seat would snitch on her. She could see herself raising a hand to motion for them to pause as she had another sip of her wine, or finished the whole glass just before common sense would prevail and the security guards would restrain her. She would snarl at the snitch and tell him how snitches get stitches. All her troubles in the weeks before had reared their ugly heads once again in the presence of Anant. She cracked a smile that was reminiscent of the one she had sported in the past, revelling in her bloodstained imagination.

Anant watched her display the array of her expressions conveying one emotion and the next until it settled on a private smile, like she had cracked a joke that she was unwilling to share with the rest of the world. The previous conversation ended along with their drinks and Aarti ordered a round of margaritas.

The transition from conversing about his parents and hers, to her brother that she was quick to broach and quicker to sidestep, and finally to her conference was seamless, as if the words previously said existed in another plane of time. She started talking about the parties that took place on the sidelines of the company's annual offsite, especially the more-often-than-not abominable aftermath. How the drug-induced political screeching had ended up in wild fists, and the calmer ones had ignored them until the saner ones had finally decided to alert the security and asked the authorities to turn off the music. Aarti imagined herself in the party, in the middle of the fight, dodging those flailing arms and putting them down one by one. Duck, weave, jab, cross, block, duck, liver shot and hook. Another time, she told Anant, the free alcohol mixed with the hash cookies that a colleague brought had crept up on her and she had been hallucinating that she was walking on clouds, her friends and Ravi had to help her to her room. A round of whisky sours in, with Aarti adamant about the eggs in it, she began talking about a series she had seen that Anant might enjoy, the smile turned into a giggle after she gulped down the remaining whisky in her glass and ordered another. The thought of punching him remained in the back of her mind, providing a steady stream of delight. 'What is it?' Anant asked, not following her lead in chugging drinks. He was happy to stay on the third.

'I could totally knock you out,' Aarti blurted out without a care about who heard her.

'You mean...'

'Knock you out. Punch you in the face and down you'll go. Hit the mat, one, two, three and you lose. I mean, one to ten, the ten count. Boxing rules.' Aarti snickered at the thought, entertained by her. Anant leaned into his chair and smiled, her happiness was contagious, and better yet, it was a reprieve from the vanished retreat. Her giddy happiness reminded him of their childhood, once upon a time before the hissing and slithering. The memory was blurred, as if looking through a frosted glass. He could make out a vague outline with the colours bleeding into one another, of her and her brother, and he was there too, sharing a bag of Cheetos and watching some cartoon. Just children being children while the adults sat together enjoying themselves. He was surprised, given his past antipathy towards her, to find that she managed to preserve a fond existence in certain memories. The darkness on her shoulder reacted in kind to this revelation and flooded him with grief for her mortality. With a heavy sigh that did not alleviate the tension that grew in him, he turned to his drink.

Anant and Aarti left the bar after another round of drinks to take a walk around the hotel. Apollo Bandar was bustling with people on a pleasant Friday night, cars rushing home from work, cars whirring by to whatever Friday night plans their owners had made. The withered flats took on a new glow, as if youth had been breathed into them. The abandoned art deco movement that left its buildings behind seemed radiant, for these were the nights they were built for, and Regal Cinema was the jewel in this abandoned crown that shone bright as ever. Leopold Café was bustling as usual, and other cafés were marked with mean mugged bouncers that were damp with sweat. Some men and women walked their dogs and others were on a stroll to the shore. Aarti's eyes came alive at the sight of a night market that was packed with people. From the gaps between bodies, you could make out parts of the tight alley that accommodated more shops, some selling bangles that glittered under the light of the bulbs, spices in tight containers like decorations on Holi, food that battled the scent of sweat in the air and clothes being draped and hung and thrown and scattered made up the rest of the market. Aarti was at a standstill with wide-eyed wonder. Anant waited for her to venture in but she only stared for some moments before she continued to walk. Anant was being led, and knowing the way they were headed, to the Gateway of India, he had no qualms following Aarti along the way.

The Gateway of India was both crowded and yet deserted. The area was crowded, but the monument was deserted. If Apollo Bandar was the living room of Mumbai, the Gateway of India was one of the many hearths for people to gather around. The monument brought snapshots of his time in the cell before his eyes, appearing and disappearing as if fitted in a vintage projector. His eyes lingered on the doorways either side of the towering gate, wondering if he could see his little cell floating on the ocean through it. Aarti's punch brought him back to reality. It was thrown to hurt but Aarti was drunk and didn't connect properly to his shoulder. 'Dammit. Come, we're walking to Marine Drive,' Aarti declared, unaware that they were on the other shore of Mumbai.

'Where are you staying?' Anant asked.

'Nariman Point.' Aarti replied and Anant convinced her to take a cab to her hotel. He would drop her there, and if she was still in her senses, then they could go to Marine Drive. 'How long?' This was all she asked.

The cab arrived in five minutes. It took them half an hour to reach her hotel, and while she was exuberant at the beginning of the drive, she had dozed off by the time they reached her hotel. Anant helped her to her room. She declared in the elevator that she would order some dine-in, her diet be damned. And something about it being wiser to be fat on your wedding day. This announcement and the walk to her room sapped the last of her energy. She fell on her bed, face buried in her pillow, and passed out while Anant was still in the room. Walking over to the window, Anant noted that she had a view of the ocean. Without the sound, the white streak of waves like strokes of paint running along the shore was the only reminder to all that stared through these windows that the ocean was alive. He booked a cab to Marine Drive while staring at the ocean that continued to crumble like paper as it neared the shore. The alcohol made him apprehensive about her state and by turning her on her side, he put these bubbling fears of her choking to rest. He pulled the blanket from under her and threw it over her like a lazy burrito that had come apart. On his way out, he paused to glance at the darkness that seemed so lithe that it could have been an ink stain. He met the cab in the driveway of the hotel.

The first thought that Anant had as he made his way along the stone boundary of Marine Drive was that on a new moon night, past the tetrapods and away from the immediate waters of the ocean that was lit by the lights of the city streaming down on it, the ocean would look like the void with the stars barely enough for even a sprinkle of silver. He stared into the endless ocean wondering if on the horizon sat the hint of the formation of the rocks that he had seen from his cell. A glance here, a look there, at times from the corner of his eye, trying different angles to find such a formation on the horizon, with no precipice in sight, Anant satisfied his curiosity by imagining it on the horizon. And past this precipice, beyond the horizon would be the abyss where the little cell would be floating. He felt like it was his obligation to hurry and sleep in his flat and wake up in the cell. It seemed the only way to sneak past the sign, to let intuition guide him back to his retreat. To try and solve the mystery of the precipice. Perhaps the little light that had accomplished what it sought to do. Maybe something from this night had reached the resident and he would be more inclined to help him. Anant stayed on the slabs of stone, legs hanging off the edge with the tetrapods below him. No doubt there were people indulging themselves, away from the prying eyes of the city. Anant's eyes did not waver from the ocean, not even when he got in a cab to return home. When the ocean was out of view, he stared at the headrest in front of him, and could still see the white streaks of the waves, as if he had left his eyes on the stone. The sound never made it to his ears for he had taken his ears with him to the cab. When he got to his flat, he turned to one of the first records he had bought, titled 'Popular Piano Pieces'. He got himself a cold bottle of water, and guided the needle to the spinning record, and Side B began with 'Sonata Pathétique', or as known by Anant 'Piano Sonata No. 8 in C Minor, Op. 13', by Beethoven as played by András Schiff. He had plans to retire to bed, but the music breathed life into him, and he went on looking at his rough notebook, knowing he could not do justice to the ocean but nonetheless trying. An hour later, with his energy spent on his failed attempts to draw the ocean and retain even an ounce of its majesty, he turned off the music, and went flat on his bed. The soundless white streaks serenaded him to sleep.

Chapter 22

The gentle strumming of an acoustic guitar, the distinctive booming of an organ in the background and a raspy voice singing incomprehensible lyrics greeted Anant as he woke up. He stirred on the mattress out of habit rather than need, for he opened his eyes without the grogginess of sleep sticking to him. The first thing Anant realized was that he wasn't lying on his mattress but he was sitting on the floor with his back against grey bricks as soft as a mattress, and his soft cotton bed sheet stripped away from his skin. The raspy voice in the distance was of Johnny Cash, repeating the tune and the beginning lyrics that Anant remembered from his college years. The familiar wooden floor greeted him. The scarlet mat underneath him and the turntable beside him, on the stool with its legs curved outwards. The speakers on either side of the turntable had disappeared, and the sound of the music boomed from outside his cell. 'Good morning,' he muttered, wondering whether the resident was present or not.

'Is it morning?' The resident sounded sharp as always.

'It's morning somewhere.' Anant found himself at the spot where the gate once stood. He looked from side to side, and was greeted by the impassive expanse of unfiltered darkness that was its all encompassing self. In what was becoming his routine in the cell, he made his way out of the window, and peered into the abyss, searching for the light, and to his relief, or to his surprise, the change in the abyss was conspicuous. The light had further cut through the void, the shades of dark blue spread along the formation of rocks as if it were being worn by the rocks, making it easier to spot the precipice. Any underlying doubt that Anant may have had about the existence of this precipice was swatted away by its now distinct silhouette. What resided on the top of the precipice was still shrouded in the mist of the void, but from time to time, the robes were lifted to give him a peak of the archway. Anant wondered if a mirage in the desert could last for days.

'Not continuing to gentrify this place today?' the resident asked him. Anant realized that their conversations weren't just said and heard, but they were understood, almost telepathically. Given how they shared this body, he thought to himself, would it be considered telepathy or the work of neurons that they were listening to one another.

'I don't plan on moving in, if that is what you're worried about,' Anant said.

'Noisy neighbours are like a bad stench, you get used to it but it doesn't mean it ceases to exist.' When the resident wasn't given a reply, he continued. 'Is that something from your world?'

'No.'

'Talkative today, aren't we?'

'Trying not to stink up the place.' The thoughts of courtesy he had planned to show the resident had since faded.

'It's just us here. How many times have I told you this?'

'Twice.'

'Touché.' A brief pause. 'I can keep repeating myself over and over again till you understand it.' The quite stretched on.

'It's just us here. It's just us here. It's just...'

'I get it. I understand. Okay. Well, how are you?'

'How am I... The company is severely lacking, that much I am certain of. Now, if that isn't from your world, and not a present for me, is it your imagination?'

'Precisely what I was wondering,' Anant replied. 'I don't know if that's real.'

'Why is it not real?'

His unwillingness to explain was overshadowed by the threat of the resident resorting to the annoying chant, and in an effort to deter the resident, he continued. 'It could be my imagination.'

'And?' Silence.

'Fine, so what if this is your imagination?'

'Then it wouldn't be real?'

'Is the record player real? Did you not give birth to it?'

'It was from my memory,' Anant said. 'I put it there. You seem to be rather normal today?' Anant tried to move the conversation away from the precipice. 'Maybe the part I am playing is you. Now, what about the cell, that too from your memory? You gave birth to this structure.'

'It didn't just pop out, I built it.'

'You created it, and now it is real. As real as any of this is to you.'

'I remember building the cell. Not as solid as it is now, but I remember creating it. Who created that?'

'A conundrum indeed.' The arrogance in the resident's voice made Anant wary of what he might know that Anant seemingly failed to perceive, and he took to silence once again.

Staring off into the distance, Anant realized that he was getting distracted. He wasn't sure if the resident was present or not. This constant one-way traffic of reminders that the resident existed alongside him, almost bearing down on him, deterred him from his task and Anant even lost sight of the precipice from time to time. He would strain to spot the silhouette again, the soft glow of the shades of dark blue was a lighthouse to alert him to the rocks, his darting eyes would look to the light like a sailor lost in a storm, and when his eyes would settle on the light, he would allow it to reveal the precipice. Time passed while Anant stood frozen by the window, unable to look away from the precipice. It felt like someone had put blinkers on him, and all he could see was what was ahead of him. But unlike a racehorse, he could not turn his head, and worse, he could not gallop on to the precipice. He was stuck by the window, put on pause; for a moment he wondered if it were the circumstances or if someone indeed had tried to freeze him, and moments later, he would be back, waiting for a gunshot that would never be heard. At one point, he rummaged through his memories of movies and shows to imagine the sound of a gunshot. He could only manage a poor imitation of the sound. And he wasn't sure if the sound was heard in the cell. Alas, there was no galloping anywhere. There was only Johnny Cash that had finally gotten tired from singing the same few broken lines of 'The Man Comes Around' and turned to strumming a new tune and repeating 'I Hung My Head' from the song titled the same.

Anant imagined a car to drive over, or a plane to fly over, or a hand glider to float over, even a cycle that he could pedal across the smooth surface of the abyss, a modern-day do-it-yourself river of Styx, but there was no Charon in sight from whom he could rent a bike. He imagined a bridge that would lead him to the top of the precipice, hundreds of thoughts like monkeys coming together to put stones that would remain level and not drift away, but neither was he Rama, nor was there a presiding deity like Varuna. Anant consoled himself with the fact that when the resident would suggest the same, and he would, no doubt in a matter-of-fact tone, Anant could tell him that he had tried it already. Anant was taken aback at how strongly the intrusive thought came across, as if born out of some rivalry that existed between them. Since when had the resident begun to affect Anant by his presence? Anant was quick to wave it off as a one-off. No doubt a one-sided affair, Anant thought to himself, no rivalry, couldn't be. Anant thought back to the last time he was in the cell. The resident had sprung up as a fleeting thought at best, something to consider in moments of lull, or to distract himself. Adamant that nothing had changed, Anant maintained that there couldn't be any rivalry, for he was Anant, and the resident only a minuscule part of him. Yet, Anant couldn't shake him off. His presence, this notion of rivalry, if not being real then at least festering in the cell. Curious or suspicious, Anant tried to tune into the resident's thoughts, as if there was a part of his mind that he could press his ears against and eavesdrop. A figurative static was all Anant was met with. There seemed to be a distinct line between where the resident ended and Anant began, despite them existing in the same body. Pops and crackles were heard in the cell as the stylus met a new record, and Johnny Cash began singing 'A Boy Named Sue'. The change of record pulled Anant out of his head. He was certain that he had heard the song before but he wasn't sure where, nor did he know the lyrics of the song. And unlike the others, the song was complete.

'Nice, isn't it?' the resident asked.

'This is you?' Anant said, mildly surprised.

'Yes.' The affirmation had come.

'You could create all this time?'

'Maybe, I had never tried before. I cannot be certain and I'd rather not feed you assumptions. It was only after your miracles the last time you visited that I tried to work some of my own magic. It worked, but nothing remained in the cell. It all just floated away.'

Anant clenched his jaw to stop himself from snapping at the resident for not revealing these developments that took place in the cell in his absence. The winds of rivalry were gathering pace, and even the adamant could be made to kneel. Anant was not one to ignore what was becoming rather obvious. The possibility that the resident and Anant weren't on the same side had become a probability, but Anant thought it was premature to believe with certainty that they were standing on opposite sides. No matter what side the resident was on, Anant was sure that reprimanding him would have been useless. 'Why do you think you can create now?' Anant inquired, thinking about how the cell that was never entirely his seemed to have drifted further away from him, and stood at the border between Anant and the resident.

'Same reason why you can create,' the resident replied defensively. So, the resident too felt competitive against him, Anant thought to himself. It was understandable, considering the cell was his home.

'I created the cell before you...appeared. Why do you think you can create now?' Silence. These possibilities, probabilities and certainties pushed Anant to an uncharted territory. Half-baked conclusions and baseless accusations lay ahead, which the resident could swat away by sticking to his defence of never having tried before. Saner thoughts prevailed. 'I suppose it no longer matters. Why don't you imagine a mode of transport, or a bridge that we can take to walk there?'

Long moments of quiet were broken by a deep sigh. 'Nothing. Not even like before, when it would appear and float away.'

'But you can still create in the cell?' Anant asked. A small emerald bourgeois chaise appeared and floated away, unaffected as it passed through the grey walls before suddenly vanishing when Anant thought that it was far too big.

'It didn't disappear before, just floated away.'

Building a premise, Anant turned to look at the record player, and 'Sam Hall' began to play.

'Try to change the song now.'

'It was stunning.' The resident mourned the loss of the chaise before following Anant's orders. 'I can't. I tried.'

'So, there is a hierarchy at play,' Anant thought to himself once his hypothesis was confirmed. The question that remained was how the resident had gained this power in the first place. Had he learned from him? Anant refused to believe it was as simple as monkey see monkey do, as the resident conveniently tried to make him believe. Anant turned to the window with a sigh, eyes languidly searching and resting on the midnight blue robes in an ocean of black, the archway on top of the precipice still out of his reach. With another heavy sigh, he returned to the mat.

'What makes you so certain that this far away land is of any consideration?' the resident asked.

'It's there, and it's beyond us. It must be of some significance.' Anant had never sounded more like a caveman.

'We have never set foot on the moon either. Once upon a time when it used to hang in the sky.'

'The moon was from my world. I had seen it there, like other memories, so it is not unheard of for it to be present in this world. This, it just appeared one day.' Anant could see no reason why the Gateway of India would appear as it did, as if it had been plucked from his memory and mutated to this current palace in the clouds.

'I hope you haven't forgotten visiting this fairy-tale far away land in your world.' The resident said. It did not merit a reply.

'How do you know that song?' Anant asked instead.

'"A Boy Name Sue?" It's a classic.'

'But how do you know it so well?'

'You must have heard it.'

'Perhaps.' Anant thought better than to tell him that he did not remember the song at all, that if he had, it would have played on its own accord along with the tatters of other tracks of 'American IV'. Anant tried to change the song and play 'A

Boy Named Sue' himself, but despite his squinting and staring, mental huffing and puffing, trying to force his thoughts on to the record player, he could not shift the needle or flip the record or whatever was required to play this song. He tried other songs that he knew the names of, but alas it was to the same result. He could not play any songs that weren't Johnny Cash's, and from his discography, only the tracks he remembered. All of which were from 'American IV'. Just knowing the title wasn't sufficient. 'Play it again.' Anant stared at the record player, waiting for the vinyl to change. 'Do it.'

'Believe me, I am trying. It's not working any more,' the resident replied. Anant leaned back with a huff. The moment he looked away from the record player, his attention occupied with his own frustration, the record reverted to 'A Boy Names Sue' with the dying of a cheer that lasted less than a second. 'It worked.'

Anant changed the record to 'Sam Hall' again and asked the resident to work his magic once more. Anant could imagine the roll of his eyes, the squinting in annoyance as he got to work again, and in the split second when Anant focused away from the record player and to the possibility that his hypothesis may be wrong, the resident managed to complete his trick and change the record. Having confirmed the existence of a hierarchy in this world already, with this exercise Anant brought clarity to how it worked. While he had learned that the cell wasn't entirely his own, not any more or perhaps never at all, he could now see that his own creations within the cell could also be affected by the resident if they were left to their own devices. Taking a calculated risk, Anant went ahead and explained the same to the resident, who responded with a half-hearted comment that Anant was merely blowing smoke up in his ass. But by feigning ignorance, Anant realized that the resident was indeed playing, and whether the side was directly opposing Anant or not, it was clear that the resident wasn't aligned with Anant. His curiosity satisfied, he returned to the task at hand. 'I am going over to the window. I want you to imagine anything that could take us to the precipice, or even close to it. A car, boat, it could be a bridge or a moving walkway. A f***ing rocket. Anything at all, go crazy.'

'I just don't want you complaining if my ways differ from yours. You are more plebeian when it comes to imagination, this place is as good an example as any,' the resident said.

Anant chose to reply with a curt nod to no one, more focused on the distant coveted land. He walked over to the window and stared into the abyss. His eyes frequently darted towards the midnight robes of the precipice but he managed to veer his mind away from trying to decipher the mystery. He had to allow the resident to create. He breathed out, time and again, readjusting his focus to the depthless abyss that was darker than a moonless sky. Darker than the colour black itself. Darker than when he would shut his eyes and no rays of light would touch his eyelids. Moments went by without Anant having to readjust his focus. Like a stone dropped in the middle of the ocean, he found himself sinking down into the quiet, away from his ambivalence towards the resident, away from the hierarchy and non-existent winds singing of battle. He thought he had found Zen for his mind no longer wandered. He couldn't focus away from the void even when he looked up or to his side. There was no precipice, no hues of dark blue from where the little light fought the void, and when his eyes fluttered open, he didn't remember ever closing them in the first place, he thought the light had finally cut through the abyss, for he was showered with vivid colours. Red, orange, yellow, green, blue, indigo and violet cascaded him. He could have sworn he saw a flash of a crescent made with sprinkles. Then the feel of the cotton cover of his pillow on the side of his face. Anant rolled around, and sure enough it was no longer his clothes but the feel of his bed sheet on his skin. He had returned to his flat.

Chapter 23

Like many aspects of their life together, the manner in which Monica and Sunil Vohra travelled differed in their method of preparation, but remained compatible in execution. Sunil had long since deemed the airport as no place of memories but one of apathy and sullen goodbyes. He felt that there were far too few positive energies floating in the airplane, like butterflies lost in the night, and at times he wanted to shake them and tell them to save themselves for the day, for when they could be admired and could brighten the day of others. But more often than not, people were on autopilot, interested in the destination rather than the plane ride itself or trying to be in harmony with the obtrusive technologies that made up the path to the plane. Sunil deemed that the time spent in airports and planes was time lost in transition between the two places, the buffer between two videos—an intermission. People came prepared to airports as if they were to duel with their arch nemesis. In the plane, buckled in, being disconnected was their greatest foe. They marched with downloaded shows and music, achieving what the schools never could—making the most energetic and lethargic people adhere to a shared structure, marking out the time they would spend on what activity, and what they would do for the rest of the journey. Sunil Vohra fell in line and merely trudged like the rest of them. Monica Vohra followed the same line, but for entirely different reasons. She did not like to travel by air. It was a source of anxiety for her. The feeling of being up in the clouds did not sit well with her. Being up in the air and floating away in her life was too much for her to bear. It made her feel uneasily light. She would strap herself to a seat before the belt light was turned on and wouldn't take the belt off until the plane landed, afraid that she might float away like a balloon and no ceiling would stop her. Or so she liked to believe, for the alternative was that she would be stuck on the ceiling and someone would eventually stick a needle in her and pop she would go. For her to travel by a plane, the window seat was a prerequisite. She had experienced the middle and aisle seat before—she had shut her eyes and soldiered on—but given her trepidation to travel by air it seemed an unnecessary burden to not have the window seat. The window allowed her to imagine that she was above the clouds, that the clouds were solid beneath her feet, and that she could walk around. It helped alleviate her fear of travelling by air. She hated it when the sun shone through the window because she suspected that she would sweat a bucket, even though there were no perspiration stains ever on her clothes. She was afraid that drenched in the extra weight, she would no longer float but fall. And just like the ceiling couldn't stop her, the floor wouldn't either and unlike Lucifer, she could not survive a fall from the clouds. She would close the window shades, and the window seat would become just like the other two. She preferred, in the order, sunset, night and sunrise. She avoided flights when the sun would be shining down on her. The only difference between sunset and sunrise was that the danger was still looming in the latter, depending on the duration of the flight.

Monica would begin packing a day before while Sunil would begin two days before they would leave. But more than the two days, he would start placing clothes in his suitcase or in a corner of his wardrobe, four or five days in advance. Monica would breeze through packing in three hours, evenly spread on the day before travelling.

The approaching wedding had festooned the house with

sprinkles of celebration that not only fooled the neighbours, but given their inclination to believe in it, the two Vohras had also been washed away by thoughts of the impending marriage. Upon clear reflection of the scenario, both would come to the same conclusion that apart from wishing for the best for Aarti, there was nothing to celebrate in the days before the wedding. Aarti, the bride, was in a different city and the wedding was also scheduled to take place in a different state. But given the rarity of such moments, they both knew better than to poke holes in this gift of a bite-sized celebration. Sunil had continued to make memories while planning all the things he would do to create further memories. He was finalizing his plans with excitement that mirrored the feelings of a child a day before his birthday. His meticulous and expansive plans, and vivid imagination had transformed his office into a war chamber that served the sole purpose of fighting the war on forgetfulness imposed by time. In the other side of the house, given Monica's new-found grasp on life, a reunion with the long-lost magic, she was in two minds long before her two days of packing, worrying about what stationery to take to the wedding and whether she would have time to dive into her world. These circumstances surrounded the residents while the festive mood patiently waited in the living room to be attended by them, and no doubt to be forgotten soon after they returned to their respective worlds, and repeated the cycle all over again.

A dozen days before the wedding, the Vohra couple sat together in the living room. Sunil had pulled out a photo album from the war chamber that hadn't been relegated to a box. They sat on the sofa going through the album. The first two pages had black-and-white photographs of their wedding. Aged and faded, the protective plastic pages made the photos shine under the warm lights of the room, and the fading looked like a by-product illusion cast by these lights. Sunil did not know what he was expecting when he pulled out the photo album, but strolling down memory lane hand in hand with Monica was not what he had imagined. Monica's siblings and her father, his mother and brother, so many faces lost in time. Time had drifted them away, like continents that were once a single great land mass, breaking up the flow of time. The others like their parents and Sunil's brother had been submerged, resting underneath with everyone and everything that time had swallowed in its belly, for Sunil and Monica both believed in an afterlife.

After her wedding Monica had tried to maintain contact with her siblings, but throughout her childhood she had looked after them as if it was her duty to do so, and when she was unchained by these fetters, it seemed only natural to drift away. They had written to her in the hope of finding their mother, even the rowdy first and the cunning second—this is what they had become, serial numbers with an adjective attached to them—had written to her, but despite their efforts and hers, she couldn't find it in herself to keep her mother's memory alive by pretending to be her any more. She tried at times to play the part but it didn't work without her being present with them. And without her, they soon learned to accept that their mother had passed, and Monica became the lost Trivedi sibling—the casualty of this ordeal, blurred and hidden behind the memory of their mother. They called her sometimes, and she did too, but everyone was busy in their respective lives and the lost Trivedi sibling wasn't high up on the list of siblings to contact. The Trivedi siblings without Monica shared a camaraderie because of their suffering of losing their mother, and Monica as well. Having grown up without a mother, the youngest Trivedi sibling still harboured a general curiosity about his sister. Not the kind that you wonder about during the lull of a day, but rather when you are waiting for the water to boil, or the microwave to warm the food. Alas, when Monica had picked up responsibilities after her mother, she had lost the part of her that allowed her to be a sister. The two converged, and the memory of a child did the rest—it blurred the roads to make them seem one, no matter how far away she looked. And the youngest Trivedi could never fulfil this curiosity. The six could never be seven again. At times, Monica would forget that she ever had siblings. That she was born eight years old, looking after children and her own father.

The photo that had blurred the most was one of the couple and both families on the day of the wedding. Everyone was present, and it seemed that the blur had taken after their memory and impacted the faces of Monica's siblings the most. Her father stood by her, and a strong resemblance could be seen between the two of them whose faces were rather clear in the photograph—Monica shared her father's neat and strong features. Sunil was visible and so was his brother and mother, and though their clothes may have begun to fade, both his family members remained untouched by the blur. It was as if out of sheer will he had kept the faces and the contrasts of their clothes from fading.

Their gander was awarded by the heavy burden of reflecting on a life that flew by, which is every life in retrospect. Sunil went to the kitchen to make them tea when the phone rang. He picked up the call while the water was boiling on the stove. It was his sister-in-law on the line. Monica could not hear the conversation. Sunil's momentary gasp pulled her away from the photo album. Minutes went by, with Sunil keeping quiet for the most of it, and other times murmuring words of comfort. When the call ended, the tea had been made. He strained the tea, poured it into transparent cups, and returned with two steaming cups of green tea and a plate of coconut biscuits atop a tray. It was jasmine green tea with ginger. In his recent endeavours, Sunil had perfected the art of tea making. He knew by instinct how much ginger to use. Monica picked up the cup and took in the aroma. Sunil blew into the cup to make sure the tea had reached the perfect temperature for a sip. Warm, but not hot. Monica waited patiently. The lines on Sunil's forehead were prominent. 'The wedding is cancelled,' Sunil told Monica, who did not know how to take the news. It didn't upset her immediately, for she did not know the reason and to declare it a watershed moment seemed premature. She turned towards Sunil and stared at him. It seemed that while the news may have upset him at first, with enough tea and time, he ended up sharing the same train of thought as her. The lines on his forehead faded like waves washing away the tyre tracks on a beach, only the ones that were engraved remained. 'We should call Aarti,' he said, and let out a deep sigh. 'After tea.'

'After tea,' Monica agreed.

Chapter 24

It was a bright humid day in Mumbai. The sun seemed to be taking centre stage by shining brighter and harsher than it had all season. The crowds of people out in the city—collectively perspiring, with sweat dripping down their bodies and soaking their clothes—walking on the pavements, and roads mirrored the thousands of people seen during Mumbai rains. Anant understood that the agitation he felt was being misdirected at the city, for he was having a bad day because of the stifling weather and hordes of people. Having been unceremoniously ripped away from the cell before he could solve the mystery of the precipice or even exhaust the possibilities that could bring him closer to the little light and the midnight robes, Anant was left with a troubled mind and a sense of frailty. The sweat trickling down his forehead and his shirt sticking to his back were on the periphery of his concerns. The real problem was his mind, and the sense of vulnerability that was ailing Anant. These were worse than the sun, leaving him on unsteady ground, as if he was missing a tangent between his mind and self, his body and self. He felt like he had been dismissed by the retreat, spat out by the cell like a bad piece of gum. And so, while his body struggled against the weather, and his mind rattled around birthing nebulous thoughts whose origin remained obscure, he now carried the aura of the other—the resident—and their fate was to float away. Anant struggled to belong anywhere, even within himself. He was perpetually caught in two minds and neither seemed to be feasible options, for he wasn't sure what would float away. He arrived at the site at two o'clock, but could only spend thirty minutes before he had to flee. His choices of refuge were limited. He couldn't return to his flat for there was nothing to do there but dive into his mind. He couldn't turn to the beach or the Gateway of India because the sun had risen with cruel intentions. A mall was the only banal answer he could come up with, but the hordes of people standing atop one another, whispering, talking, and shouting, would have made his unsteady ground tremble under the weight of it all. All Anant could do was follow the immediate—believing and hoping that the immediate was his, for he was the first to perceive the world around him.

Anant arrived at the local market near Rajat's flat, leaving a trail of sweat along his path like a snail. He entered a restaurant that predominantly delivered food but it seemed that some wayward souls managed to find their way to the glass door because they kept a handful of plastic chairs for these damned few. A bottle of ketchup sat in the middle of every wooden table, all five of them, each progressively flimsier than the last. The joints of the ceiling fans creaked with each rotation, showing their age. But his impulse to follow a thought hadn't been futile, for he found momentary stillness when he sat down and browsed through the menu. He ordered a vada pao, the Indian burger. Anticipation bubbled in his stomach at the thought of the food. And then, as if to spite his heart and stomach, his mind decided that it had been ignored long enough and began to jump around once again, rolling down thoughts like boulders falling from the sky, the tremors of which ravaged his unsteady self and all his efforts to stretch the momentary peace were undone. The sound of utensils, the constant phone calls for orders and the chatter that leaked out of the ktichen, TV anchors screaming at the top of their lungs, a repeat telecast as if news no longer needed to be recent, but like TV soaps only needed to have the masala. Without the awareness to guide it away, the noise began to invade his ears till his mind had a ringing soundtrack to accompany its frolic. He left the restaurant in a hurry after finishing his food in large barely chewed bites. The sun resumed barbequing him while he called for a cab, thinking he'd head to a museum, that it had been a long time since he had visited Dr. Bhau Daji Lad Museum, and again, his mind paved two roads ahead, as he remembered a place Rajat had told him that he had visited, a place that allowed him to be still. He took the long cab drive to the Jehangir Art Gallery. The cab drive itself was torturous, sitting still in the back with nothing to defend him against his mind's onslaught of suggestions that were being flung at him one after another. 'F*** this, let's go to a bar,' his mind screamed at him. 'What good will a bar do, let's head to the beach,' his mind screamed back. 'You're a piece of shit, you know that? You can't decide what to do. Are you even real?' the mind retorted. And on and on, plucking out different locations, foods, drinks, songs, following it by offering a different suggestion, and in the midst of this confusion, pestering Anant who had labelled the suggestions as fake. The radio was too loud, which pushed him to tell the driver to lower the volume; the barrage of ads, the posters and billboards outside the window—everything was screeching at him while the trepidation over his choice of the museum screamed from within. 'A museum, really? Why don't you hide in your little corner?' Retreat, Anant thought to himself with biting irony, what he needed was a retreat, perhaps one that he could enter at any time.

Anant stepped into the art gallery, ignoring the prints lined along the footpath, only to pause and continue jumping from painting to installation, mimicking his mind. His mind just wouldn't allow him to settle on any art nor be still in the café or the antique dealer in the basement. The surreal paintings made him uneasy and sculptures and artefacts weighed him down, as if a coil was tightening in his chest and was beginning to crush his lungs. The last thing he wanted was to further blur the line between this world and the other. He didn't last half an hour before he was outside on the portico of the gallery gasping for air. Mumbai had finally managed to turn away from the sun, which was bleeding into the sky. As the sun continued to set, Anant berated himself for taking the fruitless long ride to Kala Ghoda. 'What now?' he asked and paused for a moment. He waited as if he was expecting an answer from someone. Be it from the resident, or his mind that seemed to have a will of its own, but he waited nonetheless. Another thought floated to the forefront of his consciousness, one that he grabbed with both hands so he wouldn't have time to consider the suggestion that followed. A ride to Malad to get a tattoo from the shop he had noticed during the time of the tree that grew from his grave. He got into a cab, but never made it to Malad. Rebelling against his mind midway through the journey, he changed the location to the flat. 'My mind be damned!' he thought. Anant refused to bow down to the whims of an uncertain mind. He remembered how he had fought against the tree, and though the times were darker, too dark to see, he had his intuition to rely on. Anant believed that the resident couldn't possibly anticipate the intuitive mind. He stopped by an alcohol shop to buy a bottle, and considered buying wine but the iconic simple black label of Jack Daniel's made the decision for him. Another way to spite his mind that had suggested a cognac. His plan was to dull his mind into obeying him, much like a doctor drugs a patient in a mental hospital. And he hoped that the entity he suspected was responsible for his unappeasable mind, for he couldn't blame himself for the sense of vulnerability, would get the message. The doughnut theory, as the resident had put it. All he needed to do was be absorbed in something, and it would reach the resident. 'Well, I will flood him with alcohol,' Anant thought to himself. He kept his eyes fixed on the bottle during the drive back to his flat, as if he were in the midst of an intimate moment.

Tormented by the duality of choices that his mind constantly projected, and a duality of self, him and Anant Vohra, him and the resident, Anant turned to the ways of the god of duality and drowned himself in Dionysian revelry until he had subdued his mind. His plan worked, eventually. Anant was unsure if it was the work of the alcohol on his mind, or if the resident had been flooded into silence, but he was pleased with the results nonetheless. He staggered back to sit on the wingback chair, put his legs on the coffee table, having brought the needle of the turntable to the edge of the record. 'No Blues' from the album *Smokin at the Half Note* started playing once more. But Anant despite his gratification remained blue, a darker blue, a midnight blue, for entirely different reasons.

Seconds ticked on and turned to minutes that became hours and Anant was drunk by the time his phone rang. It was a call from his father. To his surprise, both his parents were on the line. The tag-team could only signal trouble, and Anant put his legs down and sat with his back straight. Small talk followed, everybody was fine, and nobody was up to anything in particular. Anant's mind had been fished out of the ocean and it began to feed him the possibilities of why this call was made. It was kinder to him, as if the time out had brought it back to its senses. Anant could feel the faint lingering hiss of death, and he struggled against the drizzle of thoughts of what could have happened. 'Have you booked your tickets for the wedding?' Sunil finally inquired.

'Not yet, when and from where should I leave for the wedding?' Anant's shoulders dropped immediately, relieved, and he slouched on the chair once more. His only focus was to keep his voice from slurring.

'Don't book the tickets,' Monica told him. Momentary anxiety erupted in Anant and disappeared just as quickly, as if his mind had remembered its disdain and tried to use this opportunity to impale him with a new problem but his clear memory of the evening in the bar with Aarti shielded him. If she had rescinded his invitation, Anant thought to himself, it would have little to do with that night. Monica broke the news. 'The wedding is cancelled.'

Anant was surprised at his own self-centred reaction. He was a lightweight, and alcohol had eroded the etiquette of the mind that helped him process information in ways as to adhere to the normal. Upon hearing the news, Anant jumped over the concern and was met with relief, relief at the validity of his memory, relief that there hadn't been any bad news concerning his parents, and then, relief at knowing that he wouldn't have to go through the tedious cycle of meeting every distant relative of someone who was once a neighbour of his grandparents whom he hardly knew, or entertain a superfluous conversation with people who had seen him as a child once upon a time and were holding it over his head as if trying to establish their importance in his life. But primarily, away from the exaggerated versions of the monotonous interactions that he found unnecessary and to be the coarse thread in the fabric of society. Anant was relieved that he wouldn't have to risk attempting to wade through the wedding with a part of his mind indulging in the overhaul of his retreat and a resident with ulterior motives that may or not may not be directly in opposition to him. Once in a fit of spiteful imagination that was either his or had been sowed by the resident, Anant had envisaged a change in power, a coup d'état while he was in the web of unavoidable distractions of the wedding. While Anant courted these thoughts, the silence stretched on and in Pune, sitting on the couch with her husband holding the phone, Monica considered the possibility that Anant could be taking the news harder than she had expected. Sunil called out his name to make sure he was still on the line, and to indicate that he should say something. 'That's too bad for her. What happened?' It wasn't like Anant to be inquisitive about either side of his parents' family.

'We haven't called her yet. Well, we did, but she hasn't returned our call. Poor thing might need some time,' Sunil said. 'Do you think we should visit her?' he added with concern for no one in particular.

'No, let her pick up the phone before we decide anything,' Monica replied. 'The worst thing we can do is just show up.'

Whether it was the alcohol that loosened his tongue or Anant could not trust his unsteady self to find a solution to his problem, but when enough time had passed Anant found it appropriate to change the topic. At great jeopardy to his hermitage that had become increasingly entangled in the world, he turned to his parents for advice. 'Hey, uh, do you two ever...and I am not trying to cause any fear...' Anant had to clarify because any troubles that he did tell them about, his parents had a tendency of overreacting. Anant understood that he was partially at fault for this reaction, it was rare for him to come to anyone for advice, making such a moment always grander, or graver, than it needed to be. But just by saying these words he opened the gates to hell and there was nothing to do but march through them. It would have been barbaric of him to not finish the thought and let their imaginations create monsters. 'Do you ever have days when your mind is just...not in alignment with you?' And then there was silence. Anant was regretting his decision already. In the Vohra house, Monica gripped Sunil's arm to quiet him. She put a finger on her lips, and waited, turning the very silence that Anant had built around himself against him. 'Hey, it's not that serious. I don't want you thinking anything is wrong. Just one of those days.' Anant broke the quiet to justify himself.

'What days?' Sunil inquired, aware through years of experience that without the comfort of silence that Monica had just seized, a direct approach would pierce through any remaining defences and cause his son to unravel. Such was the cunning duo of Monica and Sunil, executing their tag-team manoeuvres in tandem with each another.

'Just on edge. Like my mind is not entirely my own,' Anant whispered the last sentence, out of fear of eavesdropping ears that could be present within him.

'Today?' Monica asked.

'Yes, today. It happens sometimes, like back when I was in school. It wasn't just puberty.' He gave out a chuckle to try and cut the tension. Neither of the two bought his superficial laughter. 'It's funny how you imagine every problem in your teenage years to merely be puberty. Of course, in hindsight, at the time it's the end of the world.' Anant tried once again before finally accepting that he failed on both counts—damage control and trying to navigate the conversation away from his troubles.

'It happens to everyone, Anant,' Monica told him. 'Try to go where your mind wants to take you. It might not be what you want, but perhaps what you need.'

'No, I say you stick to a routine. These things happen in passing. Your mind will eventually fall in line,' Sunil added. 'Just stick to what you do, okay. Do not drift between the lines.' Sunil had channelled Nostradamus, and neither of the three realized it.

'Yes, it was just an odd day, that's all. Nothing to worry about.' Under the excuse of trying to ease his parents' concern, Anant tried to reassure himself that nothing was wrong. 'I will see you soon. Have a good evening…good night,' he said, and after his parents wished him the same, the call came to an end.

Anant leaned back in the leather chair and let out a heavy sigh of defeat. He had shared more with his parents than he had intended to. For a bleeding heart, hospitable ears are akin to medicine. Yet, he did not see his loose tongue as a product of his mind teetering between his thoughts and that of the resident's, nor did he see it as the result his parents' smarts, but instead he chose to believe it was the effect of the alcohol. He poured himself another drink while considering their advice. A routine, or to allow himself to drift away with his mind. He found it strange that his mother had given him advice that was the opposite of what she would have done. And his father had followed suit. Anant had already spent the day doing the opposite of what his father told him, constantly allowing himself to be pulled to both, and doing neither. When he had returned home with the bottle of bourbon, he attempted to drift away with his mind, like he was hitchhiking with these thoughts that never took him with them as they floated away. But upon further scrutiny, Anant realized that his attempts were destined to fail because he had a foot on the ground. He was wary of these diluted thoughts, and the source of these thoughts. He was jumping off before he floated away with them. It took him some time to dissect the advice, and choose which direction he wanted to take. He put the record back in the sleeve and took out another, Godowsky's *Renaissance*. With his drink in hand, he stretched his back, positioned the arm on the edge of the record, and sat on the mat with his notebook in the other hand. Maybe he would read a book if he couldn't sketch, he thought to himself. And stick to it. Like a routine. A routine for one day. And if this didn't work, he told himself he would fly away with thoughts, to the moon or even to the cell.

Anant paused in his reading to take a moment to stretch once again, the notebook resting on the mat underneath his thigh.

There was a numbness in him that stretching could not diminish, as if he were a bomb slowly ticking away. The explosion of all he had been drinking was unavoidable but underneath it, the coil that tightened in his chest had remained, as if attached to a greater explosion. One that slithered from his chest to his stomach. A bomb without any ticking, growing in heat as it concocted its own explosion. Anant was unsure if the explosion was avoidable, and thoughts of mortality returned with an impassive acceptance of the after-effects. A bomb that would not harm the body or even the resident, but only him, the one behind the name and the decisions. He shook his head and pulled the notebook from underneath his thigh, flipping through the pages to his recent drawing. He had sketched an archway on top of a precipice overlooking the abyss with the sequestered cell lost in the distance, like a bottle with a message of what once was, floating amidst the invisible tides of the abyss. It was rough work with shoddy lines, but it was what he had had in mind when he had begun sketching. He thought if he could visualize the precipice, he would be able to work more efficiently in his next visit to the cell. The only goal in sight was to reach the bedrock, and climb to the precipice. The light at the end of the tunnel, vying to be seen, to be reached. How he would reach the light, reach the precipice, he did not know. The sketch helped him clean the image that was in his mind, even though he had taken creative liberties as he progressed in his sketch of what lay hidden in the midnight robes that clouded the structure. He had added bas-reliefs and engravings on the archway, mostly mindless doodles of reapers, with or without skulls, and scythes. He also drew eyes. Single eyes, pairs of eyes, human eyes, blank eyes, crow eyes and cat eyes, eyes with different flecks and irises, varied in shading, the archway was full of eyes. It was beginning to look like a long-lost recount of the battle between reapers and eyes. And engraved on the very top of the archway was a giant doughnut with a crescent of sprinkles. Away from this sketch, he had read thirty-something pages of a book. He was a slow reader, and took his time to appreciate sentences and in his state, slur them to see how they sounded. It was equal parts carpentry and design. Certain details caught his eye and he would reread paragraphs or ponder over what Carl Jung had seen. He was reading Jung's semi-autobiography titled *Memories, Dreams and Reflections*. The title had caught his eye when he was browsing through art books online, months ago. He had never got around to reading it until now. 'It is a shame that I won't remember much of it tomorrow,' Anant thought to himself. 'Maybe I will begin reading it again tomorrow.'

Five and a half hours of the bottle later, Anant got up from his mat to a wobbling world that he met with false steps until finally his feet were firmly planted on the floor. Anant wasn't a heavy drinker, in fact he mostly avoided drinking, despite the increased frequency in these past few weeks, and half of a bottle was raging a storm in him. He closed the notebook and slid it in the shelf beneath the record player before striding over to the balcony, chewing on the back of a pencil. A lonely moon hung up above, looking down at the city with indifference. It was a solemn night and the absence of stars made for a dismal mood. The ecstasy had faded, Anant wondered if madness awaited him now. He continued to gaze into the sky, focused, now used to trying to decipher distant images, and managed to make out one or two stars, like flecks of chalk dust on an otherwise pristine blackboard. Cars, bikes and autos, along with people on foot were scattered all over the road, trudging their way back home— having lived through the malicious sun, hoping that it would be more benevolent tomorrow. And some, in a twist of all they had been told about waking up and going to sleep early, were

headed to work. Anant checked the time again. It was thirty
minutes past eleven. Four hours and fifteen minutes since the
call. Anant kept track of the call to quantify how long he had
stuck to a routine. The advice had worked. He had coaxed his
mind into burying itself in the book and the music. He declared
to himself that he would spend the next few minutes watching
the movements on the road, coming and going like the ticking
of a clock. Like the ticking of the bomb that he couldn't hear.
Every now and then, a car or a bike louder than the rest would
cut through the clamour of the streets, and he would jerk back
not knowing why, before he would listen to the noise as it would
slowly fade away. He was alive, he muttered to himself. Was it
a statement or a reminder? Anant peered into the palms of his
hands, staring at the lines of his hands, of his wrist. His eyes
travelled up his forearms and back to his palms. 'Anant Vohra,'
he said to himself. 'The other... The resident.' It wasn't the
same. He was still Anant Vohra, despite any control the resident
may have over his mind, his body remained his own. Had the
resident sowed the seeds of such a possibility while he was in
the cell, much like he had sowed the rivalry that Anant had
never felt before this visit? More questions cloaked in obscurity,
more answers that demanded leaps of faith. He returned to the
living room and sat on the grand chair, his heavy eyes shut to
distance him from his surroundings. The world spinning seemed
far away now, like he was watching it from a secure bunker. Or
from up above, as if he were sitting on the moon, bathing in the
silver light that cleansed him of the resident. 'Anant Vohra,' he
repeated to himself out loud. The sound seemed more real than
the music that somehow managed to follow him to the moon
while the world continued to spin. 'Anant Vohra.' He continued
to repeat at irregular intervals like a chant.

'Anant Vohra.' There was no longer any sound. He tried

again, and once more, it came out a thought. He opened his eyes to find himself on a mat similar to the one in his flat, a mahogany floor beneath him, and grey brick walls around him. Anant did not take long to adjust to his new surroundings. He jumped up to his feet and ambled to the window. The abyss awaited him. It was as it was before. The little light, it seemed, had done all it could. No more did it cut through the abyss, the same dark hues of blue cascaded around the silhouette of the precipice.

'You should take a peek out of the door,' the resident remarked.

Without replying, Anant walked to the doorway and peered out. Nothing. A void. He looked around, wondering what the resident was talking about. And finally, Anant looked up and found in the distance the doughnut with a crescent of sparkling sprinkles pinned up to what seemed like the ceiling of the abyss. It was like a full moon hung on a starless sky. 'The doughnut theory.' The resident was pleased with himself. Anant could hear the grin in his voice.

'Did you do that?'

'Would I have the power to?' the resident retorted.

Anant sighed and shook his head when out of the corner of his eye he caught a new entrant in the cell. In the corner, coiled in a bottle, was *Memories, Dreams and Reflections*. 'I'm afraid I'm unacquainted with the book,' the resident said.

'Were you creating a lot while I was gone?' Anant asked. He knew the answer, and when the resident affirmed it, Anant closed his eyes and reminded himself that he was indeed Anant Vohra. 'But managed nothing to take us there.'

'I tried.' The resident paused, and chose to indulge Anant. 'Nothing worked. I even thought of a catapult, like in that game...' the resident trailed off trying to remember it.

Anant knew which game he was talking about. He used to

play it every day during his free time on the computer when he was growing up. He waited for the resident to move on, but finally, he said 'Age of Empires'.

'Age of Empires 2,' the resident was quick to correct Anant, satisfied at having baited him so easily.

'You planned to have us shot?'

'Catapulted,' the resident corrected him once again. 'And you said you wouldn't comment on my creative prowess.' No wonder Anant was jumping here and there, when a part of him was dreaming of being catapulted.

If walking was a possibility, Anant considered, if he knew that he could climb out of the window and not fall into the depthless void, Anant knew he would find himself back in the cell every time he blinked. Running through the various scenarios in his mind, there seemed to be only one logical step to take. 'If we can't go to the precipice, is there no way to push the cell itself to it?' Anant inquired, aware of where this was leading to. If it worked, Anant would gladly let the resident have his glory.

Silence. Anant could almost hear the resident taking his time to register the words that had been spoken. 'You mean a massive catapult?' The resident was giddy and astonished that Anant would not only agree with his stratagem, but encourage him to think even bigger. Anant swore that he could hear him laugh a silent laugh, ruminating over the possibilities.

An abrupt sound cut through their conversation, echoing in Anant's mind and reverberating in the cell. Before the reverberations could end, the echo began again, giving further life to the reverberations, and on and on. There was no record on the turntable, the needle sitting pretty in its position. 'What is that?' Anant asked but there was no reply. There was no other sound but the ringing that began to slice through the cell, more and more of the structure was cut through at regular intervals and would dissipate, leaving Anant standing on the floor with the void flooding in. Anant hurried around the disintegrating cell to inspect what was happening, but before he knew it, the floor that remained crumbled and he fell. A brief flash of colours later, the same sequence of colours, Anant noted despite his confusion—red, orange, yellow, green, blue, indigo and finally violet—he opened his eyes to find himself back on the chair, his hands instinctively reaching for the arms of the chair. The ringing died while Anant was trying to collect himself and calm his racing heart. The source of the sound was the phone in his pocket, Anant noted. He was in his flat in Mumbai. He was Anant Vohra. He slipped the phone out to check who had called him at this hour of the night. In the back of his mind was an image, Anant could have sworn that he landed on the moon after he fell, right after the explosion of colours and before he woke up in the real world. The moon that was the doughnut in that world. He rubbed his eyes before squinting at the screen. He had a missed call from Aarti.

Chapter 25

'I didn't wake you up, did I?' came Aarti's voice from the other end of the line. There was a weight in her voice that was absent when Anant had last met her, making her sound older and weary.

'I was up.' The small nap in the form of a brief visit to the cell had cured Anant of his slurring.

'Oh, that's good,' Aarti replied, and silence settled on the phone. She could hear him breathe, ragged and hurried, like he had just stopped jogging and was trying to steady his breath before she had called him. 'So…my wedding is cancelled.' Despite all that had happened, sitting alone in her hotel room with a drink in her hand, she allowed herself to smile at the thought. It was her little secret, and as long as she had the power over the story, she could bask in the comfort that this secret brought her.

'What happened?' Anant asked.

'It's a long story. I don't…' Aarti trailed off. 'But it is why I called you,' she said and mused, as though she was going over her options of what to say next. For a moment, she wanted to keep the story a mystery, something hers forever. But she had called him to say her piece. When had he become a telephonic confessional booth, she didn't know, but a part of her, having seen her father's face in place of Anant's on that fated day in the Vohra household, believed she could be talking to both, to Anant, and through Anant, by merely sharing what she had to say, she believed that her father could hear her as well. He definitely could, she thought. And there was another part of her that was bursting at the seams from the constant effort and strain of keeping the details, despite the power that the secret brought her.

'Go on.' Anant got up and walked to the balcony to be away from the music. There was a fleeting thought of a catapult once again, but out of sheer will he put a cork in the hole that was leaking such thoughts to him. He could do nothing about the thoughts that were floating in his mind, but he could at least make the resident wait. 'What happened?'

As Aarti ventured into her story, she was faced with a turmoil of emotions, and the only thing that kept her from being blown away by the storm and the uncertainty of her morals and emotions was a single truth, that she was no longer resigned to being a passive spectator of life. Whether what she had done was just or unjust, she did not care. Life, she considered, was not just or unjust either. Samsa, in *The Metamorphosis*, had to die so his family could change. What was just in his death? Who was dying here? No one, she thought to herself. Only an idea. The circumstances were changing because of it. And she was at the helm of it, no longer content in deluding herself that her cocoon was contentment. That things no longer just happened or were merely happening to her, but happening because of her. Perhaps they always did, she thought to herself, collecting her thoughts to bring forth her story. She decided to begin from the time when Anant had helped her to her room. Two people from the conference had seen her leaning on him as the Vohra cousins staggered up to her room. She had been leaning for support, but her colleagues had a tendency, or rather it was ingrained in them by being constantly injected with gossip, a tendency to jump to a conclusion that reeked of bias since it would invariably be a confirmation of what they already believed, of things they could giggle and gasp at later. One of them called Ravi. It was a simple misunderstanding, but caught in a hangover she wasn't ready for the bombardment from the anxious Ravi who was aware of the debauchery that took place on the last day of a conference. He charged with an attack rather than an inquisition, which perhaps could be understandable given the situation. When her lack of an answer did not ease his worries, and she was rather glad that she did not feel obligated to answer the questions posed by her fiancé for it had only been a case of confusion for her, her clouded mind unable to comprehend what was happening, the outburst that followed gave her a rare chance at life once again. There she was, with a phone lying beside her on the bed, the loudspeaker on, a scarlet "A" pinned on her chest, not for adultery but apathy. She felt like Meursault from Albert Camus' *The Stranger*, but she had committed no murder. She remained sprawled on the bed staring at the ceiling, at the recently cleaned white vents of the air conditioner, no longer sure if he continued his accusations, or they became indictments, or judgements.

The other person who had seen Anant enter her room was a friend who helped track the one that had called Ravi. He was a colleague, they both worked in the same office in Gurugram. Can a cog of the machine be beyond redemption? Are the manipulated as much to blame as the manipulator, if the crimes are damning? What if the crimes are merely hollow, with whom does the fault lie? With an aspirin-induced clarity of mind, Aarti was able to clear the confusion with ease. With some persuasion and a monetary offer that was too good to refuse, Aarti was able to convince the hotel authorities to show the camera footage which revealed Anant entering the hotel with Aarti and leaving without her within minutes. She recorded the video and sent it to Ravi, who had been told that he had stayed overnight. When this colleague of hers saw the tide change, saw the fire he had sparked roar around him, much to the shock of Aarti and her friend, he began to defend himself by saying things still could have taken place, that it wasn't proper. He would have continued, living in his own world woven by the gossip until her friend silenced him with a glare. And then, for the final act that led to the end, Aarti sent him some childhood and family photos after the person's face was confirmed. They were cousins who grew up around each other. They shared the same last name. It wasn't needed, but she continued, seizing the opportunity that fate had given her, an exit from the ride that she had stumbled on. To paraphrase Camus, she did not know what ride interested her, but she knew which didn't. And so, message after message, she continued to bombard Ravi with proof even when he accepted his fault. He apologized saying she did not need to offer any proof and that he trusted her. 'What trust?' Aarti had spat back at him over the phone. Her colleague flinched, having to stand by her side to live through his embarrassment in front of Aarti and her friend.

'What trust falls at the first sight of suspicion,' she said with Anant on the other side of the conversation. Hysteria, no doubt in Aarti's mind, was the conclusion that Ravi must have arrived at. She found it hilarious how his own jumble of emotions had never been branded as hysteria, but hers, given that her chromosome repeated while he had the variety of two, had been relegated to hysteria. He said he was booking a flight to Mumbai. That he would meet her in the hotel, have a chat in his flat.

'Like a Band-Aid,' Aarti said. 'I told him I couldn't marry a man who would behave in such a way because of gossip. He wanted to call my outburst hysteria, he did call me irrational, accidentally I think, because he very quickly tried to make me believe that I was just hearing things. Because of course it was better that my ears were to be blamed rather than his hypocrisy...' Aarti trailed off with a sigh. 'I knew that he could be insecure, that much of his screaming was harmless anger, but...'

'You ripped the Band-Aid.' Anant knew that he felt something about being involved in this mess, but it was increasingly taking more attention to grasp the emotions he was feeling and he decided that now wasn't the time to try and decipher them.

'You know, just like that person who had called Ravi must have added his own masala to it, I am sure people will add masala to what he must have shouted at me. If they haven't already. And it might hurt, perhaps, it must, mustn't it, but for now, at least, the pain of the Band-Aid has subsided and before the irritation from the scarring begins, I have a few moments to wash the wound in peace.'

'Is there a wound?'

'I think I want there to be one. I hope so. If losing something doesn't hurt, would keeping it have been any different? I did like Ravi. I don't want you to believe that he is a bad person.' Aarti clenched her jaw, trying to find the right words. 'Just... I don't know. I don't.' Anant remained quiet, giving little sounds to let her know he was listening. 'Bad timing, maybe,' Aarti murmured.

And silence presided over them once again. What was there to be said. Anant knew they weren't close enough for his condolences to matter and Aarti believed that the Vohra cousins were distant enough for Anant to not be bothered with any attempts at consoling her. There was an unsaid agreement between the two to simply sit in silence, and let time wash away the story. A morose minute passed and Aarti was comfortable to bring the conversation to an end. 'Anant, thank you. Even if just for meeting me. I feel better than I sound. And it...this wouldn't have happened if you had declined in the first place. And also for helping me up to my room. That was nice of you.'

'You're welcome.' Anant had questions he wanted to ask, but these were birthed in momentary curiosity that he would soon forget himself. He had no interest in this voyeuristic eagerness to know someone's personal life. Perhaps this indifference was to a fault, given how the person in question was his own cousin. Distant cousin, a reoccurring meteor shining by his planet. Too distant to hold any weight in the interaction. 'And I am happy for you.' Anant realized that the faded resentment he held for her had disappeared completely somewhere between the announcement of her marriage, and this declaration of having cancelled the wedding. If such a resentment ever existed, and wasn't the product of a child's tendency to dramatize his emotions, which had been projected as the truth, for he remembered how he had fondly looked back to her presence in his memories of childhood. The only problem he ever had was with her smile that had recently receded and lost its naivety. It made Aarti more real to him than ever before.

Aarti cut the call with a smile that she greeted like an old friend that had been lost in her hectic life. She stared at the mirror to admire this smile, not for its charm, nor symmetry, but for the purity of it. Untouched by people and the collective will of the muscles around her lips, it had risen from her heart. Life had slipped by somewhere along the way, and the cocoon she had built had been swarmed by time, till it loosened, till the bubble wraps that once protected her from the shock of her father's passing fell. Her inaction drowned her, and now that she had finally made the right decisions, or at least finally made decisions that were of substance, the waters were calmer, and this heart-stirring, stomach-warming happiness was her reward. And relief from finally breathing without any bubble-wrap confinement. She stared at the mirror, eyes caressing her reflection, alone in the bathroom and alone in her mind. When she shut off the light to return to her room, she caught a brief glimpse of her face and the smile on her face had waned. For happiness was as rewarding as it was fleeting, and her future still lay ahead of her. What now?

Chapter 26

Boxes on top of boxes had begun piling on the plastic covering the grey marbled floor in Rajat's flat. Iqbal walked from box to box, inspecting it for damages, and orchestrating the workers to carefully unbox the myriad of products that had begun to arrive since the morning. Dandekar sahib, who had overseen the electrical work, was guiding multiple electricians as they connected the ACs and the water softener, checking every socket with a TV or a lamp, while the rest of the TVs were being installed by Aamir and other carpenters. The fridge was to arrive in two to three hours. The final coat of the navy paint had dried, and the fumes of polish had dwindled to leave the flat in a rather relaxing aroma. Watching the flat come together, Anant struggled to believe the work done by him. He had never worked on a site like this, never had an assignment like this—the sheer volume of the job, the number of hands that built this site, many of whom had moved on to other jobs, the daily visits to the flat, the inspection of work, the constant intrusions of Rajat. It was clear that the assignment demanded more than any previous job, but it had required more than Anant thought he was capable of. The array of sketches in a range of designs that once filled his portfolio briefcase now sealed in the envelope, the trade he had made complete. He received half of the payment in an envelope and Dandekar sahib told him that the other half would be transferred to his account.

A beautiful sofa with intricate woodwork, starting from the precisely carved legs going up to the delicately turned armrest, that had arrived in the morning had been the centre of attention of the flat ever since. It was a stunning Biedermeier sofa that would have caught the eye of any onlooker. The print on the couch was of lilies, peonies, roses and carnations, all in a variety of colours as if remembering a spring in Eden. It was a gift from Rajat's dad. Rajat sat on the couch with an ease as if the couch had been built to accommodate him. The beauty had enchanted him just as it had done the workers, and he glanced around the room pleased with the reactions. The contractors adhered to his unspoken wish and showered him with compliments, and the workers followed their lead. Rajat revelled in the unwavering charm of the sofa. Aamir was in awe of the work, as if it hurt to see something that may just be beyond his capabilities. His contractor took a sharp intake of breath every time Aamir would glance at the couch, even in passing as he scurried here and there, installing TVs, and making last-minute adjustments to screws and nails. Kartik had gone down to help with the unloading, and to oversee all that was coming, along with some labour to assist him. Somehow, the pair had been separated, and Marathi, now without Kartik to steer him around, walked up to Rajat with wide eyes and a grin revealing his missing teeth, telling him he looked like a maharaja while sitting on the couch, and the world would be in awe if they saw him. Rajat joked that he should sit and feel like a raja too. The demotion of position in the compliment was lost to everyone in the room but Rajat. Although he did not wish to come across as a person who was too keen to receive compliments, Rajat could barely contain the big smile on his face after hearing Marathi's remark.

Anant finished his glass of water and announced that he was leaving. 'I'll walk you out,' Rajat said, and swaggered past the door and to the lobby. 'My man, you have done great work.' Rajat complimented him while they waited for the lift to ascend. 'This is what I envisioned. You have helped me bring it to life.'

'Except the couch.' Anant paused, as if testing the effect of the words, watching them stretch and cast a shadow on Rajat's face. Though Rajat liked to portray his mind as this entangled mess of a genius, Anant had learned that a pull at any string would unravel this mirage that Rajat's convictions had created, leaving him subject to his baser instincts. The current lack of stability of own mind had propelled Anant to this childish and rather malevolent course of action. As if by proving himself right about Rajat and the workings of his mind he would somehow become more qualified with his own mind. Anant had never thought any more or less of Rajat because of this, every person has a weakness, he told himself that he was merely confirming what had been floating between a hypothesis and a theory. And the clench of Rajat's jaw, the sudden darting of his eyes, the nervous tick in his jerky movements that he hid behind bravado, Anant confirmed the theory before continuing. 'It's the jewel that makes the crown.' Anant was immediately ashamed by his tasteless action, even before he finished the compliment, seeing it for the malicious and unneeded drama that it was. 'Perhaps Rajat managed to rub off on me,' Anant thought to himself.

A smile threatened to appear on Rajat's face that he quickly hid behind the clenching of his jaw. Anant's stunt did not register with him, only the compliment. 'We talked one day, and this is what I suppose we came up with,' he said with a self-satisfied shrug. Anant wondered whether Rajat would have taken the credit for the woodwork as well, had he met their craftsmen before the work had begun. For far too long, Rajat had marched to his own tune which to him was a symphony that would have put Mozart or Paganini to shame. He moved as if he was not only capable of greatness but he was great already. As if any wave of inspiration never led to a mess, was never spoiled by the needless indulgence of creation, but led straight to the blinding bedazzlement of self-congratulation. Staring at Rajat, Anant wondered whether this unnerving confidence was what greatness demanded, wondered if it was his own shortcomings that failed him in comprehending Rajat, for he knew that his own limited aims and capabilities would never amount to greatness. He hoped that Rajat could get down to the dirty nitty-gritty of creation so perhaps, one day, Anant would see exactly what he himself lacked. 'I will see you in a couple of weeks...' Rajat said, 'housewarming party.'

'Yes, you will.' Anant nodded, and they shook hands. Neither knew that this was the last time they were going to meet. Rajat would end up sending an invitation too late, caught up in the magic of travelling, for inspiration he would tell others. Because the entangled mess that was reality had been shrouded in dreams and aspirations that Rajat had woven to keep reality at a distance, and the fact was that he had the means to keep the play going.

Anant kept his briefcase attached to his hip during the cab drive. To celebrate, he and his bag took a detour to a liquor store where Anant bought a bottle of Glenfiddich 18 years. He took another detour to an electronics repair store that also happened to sell music CDs and records. The vinyl records were stacked standing up in a single box on a low shelf amidst a sea of speakers, headphones, phone cases and an array of other accessories. Scattered on top of speakers were a few more records. Anant did not go through the records because amongst the stack, hidden behind a duet album of Jagjit Singh and Lata Mangeshkar, among Nusrat Fateh Ali Khan, Pink Floyd, Fleetwood Mac, Bach, and S.D. Burman, there was one record that had a side profile of an Arkansas-born Kentucky-declared-by-the-listeners singer printed on the front side with his last name 'Cash' in bold white letters on the top of the album. Anant picked up the record with trembling hands. The two-disc album was light, and yet felt far heavier than the briefcase. A profound silence enveloped Anant, so much so that he was almost taken back to another world entirely. All his senses tethered on the edge of the void. He wondered if he was in the real world or in an elaborate construction of his mind. 'I am Anant Vohra,' he whispered to the album, Johnny Cash, *America IV: The Man Comes Around*. Anant bought the album while gripping his briefcase to remind him that he could feel its leather material. He made sure to stand against the table, the edge kneading him in his thigh. He was afraid that one false step would cause the world to unravel and reveal that he was in the cell. He walked to the cab with his eyes wide open, making sure every step was met with sturdy ground. Like his mother during air travel, he wore the seat belt in the rear of the cab, drawing an amused expression from the driver whose remark died in his throat seeing the frantic state of Anant. Anant leaned into the seat and stared out of the window to reassure himself that he wasn't going to drift away or fall down.

In his flat with two cubes of ice in a tumbler, Anant sipped the whisky while carefully keeping the money in his drawer. The whisky had helped him return to the world again. His senses were no longer being choked in the vice-like grip of silence. He recalled his father's words of sticking to a routine. He took out a quarter of the cash and slipped it in his wallet before hiding the envelope between his notebooks. He kept the whisky by the record player, slipped *American IV* out of the sleeve and began to caress and later clean its grooves with a cloth from his sunglasses box, unable to believe that he had the record in his hands. 'I am Anant Vohra,' he said out loud once again to strengthen his belief that it was indeed him in the real world. His phone began to ring, cutting through this unreality that he was experiencing, this dream that he was having while wide awake. He ignored it. The sun was setting, he would have the evening and the night to listen to the album. A sense of finality hung in the air, as if there were two paths in front of him, and his choice would come to define who he was, or worse, what he was. He held the record that fate had placed in his hands, his fingers along its sharp edges. He placed the record on the turntable. But before he could guide the arm to the record that began to spin, his phone rang again. Not wanting to be disturbed, he marched over to his phone thinking to himself that he would put it on 'Do Not Disturb' so only his parents could reach him, who only called him once a week, so he would be left undisturbed given there was no emergency. The thought of the Titan sent a tremor down his spine, his already withered and overworked nerves managed to weather the storm. Picking up the phone believing it was Rajat, his eyebrows shot up in surprise as he stared at the screen. It was Aarti. Anant debated letting the phone ring before finally he brought the phone to his ear.

'Hey.' Aarti greeted him.

'Hello,' Anant replied and paused. 'How is unmarried life treating you?' He owed her this question for the heart she had ripped out in front of him yesterday.

'It has its ups and downs,' Aarti replied.

'And is it up or down right now?' Anant asked, trying to get to the point so he could return to his whisky that was getting diluted by the melting ice every passing second and the record that was sitting pretty on the record player.

'Down. I... I am sorry but I need to ask you a favour.' Aarti's apology for asking a favour made Anant pause.

In her hotel room, after Aarti caught her faltering smile, she had chosen to hide behind another celebratory drink before she went to sleep. The sun rose and she went down to the buffet. She had extended her stay at the hotel past the weekend. She indulged in the food that she had to discard because of the approaching wedding. She had chocolate mousse with wine in it, waffles drizzled with chocolate syrup and a banana lime ice cream on top of it. She returned to her room and prepared for a long shower. Ravi had called her for the seventh time and the call was met with the same fate as the rest. She ignored it. She had decided to leave her phone on her bed so she could enjoy her shower without the disturbance. This moment of solitude and pause from the excessive indulgence finally allowed the insidious thoughts that had been lingering and growing over the night to catch her unawares. With nowhere to turn and shampoo in her hair, doubt creeped and wormed its way into her. She washed her hair hurriedly, but these doubts, of her actions and now of her future, were etched in her by the time she had rinsed off the shampoo, and thereon merely stood under the shower with an unease of the future that lay ahead of her.

'What is the favour?' Anant inquired, breaking the silence after waiting patiently for a minute to give her time to continue.

'I am booking a flight for tonight, to Varanasi. I want you to come with me,' Aarti said.

Anant had plenty of questions to ask. Why tonight? He assumed that it must have something to do with a distraction from the fallout of the wedding. Why Varanasi of all places? Anant was unaware that the wedding was to have taken place in the city, and instead thought that she was seeking divine intervention in her life. Why him? There was no assumption for him to jump to, he had nothing.

'Why me?' he asked her.

'I know this is out of the blue, but I want to go to Varanasi. To see what could have been. And... I don't want to go alone. You are my cousin. And the only one in this damned city that I know.' She hesitated to say trust. 'Despite our troubles, despite our whatever, cold war or whatever, you have been helpful. And you were involved in the break-up of the marriage.' It was the first time their age-old rancour had been stated out loud, but it was overshadowed by the circumstances.

'Involved would suggest that I had done anything out of the ordinary, intentionally or unintentionally, to break up your marriage.' He was merely an outsider that circumstances had turned into a tool, one that Aarti had no hesitation in using to free herself of her marriage.

'I wasn't suggesting anything. You were trying to help me. I am simply asking that you continue to do so. I don't need a babysitter, just a set of eyes to hold me accountable. Just this once. Please.'

No. It is such a simple one-syllable world. One that Anant had no qualms using throughout his life. All he had to do was to utter a single word and no doubt Aarti would have been embarrassed to even ask for a reason. Just a simple word, and he could return to his drink and begin listening to Johnny Cash. His date with fate awaited him. His tryst with destiny, though whether he would remain independent was still a worry. There was the mystery of the precipice. And also, more than a footnote than it seemed, his own life outside of the other world. He needed to start looking for projects once again. Anant had every reason to not go with her. Why dive into the muddied waters of a break-up, he asked himself. He and Aarti weren't close, while they happened to have similar blood in their veins, they weren't family. Nor were they friends. He wasn't necessarily concerned with what would happen to her, whether her decision was for the better or worse wasn't a concern to him. All logic dictated that he should sever himself from such obligations before he was pulled into her troubles. A monosyllabic response and yet his lips had found a word with two syllables. 'Okay.' He pressed his lips together into a fine line before letting out a deep breath, conceding his defeat, and said, 'When?'

'Meet me at the airport around eight. I'll take care of everything,' she told him. 'Thank you.' She cut the call just after she muttered her gratitude, as if worried that he would change his mind. Or that she would.

With downcast eyes, ashamed to look at the record, Anant took to his glass. Why had he agreed to it? Anant refused to believe that it was out of the goodness of his heart, to help a fellow human being in a time of need, even if this human being happened to be his cousin. The fallacious resentment for her that he had held in the past had no sway over him. Anant realized as he parted the many titbits of their past together, that all that remained in him for her was indifference. That the past, irrespective of whether she was liked or disliked, was in the past. A true indifference not dressed by lies or lack of information, for he believed that he had come to know her to an extent, nor was this indifference marred by judgement. Remembering his cruel antics with Rajat, Anant realized why he had chosen to go. He saw how increasingly entangled he had become in his own byzantine life over the past few weeks, and some time away could help him detach from himself, to return to clarity. As he did with his designs when his mind had been overworked and the only choice was either to pull his hair trying to finish it or let the pages rest for a few days. A case could be made that his life had gone haywire once he had stumbled into the lives of Aarti and Rajat, but he had enough clarity to see that the metamorphosis of the cell was only the next step of evolution. This becoming, what he was becoming, he did not know. Yet, he refused to seek comfort by lying to himself and dressed his own troubles with exasperation towards others. The truth, the whole truth and nothing but the truth remained that he had long since left things in his mind to exist with their own free will, just as the hissing and slithering once had, and over time these things grew out of his control, wrote their own constitution and declared independence. They became distorted. Perhaps the answer lay in this indifference that he felt towards Aarti's plight, that if cultivated, could give him a different outlook towards his own problem. Detachment was the key, Anant thought to himself, and which better city than Varanasi to learn of these stoic ways. Or, Anant continued, perhaps he was once again complicating things by theorizing them, and perhaps all he needed was simply a break from his own life, to indulge in a story other than his own. His handicapped mind, still reeling from the sudden silence that descended and coiled around him in the electronics store, managed to convince him that this was for the best. That the record would be waiting for him.

'At eight,' Anant mumbled and dared to look at the record player again, and put the glass case attached to the turntable down to protect the record. He then turned off the switch, finished his drink, packed his bag and went to take a shower.

Chapter 27

The flight to Varanasi was uneventful. Anant and Aarti had an unspoken pact of silence between them that was broken once, to greet each other outside Chhatrapati Shivaji airport. They checked in their bags and made their way past the security check to reach the gate before the boarding would begin. They were early. Anant watched Aarti head to a bookstore. Following her lead, Anant took to wandering in the airport. The airport was hoisted on columns that were made to look like ornate man-made trees of plaster. Shops greeted him every few steps, shops full of books, bags, clothes, electronics, along with restaurants, cafés and bars, and vending machines sprinkled in the few steps from one shop to the next. It was truly the century of malls. The airport itself was a giant mall. He walked with his headphones on his ears, but he did not turn on the noise cancellation. Without any thoughts of being shot out of a catapult, or thoughts appearing and disappearing, his mind was quiet and the noise of the airport was a constant reassurance that he was in the real world. A white leather jacket hanging at the edge of a leather goods shop, a man dusting a handcrafted stained-glass lantern in a pop-up shop, a child browsing through candy with eyes red and wide in wonder, a stocky old man with a Hawaiian half-sleeve shirt sitting in the bar with a book beside his mug of beer and his shades protecting his eyes from the light, a group of backpackers resting on their bags with purple and orange kurtas and pants, men and women on their work trips sipping coffee with their sleek leather messenger bags or cabin suitcases beside them for company. Mumbai airport was alive and bustling. Anant returned when the announcement was made that the gate was open for boarding, and he found Aarti sitting on a chair with her legs tucked beneath her. She flipped through the pages of a book she bought on an impulse. *The Golden House* by Salman Rushdie, the cage-like house on the cover of the book resonated with her. As if she had managed to escape before the construction of the house was completed.

The flight did not change the pact. Aarti had the window seat, and Anant had the seat next to the aisle. A younger man was stuck between the two, his sinuses flaring up due to the altitude, ready with an arsenal of entertainment to battle boredom. Aarti flipped through more pages when she wasn't looking out of the window. From time to time, she glanced at Anant, envious of his noise cancelling headphones. If she could be away from the noise, she told herself, she could imagine she was alone above the dark clouds. Aarti amused herself with the thought of surfing clouds all over the world. Like Goku on his flying cloud in the *Dragon Ball* series, or like the fighting Buddha, she thought, remembering a cartoon she used to watch in times gone by, and whom he was based on. She wondered if these clouds would grow weary of her and spit her out along with the rain. Would the weight she felt in the pit of her stomach remain? She had constructed a wall between her thoughts and herself, specifically the thoughts concerning her recent actions. The what-ifs had become too many, and she feared being swept away by these thoughts. She feared that maybe she would be swept too far to return to herself. Like the cocoon she had once built, that once again, fated to repeat the past, the choices would be made by the time she got to her feet. Though she had managed to block these thoughts, suppress them and push them down into her subconscious, the weight remained, reminding her of their presence. It happened, they said to her. You must live with it, they preached. That's life, they philosophized.

Anant broke the sacrosanct silence when they were at the conveyer belt waiting for their luggage. 'Have you booked a hotel?' he inquired.

Aarti took her time to process the simple question, as if she were sending a telegram to her mind and then awaiting a response. 'Not yet. I will have a look.' She pulled out her phone, and Anant moved closer to the conveyer belt to be on the lookout for their bags. Silence settled between them once more, like the third amigo, and followed them from the luggage merry-go-round to waiting for the cab amidst the dogs that sat just past the airport, and finally waiting for the rooms in a cosy five-star hotel. The traffic was sparse, the main road from the airport to the hotel was deceptively wide and clean if one only looked at the road and not around, for it was in stark contrast to the city it pierced through. The lobby of the hotel sparkled, floors shining from being scrubbed daily, but Anant found the interiors to be disappointingly uninspired. A sober beige and cream theme with the same shades of marble and walls. In the city of moksha, the hotel had chosen to remain constrained. The hotel lacked any life. The bar near the entry was hidden, facing shops that were going through renovations. Anant and Aarti were given identical rooms, the only difference was the little painting over the desk in the corner to unsuccessfully try and resuscitate the rooms. Aarti insisted on paying for the accommodation, but Anant was successful in making her see reason.

'Freshen up and come to my room. I'll order food and we'll plan the day ahead,' she said with a zest for life that the walls had been designed to be deprived of. Arriving in the city had been far more daunting in thought than in reality, and now, standing in the city where she was meant to get married, without apprehension, she began to feel alive once again. The weight had eroded somewhat, as if her stomach had digested part of it.

Anant pulled the tan curtains of his room to find a view of a small pool outside that had been closed for the night. A few of the hotel's guests could be seen sprawled on the lounge chairs alongside the pool. Their partly illuminated hands made animated gestures as they continued their discussion. Anant watched them from his window, his eyes trailing their hands as they jerked forward and back, pointed at one another, and when laughter followed, Anant took it as a cue to let them be. He took a quick shower to wash the scent of the airport off him, and took out a bottle of water from the fridge, replacing it with the complimentary tepid water that rested on the dresser. He sat on the armchair, put his feet up on the footrest, and closed his eyes to try and peek into his mind from afar, as if seeing it through a telescope.

'What is the resident up to?' he thought. Finding no answers, he put his feet down on the floor and sat straighter. He breathed in, and out, and allowed himself to be sucked into a world where seconds that ticked on never turned to minutes. Yet, time continued to pass. Anant kept his eyes closed, he continued to breathe, but it was clear that something was missing. There was no renovation sign hung outside, no vanished cell, nor had the world dissipated; instead, Anant felt that the rope he tugged and used to climb into himself had been severed. Anant wondered if his own mind was imposing the vacation on him. He stirred in his chair, unsure of how to react. He began to sweat, a vague profusion of thoughts swarmed in the darkness that he could no longer pierce. He couldn't fathom being exiled from this world, from his world. Objectively, Anant tried to tell himself as he struggled to maintain a steady breath, to say that the cell was merely his imagination might be dismissive but not untrue. Anant knew the cell was a product of his imagination. That he had never really put up brick by brick to create a cell. It was an imaginary place where an imaginary foe resided. But yet, it was his world. He was Prometheus and he was Athena. He had created the world, and breathed life into it. This world became more real every moment Anant spent in the retreat, and the independence he bestowed on this world only felt natural. Free will is paramount for any creation. The doughnut theory, Anant recalled, as the resident coined it, this exchange of the real world for time in the retreat, these gifts of ideas and visions from the real world that further decorated this unreal world. Alas, he wasn't Krishna, he didn't know what his future held. He couldn't have foreseen his creation declare itself Mount Olympus. That the channel he created would be used through his imagination to reach him in reality. That it would hold the strings of his self, which self he did not know, but an image of himself, in an array of selves that had been made and discarded over time. The real and the unreal were perilously interweaving with one another, the definitions of which were no longer bound. Anant was a part of a deformed collective reality. One where his mind could decree that he wasn't allowed in, not now. Now wasn't the time, Anant told himself. He was taking a break, and his mind was merely helping him stick to his decision. If Anant dared to, he could even have hoped that he was getting better, that this time away from the cell, imposed or otherwise, was a way for him to mend the cracks that were appearing in his mind, at the meeting of the unreal and the real world. Even the darkness dancing on the shoulders of people had become just decoration. There was no unticking bomb. His mind was quiet, and Anant decided to leave it that way. He got up from the chair and made his way four doors down to Aarti's room.

Aarti hadn't changed out of her airport clothes after she entered her room. She had a call from her somewhat placated, still-frenzied-but-not-berserk mother, to whom she talked for a few minutes. She was finally making headway in trying to calm her nerves, in making her understand her choice. She had managed to do so by feeding her harmless lies of seeking god. Her mother was trying, and that was good enough for Aarti. She ended the call and washed her face. The zest she had felt when she arrived at the lobby had begun to fade. She shook her head and took out the hardcover novel from her purse. She settled in the chair and began to read about the Goldens, about an Eden where no one bit the apple, and Eden itself became a prison. Half an hour passed and she ordered dinner. The food arrived within minutes of Anant entering her room. Pizza and two pints of much deserved beer. Aarti hadn't ordered any drink for Anant, expecting him to choose his poison, but when she picked up one bottle, he picked the other.

'I plan on going after noon. You can come with me if you want,' she told him. For a moment, she questioned whether she wanted him to come with her. A little support wouldn't harm her, she thought.

Anant sipped his beer and ate the margarita pizza as she continued.

'There are plenty of sights to see, so whatever your choice is, it is fine with me. The flight is in the morning, the day after.'

'I've come this far, I might as well,' Anant replied with a shrug. Another's story, he reminded himself. His vacation entailed taking a break from himself.

Aarti had already gone through half the pint, and called in-room dining for another two beers, making it a point to ask Anant if he wanted something, to have it known that she was ordering the two beers for herself. 'One for me,' he told her. She changed the order to four. The first few slices of pizza swiftly disappeared, but Anant, on his second brew, was beginning to feel more tired than hungry. Aarti's pace slowed but she still picked up a slice every few minutes, quietly chewing away and returning to her beer. 'How do you feel?' Anant caught both of them off guard by the question.

Aarti ruminated on the question, and for a moment, Anant thought that she wouldn't reply. 'Strangely, I think I am at ease,' she answered. Neither of the Vohra cousins realized how their struggles grew from the same roots of a fallen relative. Nor did they see how their solitude had come to mirror that of others. And sitting within five feet of each other, the tragedy of the dinner was that no one said a thing, they both behaved like they got it, that they understood it, that they weren't 'full of shit', that their silence muted their suffering. They could have stumbled into the fellowship of the troubled, but alas, they stuck to their silence, a silence deprived of resonance, a deathly-still silence nurturing the thought that their solitude was their own, not too unique to them but the depth of which only they could see. That the circumstances that surrounded their isolation were inherently unique. But death, doubt and destiny, if a collective reality existed, more than life, conviction and nihilism, or absurdity to the absurdist, these former and graver emotions were the unifying bonds of such a reality. Felt by everyone despite their differences emotionally, financially, morally and spiritually. It was a moment lost in time, *ichi-go ichi-e,* for this time only. Aarti would be leaving the following night, flying to America to stay at her brother's, for a fresh start, leaving behind a text and a box of sweets. No explanation. Anant wouldn't require one.

Chapter 28

The following night, Anant received Aarti's message, he was seated in the armchair in the corner of his room, drenched in sweat, shivering and staring at the walls of his room, a pound of flesh lighter. How a day changes as the seconds tick and turn to minutes.

Earlier in the day, just as the hustle-bustle of a busy hotel had begun, Anant had woken up feeling tired despite a good night's sleep. A dull ache in his body made stretching on the bed more satisfying than usual. His stiff back purred as he twisted and turned. Having brushed his teeth, Anant decided against a coffee in his room and went down to the buffet instead, each step taken with an intent to dedicate himself to the vacation. He was joined by Aarti, whose expression showed that she was wearing the day ahead on her face. He had two glasses of fresh watermelon juice, and a walnut brownie that looked better than it tasted, while she had decided to look around and weigh her options before taking a small portion of whatever suited her palate, and ate with nervous eyes darting around the room, and a cup of black coffee with a single cube of sugar sitting beside her plate. They ate in a new silence which reflected Aarti's nervousness, an uneasy silence, as if the third amigo had gone through his own set of ordeals. Given the circumstance, Anant thought that her anxiousness was understandable, and decided that giving her the space was the correct step to take. They had arrived in Varanasi at night, and now, near noon, the roads had come alive, with people, often covering a whole lane, disappearing here and reappearing there. A bleak sun struggled to cast the day in light. They were at Dharm Vatika, the venue that had been booked for Aarti and Ravi's wedding, just after twelve. The iron gates were open, revealing a lawn that looked like an elongated backyard of a mansion. People carrying carpets and rods on their shoulders marched past them, stalls were being set up along the boundary. Anant watched Aarti stand at the edge of the ground just past the door, her eyes shut and her mouth open as she tried to concentrate, and recreate a night that perhaps still could be. Some workers stared at them. Others stared at her. Anant wondered what was going on in her mind as he began to grow uneasy. Moments went by, and finally, she let out a breath that she didn't know she had been holding, and her discomfort along with it, for when she opened her eyes, it seemed that peace had prevailed in her battle against the city and her mind.

Seeing the venue, standing a step away from its manicured grass, being present in the city and feeling the distant sun on her skin, she realized that no matter what could have been, and sure, she accepted the possibility that it could have been a good day, even a great day, but she refused to accept that she had sacrificed the best day of her life. That she had carried this niggling thought with her was a revelation in itself. And by putting it to rest, she found that she had resolved the conundrum of her decision and turned it into a fact of life. As if she rode a horse and plucked herself away from the midst of battle. And without Helen, there was no war. There was still a possibility that she could have convinced Ravi to get married, but she chose instead to believe that the option was no longer available. Like she was a child and had let go of her balloons, watching them float up and into the cloudy sky. That she had made her decision like the ones that had chosen to get married that night, for whom the lawn was being prepared. The decorations themselves mattered very little to her, and would become a subject of curiosity during the times she would be waiting for the bus in her travels across America. How the studded white couch set up on the stage overlooking the lawn would have been uncomfortable, leaving a sore behind for both. The weather would have soaked her makeup, and made him miserable in his heavy clothes. Ravi never was one for dirt and sweat, his struggle to maintain decorum as each and every guest took the small steps up to the stage would have been visible.

Aarti had come to Varanasi, like many others, to put the dead to rest. Though for her it was the death of an option, of a life that could have been. The smile in her reflection after she had broken the marriage, however fleeting, was what she craved. The freedom to choose was the freedom to live. To not exercise free will was to not live at all. It was inherent in human nature to choose liberty, she told herself. And as she set fire and watched the last hopes of a wedding ablaze, she was overcome with the cathartic relief of having chosen correctly. She smiled wide, and yearned for life to make her smile again, for a world to reveal itself and try to get her to smile. She believed it was owed to her. That through the limbo of uncertainty that followed happiness, there was always the possibility of more happiness. After sadness, happiness. It was a cycle, and one where the happiness followed, one where it ended with happiness. A cycle not of sadness following happiness, but of happiness after sadness. She thought of her father, of the distant image of a man who had been her father, of whom she remembered very little, alive in stories than in memories. And she realized, now, in the post-euphoric clarity, that she had, on her own, managed to leave that wretched day far behind. She had been carrying his dead carcass for she was afraid to let go. But she had the stories, and the few memories, and that was enough. The feeling grew as they got back in the cab. She didn't know when she decided to take a gap year from life itself, to shed the old skin and cleanse herself. Gregor Samsa had died in his bedroom, unable to move. The Goldens had fled to America, unable to shed the curse of the past. There was a harmony somewhere between the two, surreal enough for her to shed her skin, real enough for her to return to life. A bridge to a new life. The wall she had erected to block herself from her thoughts disappeared, the rush of thoughts was but a gentle stream that went past her, like cars on a wide empty street and she on the footpath, watching them skate away. She finally allowed herself to enjoy the city while they drove out of Dharm Vatika. She suggested a boat ride. She had always heard of the Varanasi ghats from her mother. She also wanted to try some sweets and browse some shops for silk sarees, but wasn't sure if she had enough time for both.

The roads were congested, with cars, with people on the roads, with stalls and rickshaws, and withered old buildings so close to the roads that they seemed to stand over them. Aarti found a charm in the old city, as if she had stepped into a world that did not adhere to the same rules as Gurugram, where she lived, or any other town that she had had a chance to visit. They made their way down a long alley, with old shops selling breakfast, selling sweets, selling stationary, and down the steps where vendors were sitting on the ground, some cutting hair, others giving massage, reading the stars. And thus, they had reached the banks of the famous Dashashwamedh ghat for a boat ride. It was this boat ride, along the banks of the Ganga, when this life that Anant believed he had stepped away from, that his mind imposed a vacation from, crept out of the shadows and made itself known. It was on the boat ride that life took its pound of flesh from Anant.

Aarti and Anant sat facing each other on the opposite flanks of the small boat, both lost in their separate worlds. A peculiar calm had come over him, severing him from the people on the ghat, and others enjoying the cloudy day on the river. He did not know how long he was lost, or how far he ventured into his mind, which wrong turn he took along the way, but when he glanced at Aarti, it felt like he was viewing her through a painting. The smoothness of her dark skin that reminded him of his uncle, the way her hair fell almost caressing her eyelashes, her eyes that carried a new-found secret, the serene expression on her face. Anant wondered what had changed in this brief visit, he wondered what she had found. Aarti seemed to reside in another world entirely, he mused. The darkness on her shoulder had vanished. Startled, Anant looked to the helmsman paddling the boat and found that he too was without this entity on his shoulder. The longer he stared at the two, the more distant they seemed, like these two were in the real world, while solitude restricted him to a place far away, as if he was the one in the painting. He lost the ability to move his body. Which painting can move, he said to himself. It wasn't him that turned his head to stare into the calm waters of the river, rippling whenever a boat rowed past them, and when bigger motorboats met them, they parted the waters in such a way that they left waves that shook their boat. He stared into this deceptively stormy water, dirtied by the sins of the people, muddied by the sins of factories, sacred to those that believe it rose from Vishnu, dripped down from Shiva's hair bun. His heart began to pound, he realized the only sound he could hear was this loud thud of his heart. His body continued to stare into the water, ignoring the warning of the helmsman. His surroundings began to disappear, the people washing themselves by the shore, washing their clothes, sitting by the steps drinking chai, the bearded and long-haired men sitting on stools or mats, all were pushed to the periphery and a fog swallowed them whole. It was just him and the river. He wondered if someone, him but not really him, a part of him, someone inside or within him, had connived to have him arrive at Varanasi for the other reason many flocked to the city from all over the country, to die. Was he being given a choice for nirvana, to be carried to the paradoxical god about whose existence he had never contemplated? Anant stayed frozen, staring into the river. Soon, the thick fog began to dissipate. The boat reached the ghat. Anant breathed easy, he had survived whatever had come over him.

Over the past few days, Anant and Aarti mirrored many of the troubles of the other, but as they stepped out of the boat, they were strangers to one another once again. Anant was worse than he had ever been. Something had happened, though he heard no crack, yet like someone who knows he's broken a bone the moment it happens, he knew his mind had fractured, and separated from his body, both of which refused to work in tandem with one another. Aarti had waded through her mind as a rite of passage, and brought herself back again. The tapestry of her mind was of life, not sickness. She had moved on with a new-found appreciation for life. She did not suggest that they have sweets, she pulled him by the arm to the shop. Anant, devoid of any will, merely allowed himself to be led. She stared at the variety of sweets with childlike wonder, the variety of colours weaved a festive mood despite the flies that buzzed around it. The customers shifted to give her space while she elbowed her way to the sweets. She got a box with her favourites. Anant stood beside her unable to show any interest in anything, his sweet tooth long forgotten. He was homogeneous on the outside, but inside, he was a collection of alien beings that were once a part of him, now vying for control of the bodysuit that was Anant Vohra. From the sweet shop, Aarti decided that it was time to return to the hotel. Her eyes were alight with a new determination, a new goal called out to her, it serenaded her with wild musings of a foreign country. She had left Anant far behind, while she could have shared his troubles, the previous day, empathized with him as he could have done the same with her, now he seemed his usual alien self again, perhaps in his mood swings choosing to hide behind the silence. Back in the hotel, Aarti informed him that she would call him after she freshened up. Anant blinked, her words incomprehensible, floating at the interstices of the other world and the real world. The darkness that rested on everyone's shoulder had disappeared. The world was quickly ceasing to make any sense. It felt like every time he blinked he had moved from where he previously existed. One moment he was in the ghat, another, he was in the hotel lobby, and now he opened his eyes to find himself in his room, sitting in the chair, covered in perspiration, staring blankly at a wall, feeling lighter than ever and even lighter as woeful seconds continued to tick on and turn to dreadful minutes. It was out of sheer soul-curling fear that Anant managed to grip the arms of the chair, and began to bleed into his wires, vying for control. His grip turned tighter and tighter till his knuckles turned white, afraid that he might just fade away this time, instead of floating away like he had dreaded during that ominous boat ride. Aarti had finished packing her bag while Anant remained glued to the chair. She booked a flight to Delhi to collect her passport from her flat in Gurugram. Ravi and Aarti had planned to travel to America for their honeymoon and both had a ten-year visa. She contemplated booking tickets to Chicago where her brother stayed. She did not plan to stay in Chicago for long, she was more or less ticking off meeting him so she would be free for the rest of her trip. She picked up one laddoo from the box for the cab drive, and left the rest for Anant. She informed the front desk to give him a key, paid the dues, and was on her way to the rest of her life, where she hoped that no one day would be the best day of her life, and she would smile only when she wanted to. She did not book tickets to Chicago. She decided to begin her journey through America with the city that had enamoured her since her childhood, New York.

Aarti sent a text to Anant when she was at the airport waiting for her flight, an hour and a half after leaving the hotel. 'Flying to America. Call the reception. Thank you and take care.' Cordial as you would be to a colleague. She wanted to add that maybe she shouldn't have punched him, but punching him, just like the wedding being called off, seemed a prerequisite for her new self to be emerging.

Reading the text, and then again, Anant was unsure of what to make of it. He had just returned to the world after life had unceremoniously shoved his face in the pompous belief that he could take a break from it. The first thought that occurred to him as he read the message the second time was that Johnny Cash was waiting for him, lying on the record player back in Mumbai. He called the front desk as he was told to, and was sent a key. Thoughts were scarce in the meantime, otherwise Anant would have tried to guess what she could have left behind for him to see. Alas, he could not bring himself to get up from the chair until someone knocked on the door. He staggered up and collected the key. With faint steps, he entered her room to find the box of sweets she had bought lying on the bed. Had she bought it for him or had she left it behind as one does flowers on a grave? A thank you, Anant concluded. He opened the box and was greeted with the scrumptious scent of ghee and sugar syrup, as if the sweets had bathed day and night until they were sweating with this very scent. There were three types of sweets in the box. He took his time inspecting each one of them before settling on the laddoo. Made with boondi, decorated with saffron and little candies in red and green, they looked like all the festivals had consummated and the result was this laddoo. Perhaps, the world made a little more sense to those who are thus entranced by the sweet joy of laddoos. Here was joy in a box, Anant told himself. After all he had suffered, Anant thought, he deserved this. But before he could take a bite and relish the laddoo, the fact that he was completely drawn towards the sweet registered. The damned doughnut theory, he recalled. Eating it meant sharing it with the resident. Slowly, the decrepit wheels of his mind turned. He remembered what he went through that resulted in him having to huff and puff his way into his own body, the effects of which had not yet waned. And the wheels brought him to a revelation. He realized that he detested the resident. That he hated him more than whatever joy the laddoo could bring him. That he would gladly sever himself from this moment of joy to rue the resident. And it felt something akin to impaling a dagger in his stomach by rejecting the sweet. But who else except the resident could have led the coup against him in the boat? But why try and jump off the boat. Anant had no answer. Had it been his body rejecting a new consciousness? His lacerated mind could barely structure comprehensible questions, let alone hold a hope for answers. All he had was this route of spite. He closed the box and made his way back to his room. The doughnut theory, what lay in the absent centre. How far did its sprinkles cast their spell? It was more than merely sharing pieces of the world, more than the resident being able to create from his own memories. Afraid of what fate awaited him in his sleep, Anant decided to stay awake all night.

Chapter 29

Though Anant had declared that he would stay awake all night, one cannot merely decide to abandon sleep and follow through with it. Preparations are needed. Anant hadn't woken up fresh, fatigue clung to him like an odd stench. The hours were long, and the room did not have much to keep him busy. It was like a beige prison. As he ventured past midnight, he realized that he wouldn't succeed in his battle against sleep if he remained in the room. Seeking distractions that would level the playing field, he ventured out of his room and into the garden. Leaves were scattered along the cobblestone path, some streaked black and other silver from the moon that managed to peer through the foliage of the trees. An eerie quiet had descended on the old city, as if it had suffered a disaster between the time Anant came back from the ghat, and returned to the city. The pool water was still, the lights turned off, and the overhead trees protected it from the illumination of the moon. Dark, like a portal to some alien land, the pool stood still. Anant walked, the fear of water, of what happened, sent his heart racing. Trying to be brave, he peered into the water from a distance, but could not make out its bottom. He imagined it to be immeasurably deep, deeper than any pool, deeper than any river, where he could remain submerged, suspended in the silence found under water. Fear snapped at his heels. He jumped away from the water. He turned around to find the path, with trees either side of it, growing wild before his very eyes. The eeriness of the night seeped into his nerves. Anant became further unsettled. There was a silence that pervaded the hotel—he couldn't hear any cars going by, no one talked even in the hotel. As if aware of the sinister night, the people had returned to their homes, leaving behind an abandoned city that had given up midway on its concrete makeover and chosen to continue breaking down. Anant touched his face, he whispered his name, he returned to his room with something akin to fear and disappointment, his fractured mind struggling to distinguish between his emotions. As he walked through the lobby of slow death, he tried to remember in parts what had interested him during their visit to the boat, tried to kindle an interest in the living. The massages on the steps of the ghat, oiled heads pressed by hands, kneaded by elbows, and cranked at the necks. The sea of faded colour, in clothes, on decrepit walls, on alleys stained with paan and betel leaf. The thick clouds of marijuana rising like chimney smoke from the sides of the steps, or from ledges, and amidst the ascetics there were surreal ash-smeared beings who seemed to live in two worlds themselves. Anant wasn't an enthusiast, but what better time than in the lap of a marijuana smoking god. Only if he had had control of his body, he could have also introduced himself to a sadhu. Not that Anant believed that a sadhu would hold any answers to his problems, but he amused himself with such thoughts while he sat in the chair that he had turned to face the window overlooking the pool that had returned to its normal self; from his angle he could see the lights that surrounded the pool gave it a vague outline and illuminated the corners of the water in a fungal green glow.

Anant hated the resident enough to stab his stomach by denying himself the laddoo, such was his resentment of the resident, and yet, Anant had come to realize that he feared sleep just as much. He surrendered himself to the second type of sweet in the box for energy, a laal peda, a regular diabetes on a plate like most Indian sweets, cardamom, rose and dried fruits added to help achieve a sugar euphoria. The laal peda was more brown than red, and helped Anant stay awake past two as he continued to take bites of it and stare at the pool. As long as I am not completely taken by it, the resident will not be able to taste it, he told himself. Three times he reached a diabetic heaven that night, each time the heaven waned in its grandeur and revealed itself to be a mirage, and at fifteen minutes to three, he turned to pack his bags and take a shower to pass the time. He checked out of the hotel despite the knowledge that there would be nobody on the road. His flight was only a few hours away. He declined the suggestion that he take a cab, and carried his bag with him to the gate of the hotel, looking for an auto. He needed to see more of the city. Further down the road, he found an auto twinkling under the moonlight, more black and silver than yellow and green. The driver of the auto was a slim greying man with a paunch, no doubt a result of all the delectable laddoos and pedas, and the breakfast of Varanasi, jalebi and kachori.

'Show me the city.' Anant knew these touristy words would inevitably result in a few more hundred-rupee notes out of his pocket, not as much as the foreigners would pay that came to the city in search of meaning or marijuana, or both, but he was too tired to think straight, and having been through what he had, he couldn't bring himself to care about a bit more money out of his pocket. 'But I don't have much time.'

'Please come,' the driver replied with a half-frown, half-smile, unsure if Anant, the man standing before him, was a potential customer or just another miscreant out in the night. The driver's name was Harish, and though he was of a quiet disposition, he was a quick-witted fellow who knew the interests of a typical tourist from decades of experience. He had a mental checklist of where to take him, but given the limited time, he turned to

Anant and read out his list in one breath, as if he were reading a menu. 'Temple, ghat, yoga centre retreat, BHU, ganja, what do you want?'

'Can I choose two?' Anant inquired, his heart racing at the sound of the ghat. The waters called out to him, he yearned to make his peace with the river.

'Ji, but then I will have to make the decision. I can't guarantee the best place, but hopefully both are available.'

'Ghat, and weed,' Anant told him.

Was Harish cognizant of his decision, or was it fate that pushed him to Manikarnika ghat, the cremation ground where Anant would have found people even if he ventured there after midnight when the rest of the city was asleep. Or was it this presence of people that Harish thought would help him buy weed? Harish drove through the ghost streets down a small road that had heavy police presence even in the dead of the night, with barricades scattered on either side of the road. Some of the shops were open, the people inside were calling out to the devotees who were walking on the road. Harish stopped before Anant could see where they were all walking. He walked with him down the hallowed steps, sanctified by tears and smoke. He dragged a foot when he walked, and frequently glanced in the direction in which the people were headed. Only after he had helped Anant secure marijuana from a closed cigarette stall fixed on top of abandoned truck tyres that was threatening to crumble, did he find the moment to ask for permission. 'If you'll take time, can I...' He pointed at a temple hidden amidst the buildings.

'Yes, sure.' The solemn temple and mosque of Varanasi, the entrances of both were guarded by police with guns hanging on their shoulders. Anant turned away from Harish and looked out to the river bathed in the silver of the moon and grey of the smoke of the still burning pyres, and men and children in the corners awaiting the fire to burn itself out so they could collect the bones and ashes. It was a surreal sight, the whole place felt as if a spell had been cast on it, separating it from the dirt and litter along the road and its own abandoned makeover, the plaster of which was crumbling. Anant sat on the steps staring into the water, his mind overwhelmed with the world that seemed to grow more and more unreal. His only anchor were the seconds that turned to minutes. The ash in the air was overwhelming. A crackle was heard every now and again. There was the sound of steps, someone had begun to clean the cremation ground where the pyres had turned to ash, the ghosts of this world, beloved to the beyond. The phantom wails of mourners pierced the silence. And in the unreality of the place, Anant knew for certain that he was himself once again. He did not smoke the weed for he did not know how to roll it, nor did he have the paper to try. When Harish returned, he offered to help him roll one and slyly suggested that he had a chlllum in his auto that they could also try. 'Will you?' Anant whispered to avoid any transgression against the quiet of the area.

Harish was taken aback at the question, and only when he went to his auto and returned with his box that he nodded. Anant gave him some money to get cigarettes. And while he pocketed the money, he did not leave for cigarettes but merely sat down beside him and like a craftsman lost in his work, began to fix them both a shot meticulously removing seeds from the weed. 'Impotence, baba,' he explained. Anant went first, with Harish holding the lighter. 'Smoke, smoke, smoke.' He encouraged him as smoke rushed into his lungs and seeped into his soul, his mind having to grab on to its scattered parts to avoid unravelling as it was shot up in the air. Anant pulled away from the chillum, coughing. Even his coughs were full of smoke, and he sat dazed for a minute until the tidal wave of high hit him. Like his mind before him, Anant shut his eyes and focused on trying to hold himself, he felt he would shatter to pieces and scatter in the air. With trembling hands, he tried to return the favour but could not hold the lighter steady, let alone find the right angle for the 'chand', as Harish called it, the full moon formed by burning weed sitting on top of the chillum. He took the lighter and did it himself. Harish made another round for them. Sadhus came and went in the distance, some drenched and dripping along the way, having taken a bath in the cold river, lost in their own world, muttering chants, greeting stray cows as they went along their way. The skies in the distance began to bleed, signalling the arrival of the sun. But the decrepit buildings remained untouched by these lights, covered in the hazy grey morning as if existing outside of time and nature. Soon, people had begun to arrive in the ghat with mats and stalls. Some more shops were being opened, selling logs of wood. Harish was unconcerned with them and held the chillum for Anant to take the hit. Anant felt his insides sway, and could barely take the hit. Harish finished it for him. They both sat on the ghat, the sun now peeking over the horizon, a reminder that everyone existed in the real world. The ghostly silence and the unreality was replaced by the sound of walking, chanting and chatting, the ash that seemed to hang in the air had settled and the stink of the litter in the streets and the many odours of the area taking its place. The crescendo of wailings could be heard, and those of condolences. 'You okay?' Harish asked.

'Was he okay?' Anant asked himself the question, and found himself to be devoid of answers. He was as close to the Titan as he could possibly be, and yet just a moment ago he had been lost in a world that existed outside Varanasi, as if a piece of land had been carved open and ascended to another plane where the sun could not reach, where the only smell was that of ash. Perhaps his cell had been present somewhere, floating amongst the broken buildings. Was Anant okay, he asked himself again, trying to focus, but unable to. He realized that he wasn't concerned with Anant just as he was unconcerned about the Titan, at least for the moment, Anant's feelings or worries held no weight. Anant would be lying on a pyre in a cremation ground much like the one beside him. He realized that he could very well be sitting beside where Anant's last rites would be done. Who was this Anant but a collection of memories, dreams and reflections. A body bag to be filled with these intangible pieces that made Anant. His baggage, from point A to point B. In that moment between the other world that the city had taken him to, and the world where the city resided, he believed he was more than Anant. Just him, perhaps an it. Who is to say if spirits have gender. Would his be in the shape of Anant, and despite the reincarnations, if such a thing existed, had his soul chosen him as its image? 'I am... I am... I am...' That was all he had. He was. He is. He won't be.

Harish chuckled seeing the high that Anant was experiencing, like a teenage boy having his first joint. 'Bum Bum Bhole!' Harish exclaimed, ecstatic seeing Anant experiencing the overwhelming city in his veins. He walked over and returned with two cups of steaming chai, with ginger and tulsi, the holy basil. 'Har Har Mahadev,' he repeated the beloved chant of the many people of Varanasi, offering him the cup. Anant took the chai. They sat side by side sipping their cup of tea.

'Time? When do you leave?' Hari inquired. The question, like a bait, lured him to it, it tethered him and slowly, like a fish, he was reeled back from wherever he had ventured to. He returned to himself, to Harish who sat beside him, to the city that was real, and its people and their prayers, their jobs, their grief, their garbage, their sweat, and their chai. He checked the time on his phone and nodded to Harish. 'Let's leave.'

The only sound during the drive to the airport was the air whizzing by him, and he still floating on the interstices of the real world and where the city had taken him, but now as Anant. A police officer stopped the auto and Anant had to show his flight ticket to him before the auto was allowed to proceed towards the airport. Harish had slowed the auto once inside the premises. 'You know, the cremation grounds used to scare me. Very much. But I realized one day that this city promises moksha. Do you know moksha?' he asked.

'Yes, I am familiar with it.' Anant wondered if nirvana was what he was after but checked himself from saying anything.

'Away from the web of this world. Sir, I don't mean to impose myself, but whatever you are feeling, it is but a web of the world, woven by maya. You visited Varanasi. There is moksha awaiting you.' These were the kind-hearted empathetic parting words from Harish, besides a thank you when Anant paid him more than the fare. He also gave him the bag of weed in his pocket that Harish patted with a grin. The words were pretty indeed, but alas, they did nothing to help Anant. No matter the divinity that Anant wasn't sure he believed in, in the present, even if he was a mere fly, he was a fly caught in the web of a world of his own creation. And all the fly could do once trapped, was struggle to escape, and await the spider that had patiently bided its time in the shadows. Moksha would just have to wait for another reincarnation, he told himself. The only cycle Anant wanted to break away from was the cycle of finding himself in the cell that he had constructed in his mind. Floating between worlds and realities, with coffee in hand that willed him to stay awake while waiting for the gate to open, he finally took his seat and the caffeine, like a genie, disappeared once his wish had been granted, and all he was left with was the overwhelming weight of his eyelids that would not stay open no matter his efforts.

Chapter 30

Anant's eyes snapped open to find a moonless sky bearing down on him. He was flat on a wooden canoe with a coarse grey border running along the opening of the boat. It was dark, darker than usual, as if decades had passed since the memory of light even existed. The boat wobbled as he tried to stand and reluctantly he remained seated on the spot he lay on. From his new elevation, he could see past the mouth of the canoe. The void above reflected the void he was floating on. Anant knew where he was, the question that was bothering him was where were the precipice and the cell? There was no horizon in the distance, only the seamless void. It was hard to tell if he was moving at all. He managed to twist and turn to get a better look behind him and found much of the same. He closed his eyes and tried to imagine his cell, with its mahogany floors and grey brick walls. He tried to recreate the record player and the mat, tried to listen to the music that resided in his memories, and the precipice in the distance. He opened his eyes to find himself seated in the middle of the canoe with nothing in sight. Anxiety snapped at his feet, he managed deep breaths to calm himself. He then decided to lie down on the canoe for a while. He brought his knees to his chest, turning to his side, then lowered his legs and turned around and lay flat on his stomach. He got up with a pushup before bringing his hands closer to his legs and finally made it to his feet without disturbing the canoe. Without the cell, Anant wondered as he was faced with the vast expanse of nothing, if he fell, would he return to the boat? 'Where are you?' he asked, but he was met with silence.

He didn't need to ask to know that he was alone. He felt it inside him, as if he had been weighed down by these recent visits and suddenly the weight had been severed, taking with it some of his own weight. He was the perfect weight to merely float away. Fear surged through him, leaving a trail of goosebumps as it enveloped his body. The change in this world, the absence of the resident, this abject isolation, Anant did not know what he feared the most. If he was here and powerless, where was the resident? If the scales were tipped away from him, they must be in favour of someone. Anant tried to imagine a paddle, and one fell from the sky and dissipated before it was within his reach. He dived into his memories of the things that he had been taken with, and he found that the stream of memories evaded him. It went around him, as if it weren't his memories but that he had become the trespasser.

How long did Anant stay in the boat that floated to nowhere? Did the seconds tick on and turn to minutes? Had the rules of the world changed? He would switch positions—standing, sitting and lying down with his back as a support. Gradually, he became careless with the canoe, frequently rocking the boat to feel something. There was no sound, no taste and no feel of the planks underneath him, not even that of a mattress. All he had was his sight, and the distant scent of something stale, concealed between the particles of the air and he had to close his eyes to catch the scent. He wondered if it was his own rotting consciousness. Anant had tried to dream, to amuse himself with thoughts, to remind him of his life, but quickly he saw that it led him nowhere. He had dreamt of people, his family, Aarti, Rajat, Kartik and he tried to breathe life into these dreams with details, other people that he remembered became the one-dimensional decorations in the foreground and background, giving a depth of field to these memories. He dreamed of music, but all he could think of was the Johnny Cash record sitting on his record player that could have been his salvation. What could have been would never be, the thought lashed at him. He moved on, and dreamt of the doughnut as if it were the sun that would bring light to this world. He stared up and imagined a doughnut in the sky. He dreamt of the dance between the silver ocean and the moon. And of the little light that could have been his North Star. Of Harish and his time in the surreal ghat in Varanasi. Nothing came to fruition. All he did was empty himself of these memories till all he could imagine was colour. Of walls being layered with patterns and wallpapers in rooms without any detail except paints. Red, orange, yellow, green, blue, indigo and violet, all beating along with his heart, whether he imagined them in pools, cans or walls, distorted colours that he feared could begin leaking out of him at any moment, leaving him behind with nothing.

Anant got to his feet once again, with a solemn grace brought by the tranquillity of his certainty in the decision he had made. He would jump over the canoe, and see where that led him. His only fear was losing the rocking sensation of the canoe, his only assurance that he could feel, that he was somebody, that he wasn't the void projecting itself. As he approached the edge of the boat, his step faltered, he paused deliberating the jump, the sudden movement and abrupt stop caused the boat to topple over and he fell. But instead of falling down, he fell forward, almost hitting the tray of food that was sitting in front of him. He was in the flight again. His seat belt was still around him. The food on his tray was untouched. The plane was still in the air. He was surrounded by people. Not Aarti, he wasn't going to Varanasi, he was coming back to Mumbai. Varanasi had been real. Harish had been real. The coffee he had in the airport had been real. The canoe, the void, had been a dream. But it didn't feel like he had woken up from a dream. There were no signs of him ever having been asleep. Somebody had to have ordered the food, taken the tray and opened it. He didn't feel groggy either. He took deep breaths through his mouth, moving his jaw side to side, and clenching and unclenching his fists. He looked around to find an elderly lady sitting diagonal to him, staring at him with disapproval. The couple beside him were half asleep, with their plates on the tray, waiting for the attendant to pick theirs up. He distinctly remembered having taken the middle seat, but somehow he was sitting in the window seat. 'I am Anant Vohra,' he whispered to himself. Never before had he liked hearing his voice as much as he did in that moment. The only question that remained was that had Anant been hallucinating, or had he been in a dream and had indeed lost control of his body?

While he deliberated over the question, his body was functioning on the assumption that it had gotten no sleep since his first night in Varanasi and he was feeling its effects. But the fear was a pick-me-up stronger than any coffee. He stayed awake during the course of the flight, staring at the clouds and the wing of the plane, which reflected the rays of the sun, allowing it to peek through the window, and sear him along the way. Back on the ground, he waited for the aisle to clear before getting up. He wished the attendant a good day. He kept his head down at the conveyer belt. He got his bag and made his way to the multilevel parking area where the cabs were waiting. He found his and was in and out of himself as he was driven to his flat. He used the front camera of his phone to check if he was wearing his own face, that he hadn't woken up as someone else. The same hair, same two eyes now bloodshot, same bent nose and thin mouth now chapped and dry. But while the man looking back at him looked like him, he did not feel like him. Like he was looking at his reflection through a distorted mirror one might see in a carnival or amusement park, but instead of his face, it distorted his insides, his heart, his mind and his soul.

Anant entered his flat and found it as he had left it, the record sat still on the turntable, waiting for him. Memory had ceased to be reliable, what he felt was true could just as easily be revealed as a lie. For a moment, standing by the couch staring through the glass balcony door, he wondered if he had left at all. Whose memory was it anyway? Perhaps he had just now returned to himself, having been a spectator throughout these days. Who was in Varanasi? Who was dreaming? But the record was there, indeed he had bought it, and left it behind. For a vacation, Anant recalled the reason why he had left Mumbai, and felt scorned by his mind, and by fate. Was the thought of a break so mortifying a thought, so blasphemous that it needed to be struck down?

Anant poured himself a glass of whisky that had been unceremoniously left in the kitchen. He guessed the name before checking the bottle to validate his memory of purchasing the bottle. It was still Glenfiddich 18 years. He went to get some ice. As he opened the freezer, he saw that there was a chunk of ice covering its walls. He tried to use a knife to cut the ice, and when that failed and all he could get were crumbles, he shaved the ice with the ice, as he had watched Aamir expertly do to wood. He put a few shards of ice in his glass, and poured whisky over it, listening to it crackle. He took the drink with him to the shower. The water washed the airport off him, and the whisky washed his soul. He changed into fresh clothes, and by that time, he needed a refill.

Anant wasn't sure if he was preparing for the trip he knew awaited him, or buying time to forget where he was going. The bomb that he had felt inside him, weeks ago, had grown hotter and Anant was beginning to feel a strange warmth inside him, as if a fire was growing, one from which he harboured no hopes of survival. But a more adamant resolve persevered, the prospect of death remained in the background of the battle he would fight, a war with his mind, for his mind. His chances of survival had little to do with his yearning for a fight. He would go down swinging, chewing, scratching. If he were to disappear tomorrow, he would make sure his wrath was felt by the resident, even if it was only felt like a mere itch, before he was gone. Like a bee, he would gladly die after having stung.

'How far into madness does one realize its descending steps?' Anant thought to himself as he stood in the washroom sipping his whisky and staring at himself in the mirror. 'Are you mad?' he asked, and for a moment, he couldn't hear himself. He whipped around in panic to see if he was in the cell or the boat, but his senses were alive, and he calmed down. And when he tried again, he could hear his voice. 'Are you mad?' he asked again. There was no reply from the mirror. Given his circumstance, was it crazy that he expected a reply? Anant went into the kitchen for another glass of whisky before he turned the record player on and moved the arm to the edge of the spinning record. He stretched his legs as he sat down on his mat. Drowsiness came carrying the reminder of his lack of sleep, his body reacted in kind.

'There is a man going around taking names, and he decides whom to free and blame.' Johnny Cash began with the first track of the album *The Man Comes Around*. He was reminded of the time when he first heard the song, first heard of Johnny Cash. How naïve he had been about the freedom he had, living in a self-imposed exile. The markings he made hadn't been permanent, they hadn't become boundaries that would only be broken when his mind fractured in multiple places. How quick he had been to believe he lived in a world away from the one around him. It is often when problems become issues that you yearn for a time when you weren't plagued. It is easy to think that you might have insomnia if you don't get a goodnight's sleep for a few days, or depression if you are experiencing changes in life that have knocked you off balance, but problems have an underlying cause, rooted to tangible reasons, while issues seem to exist having shed any notion of cause, unconstrained by any sense of propriety or reason. How naïve he had been indeed. The world used to be real, death used to be real, his cell was merely a retreat from the Titan, which existed in his imagination rather than as a resident present in his mind. And now the cell was becoming a battleground. 'Where to?' Anant asked himself, unaware until this moment that he had been talking to himself ever since he entered the flat.

'Where to?' Anant wanted to say that he wasn't going anywhere. That he would catch up on sleep. How many times had he used sleep as an excuse to lie on his bed and retreat into his cell. In his younger days, the visit to his cell had been a return to his equilibrium, while he was reeling with reminders of the Titan from the darkness that used to rest on people's shoulders. Why did he keep returning to his cell after he had learned to live with this darkness, when the horrors of it had largely disappeared, only to catch him at odd times? To be disturbed by death, twice or thrice a week, Anant believed was normal. Now thoughts of the Titan no longer troubled him, and the darkness itself had disappeared, and he could no longer avoid his cell. 'I have a world, after all,' he thought to himself. Anant was going somewhere. Sleep was a road to his cell. He sipped his whisky. Johnny Cash began singing 'Give My Love to Rose'.

Anant woke up on the mat with the record player beside him. 'A return to my cell,' he thought with the authority of one prepared to take ownership of his creation, and steadied his breath in preparation of whatever awaited him. It soon dawned on him that there was no mahogany floor beneath him, nor any grey brick walls surrounding him. He had a glass beside him. He had woken up to himself, not in his mind but in the 'real' world, if such a distinction was even apt any more. He was in his living room.

'Hello.' Anant had decided to speak out loud, if only to reassure himself that he was indeed in the real world. 'I am Anant Vohra,' he said as though to confirm that the room wasn't a figment of the imagination, his or the resident's. He wasn't sure what he was supposed to do. 'What now?' The age-old question thundered and its reverberations filled him with dread. His neck hurt from the angle he had slept at, but it was his stomach that was bothering him the most. He felt like there was a bomb there that was about to explode, his insides the ingredients that would blow him to smithereens while the body would remain unscathed. He began to feel like a prey that had felt the presence of the predator, seen its cold eyes sharpen at the sight of weakness, and he could do nothing but await the rustling leaves, the sharp intake of breath, and the moment the predator would pounce. What was he to do?

Anant rose from his spot and walked around the flat, paranoid about his surroundings, his eyes darting around to find a shadow of the predator. He poured himself a glass of whisky, and sat in his armchair, looking at the windows as if the predator would burst through to charge at him. Was the predator the resident? Or was it the Titan that had written his fate the moment Anant pocketed its fragment in his mind? Anant was unsure who was who, he felt exasperated at the question he had asked himself. How could he undertake such an audacious task of differentiation with the assiduity that it demanded, given the state he was in. Certainty of anything evaded him. He felt transparent, a being with too many holes to capture anything. The absence of the predator was just as terrifying as the possibility of one. He feared a reckoning but believed that there had to be a reckoning, or else… Anant couldn't even image an 'or else'. There was nothing else. Anant drank and listened to Chopin's Nocturnes by Arthur Rubinstein. He remained in his leather chair and stared at the windows, not looking past them, stared at the floor and then at the ceiling. By the time he passed out in the chair, he knew every nook and cranny, every speck of dust in the living room, the angle from which the windowsills hadn't been cleaned, the furniture that hadn't been dusted, the ceiling that had the premature cobwebs, the floors that had collected dust from a week of the maid's absence who came every weekend. His apartment looked clean, he thought, but it was covered in dust, much like himself. Thoughts about the predator continued to afflict him till the moment he passed out, his imagination had given birth to the image of the predator ripping through him to emerge from the inside, as the Titan had ripped through the depths of his mind to emerge at its forefront, and in those moments, the fear gave him the clarity to distinguish between himself and the resident, and the Titan that existed above them all, it was in these intoxicated moments that he believed with certainty that this was the malicious work of the resident. Passing out was the only way he would have gone to sleep. He was fidgety and suspicious of even the mundane parts of reality, unsure whether he wanted to open his eyes to find himself in his living room or in his cell. Funny what was once a cell, or the cell, had become his cell.

There is a sense of self in every person that enables one to perceive reality. Who am I? What am I? One may concentrate on the latter if the feelings of insufficiency grow, choosing to attach itself, much like a leech, to distinguishing preset identity. I am only my religion. I am only my politics. I am only my gender. I am only my caste. I am within whatever this boundary marks me, and thus while imprisoning me it allows me to be more than myself. Therein follows 'Where am I' and 'When am I'. But all Anant had was a cocktail of rudimentary selves. Unconstrained by afflictions and superfluous convictions, who I am could be shaped by one's core value, and what I am, where one often shovels their rigid identity, could be determined by one's actions. All Anant had to these questions were spoon-fed answers, markers that had been laid down since he was a child. Who was he? Anant, and this, he clung to. Repeating it to himself constantly. What was he? An individual, often followed by thoughts of the resident. Where was he? Flat. When was he? He would look to the time of the day, the date and the month, which with no work had become redundant, but not obsolete as in the cell. What it all meant, whether it was real, Anant went through the coming days as a crumbling hollow shell of any self that might have once been. His identity fractured, his emotions incomprehensible, the lines he had made along his journey that he had once defined as one from point A to point B had blurred, and the rest washed away. Unable to concentrate, without any work, with sleep unfaithful to him, the bomb continued to tick in his stomach. The only time he got any rest was when he passed out on the mat or in the chair believing he would wake up in his cell, needing to wake up in the cell, but it remained swallowed by the void that continued to be daunting and impenetrable.

He spent his days looking for anything when he wasn't crippled by anxiety of the world outside that seemed real and just as likely may not be. He looked for life in coffee shops, parks and art galleries. He would catch himself staring at people's shoulders wondering if the darkness had left any trace behind. He had finished the book he was reading, and added a collection of non-fiction books that he had either bought and glanced over, or was on his reading list. He would read night and day, or at least pretend to, for more often than not, he would catch himself merely skating from word to word, or worse, tumbling down from line to line, and he would return to the last passage, or turn back pages to restart from where he had drifted away, often from where he had started. When he wasn't trying to indulge in books, or in the world outside, he would listen to music, and sometimes even watch movies. He couldn't lose himself while watching movies because he was a passive spectator, not unlike music, but music would often be accompanied by him pacing around the flat. Movies, despite it being an easy way to pass the time, were not reliable, for he thought it was too risky for his mind to be dormant for too long, considering it was susceptible to mutiny at any given moment. He preferred staying active, even when he couldn't take a step outside his flat. It was a reminder, or a reassurance, that he still had some ownership over his body and mind. When he did watch something, it was children's' cartoons because he was afraid of what his mind might pick up from the movies and make its own. If he were to ever return to the cell, the last thing he needed was guns waiting for him. This fear of his imagination was why he stuck to non-fiction books, and why he barely touched his notebooks, and never for an extended period of time. He did not touch the Johnny Cash record again.

Dostoevsky, perhaps recalling his own experience with the death penalty, wrote in *The Idiot* about how a prisoner facing the death penalty met a fate far worse than the end itself, the crippling certainty of death that hung over him every day, and the daily death of the hope of a pardon that a prisoner carries till he reaches the steps of the guillotine or the firing squad. Anant was tormented not with the hope of a pardon, but a hope of war, that he still had a say in the matter, that he was a bee, and it was a divine right that he not be swatted by a newspaper, but die by his sting. And every day he did not wake up in the cell, he believed that he had taken his last stand on quicksand. That he was being swallowed whole.

Having been stripped of his identity, and the nightmare of the predator lurking within his consciousness, the next step in Anant's self-engineered ostracism was stripping him of the simple things that brought him comfort. The shower ceased to be soothing. The water cascaded down imploring his body to assent yet the silent words of the water never reached him. He who enjoyed sweet coffee, had to turn to the bottle, if only to put off the impending hangover that he could feel tightening around him, other times he would take a pill or two to cure him of the otherwise perpetual dull throbbing of his head. The pills added to his nausea that wasn't the culmination of Glen and Jack, just his body responding to the bomb that didn't tick preparing for its explosion. He would routinely swallow half-chewed food or a drink down the wrong pipe, and collapse into a fit of coughing. Anxiety made him relive his memories of the previous few hours, struggling to distinguish what was real and what was his imagination. The predator he had seen standing past the glass door was a mirage, him barging into his balcony was real. A wolf charging at him as he walked in a park was a mirage, him having to hold himself off kicking a dog being walked by a child was not. Anant wondered if the latter was a mirage or not, for he couldn't recall going out recently. Perhaps it was a memory of another day, and perhaps one night a dog made larger in the shadows had come charging at him. His compulsive fear that he was being toyed around by his mind made him attempt to resurrect his fragmented memories of the day and yesterday to put the uncertainty of these memories to rest. The cascade of memories that washed over him pummelled him into submission, to suffer in silence. 'I am Anant Vohra.' He muttered to himself to calm himself down.

Control was slipping out of his fingers like sand, and he was trying to grasp at the little he had with all his might. As you well know, might has nothing to do with holding sand, but all Anant was left with was his might, his fleeting strength. He had withered over the course of a few days, was a man devoid of defences, devoid of reason, devoid of intuition that did not lead him astray. He was only a reactionary being, like a baser animal. One night, Anant woke up in the plastic chair in the balcony where he had passed out, a glass sitting on the floor beside the chair, inviting a number of flies to get drunk and seek the ground for blood. He noiselessly prepared a bag and decided that he would drive to Pune. Control, he thought to himself, he needed control. This was his decision, and off he went into the illuminated streets of Mumbai. Anant began his journey with the certainty that he wasn't drunk, not any more, but the certainty itself quickly became fleeting and he had to convince himself of it by checking his breath every fifteen minutes. The car seemed to glide from time to time, as if it did not have a grip on the road and any time it would begin its take-off and float away. He clung to the steering wheel, his back hunched over and sweat collecting on his forehead and dripping down on to the seat. At times when he blinked, he would frantically inspect his side-view and the rear-view mirrors to see if he had hit someone. To remain in a lane was a struggle in itself. As he departed the city and drove on the expressway, Mumbai wept from the skies, as if mourning him, bidding him farewell. Whenever he stopped, not to take rest but because he just could not continue, he would walk around the car in a circle looking for damage, for blood, broken glass, and punctured tyres, that were never there. Every time he returned to his seat, shivering with each step, he would find it stained with a bigger patch of sweat.

He arrived at the house an hour before the morning traffic would take the Pune roads by storm. With frequent stops and at pedestrian speed, it took him three hours more than usual to reach his home. He remained in his seat long after he had turned the engine off, and for a moment, his eyes swept around his surroundings, expecting Aarti to pop up to help him with his bag and show him her ring. The sense of déjà vu had little to do with his present, and more with his mind making him believe that he was back at the start of the cycle, to relive these past few months all over again. With no sign of Aarti, he wobbled out and made his round around the car, inspecting it for the blood that he suspected was there.

The Vohra house had seen celebrations meticulously imagined under Sunil Vohra, and was swarmed with the quiet routine of Monica Vohra, sprinkled with the magic that had reunited with the lost Trivedi sister. The house stood distinct from its peers, Anant believed it existed on a different plane from its surrounding. With oblivious eyes, he found the house to be as it always was, it could have been taken from his childhood to be presented to him now. The many memories of the house had been superimposed till all that remained was a vague idea of his house. He wondered if the house was real at all, and the thought struck him with such a blow in the stomach that he wanted to keel over and retch his guts out. 'I am Anant Vohra,' he muttered.

Walking up to the door, Anant did not notice that his parents' car was missing. He trudged on and rang the bell. No one answered. He waited, and rang the bell again. His wretched gut that he couldn't retch wedged itself between his lungs, adding to the weight he felt on his chest. Anant recalled that he had alerted them via a message at night, and they had replied in the morning informing him that they would be here. Old discarded nightmares returned to torment him, like a murder of crows pecking and clawing one feeble prey. He checked his phone to confirm whether he had sent the message at all. There was a new message from both his parents. His mother had sent him a message telling him that they would be back by eleven, that it was a prior arrangement which was unavoidable and that they had waited for him. Anant now took note of the three extra hours it took him to reach the house.

Furthermore, Monica added that if he didn't have his key, he could wait in a nearby hotel. His father had messaged him explaining that Monica had an appointment with a doctor, that they would have postponed it but it was important. There was more to the message, something about waiting with the neighbours or to at least approach them if he wanted something. Anant's heart was palpitating by the time he finished the message, and he was leaning against the door with sweat dripping down his brow. The weight on his chest grew heavier, and his liver seemed to jut out, pressing itself against his ribs, as if making way for the bomb. He was heaving his breath like he had to manually pump his lungs for them to work. He always carried the keys of the house when he came to Pune, and he patted himself in a hurry to find them. The feel of his clothes, the texture of his jeans, everything felt coarse to his hand that rummaged through his pockets, his heart in a mad frenzy that demanded all his attention. He could hardly feel the key in his hand when he held it. He finally managed to unlock the door. He gasped and stumbled inside, leaving the key in the gate and the outer door ajar, he nudged the inside door away so it would form a crevice that gave him privacy. The weight on his chest had grown too heavy for him to carry, it restricted his breath and the pressure was crushing him. Left with a lump in his throat, Anant found himself sandwiched between the door and the wall even as his eyes remained closed. His retreat, his retreat, his retreat, it sang.

He repeated it like a chant to summon it.

He would take the confines of his cell, Anant would gladly lose himself on a canoe, he had become lax and forgotten the Titan that had made him build the cell in the first place, brick by brick, with hissing and slithering in the coves of his mind. The insidious nature of death that he had pocketed in his mind gripped his very soul, baring its immortal fangs. And now with nowhere to run, merely the sound of its daunting march brought him to his knees, it made him crumble. And he felt it. The bomb that did not tick, with its now crushing pressure, found its missing piece. The bomb had waited, it distracted, it ticked, oh how it ticked now that it was complete, from a world where seconds never ticked on to become minutes, and finally, it exploded. The explosion was both scalding hot and piercing cold. It oozed out of his nose, leaked out of his eyes, dribbled down his ears, rushed out of his mouth, and soon it enveloped him and spread through the living room while he lay on the floor gasping for breath. It reduced the world around him into a bleaker version of itself, as Anant heaved and cried tears that now would not stop. He felt himself being dragged into a pit, slammed into a hole, his vision blurred and he sat shivering, cold and sweating fire at the same time. He couldn't move. He was stuck between the wall and the door. Covered in sweat and tears, he was barely able to breathe. There he was, at the edge of existence, on the cusp of infinity, watching his own cataclysm, both void and man, more void than man, and slowly, as if bringing the play to an end, the waves of time eventually reeled him back, eased him of the fire he had been set on, and warmed the parts of him that were freezing, and returned him to his hollow body. His heart finally began to slow down like a train running out of steam. His soul quivered, his fractured mind was static, and his body tired from the exhaustion of merely trying to exist. Contemptuous seconds languidly ticked on, and turned to minutes, and Anant realized that he had a new companion beside him, now resting on his shoulder was a blot of darkness.

The reason behind the doctor's visit was the result of a blood test among many that Monica Vohra had taken. While the rest of her bloodwork was fine, a single excess caused Sunil to worry. It was the result of a medicine that she no longer needed to take. On the drive back to their house, Sunil suggested getting something for Anant, as if he had come back home after months. It would be a good moment, he thought. They stopped by a small café near the house to get a banana smoothie that he enjoyed when he was younger.

It was Monica who walked up to the door while Sunil was parking the car when she noticed the door ajar with the key still in it. When brought to Sunil's attention, he motioned for her to be quiet and bravely stepped into the flat with her close behind. The door hit something that stopped it from opening completely, and Sunil shuffled past the door and pivoted around it to find Anant's shoes along the wall behind the door. With the belief that it was better to be cautious than regretful, Sunil checked the rest of the house while Monica marched to the living room to put down her bag and off she went to Anant's room. The bedroom door was open and Anant lay lifeless on the bed, looking like he had taken a shower with his clothes on. The air-conditioned room was far too cold and yet sweat continued to trickle down his face and neck. Sunil arrived in the room while Monica observed Anant. Unable to follow his wife's circuitous approach, he strode over to his son and checked his forehead for fever. 'What is wrong?' he asked, relieved that there was no fever.

Anant blinked, his unfocused eyes were open but it was only when he felt a hand and heard a voice that he slowly recognized his father looking down at him. He noticed his mother standing at the foot of the bed. People, he thought to himself, people he recognized. The pieces of his mind passed the information, and slowly, the will that could not hold sand, managed to pull his drifting body and mind together as he observed with his unmoving eyes. Pain lingered behind his now blank eyes as he observed his parents. How they had aged, he thought to himself, withered, shrunk, spine rounded, hair whiter than ash, and yet, eyes carrying the twinkle of old age rather than the emptiness of it. His fleeting energy was spent by his heart to ache one last time. He remained on the bed until his father helped him sit up against the headboard. He felt worse than he looked, and he looked dreadful. 'Nothing. I just didn't eat last night, it was a busy night. I was packing. And during the drive I felt light-headed. I drove slowly which is why I am late. When I finally came to the house, I was just too tired to work.' These were far too many words for Monica and Sunil to believe their son's excuse. Anant stuttered in places, and took long pauses in between his excuse to collect himself. Sunil did not continue with his hands-on approach. In matters of deceit, it was best to allow the lie to be peeled open, and Monica was better with the subtlety it required than he was. He glanced at her, and without a word, they both knew who had been chosen as the first point of attack.

'We got a smoothie for you. I'll put it in the freezer and bring it to you in a few minutes,' Sunil told him, thinking to himself that it wasn't subtlety that he was missing, but something else entirely. And despite Monica's observant nature and Anant's flare for introspection, it was only Sunil who could notice it in his family. It wasn't his taste for memories, nor was it his direct approach to people, but people themselves separated him from the two. That despite his own isolation, he still held on to the threads that lead to people, he cherished them, while Monica had learned when she had to manoeuvre along these threads when time itself brought her to people. Anant had taken after both of them and made something worse out of it, holding on to threads as if they were paddles to be used to stir himself away from people on the waters of time.

'How are you?' Anant asked Monica. Sunil waited by the door to listen to her answer, and when the question was met with the absolute silence that only Monica was capable of, Sunil shook his head and left. He couldn't bring himself to try and understand the intricacies of this strange language. He felt it would corrupt him.

The silence radiated off Monica, dressing the room in its calm. Whenever Monica managed such an absolute silence, in any given circumstance, she appeared to be the most serene in the situation. A lifetime of being a mother, first to her siblings and her father, and then to her own son, had taught her much.

'Good. How are you?' Monica inquired after long seconds had passed. It wasn't her words, but the concern behind them that would have made Anant jump and try and avoid unravelling in front of her, if he had had the energy to jump or unravel.

'Just tired.' Anant's reply was met with silence. Expectant eyes were not rude enough to stare, no, Monica wasn't prone to such novice mistakes. Whenever he glanced at her, he found her looking at him, but he never felt her eyes on him. It never felt like she was trying to pull out his soul and read it as if it were a newspaper. But if she had, what would she find? Was the editor still him or someone else? Was the newspaper in tatters? 'It's been a long month.' Anant's words seemed like a confession.

Monica did not put her hand up and exclaim that he was hiding the truth even if he wasn't lying. It was understood by both that she knew. She nodded and used a hand towel on the nightstand to wipe the sweat off his forehead. She waited for him to say something , then patted his head before getting up.

'Smoothie?' she asked. He nodded. She left. Her work here was done.

Sunil arrived with the smoothie in hand. He sat down on the bed and held the smoothie out for him. Anant pushed himself to sit up straighter despite his muscles wanting to collapse, barely managing to hold on to the cup and not shake. He took a weak sip of the drink, barely able to taste or swallow the smoothie. The silence between father and son was different from the one before. It was loud with the both of them. Slowly, sip by sip, Anant managed to wet his mouth, and later, taste the smoothie. The smoothie was cold and thick, the balance of strawberry and banana was tantalizing, and while a pleasant offering, it lurched in his stomach that was incapable of digestion. Anant felt impelled to fill the silence with words. Anant knew that it was not Sunil's intention to subjugate the mood of the room to his whims, it was a habit learned through the years of Sunil getting lost midway or Anant walking away to return to his solace, where both of them had to try and entertain the other. Together, they contributed to this corrosion of the quiet. Anant was taken aback not at what he felt, but that he felt at all. That despite his existence barely holding on, he could still feel the faint remnants of this cocktail of silences. He was being worked upon, despite these defences that Anant believed hid his innate nature, he was being read, it was the reason why Monica had left after calming Anant down and tagged Sunil in. It was another tag-team manoeuvre that they were using on Anant.

'How was the visit?' All he could muster was the question, his chapped lips barely moving.

'Ah, you know, the usual.' Sunil shrugged.

'You know, you should take care of yourself. Be more aware of your body.' Sunil's voice was made deeper by concern, and he cleared his throat with a cough. 'Should I make a doctor's appointment?' he inquired. '...Or will the smoothie do?' Sunil did not believe in his own joke.

'No, no. Maybe if I feel the same after I have rested.' Anant knew from experience that he had to give something to his father if he wanted him to back away. There was no fight left in him, not even for a disagreement. Nor had he any energy in him to muster guilt for lying, for he knew what plagued him would not just go away with some sleep. His father was placated by the 'maybe', and closed the door behind him as he left the room. It wasn't abrupt, he had paused before standing up, waiting for Anant to say something, even when he was at the door, he stood still and waited. Waited for what? Sunil did not know. Yet he had paused and waited. For something. Anything. He could see that Anant needed some time alone, and that Monica must be waiting in the kitchen to discuss what had happened. And so, he left.

For better or worse, most parents try to be experts when it comes to their children, often but not always, born out of a need to keep their child away from danger. The children turn into teenagers who copy their parents while they revolt against them, vying to take control of their lives by behaving as if they were the experts. Given their own childhood, Monica and Sunil were never swept away by this phenomenon. But they believed that as a team, while they were not experts, they made a good duo with their varying perspectives to try and figure out the troubles in the family. If there was anything to figure out at all. And with the state that they had found the house and Anant himself in, the worry made the possibility that there was something to unearth into a certainty.

Chapter 31

If his childhood had a taste, Anant thought as he was in bed, it would be a banana-and-strawberry smoothie. Throughout his younger years he would often be seated in the nearby café, indulging in this smoothie. It was one of the founding fathers of his sweet tooth. His childhood, these younger years, Anant wondered when his life moved on from tasting like the smoothie. How big a net did his childhood cast? Anant knew that his uncle's death had triggered a change in him. It had aged him, yet he had managed to hold on to a part of his childhood. And while his teenage years went on in the ambiguity of adolescence, teenagers believing they were adults while adults treated them like children, when he zoomed in on his teenage life and looked at it as more than just a lump sum span of time, he found that the smoothie managed to find a space in his memories where it was possible for him to pull it over parts of his teenage life and cover it. Perhaps, he momentarily considered, that some of his childhood had seeped into his teenage years. But hadn't his childhood ended with the passing of his friend? He was tormented by death to find that there was something so final about losing a staple in his life that simply wasn't compatible with the carelessness of childhood. As he lay on his bed, exhausted and with a belief that he was recuperating, he was weaving his memories in such a way that the possibility of covering his teenage life with the comforting blanket of the smoothie was possible. Why? To cling on to something that served as a reminder that his past had been real, that it hadn't been a creation of his mind, a dream that he had while wide awake. That as he wandered through his memories, he would have the crutch of a smoothie that existed outside the dualities of him and himself. That despite the fickle nature of his recent memories, his childhood had been real, that it was concrete. That he had existed, had lived. He tried to put every good memory that he could think of and tried to cram it in the plastic cup that he could drink in his time of need. A sip and there it would be, euphoria showering down on him from the sweet heaven above, ruled by the doughnut god, soothing him with the reality of better times.

Sitting against the headboard with the cup in hand, he sipped from a cardboard straw that had a whirling line of turquoise. His body yearned for sleep, but sleep refused to cooperate. His breathing was normal, albeit a little laboured, and his heart was no longer trying to burst through his chest. He had been through the explosion and survived, had managed to drag himself to his bed eventually, though he barely remembered how, but all was not well. It felt like the fragments of his fractured mind had drifted further away and could no longer communicate with one another. All his soul could do was quiver. The bomb had exploded, shouldn't it have taken him with it? He survived, left to cling to each and every moment, for the validity of his existence outside of it was in doubt. The explosion had left him with a companion that sat on his shoulder, weightless, formless. A stain of ink suspended in air. Was it a sign that the Titan was on its way towards him? Or worse, was it the work of the wicked resident?

As he grew weary of time, he had enough of the smoothie to momentarily replenish his soul and before it would leak out of him, he ventured to wonder about the Titan, and time. In all his feelings, thoughts and convictions that he ever had towards death, there was hardly anything about time. How far did Anant need to go before he could find trinkets at the altar of time? At what age? Anant found that he was devoid of notions of time. The sacrosanct was and wasn't, had relegated all other notions to a place where he could not venture. How self-indulgent he had been towards the Titan, how ignorant of time. Time that moves on just the same, not sparing a second, ticking and turning, swallowing minutes and hours, sunrises and sunsets. For what about this primordial being whose currents brought on the tremors of death. Anant couldn't believe how ignorant he had been. He had failed to realize that time was a partner of the Titan, a tag-team rather than luggage to be carried along with the thoughts of death. Anant was slowly dying every day. He would not merely drop dead one day. And so was everyone, all the same.

And behold a pale horse, and his name that sat on it was Death, carried by the immortal white stallion known as time. As Anant lay broken, lacerated, burnt and frozen, he began to dissect his delusions. 'Is this the life flashing before my eyes?' He spared a thought in passing, returning to his ruminations. The writing had been on the wall, as Anant stepped into adolescence, he ushered the hissing and slithering to a new age where it could manifest itself as the darkness on the shoulder of everyone, his subconscious, his shadow trying to make him understand that everyone was passing, that death was upon everybody already. The tree that rose from his grave tried to help him accept the side effects of his own life. Pain, suffering and mourning. And in his stoic fervour which had bloomed from his lifelong obsession with death and a profane ignorance of time, he continued to try and turn the spotlight on him—a desperate attempt to hide the bodies withering and ageing, to hide the rounding spines and white hair. And for others, the abrupt end, where it seemed death had leapt at them, but such wasn't the case. Death wasn't marching towards them, they were being carried by time to death. Oh, how foolishly he had sowed the seeds of this stoic hermitage in his childhood, fooling himself into believing that he accepted the two entities that he foolishly viewed as one. Death and Time, Time and Death, ruminated upon by philosophers and spiritualists throughout centuries, and somehow reduced to a whimsy of an insolent child who had deluded himself into believing he had mastered it. As long as there is heart in man and it beats not with the sole purpose of pumping blood but is courted by life, unshackled by the notions of afterlife—be it heaven or reincarnation—no man can be unaffected by time and death. To do so would be to rip your soul in two, and use one to cover yourself from life while the other is used to deceive yourself into believing that you are living. And Anant wasn't living. In his efforts to detach himself from death, he hid from the fleeting present. While he continued to pay respects to the Titan, he ignored time and the effects of time on those around him, continued to turn to his cell that existed in the past. The audacity of his childhood naivety, Anant couldn't help but smile at himself. Perhaps, he considered, he had never ceased being a child in some ways.

His lips chapped and greying. His hair stuck together like a used mop. He couldn't believe how in his fear of the Titan he had tried to freeze the primordial being that is time itself. Every time he repeated it to himself, he thought it ever more absurd. His memory of the waning aftershocks of the Titan that were once feathers in his cap, were thorns he had pierced into his crown. There lay Anant, he died for nothing. He remembered now, his friend, a ghost of a figure, without a face, without memories, an artefact desecrated by his whimsy, the loss of this friend hadn't pierced him as deep as when his uncle passed away. It was more confusion than sorrow, more shock than grief. Rather than suffering through the consequences of the Titan, rather than mourning his loss or trying to grasp what had happened, he merely draped himself with the fact that death happened. Death happened indeed, but severing himself from mourning, he could never heal. And there were times he fought, as if he could save them, those he loved, those he knew, while hiding behind the construction of a retreat that would exist away from the world, and where later he would spend his time, in an act of contempt, in his cell where seconds did not turn to minutes. Where in his juvenile audacity he had come to believe that he had frozen time itself. And thus, he failed to not only process the death of those he loved, but also the fact that seconds tick on to become minutes which turn into years and in a blink of an eye, time has washed away a decade. In a way, the darkness was a needed reminder, but Anant saw what he had failed to perceive then, that it wasn't that everybody was fated to die, but that everybody was closer to the finish now than ever before.

There were more deaths that followed. He remembered his contempt in all his glorious faux-wisdom, as if he knew all along. He was driven, and later drove to processions, seeing life fall again and again, a fall that sends tremors which are felt by those closest to the tree. Except him. Though he would fight against death from a distance, battle against this idea of death, the moment the Titan struck, he would see it from another world entirely, sitting in the comfort of his cell, and thus not only severing himself from healing, but also fooling himself into believing he accepted death. And he considered it a triumph. He was so pleased with himself, but the bomb kept ticking, although Anant could not hear it, for he left no notion of time in the world where it concocted its explosion. And his poor heart wept, and his soul tried to warn him as his actions led to its confinement to a coffin, to savour the world in bits, which Anant in benign maliciousness considered other-worldly. As if the world itself was beneath him, and what was worthy of his interest was somehow christened as divine.

Anant was pulled out of his head by the sound of slurping when he tried to take another sip of the smoothie. The darkness on his shoulder, the smoothie, the exhaustion of his body, the tattered mind, the ailing soul, he wondered where this insight was originating from. Once again, the question of whether this was his life flashing by him arose. Or was there a little light in him that was still trying? He pushed himself away from the headboard to lie on the bed and stared at the ceiling that had retained its pristine white coat despite its years. 'I am Anant Vohra,' he muttered to make sure he was in the real world. All the signs suggested that he was, but the untouched white coat tried to rekindle the doubt in his mind, as if trying to burst the bubble of clarity that had stretched over him till now.

He went through the snapshots of various funerals and processions he had been to over the years. His uncle, the radio-baby, his friend, the college classmates who had died in a car crash, the middle-aged daughter of an old couple who lived around the corner. And he imagined processions of those who might have passed away, teachers who were nearing seventy back when he was in school, the drunk colleague at his internship who was trying to cure the diseases that were the effects of his raging alcoholism with more alcohol, and on and on. People he never talked to would come alive on the ceiling, in a flat makeshift creation of sticks, dressed with bones, muscle and clothes, drained of colour, fated to meet their end again. Anant watched their processions, those he had never seen because he was a child, he imagined. Burned, buried, lying in a casket or on a white blanket for people to pay their respects. The white backdrop of the ceiling made it seem like a projector was at work. Anant went to sleep counting processions.

When his eyes fluttered open, Anant knew where he was before the world revealed itself to him. The subtle differences between waking up in his world and in his mind were magnified given how his body felt before he passed out. He felt like a new man entirely, as if he had been pieced together, cleaned and wrung. Or rather the same man in a new body, for the metaphysical troubles that plagued him had not abandoned him. He was on the canoe once more. The world around him had changed. It was brighter than before. He got to his feet without rocking the boat, and saw the cell in the distance, in ruin. The grey brick walls were in tatters, the mahogany floor had come apart, pieces of the bricks and planks floating amid the nothingness that surrounded it. The door that would not open was rusted amongst the floating pieces of the cell. Amidst these ruins swam the bottle with the book coiled in it. His surroundings had always been clear, but a brightness illuminated the world. The source of this new-found light was above him, cutting through the darkness to illuminate the world, and Anant realized with open-mouth wonder that the little light could have in fact cut the abyss deep enough for life to escape and etch itself on the sky. The sky was alive with memories. The scene overhead was much like watching a million screens at once, each playing something different. Anant stood there overwhelmed with emotion, and his eyes traced the memories, leading him to turn around, away from the cell, and there in the sky was the doughnut moon with the crescent of sprinkles, and underneath it, in a way that the hollow of the centre of the doughnut allowed it to keep its cloak of dark hues of blue, stood the precipice.

It is only in relation to situations and markers that we can assess our journey. Whether it is from the early beginnings, from the little accomplishments or failures picked along the way. Trees running past, tunnels to go through, heart breaking and resurrecting, of achieving goals and dreams crumbling, before and after people, not just Christ, the transformative arts and on and on. These are the markers of life, and with the doughnut moon coming closer, and the cell drifting away, Anant knew that he was moving towards the precipice. Only when the enigma of his situation waned did Anant ask himself what had changed. His eyes never moved away from the formation of rocks that had formed a small island of sorts, afraid that it would turn out to be a mirage. Yet, he could not stop looking at the vivid colourful sky above. Any image of a spring evening sky bleeding purple and orange, or any image of a post-rain sun amidst the scattering leaden clouds, would pale in comparison to the multitude of colours playing above his head. How were things different from the time he was in the cell, and when he was drifting away in a void, to now when he was headed somewhere, and leaving something behind? He circled back to the question again. And he remembered Dandekar sahib, who had put hammer to the floor and walls, removing tiles and plaster, to give him more space to manoeuvre. Destruction beckons creation, this is the tag-team of Shiva and Shakti in their eternal dance. The bomb that had detonated within him, which had not only swept him with panic, but caused his self to finally submit and weather his impending fate, allowed space for something more, or just something else. For the light to move. Destruction allowed time to flood into the world once again.

Anant had accepted its ticking, for the end does not merely signify that there had been a start, but that there had been the journey, not suspended over a moment but laid over a course of time, and Anant finally heard the seconds turn to minutes and ushered the cell that had existed to the present. Anant sat on the canoe that glided on the waterless abyss and let himself be rowed, the invisible helmsman achieving the obscurity that the rower in Varanasi had strived for.

Anant waded into the once-out-of-reach hues of blue that surrounded the precipice, each dense shade giving way to a darker one as he got closer and closer to the rocks. Upon closer inspection, Anant noted that the whole piece of land existed so perfectly within the hole, at times edging close to the circumference but never stepping into the light of the overhead doughnut that seemed to hang like an archetypical figure of a higher being, it seemed to Anant like the land had been carved to accommodate the doughnut. The canoe stopped short of a silver beach illuminated by the light of an absent moon. He thanked the invisible man who did not exist, and took his first steps on the once allegorical land. He had never noticed that he wasn't wearing any shoes in this world, he had never felt any texture before. All he had was the softness of his mattress when he was in his cell. But as he walked on the beach, serenaded by the sounds of the void that was once an ocean, he felt the sand underneath him, felt its cool coarse texture. Standing below the protruding precipice, Anant stared into the darker hues of blue that awaited him at its heights; sapphire, cobalt, navy and midnight, like still opaque clouds getting progressively darker as they reached the peak, the precipice.

There was a steep trail full of bushes and trees right by the beach. An uneasy energy compelled him to move as soon as possible and he began his journey amidst the wild vegetation. The first thing Anant noticed was the pleasant dampness of the grass, manicured to be the perfect length, not too dense as to cover his toes, but not too sparse for his feet to touch dirt. A flawless coating on the ground, against which the wild trees, bushes and moss stood in a stark contrast. Anant made his way up the trek, the bushes became manicured and sprouted beautiful flowers, roses and lilies in patchy shades red, orange and yellow, as if someone had coloured them with crayons. The chestnut trees gave way to jamun trees wreathed in vines. The green grass remained pristine. Traversing the weeping willows made Anant slow down as he crouched and pushed the dense green foliage out of his face. The peonies and carnations were in blue and indigo and surrounded by bright violet cherry blossom trees. The vivid colours were a sight for sore eyes, the crayons had given way to colours so mesmerizing that it felt like nostalgia itself had bled on to it. The Japanese maple trees that followed were when the oddity of the situation dawned on Anant, for the trees were incandescent, as if little fireflies in surreal colours made up the leaves of the tree. Anant did not stop. To stop was to contemplate, to stop was to get lost. The pathway to the top was in a spiral, and he made his way round and round, getting closer to the precipice. The shades of blue became denser and darker, approaching navy. Near the top were peepal trees plucked out of a dream, a flickering hallucination that seemed to grow with every blink. They hosted thick crowns and aerial roots that hid its colour with the fog of midnight blue. Anant could have sworn that he heard the flute, but it could have just as easily been the roots calling out to Anant like sirens, tempting him to climb its trunk and try and reach for the doughnut.

The grass ended just past the thicket and was replaced with a red mat that differed from the scarlet mat of his apartment and his cell. The Eden-red mat disappeared into the condensed murky midnight blue that was reminiscent of the abyss. The banyan trees that replaced the peepal were sparse, bent and dying, the leaves grey as a dead body, some hanging on to the tree out of sheer will and others slowly disappearing into the non-existent wind. Anant stopped at the edge of the grass, at the edge of his consciousness. Here he was, he thought, on the edge of eternity. He turned around and realized that the thicket he had come from had disappeared, and the trees in the distance that still existed had begun to wither like the ones that stood around him. It felt like autumn had come with death in its arms. The bushes and the various plants and flowers lost their colour, leaving behind a putrid yellow and grey. The dirty brown of the ground had reared its jarring head, slowly replacing the lush green grass in bald spots.

Anant took a deep breath, the air carrying phantoms of wailing cries within filled his lungs, his stomach suddenly expanded to accommodate a gust of wind that rushed into him. His heart that had been on a jog began to thud in his chest. As he exhaled, smoke came out of his mouth. He hunched over in a fit of coughing with more and more dense smoke coming out of him, he felt the high he had felt on the bank of Manikarnika ghat, felt himself suspended over the grass, which had all but disappeared down the slope and only within a few feet around him was in its pristine length, a reminder that the once fine coat had been real in this unreal world.

Anant got to his feet, his steps felt as if they never touched the ground yet he never faltered, he stepped on to the mat with trepidation in his heart and dying echoes of his stoic fervour in his soul. 'Whatever happens, happens,' he told himself. Johnny Cash began to play in the distance. 'Give My Love to Rose', he had read the tracks on the back of the record over and over, far more than he had listened to it. It was the third track on side A of the two-record album, he remembered. As Anant made his way to the precipice, the murky midnight blue fog began to lift, revealing the large daunting structure that stood on the edge of the protrusion. And beyond it was a world that had completed its metamorphosis. The seamless abyss that had been cut by the 'little light that could' and flooded by a stream of memories that etched themselves on the sky, had left the ground alone to give way to an expansive and evocative world full of ethereal colours that spread in each direction. There before him, with the archway as his witness, bleeding into the ground and waterless ocean alike, spread in a surreal utopian harmony, were the colours he had seen while making the trek up the precipice. Red, orange, yellow, green, blue, indigo and violet. The doughnut in the sky was within his reach, the sprinkles making a crescent were incandescent, and in the hole…in the hole of the doughnut existed everything. The sound of dreams, the taste of space, the texture of memories, the scent of abyss and the visions of infinity. In the middle of the doughnut rested everything that never was, that never would be.

The structure made of grey bricks in front of him had for long captured his imagination. It was a towering archway with massive columns on either side, on top of which was water burning like fire, not fire in the shade of blue, for if it wasn't for the light from the sky and the doughnut, it wouldn't have been visible. The record player that he just noticed, that sat on a stool playing Johnny Cash paused, the needle was lifted and the arm moved away while he stood transfixed with the doughnut, with the structure, the world, and it returned to the edge of the record to play the first track. 'The Man Comes Around' blared from the non-existent speakers, but unlike before the track wasn't pulled from his college memory. It did not repeat the same few lines over and over again, it found the missing words, the melody was complete. 'A taste for drama.' A dry thought appeared and disappeared in front of the great magnitude of emotions he felt. Despite the force of the sound making the whole world shake, the music did not seem loud. The darkness returned to his shoulder.

Anant waited. He knew who it was instinctively. Once his helper with whom he had shared pieces of his world, and who in turn had shared pieces of himself with Anant, it was the same entity that had waited till there were enough pieces to manifest himself in the real world, disguised as the darkness that was once a reminder of the Titan. The reality and the unreality had arrived at the Armageddon, or perhaps more fitting would be the Mahabharata with no sign of Krishna. His soul was like Draupadi— the hunted, the haunted, the sufferer, the vengeance seeker; and his body was the throne. The one sitting on the throne, no longer knew which side he represented, as blind as Dhritarashtra. Whom had he wronged, and whom had the resident wronged? Whose hair would be washed in the other's blood?

Anant walked over to the towering archway while he waited. Inspired by the Gateway of India, if not used as a prototype upon which changes had been made. Gone were the two smaller doorways that were found on either side of the Gateway of India. There was but one massive archway, missing a door that should be pulled by a trio of elephants. 'I wonder if an elephant could have opened that door.' The resident made first contact after all, referencing the jammed door of the cell, and making it clear that he had crossed the diminished boundary of the once impenetrable separation that had dismissed Anant's efforts to listen in on the resident's thoughts. Anant did not respond, and walked closer to the archway that stood like a gravestone. Layers of dust collected amidst the cracking bricks. Upon narrowing the distance, Anant felt the cool coastal winds from another world. He stared through the gateway, and felt a strange oppressing yearning to step through it. It seemed to be the next step to take, having come all the way to the top of the precipice. The memories and the colours that had erupted in the world, that still existed around the gateway, and no doubt behind it, disappeared if you would look through it as if it were a portal to a new world, or a return to the unending abyss. Anant was in two minds, the two fated paths had revealed themselves to him, to step through its gate or remain and inspect the archway, its inscriptions and bas-reliefs. Intuition and rationale tugged him in opposite directions. 'You are awfully quiet,' the resident commented.

'It's been the case since forever it seems,' Anant replied.

'Yes, I always found it disrespectful.' There was a pause. 'But what is unforgivable, a crime against all good sense and decorum, absolutely revolting and downright unacceptable, is how you denied me that laddoo. How gratuitous can one be! Just plain mean.' The resident's voice reflected his belief that he now stood at the top of the hierarchy, the apex predator destined to ascend to the throne. Anant tried to ignore his words, tried to focus, tried to ponder over his options, and it dawned on him that he could no longer move. The resident had imposed himself on Anant once more, just as he had done on the boat in Varanasi. In the moment when Anant stood vulnerable, his mind plastered over the sky and life standing before him, this apocalyptic moment when he was stripped of choice, Anant instinctively knew which route he would have taken. In a previous life, before the explosion of the bomb, he might have, would have, chosen to inspect the bas-reliefs and the inscriptions etched on the pillars and the archway. To hide his stagnation in the depthless arms of aesthetics. But now, reborn through fractures, lacerations, burns, freezes, he knew that he would have stepped through the archway, to see what would happen if he walked through it, even if it meant falling off the edge. He would have taken the next step.

For too long, he told himself, he had lived with a foot in the comfort of a retreat that was frozen in time, too long he had been running, too long he had been hiding, siphoning himself to his shadow that had pieced together a grotesque consciousness, for to not hide, to not run, to not remain in comfort, whatever abhorrent form this comfort had mutated to, would be to risk being vulnerable to time and the Titan once again, and only then could he welcome back life. But what a daunting task it had seemed to not remain in the past that was inherently familiar; it meant living in the uncertain present that was life, with all its dangers, by-products and side effects, that included witnessing and straying into the one-way warpath of the Titan and becoming conscious of the currents of time that led to it. Or that led everyone to it. The bas-reliefs and the inscriptions were the product of his imagination and reflections gone by, of dreams forgotten. They did not require any more work, they did not need any more attention. They stood before him finished. Not only finished, but aged, for they were chipped, cracked and withered. He had paid his dues and the structure was complete, there had been a design and it had been fulfilled. It was in the past, gone in the wind. The only way was forward.

Alas! Anant could not move forward. He could not move at all. Often in internal struggles, and always in depictions of such struggles when manifested into separate beings, the conflict that follows is loud. It was what Anant had come to expect, one last heroic stand, one big final confrontation after which one party disappears as if the beast has been slain in a fantasy novel and the princess rescued. Gone forever. It is indeed fantasy that such struggles end and the hero ushers an age of everlasting peace. In a world where the beast cannot be slain, where there is no grand blanket of atonement, the hero's journey can never come full circle. The only end to the struggle is brought by the Titan. To come full circle any other way would merely return one to live it all once again, and again, and again. Perhaps such is life, a continuous circle that gives plenty of chances to be a hero, and just as many to be deemed a failure. How many conflicts and great final battles had Anant been privy to, how many had been waged already, how many more could have been waged until the noise fades away? For these struggles in their essence are quiet, following in the steps of addictions and mental illness. A lifetime of working peace could be fabricated on the foundations of meticulous and unceasing attention that would rival Sunil Vohra's, and relinquishment to a routine and to the world, like Monica Vohra, but never an everlasting one. For the threat remains on the edges of consciousness. The poison chalice has been drunk, the apple has been bitten into. The predator lives, and lingers in the shadows, at times corrupting the shadow itself, buying his time for the moment to pounce. Anant did not know how long he stood there with the darkness resting on his shoulder. He did not know if by constraining him, the resident had sacrificed his own movements as well. Fated to die together, Anant told himself, perhaps the resident had never wanted control, but only to punish him. For not listening, for not adhering, for rebelling. Cast out from heaven, cast into the Ganga. In the limbo he found himself in, these musings came to an abrupt halt when a precarious notion struck him: would his body continue to move in the real world? Would the reins of his life fall in the hands of the resident, or would his body birth a new consciousness, a new him?

Perhaps he was merely one piece in a large puzzle, and the resident was another, and the two of them could be fitted together. Or had time come to a standstill in the real world? But time continued to flow, it continued to sweep, carry and drown, flowing in the same direction as always. It continued to tick, even if unheard. Did the seconds that ticked on and became minutes in the world that had come alive with reflections, with colours, with memories, with dreams, mirror the time in the real world where hairs were greying, bones rounding, battle-weary immune system beginning to succumb to age and lines marrying the drooping skin. If he were to return one day, would he find himself in his bed as he had left himself, or in a new routine altogether, living his life? Had the seconds merely turned to minutes, or hours, or worse, years? When the thought of having lost months struck panic in him, Anant found that his only solace came from the Titan, and the certainty of crossing its world-shaking path whose tremors would be felt in this world. Anant believed that it couldn't have been too long, for like the tag-team of his parents, like Kartik and Marathi, like Shiva and Shakti, Time and the Titan were a pair. Their effects would eclipse notions of dimensions, traverse realms and cause rips in this world. Even the false scares would make his mind tremble, just the fear of death would cause ripples. It was irrefutable that he would come across the Titan once again, and it would set him free. Death, the liberator.

Chapter 32

'Where am I?'
    'You are here.'
'Who are you?'
'I am you."
'Me? The resident?'
'No, you. Your self.'
'My self?'
'You who you banished in your fears.'
'Of death.'
'You who you forsake every minute you do not return to your self.'
'Crippled.'
'No, merely in need.'
'Of what?'
'Your own attention.'
'Why?'
'For who are you if not your self?'
'An image.'
'Artificial.'
'I am my own creation. I have abandoned myself to become myself.'
'And what did you create?'
'...A hollow being.'
'An effigy.'
'Frozen.'
'An infantile man.'

'Not an individual.'
'Swallowed by the past.'

.

.

.

'Who are you?'
'I am you.'
'Will I return to the real world?'
'Is this not real?'
'No.'
'What makes a world real?'
Silence.
'What makes a world real?'
'What makes me real?'
'You are a perpetual reinforcement of your experiences.'
'My experiences make me real?'
'What makes a world real?'
'Bonds anchor me to the world; their weight is reality.'
'If you are cast away into a deserted forest, are you real?'
'If I am attached to the forest, its weight is reality.'
'What happens when those bonds are severed?'
'No.'
'What happens when you drift away into the abyss?'
'No, please.'
'What happens when you lose the cell, the island, the resident?'
'I don't know.'
'What happens when you are entrapped in a blank nomadic solitude?'
'...I cease to exist.'
'Did you not want to hide in your shell, to merely pass away your days?'
'No.'

'Did you not want to hide in your fears, to merely protect yourself from pain?'

Silence.

'Yes?'

'Yes.'

'Now you are free.'

'Now I am abstract.'

'Is realism not contained within clear boundaries?'

'I... '

'Is realism not weighed down by laws?'

Silence.

'Is realism not restrictive?'

'Yes... No.'

'Is realism not a pain?'

'Yes.'

'Yes.'

'I understand.'

'It has been a long road to understanding.'

'What now?'

'I don't know.'

.

.

.

'Where am I?'

'You are here.'

'Where is here?'

'On this page.'

'This is a page?'

'And this, a line.'

'Is this the sum of my existence?'

'We all exist on some plane.'

'Is this the end?'

'This is the end.'